THE LAST KING

THE MERCIAN NINTH CENTURY
BOOK 1

MJ PORTER

MJ PUBLISHING

Copyright notice
Porter, M J
The Last King
Copyright ©2020, Porter, M J Amazon Edition
All characters and events in this publication, other than those clearly in the public domain, are fictitious and any resemblance to actual persons, living or dead, is purely coincidental.

ALL RIGHTS RESERVED. No part of this publication may be reproduced, stored in a retrieval system or transmitted in any form or by any means without the prior written permission of the author, nor be otherwise circulated in any form of binding or cover other than that in which it is published and without a similar condition being imposed on the subsequent buyer.

Cover design by MJ Porter
Cover image by Shaun at Flintlock Covers
Map by Shaun at Flintlock Covers
ISBN: 978-1-914332-27-2 hardback
ISBN: 978-1-914332-28-9 kindle
ISBN: 978-1-914332-66-1 Ingram paperback
ISBN: 9798624114722 Amazon paperback

Created with Vellum

CONTENTS

Summer AD874	7
Chapter 1	17
Chapter 2	35
Chapter 3	52
Chapter 4	64
Chapter 5	87
Chapter 6	101
Chapter 7	127
Chapter 8	144
Chapter 9	157
Chapter 10	167
Chapter 11	183
Chapter 12	198
Chapter 13	208
Chapter 14	216
Chapter 15	233
Chapter 16	251
Chapter 17	266
Chapter 18	289
Thank you for reading The Last King	293
What to read next?	295
Cast of Characters	297
Historical Notes	301
Meet the Author	305
Books by M J Porter (in chronological order)	307

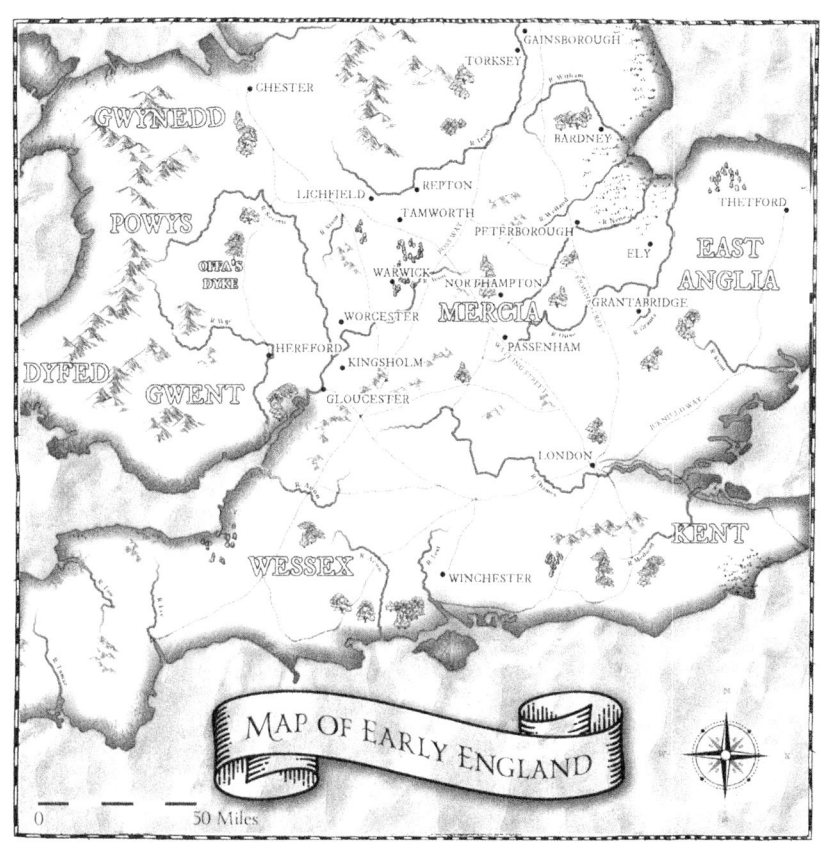

SUMMER AD874

My hands are bound too tightly. I've told the fuckers that, but they've ignored every word I've said since my capture.

My wrists, I know, are red-raw from trying to work my hands loose. The bastard who tied me up did far too good a job.

And yet I'm tied to the horse more by luck than any great skill. It seems they don't mind if I fall off, as long as my damn hands don't come untied.

It's about how it looks, I know that, and yet I'm fucking furious all the same.

Ahead, the settlement of Repton is coming into view far too quickly for my liking. Not that I like any of this. That emotion couldn't be further from what I'm experiencing right now.

Inside my trews, my legs are slick from trying to grip the damn horse's sides. It's not even a bad horse, but without my hands on the rein, I can only use my knees, and he seems particularly stubborn about taking such half-hearted commands.

He's a fucking bastard as well.

I'd use my boots, but they've been taken from me. My heels lack the impact they need to convince the damn brut to follow my instructions.

The warriors who escort me are dour-faced and sheeted in their battle gear, complete with helms, and weapons close to hand.

I've tired myself out trying to talk to them. Now I await my fate. I hope it won't be long in coming.

In the far distance, I can see the sails on the ships as they bob on the River Trent that the Viking raiders have used to infiltrate to the heart of Mercia. They flash in all shades of colour, from bleached white to vibrant red, a reminder that the four men I'm about to face are allies by chance, and not by choice.

If only I could exploit that.

Beneath me, the horse stumbles. A cry rips from my throat, fearing I'll fall and land head first on the hard-packed earth we travel over. The summer has been hot, the threat of drought a persistent problem, although so far the crops have survived. The people will be fed come the winter. I'm not sure that I'll be here to see it.

I angrily shake off a hand on my shoulder that attempts to right me, aware that the fingers bite too deep for it to be a kindness. Hard eyes greet mine. I refuse to offer any thanks, even a muffled one. I decline to even think it.

I do not like this. Not at all.

The church at Repton, St Wystan's, houses the Mercian royal dead. I hope I won't soon become an addition. It's not a huge settlement, but at the moment, it stretches long beyond the splattering of defences and canvases crammed with the Viking raiders, that spill beyond the makeshift ditch surrounding the church. There are bloody thousands of them, and the jeering has only just begun.

They sent three hundred and more men to bring me to Repton. It was supposed to be a peaceful endeavour. I ensured it was none of those things. Now they bring me, bound and gagged, my tongue stuck to the linen rag in my mouth. If I could, I'd kill the fucking lot of them.

My escort raises their heads, still helmed in iron, daubed black to look even more menacing, and with leather encasing almost all of their bodies. Only a flicker of flesh shows here and there, mostly where chinstraps hold helms in place. They look fearless but take the acclaim with heads held high, as though it's all to be expected.

The fuckers.

A gloved hand reaches over and grips the reins of my horse. I refuse to meet the eyes that belong to the hand. I do prepare for my horse to halt at the barricade that blocks the entrance to the interior of Repton. Many warriors watch our progress with suspicious eyes.

Smoke erupts from the fires behind us. Inside Repton, only three tendrils of smoke drift toward the sky, one from the monastery, one from the church, and I would suspect the third from a forge where a blacksmith labours to keep the enemy in the weapons they require.

'Jarl Sigurd,' the gate warden speaks Danish, but I understand the intent. I've been listening to the Viking raiders for almost all my adult life. 'I see you've found him. The other jarls were becoming concerned.' I don't hear the rest of the conversation, my eyes raking in the scene in Repton itself.

Few people walk about, but it's early, daybreak a myriad selection of yellows and mauves on the distant horizon behind me. I stare into the darkness of the night not yet touched by the sun. I don't like what I see. Not at all.

My heart pounds in my chest, my breath coming shallow around the rag in my mouth. I wish it hadn't been needed. I feel my head pulsing and my breath growing ragged. My horse lurches forward and once more, a hand reaches to steady me in the saddle. Fuckers. Maybe I'd rather fall here, splinter my head on the well-trodden ground and know nothing ever again.

I'm not given the option, and then I'm through the barricade and being forced from my horse by eager hands, their breath too hot on my face.

I wince. My eyes bulge. I start to choke.

In one swift movement, the rag's ripped from my mouth, and liberal water poured into my parched mouth. I swallow with the hunger of a starving man, beckoning for more, dismayed when the rag is once more thrust into place, and I'm being led to the next set of defences.

This one includes the ancient church, beneath which the royal families of Mercia have buried their dead throughout the last fifty years. More warriors stand guard here, similar to those who escort me. They don't have helms. I can clearly see eyes, moustaches, beards and the inkings that mark them as Viking raiders and not Mercians.

Fucking bastards.

There are more derisive cries from them as they scamper to open the wooden door to allow me inside the most heavily protected area of the compound. There'll be no escape once I'm inside. I struggle against my bonds, uncaring of the fact that blood drips from my fingers and while each movement is agony.

Two hands on my shoulder force me through the open door, my feet walking over the rough terrain before finding the smoothness of well-worn stone. Bastard cold stone as well.

I shiver, the hands lingering on my shoulders for too long. I think to dislodge them, but what's the point?

The interior of the church is dark. Only a handful of candles blaze where the altar stands. There are no priests and no monks. I bow my head, mourning their loss.

All of my escort crowd into the church. I'm pushed deeper and deeper inside, blinking to try and acclimatise my eyes to the half-dark. The loud scratch of leather boots on the stone almost makes me wince. There is a vast quantity of weaponry on show on the weapons belts of my guards. In a holy church, no less.

It's not fucking right, and I'm not even overly religious. But there's no respect, and that boils me again.

Rough hands clamp my tied hands. I wince at the touch. If I wasn't gagged, I'd have cried out in pain. Fuck. I mustn't appear weak, even here, surrounded by the blank faces of enemy warriors.

More and more warriors surge into the church, seeming to come from openings I didn't even know existed, not just from the main door I've travelled through. The men, sodden with sleep and no doubt ale, barely perk up at the sight of their much-longed-for prisoner. I hear mumbled comments as I swivel my head, trying to see all I can.

There are shitting hundreds of Viking raiders, all wearing similar equipment. These, I deduce, must be the sworn men of the four jarls of Repton. Jarl Guthrum, Jarl Oscetel, Jarl Anwend and Jarl Halfdan, brother of the Ivarr who caused so many problems for the Wessex kings before his death.

I watch the men, making a note of how they line up, as though used to such summonings. They wait, expectantly.

A large space remains around me, and my abductees despite those coming to witness this humiliation. It's as though none wishes to get too close to Jarl Sigurd and his men. I wonder then what sort of reputation the bastard has? Maybe he's a mean fighter, a terrible drunk or just a bloodthirsty bastard known for being cruel to those who take him as their master.

I'll never know. Not now.

A hush falls.

In the distance, I hear strident footsteps over the stone floor. Four men emerge from the door leading into the area between the church and the River Trent where the ships are moored.

They're all shapes and sizes. In the lead is a large man, a wicked scar gleaming in the suddenly growing candlelight as more and more flames spring up, as though lighting the path for him. I take him to be Jarl Halfdan. He looks as mean as his reputation. That he comes without his byrnie or weapons speaks of a cocky fucker. The Viking raiders never lack for stones.

Behind him is a smaller man. I know him to be Jarl Anwend, although he doesn't know me. Surprised eyes rake me in from behind a long nose and elongated chin. Not an attractive man, but he seems to make up for that with his warrior's build Here's a man who can fight, and probably very well. I'm unsurprised to find his weapons belt in place. He can fight and has learned to plan for all eventualities. I might have respected him had we met elsewhere.

Two men follow him. I don't know which is Guthrum and which

Oscetel. They could almost be brothers. They share many of the same features and walk like men who know the reach of their influence and power. Yet, they follow the two other jarls, which must mean they're less powerful. At least, here, in the strange little collective they've decided upon to rule Repton.

I'm shuffled forward by booted feet, hands on my shoulders, one digging in far too deeply, as though I'm their anchor and not vice versa.

A silence falls as the Viking raider bastards seek chairs and settle at the front of the church. It affronts me, once more, to see such men when a priest should stand there, wearing only his holy robes, his hands raised to praise God.

Jarls Guthrum and Oscetel mirror Halfdan in coming unarmed. Cocky arseholes.

I reconsider. There are near-enough a hundred armed men in the church. Perhaps they're right to rely on them for protection.

Candles have been lit behind the backs of the jarls, and a fire blazes on the floor. I'd not noticed it before. Fuckers. The church shouldn't have had a fire in it, and it accounts for the thick air. I can almost taste it rather than smell it. For a moment, the stench fills my nose. I think I'll choke again, only then I'm distracted from my panic.

'Jarl Sigurd,' it's Jarl Halfdan who speaks. His voice is rich and commanding, and again, I understand him even though he speaks Danish.

Jarl Sigurd, now standing close enough to me that I can smell him, inclines his head.

'Jarls, I have your prisoner for you.' If the accent is less thick and the words muffled, I'm sure that everyone will blame the swollen chin and cheeks that Jarl Sigurd has earned himself in capturing me.

I wait, as does the entire church, expectant eyes on Jarl Halfdan as he gazes at me.

'Jarl Anwend, bring forth your son, I would know if this man is truly Lord Coelwulf. He certainly doesn't look the part.'

I bristle at the words, even though I anticipate them.

A youth I know to be Anwend's son rushes forward to stand by his father, an awed expression on his face as he looks from Jarl Sigurd to me.

'Yes, yes, that's him,' Anwend Anwendsson splutters in Danish. The tension in my shoulders doesn't diminish, not one bit, because someone else is being thrust through the crowd at the instigation of Jarl Halfdan.

'Fuck,' my head all but explodes because I can't get the word beyond the rag.

Goda, beaten and bloodied, his head hanging at a strange angle, turns pain-filled eyes my way and startles, horror on his bruised face.

'Yes, it must be. Take him away.' Jarl Halfdan watches Goda's reaction carefully and dismisses him as quickly as he's had him brought before him. I try to reassure Goda with my eyes, but I know I can't convey everything he needs to know.

Two large men drag Goda from the hall. His eyes never leave mine. The black-clad warrior at my side stiffens, his stance no longer as casual as it should be.

I can't even hiss at him because of the rag in my mouth and the hundreds of eyes that watch everything I do.

'So Lord Coelwulf, you have finally accepted my invitation to join me in Repton.'

This isn't my idea of an invitation, but I'm powerless to say anything. Not bound and gagged as I am.

'I expected someone with better clothes,' Jarl Halfdan laughs as he speaks, the rest of the warriors in the hall joining in, for all the jarl taunts me in Danish.

I can't reply, and he doesn't expect one.

'It appears you don't wish to willingly pledge your oath to the new rulers of Mercia. We had, obviously, expected some resentment.' Jarl Halfdan's switched to my language, perhaps worrying that I won't understand him. I need only look at his eyes to comprehend his fucking intent.

'We allowed King Burgred to leave here, go to Rome to live out the last of his days,' his tone is filled with false compassion. I struggle against my bonds, for all I've come to hate King Burgred.

'But of course, the agreement could only be reached after he'd informed us of all who might object to the change in .... leadership. Your name was offered immediately. I can see I should have sent Jarl Sigurd to retrieve you first of all. My mistake,' Jarl Halfdan speaks as though he's the king here. I can see unease on Jarl Anwend's face. His son speaks frantically into his ear, and I curse.

I should have realised the lad would be here.

Yet Jarl Anwend holds his tongue, uncertainty on his ugly face. Perhaps he's pleased he came armed to this impromptu meeting.

'Now, the choice is yours. You can still pledge your oath to my fellow jarls and I, or we can simply end your life. I'd sooner the latter. I don't believe you'll be a good ally after all. If you're here, then I imagine your men are dead, and that means you're the lord of no one and fuck all.'

I incline my head as though accepting the point. I can't reply, and the unease amongst the men who captured me seems to prove the point as well. What more should I say?

'So what will it be then?' Jarl Halfdan laughs, sitting forward eagerly on his chair. He flicks his eyes over the other jarls he says he rules with but who've not been consulted before he speaks.

I remain still. I want to rip my bound hands free and grip them tightly around Jarl Halfdan's throat, but I can't. I feel small and insignificant, my hands covered in blood that I've spilt trying to fight my way free.

I don't fucking like it, not at all.

'As you will,' Jarl Halfdan leans back, a satisfied grin on his face.

'We should do this immediately,' he exclaims, standing as though about to take a sword and swipe my head from my shoulders without further thought. Only then he pauses, glancing at Jarl Sigurd and the black-clad warriors who surround me.

'You found him. You'll have the honour for exhibiting such restraint until now.' Jarl Halfdan nods to himself, pleased with the solution he's proposed.

I turn aside from him, instead taking in the church's interior and looking for a chance to escape, even now. In my head, I count the number of enemies arranged against me. I begin to appreciate just how overwhelming the odds are.

There's a flurry of activity around me, men pushed aside and others coming closer, as though to get the chance to see me before my death.

I would grin at them and show them my bloodied teeth, but the fucking rag is still in my mouth.

Do they fear me so much that they must kill me both bound and gagged? Is my reputation really so massive?

I hope so.

Yet my guard remains close, fending off those who become too inquisitive none too gently. I'm theirs, and they mean to ensure everyone knows that.

Leering faces swim in and out of my vision, and I stand tall despite my appearance. I'm a Mercian warrior, a man of royal birth, a warrior who's fought for Mercian independence, both from Wessex and from the Viking raiders. While I face my death, I'll show them what that means. I don't believe they understand what it means to be Mercian.

Too soon, the Viking raiders are forced back as Jarl Sigurd approaches me with a sharp blade in his gloved hands, a small smirk on his tight lips, his blond moustache gleaming in the reflected glow from the fire.

I'm forced to my hands and knees. With my entire body trembling, I find long-forgotten words of prayer on my lips, for the bastards haven't provided me with the opportunity to confess my sins.

I knew this moment would come, yet nothing prepared me for it. Nothing.

Strange thoughts cascade through my mind. Foremost of them all is the fact that I have fucking cold feet. I hate having cold feet.

I fucking hate it.

A pair of boots strides into my restricted vision and I envy those boots.

I don't look up. I don't beg. I don't plead. I'm resolved.

But fuck, my feet are bloody cold.

1

A MONTH EARLIER, AD874

I taste it on my lips and over the salt of my sweat.

I scowl. It's not a flavour I wish to get used to. All the same, I know what it is without a second thought.

My seax glistens slickly in the dull light, the gleaming claret reminding me more of an exotic wine from the south than the lifeblood it truly is. The double-headed-eagle impeccably depicted on the handle seems to wink at me as the eyes fill with the ruby mixture.

Not that I focus on it for more than the time it takes me to blink.

This horde feels as though it'll never stop. I'm determined to end the lives of as many of them as possible. Such slaughter doesn't bring me joy, but this is my skill. I wield it because I must. My weapon, so sharp it cuts through byrnies as though they're no more than spider webs, is busy today.

They come against my force, as small as it is, and they mean to annihilate us. But we will not go without sacrificing to their god of war. My seax sweeps effortlessly along the abruptly exposed throat of my enemy, the realisation of what's befallen him only reaching his eyes as he falls to the ground. I step over him, already sighting my next enemy.

This one swirls an axe in his left hand as I reveal my bloodied teeth. His entire body recoils, almost a backward step. Before he can consider his move, I've sliced through his belly, the gut threatening to spill at my feet. I dismiss him and move to the next man.

The ground beneath my feet squelches with each step, slick, more like a flooded river than the solid ground it should be. It's awash with the dead and wounded, the long shield wall that tried to defeat us long since disintegrated to small spots of desperate one to one fighting. This is my favourite part of any battle.

I turn, noting the angle of the sun, the brush of the breeze against my slick body, breathing deeply through my nose. This is not my first battle. Far from it.

I hear the cries of those boys who thought themselves men, and equally of those men who've found they are but boys when their lives are threatened. I scorn them. They're not worthy of my attention.

Quickly, I reach for my weapons belt, keen to know that all is where it should be. My hand brushes over the sharpened edges and deadly blades that make a home there. For now. Satisfied, I pick my next target, a tight knot of men fighting not five steps away, and move forward.

I don't hurry. Not this time. Neither, as I've seen others do, do I check the weight of my weapon or test the strength of my arm as I consider my next move. Instinctively, I know that all is well.

They'll not fail me. They haven't before.

The sun is high above my head, with few clouds to be seen, other than high up, more wisps than anything substantial.

This battle has been long. It began with the streak of fire across the eastern sky, and I don't foresee it ending other than when that same stripe sinks below the western horizon. Those who met their death in the first wave of the assault will be cold and stiff by then, the heat of the sun of no help to them.

Those still shivering with their mortal injuries will fearfully watch for the flashes of disappearing gold. They'll not see it rise again.

I mark it with detachment. There are more warriors to kill.

There are always more enemies to kill.

My seax arm sweeps to the right. I'd sooner not kill a man who doesn't know I'm there, but he should be paying more attention.

The wound along the back of his neck opens up with unsurprising ease, and I notice how my sworn man takes advantage of the action to slice across the throat.

The enemy wobbles, his head bobbing. I fear it will topple to the floor before he does, so I step around him. Icel grins at me, his black beard dripping with the blood of his foe, as I grunt an acknowledgement and nothing more.

Icel pivots to face the next enemy as I stride beyond him. Coldly, I count how many face us, how many are my warriors, almost pleased to see that the numbers, with my presence, are now equal.

That's not how we started this battle. And it's not how I plan on ending it, either.

I'll ensure we roundly defeat our enemy, and when they're dead, I'll plan my next move.

I focus my thoughts, sight my target, and rush toward them. He barely has time to raise his seax before I slice across his body. Blood spurts as the links of his metal coat burst open under the blow from my weapon. Another step, and a slash of the seax from left to right, and blood is falling like rain.

Sometimes, I think the enemy makes it too easy for me. I'm fast and relentless and always have been. But, I'm cautious against my arrogance. My men tell me that my strength is prodigious. For one always used to being so strong, it's impossible to know what it must feel like not to be.

My enemy staggers, perhaps not appreciating the extent of the injury. I take a cold moment of pity and allow him to fall onto the edge of my seax. His final gasp of air is filled with fluid as I reverse my hold, letting him slide to the floor.

I step gingerly over the rapidly growing pool of blood, grimacing at the stench of opened bowels and salty iron, at the result of my particular talents. Each kill is more than a number. But only just.

I feel as though I sweep through the enemy. They are warriors of all shapes and sizes, ages and skill levels. They all fall beneath my weapons as though I fell defenceless saplings. This butchery gives me pleasure and a burst of adrenaline only found in battle.

Only when I glance up, finding no enemy before me, do I stand upright, bring my legs together, menacing with my seax, and glance at the field of slaughter.

I lead twenty men. The enemy must have numbered at least double that. Of those who remain, three are standing, angled to protect the back of each other, while three of my warriors threaten them. Another five wait to take the place of any who might fall. I think they'll wait forever. My sworn warriors know how to make a kill, but some of them will insist on enjoying it first.

To the far right, I see where one lone figure attempts to escape into the muddy field ditch, alive for now but not for much longer.

Other than those four opponents, all others are dead, have fled or are pretending to be dead.

I sigh heavily, abruptly aware of the ache in my shoulders and the dryness of my mouth. I could drink a barrel of cold water. But it's not yet time to declare this battle won.

'How many?' I call as though to no one, but Edmund answers as quickly as always, his voice rich with the joy of battle.

'Two who will die, three with injuries that should recover, and Pybba who lost his hand. The damn fool.'

I turn to meet the eyes of Edmund. He grins at me, as cocky as ever when the battle seems to be won. It's not the same when a battle starts. When a battle commences, I almost expect him to run from the attack, or if he stays, to shit himself there and then.

His courage is slow to arrive and takes days to dissipate. But he fights with a tenacity I admire. I'd never wish to go into battle without him.

'Leave one alive,' I turn and bellow, reminding my warriors that we must employ the tactics of the Viking raiders, even if I don't want to do so. One must always live to tell of what befell their friends and comrades on the field of slaughter.

'Too late,' Edmund's voice is soaring with laughter as he watches the remnants of the three Viking raiders losing their fight to live. 'They always get bloody carried away,' he complains, but amusement thrums through the words rather than anger.

'Then bring me the one over there, heading toward the field ditch. We'll stitch him up and send him on his way.' Once the killing begins, it's almost impossible to stop until everyone on the battlefield lies unmoving.

Edmund turns to stride away, his hair hanging lank and greasy, his beard filled with spittle and blood. He's a tall man, but nowhere near my height. His eyes are the green of new growth, and women fall at his knee. Or rather his crotch. Men as well. Edmund admires a fine flank above all else.

'I think he's the one took Pybba's arm,' each step Edmund takes gurgles. I grimace at the reminder of just how much blood a man can lose and still fight on. It makes for a messy battlefield.

'Then let Pybba have him, and then send him on his way. Perhaps Pybba can repay the kindness. An arm for an arm, or something like that.' I know the phrase is an 'eye for an eye', but I don't much care. I just need a survivor to scamper back to wherever the Viking raiders have made their encampment. Fear itself is a tool.

My men disperse around the ad hoc battle site, looking for any who yet live, any great prizes or even their friends. More than one head bows low, and more than one groan rumbles as they come upon the dead.

'Bloody bastards,' I offer to no one in particular, moving to the side of the saturated ground, where a ragtag collection of horses and a few young lads shelter. The lads watch what's happening with the eagerness of the young and the horses with the experience of too many previous battles. They know this part of the day will be tediously long.

I can smell the smoke from the fire that's been left burning since the fight began. I hope it's damn hot.

'Bring me water,' I bellow. A small figure grabs something from my tall piebald horse and dashes toward me, not seeming to notice the ruin of the field beneath his feet.

Rudolf is all elbows and knees. I know he'll trip in his haste. I almost shout a caution, but it would be a waste of my breath. At least when he falls, it's a soft landing and avoids a body or a blade. He'll live to serve me for another day. I'm almost thankful.

'My thanks,' I state as I take the object thrust into my hand. Rudolf grins, his face smeared with muck, his white teeth a stark contrast.

'Why don't you pilfer?' Rudolf asks in his high voice. It's the same question that follows every success.

'I don't need to. I have you to do it for me.' It's all the invitation Rudolf needs. His legs pelt across the battle site. He's already decided where the richest pickings will be.

I unlace the water bottle and drink deeply.

The water is too warm, almost failing to quench my thirst.

I swill the first mouthful, and then spit it out, only then drinking deeply, wishing it came fresh from a stream. But it's a day old, and from the brackish water we found at the same time we realised we'd have to fight if we wanted to protect our lands.

'Pybba,' I bellow his name as I stride toward the fire. The young lads have almost all scattered, but one of them has had the wits to feed the flames. I add another few sticks, wishing it were as hot as a blacksmith's forge, but it'll have to do.

I turn once more. Where the fuck's Pybba?

'Pybba,' I roar his name, already bending to place my eating knife in the heart of the flames. The fire burns orange, not blue, all the same an acrid stench hits my nostrils, and I snatch back my hand quickly, smacking down on where my arm hair sizzles.

'I'm here,' Pybba's voice sounds ancient. I turn, lips downcast to gaze at the other man, as he stumbles to the well-trodden ground. He's older than I am. We've ridden together for over a decade. I won't let the bastard die, not today.

His face is white, his arm sheeted in crimson, his helm knocked askew so that I can see his rapidly balding head.

'Here, drink this.' I might not drink ale myself, but we never ride without it.

I take the beaker to him, mindful that he's going to need a fair few of them before I can begin the grisly work. He's slumped to the ground close to the fire.

Pybba snatches the beaker from me, with his left hand shaking and his eyes white with pain.

'Show me.' Pybba nods and holds his right arm out toward me. Hastily, I undo the piece of cloth tied over the wound. It seems that he's already made use of fire to cauterise the injury, but I know it needs to be a more thorough cleansing because it still oozes.

Other men might die of such a wound, but Pybba has enough battle experience to survive.

'Do it,' he grimaces, acceptance on his drained face. It looks as though Pybba has added more than enough of his life force to the ruin of the battle site.

'I will,' I confirm, my eyes on the wound. Rudolf has made himself useful by refilling Pybba's beaker again, and then one more, as he scampers between the dead and the living. Rudolf angles his body so that he can see the injury, a look of fascination on his young face. It holds his attention more than the dead.

'Stay out of the way,' I command fiercely. Rudolf skips out of my arm's reach. I wrap my glove around the blade of the knife, aware of the heat, even through the thick leather.

With swift movements, I press the heated blade across the bloodied stump. Pybba's eyes bulge, his cheeks puff out, and then he sags into Rudolf, as ever in the right place at the right time, and still, I hold the knife against the stump.

I know this is the only way to save Pybba's life from the creeping rot.

The blood flow has been stopped, not quickly enough, but well enough. Now, the skin needs time to cover the wound site. And it can't do it if there's muck and filth in the way and if the wound still weeps.

I swallow my unease and hold the knife long beyond the time the heat has crept through my leather glove and become beyond uncomfortable.

'Bind it,' I instruct Rudolf when I finally drag the knife away, thrusting it back into the flames, keen to cleanse it thoroughly from the work it's performed. I shake my hand and then pull the leather glove from it quickly, the foul stench making me wrinkle my nose again.

The boy works quickly and cleanly. By the time I turn back, Pybba's arm is covered in clean linen, and even the reek of burning flesh has blown away on the stiffening breeze. Now, I can only smell the burning leather.

I sigh. I'll not take the loss of him easily.

I turn to watch the rest of my warriors thoughtfully, considering the events of the day. I knew the Viking raiders sometimes penetrated deep inside Mercia, I didn't expect to find them on the land borders with the kingdom of the Hwicce when they're supposed to be in Torksey.

If they'd come by ship, I would have been less surprised. Riding here, now I have time to consider it, fills me with questions. Why weren't they stopped? What is King Burgred doing now? What ineffectual battle has he lost? When the witan next meet, I'll demand an explanation for this outrage.

The accord said the Viking raiders must stay at Torksey far to the north. It's evident they've broken that agreement. Why, then, have I not been summoned to fight for my kingdom?

Our bargain has been made, and my oath has been given to Mercia's king. The least King Burgred could do is to abide by his half of the arrangement.

'Look at this?' Rudolf brings the treasure to me. He still grins, although his hands flash redly. He's been elbow-deep in blood and gore after all. As always.

'What is it?' Rudolf asks. He has a thirst to know things. All sorts of things. I find his questions tedious and occasionally intriguing. I've long resolved always to have an answer for him even if I have to think of something on the spot.

'It's a coin, nothing more. But not one from here. Have you felt the weight in it?' I have, and it surprises me as I heft it in my glove-free hand, my seax loosely held in the other.

'Where's it from?' Rudolf asks, waiting for me to return it to him, his eyes as round as the coin.

'Maybe it's from the homelands of our enemy. I don't know, though. I didn't think they had coins,' I grimace, fearing I may regret my indecisive comment. His ready acceptance of such a terrible answer should have warned me.

Rudolf bites his lips in thought and pulls the rest of his treasure from behind his back. I laugh then. The little shit didn't just find a coin. He found a leather bag of coins, almost too heavy to hold in one hand. He grins at me.

'What they worth?' he asks, jiggling from foot to foot in his excitement.

'Whatever they weigh.'

'A lot then,' Rudolf's eyes widen in delight. I reach out and run my hand through his mucky hair. He's not my child. I have no children to call my own. But I feel I care for Rudolf as much as I could if I ever did father a child.

'Keep them safe. Don't let the others see,' the caution is well given. Rudolf turns his head quickly to ensure no one has seen our conversation. The other boys still crawl amongst the dead, occasionally shouting when they find something worthy of note. As always, Rudolf will have found the best of the spoils. Why else do I protect him and keep him safe?

By then, Icel has joined me. By rights, he should have been long dead, his hair turned grey, his black beard trailing almost to his weapons belt, but he lives for battle. Each time we vanquish our foe, he seems to turn back time and gain more years for his life. I've given up asking how old he is. The daft bastard never gives me a straight answer.

'In the reign of King Wiglaf I first became a man,' he's fond of saying, although he never explains what act made him a man. Again, I've stopped questioning him, although Edmund likes to when he's either drunk too much or is trying to distract himself from whatever attack we're about to begin. And, of course, Rudolf hangs on Icel's every word. They're an excellent match for each other, the boy who never runs out of questions, and the man who never answers them.

Rudolf's patience, cunning and deceit, far outweighs mine. Soon, he's going to be challenging to contain.

'In the reign of King Wigstan, I learned the true nature of being a warrior.' Damn the shitting fool. His riddles are unbecoming in one so damn, bloody old. That he enjoys my frustration only adds to it.

'Keen for their death, these lot. They aren't always,' Icel's voice rumbles. He's so big that if my eyes were closed when he speaks, I'd think he was a troll from the legends and not a man at all.

'They always are. I would have thought they'd have learned not to take on the Mercians by now. There's never any guarantee of victory for them. And if it's us they encounter, then there's no chance of victory at all.' Icel continues to comment on our success, his voice showing neither pleasure nor dismay at such an attack.

'I think we need to build on your reputation. This lot almost laughed when they saw us. I'll not have it.'

It's Edmund who speaks, his voice querulous as he slumps to the ground beside me. I look behind him, but I see no sign of the man he was supposed to bring to me from the field ditch. Edmund shrugs with his 'what can you do,' attitude, and I growl in frustration.

'We need to find us a scop. A skilled one, and not a shit one who can't get the name of the Goddodin right. Damn outrage.' This is one of his constant complaints. Why he believes the names of those long-dead warriors can have been kept in the correct order after all these years is beyond my ken. I can barely remember the names of my warriors, and I'm forced to speak to them every damn day.

'A scop? Why? To tell of Coelwulf's battle skills? It's not as though there aren't many warriors capable of such feats.'

'No, I know that.' I try not to listen to another tedious argument, but I do, all the same, as I check Pybba is well, if unconscious.

'No one kills the way he does. It's so smooth, so assured, never any doubt that he'll win. It's as though he dances with the fuckers who try and kill him. Others should hear of that. I've never seen anyone else do it that way.' Edmund's voice is filled with enthusiasm.

Icel chuckles darkly at the laudatory comment.

'In the reign of Beorhtwulf, you would have met a man who danced like our lord, here. Coelwulf's not unique.'

'Well, he's alive in the reign of Burgred. No one kills the way he does. And when you're dead, there'll be no one else to say there ever was a man who killed in such a way. We need a scop.' The final four words are spoken with the decisiveness Edmund hopes will end the conversation. I hope it does as well.

'What's a scop?' Of course, I'd forgotten young ears.

'You know what a bloody scop is,' Icel grumbles irritably. 'You've listened to enough of them.'

'Do you mean the stinky old bastard who fell asleep in his ale having recited about three lines and then slept himself to death.'

This statement stumps Icel, and I feel a tight smile on my lips, as his mouth hangs open in surprise.

Rudolf has proven that he hasn't, in fact, ever heard a scop perform. He's usually the one asleep after three sips of ale.

'Well, now, see, we need a scop because young Rudolf has no idea what one is. It's a bloody outrage.' Edmund persists with his tedious argument, as he works to clean his blade, interspersing his comments by drinking from his bottle. His young squire stands smartly to attention. How that boy keeps his clothes so clean, I'll never know.

More of my men are migrating to where I sit and drink my water. Some of them come with treasures clutched in their hands, others with the trace of old tears on their faces. I've not yet asked for the final body count, content to spend some time thinking that all of my warriors have survived this attack. The time will come soon enough when we have to dig another grave and say our farewells to yet more men who would have lived longer had it not been for the bloody Viking raiders.

'We don't need a scop. I don't need you sucking up and trying to make me feel as though I'm different in some way from the rest of you. All men can fight, bleed and die if they choose to do so. I don't do anything that the rest of you don't do.' And yet, even as I say the words, I know I'm lying.

I've watched other men in battle. Their movements don't flow as I feel mine do. And I'm never sure who'll be the victor. Apart from when Icel fights. He always wins. If not with the blade, then by forcing their faces into whatever stinking puddle he can find and holding them tight until their bodies stop convulsing.

He's a dirty fighter.

I like it when he stands at my back. Between the two of us, I'm sure that we'll both live to fight another day.

'We need a scop,' I hear Edmund's muttered response, but refrain from replying because I've realised that someone important is missing from our group. I stand, surveying my warriors, seeking out his dun-coloured horse, noting that his small squire is standing alone, his lower lip trembling, snot dripping from his nose.

'Fuck. Where the bloody hell's Hereman?' I direct the question at Edmund. He startles, his complaints forgotten about immediately.

'Damn the bastard,' they're brothers. Or so they say. But this is the greatest concern I've ever seen Edmund show for Hereman in the many years we've fought together.

I'm surveying the field of slaughter, and the realisation that he's dead and gone from me has already started to percolate through my body.

He's been my warrior for over a decade. The thought of going into battle without him is unsettling. Not, I admit, that he's overly skilled. But he's reassuring and can be relied upon, whereas some of the other men can be unpredictable.

Edmund's striding amongst the detritus of the battle site, looking, I know, for the brightly coloured shield that Hereman has always insisted upon. Why he's always wished to make himself a target, I don't know, but it works. Or it has. Until now.

'The daft bastard's not here,' Edmund's strained voice reaches me clearly, even though I've not moved from my position close to the horses, and he's at the edges of the churned grass.

The young lad, aware of my scrutiny, is trying to stop his tears from falling, attempting to look brave. I feel a twinge of pity for him. If Hereman is dead, then the lad will lose his place amongst my warriors. No one else will have any use for him, and certainly not Edmund.

What will become of him is not my concern.

'He's here,' the voice that reaches my ears is that of Rudolf's. I turn to where he points.

The first thing I realise is that Hereman is very much alive. His face glistens with sweat, a perplexed expression playing on his lips, his helm held in his hand alongside his sword and brightly coloured shield. Over his shoulder, he carries a limp form. Now I feel a flicker of annoyance.

Who else is fucking missing? I thought my men would have taken better care of each other than to be pillaging and drinking after the battle while we should have been mourning.

'My lord,' Hereman inclines his head as he lowers his prize to the ground.

Edmund slaps him angrily on the shoulder as he returns as well.

'Where the fuck you been?' Edmund demands.

'This little shit. He's still alive. He shouted some things while I fought him that I thought you might want to hear?'

It's not like Hereman to show any initiative, and that more than a desire to talk to one of the Viking raiders sparks my interest. His behaviour, for once, is entirely unpredictable. That'll teach me to have such thoughts.

'What did he say then?' I finally ask when silence falls amongst the milling men and boys.

'He says King Burgred's surrendered the kingdom, gone to that holy place, Rome, and that the Viking raiders claim all of Mercia for themselves.'

'Fuck that.'

'Bollocks.'

'Total arse.'

All ears are alert to Hereman's words. The responses are many but all on the same theme.

'King Burgred might not know a seax from a shield, but he wouldn't do that to Mercia. He's been fighting the damn Viking raiders for two decades. He wouldn't just give up now.'

'That's what I thought, but the little fucker was adamant. He kept asking me why I was fighting him now that the Viking raiders are in charge. He threatened me, the little tit, with all sorts of revenge. Little fucker.' Hereman sounds as furious as I've ever known him. I've never seen him lose control, but now he verges on it.

The man's lying on the floor, his face a welter of blood and forming bruises and it looks as though Hereman has taken out his irritation on him.

'You should have left him conscious if you wanted us all to hear his truth,' I say, annoyed.

'Gobby little shit wouldn't shut up, even when I head-butted him. I didn't mind bringing him to you, but I wasn't putting up with the verbal diarrhoea. Spoke our language as well.'

'Give him some water,' I order. Rudolf scampers to do as I ask. When he returns, Rudolf eyes the stranger critically, fascinated as always by the marks that seem to cover many of the Viking raiders bodies, and which show on his exposed shoulder. Hereman must have ripped his byrnie while dragging him. The black ink can't be removed once applied. Only then does Rudolf force the man's head upright and pour water over his sore looking lips.

The man does nothing, and then abruptly chokes, as his eyes flicker open in panic. Edmund's there to give him a helpful whack on the back as cloudy blue eyes survey the scene.

'Fuck.'

'Indeed. Now, tell me who you are and what's all this crap about King Burgred.'

The man's head bobs from side to side. I think he'll pass out once more.

'Give him the rest of the water,' I instruct Rudolf. He hands over the water bottle carefully, as though the Viking raider carries a contagion.

The enemy is covered in blood and mud. It's almost impossible to see any skin tone other than on his face, for the mass of brown and red from the battlefield has intermingled. His byrnie's shredded, held together by a thin strip of fabric, and only one of his feet remains covered by a boot. I wonder where the other one is, peering along the path that Hereman has just taken but not seeing it.

The enemy's lips seem to pulse, swollen by his fight with Hereman. Although silver arm rings snake their way along his left arm, they, too, are clogged with mud.

If he were one of my warriors, I'd send him to the river before I'd ever feed him, but I'm curious to hear these lies about King Burgred.

'Mercia belongs to us now. Your damn king has given Mercia for his life, the weak bastard. You've just killed your new lord's son, and I look forward to seeing you punished for it.' He speaks with a sneer of contempt. I don't miss that it's English, not Danish.

'When did this happen?' I still can't believe it. Mercia has been embattled for decades, why would Burgred have chosen now to turn traitor?

'A month ago, at Repton. King Burgred and his wife left for the Holy City immediately.' He's swallowed all of his water and takes the time to take in his surroundings, recognition flickering on his face.

'Lord Coelwulf, my men and I were sent to bring you to Repton. You have oaths to give to your new rulers in the royal hall there. Jarls Halfdan, Guthrum, Oscetel and Anwend are keen to meet the man who claims to keep Western Mercia safe. Although Oscetel may be less keen now.'

I turn aside and spit. I never expected to hear such words, even as muffled as they are by the Viking raider's puffy lips. I've done nothing but fight for Mercian independence since I could swing a sword. His mocking tone infuriates me, and I think of my seax. How easy would it be just to kill him now?

'Fuck that.' I don't speak, but I share Edmund's murmured sentiment.

'You don't have any choice,' the Viking raider comments and a stunned silence falls between us all. And then we laugh, all of us. It's laughter only found after a battle has been won. It's relief and grief and the last vestige of the battle joy that all good warriors need to live through each attack.

'And you and what army are going to take me to Repton?' I chide. The Viking raider looks around wide-eyed, perhaps only becoming aware that he's captured and alone.

'Well, the one I came with.' His voice trails off, as his eyes rake the slaughter field, noticing the fallen men, realisation dawning.

'Food for the crows, I'm afraid as you might be if you don't watch what you say.' The Viking raider sneers at me, forgetting how exposed he is.

I watch him, an uncomfortable awareness starting to take hold.

I can't allow this man his freedom. Neither do I want him as a member of my war band. I've no time for prisoners, either. That means he must die, and I've never enjoyed taking the life of an unarmed man.

'Here,' I grunt, handing him a sword. He clutches it, a furtive look in his blue eyes.

Does he realise what this means? Certainly, the remainder of my men do. They turn aside, watch, or walk away as I grip my seax.

I respect the religion of the Viking raiders. No man must be in peril for his soul, or whatever it is that my enemy possesses.

I stand before him, the movement effortless despite the day of fighting behind me. With no time for thought, I swing my seax, aiming perfectly to slice open his throat with the sharpened blade.

The man, still examining his sword, almost doesn't seem to notice the action until the river of crimson collects on the hand gripped around the pommel of the seax. He turns to look at me, eyes already losing the sparkle of life, but a grimace touches his cheeks.

I take it as thanks for ensuring he died with his weapon in hand.

It brings me no peace, but neither do I think much more about it as I walk away and Rudolf rushes to pilfer the body.

My thoughts are elsewhere as I peer into the glowing gloom of night.

If the man spoke the truth, my kingdom is in ruin.

If he spoke the truth.

Quickly, Edmund joins me as I walk the place of slaughter.

I rode here with twenty warriors and perhaps half as many young lads who didn't fight. As far as I can tell, the force that faced us was double that. And they came with horses. Rudolf and his ilk have found the mounts and are slowly bringing them to join our beasts, picking a path through the detritus of the dead.

My men can take a spare mount, the young lads as well, although it'll be expensive to keep them all fed. Perhaps I can sell a few to afford the grain to feed the others? Or maybe I'll just keep them all. I'm sure Edmund can tell me how much each horse is worth. He has a way with numbers.

I've abruptly become rich in horses and responsibilities.

'What will you do?' Of all my men, only Edmund would ask such a question. The others are always keen to follow my orders. What they are rarely concerns them.

'We carry on fighting,' I rumble. But I know that's not what he means. He's not alone in wondering what I'll do in light of the news I've been given. I wish I knew too.

'If they have a base in Repton, they'll be more organised than in the past, and they have control of the dead Mercian royal family, which is something they didn't have in Torksey.'

'Yes, but they'll be no less lacking in skills.'

I can feel the smile touching his cheeks, although he holds his tongue. We know each other well.

'Western Mercia has always been our concern, Worcester, Gloucester and Hereford. Does it truly matter if the north and east have fallen?'

Edmund's continued silence tells me more than any words could.

It convinces me, as well.

'Fuck it,' I growl, turning to walk back toward the impromptu camp. 'We'll go and find out the truth for ourselves. And hopefully, kill a lot more of the damn bastards along the way.'

Edmund nods, although I only hear it as a rustle of his beard over the byrnie he wears.

'Then we'd better get those weapons cleaned,' Edmund confirms, striding out before me, keen to be about his task.

I watch him go.

I've fought for Mercia's freedom all my life. I'm not about to fucking stop.

2

Come the morning, there are sore heads and angry voices. Too much ale and grief will do that to a man.

Last night, I was reluctant to leave, more concerned with the burial of my two dead warriors, Athelstan and Beornberht. And I was caring for the injured Pybba, Ingwald, Oda and Eahric. But now I feel desperate to be gone.

'Get up,' I move around my men, kicking stomachs and backs when they seem insensible to my words.

'Get up, you worthless fleabags.' Rudolf rushes around behind me, offering me hunks of days-old bread we purchased in Gloucester when we were last there and a flagon of freshwater. I swig it gratefully, watching his dancing eyes. If he ever develops any muscles to aid him in his warrior skills, he'll be the sort of man who looks forward to each battle.

'Clean your face,' I demand of him when his good cheer has become too much to tolerate. 'You filthy bugger,' I continue, but still he grins. I'd slap the smirk from his face, but it'd only get wider.

His excellent cheer has never faltered. I almost fear the day that it does, while knowing that the day will come. Probably far sooner than I'd like it to do.

The decision I have to make is how to get to Repton.

I'm near Gloucester, which is close to the Welsh kingdom of Gwent. I expected to face a force of Welshmen from Gwent, not the Viking raiders when the enemy was sighted. Sometimes the Gwent Welshmen skip over the border, and then, forgetting the purpose of their expedition, get carried away. I'm sure many Welsh warriors brag that they've seen the River Thames rather than the Severn.

Damn fools. What they should hope to do is to secure their borders, rather than seeing how far they can get evading detection.

But still, should I go north or east?

The Foss Way runs to Leicester. Leicester is an easy ride to Repton. But, if the Viking raiders have Repton, they may also have Leicester or any of the other nearby settlements. It could make it impossible to get close. Alternatively, I could ride north, along smaller roads, and come to Repton by a slower, less obvious route. I'm assuming the Viking raiders have taken Foss Way to reach the western regions. It accounts for finding them here.

How, I consider, did the Viking raiders even take Repton? The last I heard they were in Torksey, in northern Mercia and had been for years. Did they ride? Did they thread their way along the rivers that split the landscape, down the River Trent, until they reached their location?

Did they know of Repton's importance to the Mercians, or has it been happenstance, if it's even happened, that they've ended up at Repton? Was it just the last place their ships took them to before they were seen?

I grunt. Too much thinking gives me a headache, no matter the lack of ale I've drunk.

'North,' I shout to my rousing men, Edmund the most vocal in his complaints that he's only just shut his eyes and can he not sleep longer. 'We go north and see if this paltry force was all the Viking raiders had to show.'

Pybba watches me from beside his horse. He's biting his lip, face pale, and I hope to God he's not about to mutter words that will ruin my day. But he nods and then winces. I go to his side. I can see the bloody stump where his hand was, and a sweet scent reaches my nostrils. His grin surprises me.

'Honey, from the monks at Gloucester,' he explains. 'And lots of fucking ale from wherever it came,' his breath is sour, but he seems steady enough on his feet. That pleases me. A lot of men would have slunk off to die in the bushes like a wounded beast. It gratifies me that Pybba will not be one of them. I'd never have thought it of him, but such a wound can make a fighting man doubt all and only think gloomily of the future.

'Then we must ensure we have lots of ale,' I smirk. Pybba nods, a flicker of his worry showing in the jerky movement.

'I've seen men fight one-handed many times,' I lower my mouth to his ear. I don't want others to hear our conversation. 'Just remember which is the sharp end and always have an ally at your back. Speak to Rudolf. I'm sure the little shit can think of a way to attach your shield to what remains of your arm. He delights in that sort of thing.'

I walk away then, not wanting to make more of his injury than that. I'm amazed he stands. I'm astounded he doesn't howl with agony. But then, Pybba has always been a tricky bastard to kill. That Viking raider deserved a more horrific death. I should have allowed Pybba to make the kill, one-handed or not. I'll apologise for that. Later.

It seems to take all morning to mount up and sort out the extra mounts. Even then, there's a trail of horses that I don't need. They'll be worth a great deal to someone, and I do consider having them taken back to Gloucester and then on to Kingsholm.

Gloucester, with its crumbling Roman stone walls, would make a safe haven for the horses. Perhaps I might even make some coin from the sale.

'They're worth more here,' Edmund comments sourly, his mood far from improved. 'If one of our beasts goes lame, then we'll have a spare, maybe even two.' His horse is far from docile beneath him, and I imagine he understands his rider's words only too well.

I hold my tongue. I don't wish to split the force I command.

Neither do I want to have stray horses that might, unwittingly, be sold to the Viking raiders, or worse, to the Gwent Welshmen who sometimes steal into Gloucester to buy Mercian goods. Especially when the craftspeople of Gloucester are desperate for money and will sell to anyone.

No, I'll keep them with me. For now.

Edmund rides at my side when we finally turn our backs on yesterday's battle site. I've already dismissed it from my thoughts and made my peace with Athelstan and Beornberht, who lost their lives fighting for me. I'm not the sort of person to replay my battle activities in great detail.

The past is done and unchangeable. It's the future that concerns me.

I send Sæbald and Gyrth to ride before the main body of the force. They'll squabble like old women. Quiet, no, but alert, yes. It'll also be pleasant not to have to listen to them argue all damn day long about anything from whether it'll rain that day to who's made the most kills in all their battles together. It's wearisome and only occasionally amusing.

Those two have caused more damage to each other when drunk as fuck than they've sustained enemy injuries.

Not that I'm sleeping in my saddle. I'm aware of all that surrounds me, from the small animals in the long grasses to the birds above my head hunting the poor sods. Every sound, every rustle from the undergrowth, has me looking. As the afternoon wears on, Edmund's chuckle reaches my ears.

'They're not likely to emerge from an underground burrow, are they?'

I'm not sure I share his certainty.

'We thought we went to fight the damn Gwent Welshmen, not the Viking raiders.'

'I thought I went to fight the enemy. I don't much care who that was as long as they're dead now.'

Edmund rides a chestnut stallion. Jethson is as damn randy as his rider. Even now, he rides with half an amused smirk on his face, eying up the new horses. No doubt there's a mare amongst them he'd like to mount. Wherever the Viking raiders found the horses, they're good stock. I almost fear to find the original owner. No doubt they'll demand them back, and my profit from the battle will be reduced to the riches Rudolf has cleverly hidden.

My horse is a piebald stallion, only mine by virtue of being the biggest horse I could find at the time. Haden's gait can be uncomfortable when fractious, but today, he seems calm. If he senses any danger, he'll buck and tug at the reins. He might even nip me, the contrary git.

Rudolf bounces along in the saddle of his pony. His riding skills are weak. I don't know how his arse takes such punishment. But the pony is the only thing he brought with him into my service. I'm loath to demand he gives the animal up, even though his legs have doubled in length in the intervening years.

Rudolf rides behind me, mingling with the rest of the warriors and young lads. I hardly need to speak to anyone any more. Rudolf always knows everything. He's an inquisitive youth. But he's quick-witted too. It didn't take him long to realise I didn't appreciate his incessant chatter, and so he took it elsewhere.

When he brings the jogging pony to my side, a gleam in his eye, I almost groan. What new titbit has he gleaned now? Do I even want to know?

But for once, he has a question to ask, rather than information to share.

'We stopping anytime soon?' he pouts, leaning close so that his words can't be overheard by anyone but Edmund. Edmund is tunelessly whistling to himself, so I doubt he hears anyway.

'Pybba needs to rest,' Rudolf explains before I can dismiss his question. I feel as though we've only just got going.

I turn then, my eyes seeking out the men who follow on behind me. It's easy to find Pybba. For all his good cheer earlier, he slumps in his saddle, and I fear he might fall from his horse. Even from here, I can see the glimmer of fresh blood on the linen that covers his wound.

'Why didn't he say?'

'Stubborn old codger,' Rudolf complains. I almost slap the smirk from his cheek. He has no understanding of just what it's taken Pybba to live such a long life. Skill, damn luck, and even more determination. Pybba's a rarity in these bloody times.

But, I remember thinking little more of those who seemed 'old' when I was Rudolf's age.

'There's a likely-looking spot coming up,' Edmund nods. I look to where he indicates. The road, with remnants of the ancient build showing here and there in long and disjointed pieces of stone and pebbles interspersed with roots, turns sharply ahead. A swathe of cleared earth hints at previous campsites.

That a beck runs to the rear of the ground only adds to its acceptability. But, there's little in the way of cover, and I hesitate. Last night, we slept on a rise, able to see a great distance around us until the cloud cover became too thick. We won't have that advantage here, and the beck could trap us, as well as provide much-needed fresh water. I'll have to set watch duty. None of the men appreciates that the day after a battle when the battle joy has finally drained away to be replaced by exhaustion.

'Halt,' I shout, all the same, looking to Edmund. He sighs heavily and encourages his mount forward. Sæbald and Gyrth are far ahead, intent on their task and unaware that we've stopped.

There's a mumble of surprise from the men and boys. I refuse to meet Pybba's eyes. He'll see that this is for him. I'll not have him think I'm so alert to his difficulties. I don't wish to wound his warrior's pride.

While the young lads rush around to set up our campsite, I take Haden to the brook. It's been a warm day, and the animal drinks thirstily. Easier to lead the horse to water than bring the water to Haden. It might look as though I'm lost in thought, but I listen to the sound of the camp being made, alert to anything that might be different.

Time stretches on and then on some more, and still, I don't see Sæbald, Gyrth or Edmund returning along the trackway. I'm not one to feel foreboding, but I'm aware that they've been gone too long. I look along the path they've taken, hoping to see them riding back. But the view stays empty.

'Icel, Goda, come with me,' I call for two of my most experienced warriors, and they rush to follow my orders.

Rudolf comes to my side as though waiting for me to impart my special favour to him.

'Help Pybba, see he has everything he needs,' I speak out of the corner of my mouth, expecting a complaint. But for once, Rudolf has no retort and happily skips away to where Pybba has found a discarded log to rest against.

'Oslac, Ordheah, keep alert. Have your weapons to hand.'

I can feel the gazes of my men. I'm not the only one to peer down the deserted trackway.

Mounting up, habitually, I reach for my seax, but content it's there, I merely wait for Icel and Goda and then lead them away.

The air's heavy and silent, sweat beading my face, although it's been cool for much of the day. A forest to one side and a slight rise to the left have obscured the stray breezes. The small animals that I might expect to hear have fallen quiet. I swallow my mounting sense of frustration. I know what such silence could mean.

If fifty Viking raiders burst from the forest now, we'd be outnumbered, but it wouldn't be an unequal fight. We ride fast horses and are all well-skilled. Anyone in the forest would have to be unmounted. And the Viking raiders have little skill with horses, even if they've managed to lead them.

Icel rides his black beast, Samson, in front of me, his eyes keen as he looks around. Goda keeps behind me on his grey horse, Magic. The animals step with more spirit than they have all day, as though they sense that all is not right.

How many Viking raiders were sent to the western part of Mercia? I should have asked that question before I permanently silenced the survivor.

On and on we ride, the forest slowly giving way to open land, farmed and growing well in the summer heat, but still, we see no one, and then the forest closes in once more.

My forehead wrinkles. This is unlike any of my warriors.

Why, I consider, would they have ridden on so far? Sæbald and Gyrth knew that the day's journey was to be leisurely. I wish to reach Tamworth, but not immediately. I don't gallop but rather trot. It's my intention, as much as possible, to keep to the shadows with my band of warriors and young lads.

I don't have a war band of five hundred men to support me. Not at the moment.

'Where are they?' As my belly rumbles loudly, I hear Goda complaining behind me. We ate with the dawn, and that was a long time ago. I detect frustration and an edge of unease in his voice.

The news the captured Viking raider gave us yesterday has perturbed my men. I wish to dismiss the nervousness with my usual biting response, but even I'm aware of my dry mouth, and the heat doesn't cause it.

Peering over my horse's head, I note hoof marks in the muddier parts of the track.

'They came this way,' I point.

'Someone did,' is Goda's less than helpful reply. I feel a sharp retort on my tongue. Only then the sound of galloping hooves reaches our ears.

'Arm yourselves,' I'm already reaching for my seax. I don't jump at shades, but the thundering sound fills me with premonition.

And it should.

Edmund bursts into view further along the track, crouched low to his stallion's back. I doubt he sees us as he hustles his animal toward us.

Behind him are five mounted warriors. They jiggle along in their saddles. I'm amazed they don't fall to their deaths. They lack all skill.

'Fuck,' Goda's voice is filled with fury, as we rein our mounts to a stop.

'They only just outnumber us,' I state flatly, my weapon ready in my hands. I'm not sure that any of the six riders have seen us. Where, I think, are my two missing men? And where have these raiding scum come from? I hope to God we're not surrounded. My small band at the side of the track suddenly seems too small. With Pybba wounded and Ingwald, Oda and Eadric with lesser wounds, there are only nine men capable of fighting.

And they have many horses to protect as well as one another.

'We can take them,' Icel's voice is rich with resolve, spittle flying from his lips as he tucks his beard tightly against his weapon's belt.

'Let Edmund through, and then we intercept them,' I command forcibly. I don't want to risk injuring Haden, but if I must fight from the saddle, then I will.

The riders are coming closer, the calls of the Viking raiders and their clattering horses breaking the oppressive silence of a summer's day.

I watch them through narrow eyes, trying to size them up.

They wear battle equipment, and the sun glints on sharp blades and mean-looking faces. None of them wears helms. I'm not surprised. At that speed, it's more likely that a helm would lead to death than an enemy strike. Helms aren't renowned for staying in place while riding.

Only then does Edmund glance up, his relief at seeing us evident in how his entire body relaxes. The huge grin on his white face isn't needed.

But Edmund isn't alone in realising he's not outnumbered anymore. The lead Viking raider carries on with his strange jig atop the horse, but the man immediately behind him barks a warning, at least that's what I take it to be.

The second warrior reins in his mount as best he can, as do three other men, reaching for their helms, while the lead rider rushes ever onwards.

'Three to four. Should be easy.' Icel's straightening his back, testing his balance, and with a lick of his lips, looking around to ensure no one's behind us. Only then does he ram his helm on his head. It's been battered back into shape so many times over the years it appears to be one big dent. But Icel trusts his helm. All of those dents show an occasion that saved his life.

I agree with his assessment of our strength against the enemy. Much of the action might take place on the ground.

And then Edmund is dashing beyond us in a rush of air, and the three of us take up a position across the trackway. We almost fill it, but not quite. The hedgerow to one side, lethal-looking, with thorns that threaten to clasp us tightly if we should get caught, will be the fourth man, for now. To the other side of the track, the ground's rocky and strewn with boulders that have fallen from the valley side.

No horse will welcome riding over that. It won't want to risk injuring itself, no matter what its rider might direct.

'Damn fuckers,' Edmund has turned his horse around and waits behind me, catching his breath. I'd ask him about my missing men, but the first Viking raider is before us. He makes no effort to stop his horse as he meets us. I think it is a new trick until I see his white eyes.

The man has no control over the horse.

I nudge my beast to the right and allow the rider to thunder beyond me. I doubt he'll be much trouble.

'Ahh,' the cry from the rider who follows him is filled with fury. At least he has his horse under control and takes the time to shout for his allies as he fumbles for a weapon.

With the lead rider gone, we're an equal force.

'He's mine,' I bellow, gripping my seax, but prepared to jump from Haden's back if the man determines to fight on foot. He doesn't, slashing widely with an enormous blade from the back of the animal. The weapon looks too heavy for the rider's build, but he manages it well enough. I decide he must be skilled to possess such a finely balanced weapon.

He comes at me, leering and with no shield evident. Although mine is draped over my horse, I leave it where it is.

My opponent slashes sideways with his sword, his intentions

evident in how he pulls up short. Just like I would, he wants to wound the animal and take the rider when the horse bucks in pain.

I turn Haden aside with my knees, depriving my opponent of successfully completing the move. His sword meets my weapon all the same. I appreciate that the blade looks broad but may be weak because of it. Certainly, there's little impact on my arm as the two clash in a shriek of iron.

To the side and rear, my men face-off against one of the other attackers. We're all busy killing the opponent who wants to kill us.

One of the men has slipped to the ground, keen to fight on a steady surface. Goda has joined him there. The two discarded horses glare at each other threateningly. I consider doing the same. My horse is more valuable to me than the wealth this man carries on him. Well, apart from the sword, which may, or may not be one of the fabled Viking raider ones.

Another reaching blow aims for my arm. I feel a flicker of appreciation for the skill being employed against me. When this warrior lies dead on the ground, my enemy will have lost one of their better fighters.

That always pleases me.

Before another blow can be struck against me, I release my boots from the stirrups. With the other beast fractiously trying to bite Haden, my opponent is temporarily distracted. I move quickly to fling my right leg over the saddle, landing heavily on my feet, reaching for my shield as I whack Haden's backside. He knows what it means and hastens to move out of the way with a clatter of his hooves.

It's all happened so quickly, my enemy is still trying to control his horse. I slice the blade down the animal's back legs and step back, shield raised, ready to defend against the rearing animal.

I nod, satisfied when from in front of my shield, I hear a thump and an 'oof' of air escaping the warrior. The horse's wound isn't deep, and it will heal with time. The rider though, well he'll be dead by then.

In three long strides, my weapon's touching the enemy's neck, horror in his blue eyes. It gives me no delight to end our short battle by slicing open the exposed throat of the figure lying before me. One leg's caught behind his body, a slither of white bone protruding from the fall. I do him a favour. I think he knows.

With the wet sound of air leaving the dead man's mouth, I turn to see how my men fare. Edmund has his opponent's horse tangled in the thorns. The animal's eyes are wide with fright, as it seeks to kick its way free, only to force the rider to the floor.

With both of them snarled, I leave Edmund to his task. Goda seems harder-pressed, but I don't interfere. He likes a good battle and never appreciates an easy kill. Icel's just standing, watching, his hand on one hip, his horse milling around with Goda's and mine.

All, apart from Edmund's opponent, opted to fight on the level ground. It's the wiser course of action, even for the two men who are dead, with the third not far behind.

'What about the other fucker?' Icel points his seax back down the trackway we've just ridden down.

'We'll find him on the way back,' I shrug. One rogue warrior on a horse he can't control will be no match for my warriors, and I'm including Rudolf in that. I'm not worried about him.

I walk to the horse I wounded, unsurprised to see suspicion in his eyes. I reach out, speaking calmly, keen to grab the reins and direct him away from the two fights that continue.

The horse has been ridden hard, froth foaming at its mouth, mixed with blood.

'Shush, shush,' I soothe. I'm keen to claim the animal as mine but also to see if the saddlebags contain valuables.

Icel watches Edmund, a faintly amused expression on his face. I feel safe enough to turn my back on the attack. It'll be over soon enough.

The animal calms at my actions, and quickly, I slip my hand over his nose and then mouth, grimacing at the froth and sweat.

'Damn bastards,' I mutter under my breath. A rider should know how to care for a horse. The Viking raiders have little or no skill in tending the mounts they steal. If they're to succeed, they must learn to honour their horse as they would their weapon.

I know too well how long the Viking raiders spend cleaning and scouring their battle equipment. But not one of them would consider doing the same for their mount. I'm surprised the animals aren't lame or their teeth grown too long. Perhaps they've not long been under the control of the Viking raiders, or maybe, until this journey, the animals were still under the care of men and women who knew how to feed them, check their hooves for stones and wipe the sweat from their backs on such hot days.

The animal's shivering beneath me, foam evident under the saddle, and keeping my hand on his coat, I work my way back to the saddlebags, taking the time to check the wound first.

It's bled freely, but the flow has stopped. I can already see a layer forming over the wound. The animal will heal. With the right aid.

There's a saddlebag, and I feel it. But it seems to have nothing but provisions inside it from my cursory inspection.

'About bloody time,' I turn to check on my men. Icel's berating Edmund, as Edmund tries to pull himself free from the few thorns embedded in his byrnie. His opponent still fights with the thorns, but they hold him, as blood sheets from a wound to the top of his leg. Not the cleanest of deaths, and not the nicest to endure, I'm sure. But dead all the same. When he realises.

'Where are Sæbald and Gyrth?' I ask before the two can fall to arguing about the sloppiness of Edmund's attack.

'Fuck knows,' Edmund sounds aggrieved as he finally wrenches his left leg free with a ripping sound. 'Fuck,' he mutters, looking down at the sizeable hole that's formed. 'I found those bastards first. The damn fools must have ridden into another force of Viking raiders.'

'Bollocks,' it's not what I want to hear. Firstly, I don't want to lose two good men, and secondly, it means my decision to come this way has been a poor choice.

'Well, that was disappointing,' Goda's finally taken the killing blow. I turn to watch him eye his enemy with interest. 'You know,' he says, as though the dead man can still hear him. 'If you'd gone for the right side, instead of the left, you wouldn't be dead now.' I shake my head. Goda fights with great skill and always appears to be three or four strokes ahead of his enemy. He kills with a cool head. 'Now,' Goda says. 'Where's the other shit?'

He turns to gaze back the way the racing horse has gone, but there's no sound to be heard. The noises of the day have returned abruptly.

'We have another four bloody horses,' Goda confirms. He's bending to retrieve whatever of value he finds from his foe. 'Here, Edmund, do you want his tunic?'

'If you think it'll fit me,' Edmund replies breathlessly. The animal that was stuck in the thorns is flailing widely, its eyes wide with fear, and its flanks covered in splotches of dark fluid against the black of its coat. It might be quicker to kill the beast than extract it, but Edmund's hacking at the spindly brown thorns with his eating knife. I turn to help him, fearing that darkness will fall before he can accomplish his task.

'Sæbald and Gyrth had gone a long way. I'd been racing back for quite a while. To begin with, more men were following me, but they must have given up long ago. I can't hear them following, either.' Edmund informs me. I peer along the trackway, but I can't hear anyone, and the day is starting to draw in. Only a fool fights in the dark.

'But why would Sæbald and Gyrth have gone so far? We couldn't have travelled even this distance at the pace I set?'

Edmund's shoulders shrug at my question.

'You asked me to bloody find them. I tried to do that. I didn't consider the why or anything.'

'The Viking raiders saw a lone man and came to ask me some questions, all cocky like, blades showing, thinking I'd be an easy kill. I called them all bastards and raced away. I don't think they liked it.'

I grunt at that. I'm always amused that you can menace a man with a sharp blade, but you can really piss 'em off by telling them their mother was a whore!

'Where are they going?'

'I didn't take the time to ask.'

With a final hacking movement through the thorns, the animal finally skips free, breathing as heavily as Edmund. All the thanks I get for my efforts are a stamp on my foot from the back hoof.

'Grateful sod, aren't you,' I move to make an ally of yet another horse while Edmund fights his way free to the sound of more and more ripping.

'I think you'll need the trews as well,' Icel complains with aggravation, thrusting the tunic at him, and turning back to the lifeless body that's half-exposed in the gathering gloom.

'Do we bury 'em?' Goda asks.

'No, we'll just drag them to the side, pile some of those loose boulders over them. We've nothing to dig with, and their comrades might want them back.'

Goda bends, and one-handed grasps the leg of his kill, hauling it to the side of the trackway. The outcome of any battle always leaves far too visible signs. I've buried many men in my time. But the Viking raiders like to burn their dead first. They're welcome to them when they find them.

Edmund turns to gaze at his kill. The thorns have their clutches well and truly embedded in the body. The killing wound wetly flashes.

'Can't I just leave him?' Edmund complains, but he's already moving to extract the body. It's far too damn grizzly to leave pegged out in such a way. It would have helped if the dead man had shut his eyes in death, but instead, he peers at us.

I move to my kill and drag him, two-handed to where Goda's already piling boulders over the enemy he killed. I notice the stark white feet with interest.

'New boots?' I ask, eyebrows high.

'Old boots where someone else has already worn out all the painful parts are my sort of boots,' Goda grumbles.

'Anything else of value?' I'm curious as to how wealthy these men were. They have horses. They have weapons, but what else have they stolen from previous kills?

'Look over there.' I peer to where Goda points and see a small pile of items taken from the dead man. There's a silver arm ring, a leather thong with a small emblem on it, no doubt worn around his neck, and a weapons belt. The man had seax and war axe. The weapons look well used. The axe's handle gleams with the sheen of a man's sweat that's been worn into the handle over many previous attacks.

'A warrior then?'

'Well, in some meanings of the word, yes,' Goda comments, standing up to admire his work.

I slide the helm from my kill and a mass of long hair cascades from beneath it. It might once have been blond, but now brown tendrils flicker through it. I gasp as well, noting the eyes and the more delicate face than I was expecting, the scars adding to the impression of a woman who'd fought many battles.

'A woman?' Goda comments, his eyebrows furrowed in consternation. 'That explains why you killed her so damn quick.'

I tilt my head from side to side, considering.

'A lighter build, I noticed, but not that she was a woman.' I ignore the rest of Goda's words. She's my enemy. I've no qualms about killing a woman. She tried to kill me, after all. Neither will I take the taunt in his voice. All of my kills are easy.

'What now?' Edmund breathes heavily as he brings the dead man beside the woman.

I'm still considering what value the body might hold for me. There are no rings or jewellery, and I feel strangely reluctant to claim the two silver arm rings that rest just above her left elbow. Neither do I have much use for the clothes. But I reach and undo the clasp on the weapons belt. It'll fit Rudolf.

The clatter of a boulder abruptly obscuring her face rouses me from my thoughts, and I glance at Goda. He's grinning at me, pleased with himself. Hastily, I place more and more boulders over the dead body. Woman or man, it little matters, but, and I consider this, it might make our rogue rider keen to seek revenge if he still lives.

'We go back to the camp. Tomorrow, we'll find Sæbald and Gyrth. For now, we need to eat and, if we're lucky, find that other rider and end his life as well.'

The three men don't complain about leaving Sæbald and Gyrth's fate unknown for the night. They know that hunting at night is a bloody waste of time.

Tomorrow, I vow, I'll find my missing men.

3

Without further thought, I grip a handful of long grasses and work as much blood as possible loose from the blade. Only then do I return it to my weapons belt.

I'm already imagining the excited questions from Rudolf and anticipating his responses when he hears I killed a woman Raider.

It's not a secret that the Raiders consist of both men and women. All the same, it's always something of a surprise to kill one.

The four horses, I've never been so rich in horse flesh before, are easily gathered together, despite the wounds two of them have. While Goda and Icel determine to ride before me, I hold back, with Edmund.

Edmund still complains as he checks his body for scratch marks from the thorns. He's changed neither his trews nor tunic and his exposed skin flashes in the afternoon sun.

'I'll wash them first,' he offers when I indicate his torn clothes. 'I'll not wear the stench as well as their clothes.' We lapse into silence. I'm busy thinking about Sæbald and Gyrth. Where have the fuckers gone?

'Bit keen for another kill, aren't they?' Edmund finally comments into the silence, watching as I do, how alert Goda and Icel are in front of us.

'They're welcome to whoever they happen to find. Damn fool. I wouldn't trust a man who mounted a horse and forced it to ride fast without the skill to bring it under control. The horse is as much a weapon as the iron he rides with. I doubt he'd think much of someone who just jabbed around with a sword or spear.'

Edmund remains silent. I know what plagues him. I'll allow him to speak first.

The silence between us stretches onwards, and I almost think we'll make it back to the campsite without meeting the lost Raider or Edmund speaking.

But no such luck.

'It's true then?' The words are filled with strain.

'It appears to be. If there's another force north of here.'

'Damn that fucker,' fury turns the complaint taut. I can't argue with Edmund. I feel the same.

'We're still going to Repton,' I state before he can argue with me. His hands on the harness tell me more about him than the new silence.

Edmund wants to go to Repton. He wants to know the truth, but equally, he wants to fight. I can tell, from the way Edmund rubs one hand over the other, in an attempt to keep them firm on the harness. If he had his way, he'd be halfway to Repton already.

'But we'll kill everyone we encounter?'

'Of course,' I'm surprised he asks the question.

'And we'll find Gyrth and Sæbald?'

'If we can.'

'And what of the horses and young lads?' This is a problem. 'And what of the fact we're missing over a quarter of our force. That's including Pybba, who won't be able to fight for weeks yet, whereas Ingwald, Oda and Eahric are hampered too.'

'Um,' is all I offer. I know what the problems are. I've just not decided on how to solve them yet.

Edmund sighs, not with frustration, but weariness. We've been fighting for many years. We've not yet come close to winning but losing has suddenly become a possibility it's never been in the past.

'I knew King Burgred was no damn good.'

'I know you did. But it was Burgred's right,' this is far from a new argument, but repetition never bothers Edmund. For once, he decides not to press the point.

Without sight of the lost rider, we round the bend and my camp is before me, a fire burning brightly as the sun sinks ever lower.

It's been a long day despite my decision to call an early camp.

But even from a distance, I can see that my orderly camp is not quite as orderly as usual.

'Why are there five men on guard duty?' Goda's question is worthwhile.

'Be wary,' I warn my three companions quietly, as we ride closer, hands reaching for weapons.

Fierce eyes peer at me from beneath helms of the men guarding the camp close to the trackway. No unease, but resolve, evident in the stances of Eoppa, Ordheah, the injured Ingwald and Hereman. Hereman peers at his brother in much the same way that Edmund did to him the day before. There's a pleasure in knowing he still lives, but also a realisation that the shit they do to each other, each and every waking moment isn't yet at an end.

'What you doing here?' I ask the question of Pybba. Behind him, Rudolf is too openly in attendance. My mouth furrows. We were supposed to be resting so that Pybba could recover his strength, Ingwald as well.

'You've been gone a long time,' Hereman speaks into the tense silence, his voice rich with a complaint as he holds his brightly coloured shield. Again, I realise that Hereman has taken the initiative. What has happened to him to change him so much in such a short space of time?

'Where are Gyrth and Sæbald?' I don't answer, but sweep my eyes around the camp noticing all the small things that are out of place. Pybba is only the most visible of them, as is the new horse and the fresh mound of covered earth on the far side of the track.

'Who killed him?' I demand to know, although I have my suspicions, and fury takes hold. I expressly delegated the task of keeping the camp safe to Oslac and Ordheah in my absence.

Ordheah's head sinks low, as though expecting the rage.

'Pybba killed the Raider.' I don't ask why the Raider was allowed to get beyond those on guard duty.

'Why weren't you resting?' I direct the complaint at Pybba, while Rudolf rushes to take Haden from me, the spare mount I've been leading, as well.

'Someone needed to be awake,' Pybba spits angrily, the top of his head flushing with his fury, and I can see there's been some unholy row in my absence. Why they can't all follow simple instructions, I don't know.

'But he's dead?' I direct my chin toward the mound of earth, away from the trackway, but not close to the brook either.

'Stupid bastard tried to ride through the camp.'

I'm starting to build an image in my mind of what's happened while I've been gone. A fucking explanation is needed and quickly.

'We fought another four. They're dead. We don't know where Sæbald and Gyrth are. We'll find them tomorrow. Now, what is there to eat?'

I stride through the tight knot of five men. The young lads are watching on keenly, bowls in their hands, spoons suspended halfway between the contents and their mouths. Whatever happened hasn't disturbed them. Such confidence in the ability of my warriors to protect them might be misplaced.

I don't berate any of my warriors. They know what I think and feel, and they'll have to live with the unease between them all. And they'll have to resolve it. I'm not about to knock heads together.

In the absence of Rudolf, young Wulfhere hurries to hand me a bowl of the meaty pottage they've prepared. Wulfhere is younger than Rudolf and seems to idolise him. Rudolf, as much as he would never admit it, enjoys teaching the younger lad what to do. Wulfhere eyes me keenly. I ignore him, other than to thank him for the food.

I sit on the log Pybba rested against earlier. I barely taste the food as I quickly chew. Rudolf silently joins me, handing me a cup of fresh, cold water that I swallow and then ask for more. The camp is far from the happy place it can be. I ignore the shifting looks being passed from one to another, as though they're waiting for me to resolve the problems.

Too much is unknown, and I'll not make rash statements.

'Tomorrow we ride on, but Goda, Icel, Edmund and I will take the front. Hopefully, we'll find our missing men. Everyone will ride armed, even the lads.' With my conversation exhausted, I hand Rudolf the empty bowl and seek out Pybba. He still stands on guard duty or rather sways.

'You need to rest,' I instruct him. The words are on his lips to argue with me, but then he shakes his head and steps away from his position. Eoppa moves closer, as does Ordheah. Only four men need to guard the area.

Pybba stumbles, and I reach out and grab him tightly.

'My thanks,' I whisper into his ear, the stench of his sweating body almost making me gag. 'The battle-rot?' I accuse, but he's shaking his head.

'No, I need to sleep. Look, the wound is clear.' He holds up the stump then, and in the flickering firelight, I can see that the white linen is clear once more. He thrusts it close to my nose, and I smell nothing but the sweetness of the honey. Before he killed a man, it seems he had the good sense to clean his wound.

'Good. I'll not lose you. Now, what happened?'

'Oslac said Ordheah could rest, and then the daft sod fell asleep at his post. The Raider got beyond him. He must have been looking to kill everyone who slept. Luckily, I was awake. The wound might be clean, but it hurts. Sleep is not my ally.' Pybba winces with the words.

'Ordheah blames himself for sleeping. Oslac has made himself scarce.'

'Rest,' I instruct my trusty warrior, as I support his weight as he tumbles to the ground. 'Rest. Tomorrow will be full of surprises.'

'I'll do what I must,' he confirms sleepily, as I walk to where Rudolf has laid out our small camp. He's already curled up and snoring noisily. I'd like to do the same, but duty dictates that I arrange replacements for my men on guard duty. I'll need to be one of them as well.

I stride back to Hereman, being careful where I step in the deep gloom of night. Above our heads, a few clouds obscure the half-moon.

'Sleep,' I tell him. 'And send Eadberht and Lyfing to change with Eoppa and Ingwald.' I don't excuse Ordheah. I know he won't want to be deprived of his duty. Having failed in it once today, he'll want to show he can do as ordered. I take my place at the front of the camp.

Silence falls amongst my men and followers, even the horses quiet in their picket. Horses. I never thought I'd have too many that it might become a problem. I think of sending them back to Gloucester or Kingsholm once more.

If I send them back, with a handful of men and young lads, then my Aunt would have responsibility for the horses, and I could summon more of my warband to my side. It's a tempting possibility, to be free of the hassle, and to have fresh men at my back. But first, we must find Sæbald and Gyrth.

But the night is not the time to start second-guessing myself, and so I clear my mind, settle only on the sounds of the night.

Of course, nothing happens, and much later, it's Edmund who taps me on the shoulder, indicating I should sleep. I go gratefully.

THE FOLLOWING MORNING, my camp is awake and ready to move on as soon as the day has truly begun. The sun is already warm on my back as I slink into my byrnie with the aid of Rudolf.

'What happened while I was gone yesterday?' I wanted to ask him last night, but he was too soundly asleep to wake.

'Pybba killed the Raider. Oslac had fallen asleep. He got a mouthful of abuse after the commotion had died down.'

'Did you bury the body?'

'I helped. Yes. There was nothing good on it,' I hold back my amusement that the lack of treasure should be Rudolf's greatest concern.

'Was it a man or a woman?'

'A man?' But I can see my question has sparked his interest.

'Edmund said you killed a woman warrior.' I thought the information might have been repressed in the wake of what was found on our return. But Edmund does like to talk on, especially when he's had some ale, and he always has ale after a battle.

'Yes, the warrior happened to be a woman. I only noticed when I removed her helm.'

'Did she fight well?'

'She fought like a Raider would, one who's not used to riding a horse.' My final comment is spoken with derision.

Rudolf's keen eyes dim at my words. He wants more but knows I'm not about to indulge in the sort of information he wants.

'Here, I got this for you,' at the reminder I give him the weapons belt and his eyes round with delight.

'For me? From the woman?'

'I thought it'd be a good fit.' I can see he wars with himself. Why he should be bothered that a woman wore it, I'm not sure. Yes, it's unusual, but not unheard of for a woman to fight.

'She was a bloody good warrior. Take her weapons. Make them yours.'

'My thanks.'

'Will you ride with Pybba again today? I need him cared for, and I trust you to do that for me.'

Rudolf nods, distractedly, already pulling the weapons belt around where his waist would be if he had one. The leather is supple and polished to a high sheen. There are three pockets attached, two filled with the war axe and short knife. The other is where the richly made sword must have sat. I've kept that for myself, keen to see how good a weapon it actually is in my hands.

Oslac has slunk back to the main camp, and I watch him work, his shoulders dejected. He knows he nearly allowed everyone to be slain. It'll take time for him to earn back the trust of his fellow warriors, and even longer to be tasked with such again. I decide that's all the punishment I need to give.

He knows he messed up. That knowledge will be enough for him.

'Remember, ride armed,' I instruct one final time, Haden weaving a path through the rest of my men and horses. I fix Pybba with a firm look, seeing how he struggles with the harness and his seax, but his return glare has me moving on. Rudolf is beside him.

I saw what I needed to see.

Pybba's eyes remain clear and bright, fierce with the desire to live.

More importantly, the white linen that covers his wound is still that.

I dare the man to die when he's survived for two full days. I just bloody dare him.

Satisfied, even with Oslac, who sits proudly and tries not to meet my eyes, I ride back to the front of the snaking line.

To the rear, Ingwald and Eoppa guard my men. Ingwald's cuts earned in the battle two days ago are almost healed, already. He thanks no one for alluding to them. To the front, Icel and Goda are keen to be released to find the missing men. Edmund waits for me.

We'll ride at the front today. Haden sidesteps beneath me, and I thwack him on the shoulder. The surly beast is feeling well used, and he has no love for Edmund's randy mount, Jethson, who keeps eyeing the mares we've gained with interest.

Even that will add some excitement to the day's ride, if more was needed.

'Let's find the daft sods,' with my nod, Icel and Goda move out at a faster pace. They're not my preferred scouts, but they understand their role today.

I'm vigilant as we move, trying to hear below the noise of my force on the march. I'm not fool enough to think that Icel and Goda will fare better than Gyrth and Sæbald, but I'm now alert to the danger we face.

Should the fifty Raiders, well, five less now, come upon us, I'll issue the order that the priority is protecting our horses and young lads as they make an escape back the way we've come. Rudolf knows the way to Gloucester, and if he and the rest arrive with the horses, they'll know to take them to my Aunt at Kingsholm. What happens to them after that is not my prime concern, although I hope she'll do the right thing. She's never failed me yet.

Edmund watches the track keenly from behind his horse's head. The ground hasn't changed since yesterday, it was a rare, dry night, and the hoof prints can be clearly seen. All of them. It takes someone more skilled than I in tracking to hunt down a deer or a boar that's gone to ground, but even I can decipher the layering, and which hoof went by first.

I expect Goda and Icel to ride back to me with news of what they find by about midday. But as we spot the four cairns we built the day before, and travel further on, I don't expect to see Sæbald coming toward me.

He's festooned in blood. There's no other means of describing him.

'What happened?' I demand to know, pleased to see him and his horse, and aware that Goda and Icel will have already encountered him.

'I tripped and fell,' Sæbald tries to joke, but the shaking movement of his chest, merely makes him groan in pain, and then he's sliding from his saddle. It takes all of my speed to dismount and intercept him before his head falls on an unfortunately placed piece of stone.

'Help me,' I gasp. Sæbald is a heavy weight. Edmund grabs Sæbald's legs, tangled in the stirrups and carefully we place him on the ground.

I'm looking for the sight of his wound, but it's Edmund who finds it, lifting a piece of sodden fabric clear from his body.

'Here, on his leg. It looks like they tried to kill him in the same way I killed that fool in the thorns.' It's an interesting observation. Have the warriors discovered their dead already? I'd ask Sæbald when and where it happened, but his eyes have fluttered shut. A hearty slap to the side of his face has no impact, and I shrug my shoulders.

'It looks like another early camp,' I peer back the way we've just come. We've been riding a good long while. The fact that Goda and Icel stay out in front assures me that no enemy has been seen. Not yet.

'Rudolf,' I call for him, and he appears, with Pybba, a complaint already forming on his lips.

'Stay here, with Pybba, the spare mounts and your friends, and the rest of the warriors,' I think the use of the word 'friends' upsets Rudolf more than anything else. Rudolf does think himself a little superior to the other lads. 'Wulfhere will help you with Sæbald.' Only then do I raise my voice. 'It's an early camp again. Ensure it's well protected.'

With the command given, I allow a few moments for everyone to sort himself out. Once more, there's an area of clear ground to the left of the trackway. I can see that trees have been cut back from the spot and that some tree stumps remain. The wood has no doubt been used to build a fine hall by some aspiring thegn.

The damn fool should have planted saplings in his wake. I shake my head at the lack of proper management of such a vital resource.

'Stay close, and stay alert,' is all I offer to Edmund, as he hands a beaker back to Wulfhere. I swallow, tasting the dryness of my tongue, but I don't want to need a piss while I seek out my final, missing, warrior.

Edmund mutters softy, and then we're on our way again.

If there are forty-five warriors up ahead, I would sooner ride with more than just Edmund, but I need my wounded men to be protected more than anything. Those who can't quickly mount up and ride away must be surrounded by those who can.

What matters to my warriors is that I won't abandon Gyrth, or leave Pybba, Oda, Eahric and Sæbald to fend for themselves. That consoles them more than the thought of another battle might.

My back is slick from wearing my byrnie and the force of the sun, and as much as I'd like to remove it, I resist the temptation. I would wish that Sæbald had been able to tell me what happened, but until he wakes up, or Goda and Icel re-join me, I have no idea.

Was he injured by the Raiders, as Edmund assumes, or did something else happen?

'He still had his horse,' Edmund's musings merge with mine. It's a significant point to make, but I'm not yet sure I know what it means.

As the trackway opens out once more, the valley side melting away to merge with more gently rolling hills, I gaze toward eastern Mercia. I expect to see nothing but dirty smoke on the horizon, a sign of our enemy infiltrating the kingdom, and its lack surprises me.

'Here come Goda and Icel,' I swing my head forward once more. My two scouts are riding toward me casually. I'd even go so far as to say they chat with each other. They show no fear, and I force my hand loose on my seax.

'Where's everyone else?' Icel asks first, craning his neck to see around me.

'I left them with Sæbald. He fell from his horse. Did he speak sense to you?'

The two peer at each other, eyebrows furrowed, and I fear their next words.

'We saw no one. We've seen no one, and certainly, no sign of the enemy.' Icel speaks in his low rumble.

'Fuck.' The news is unwelcome. But I don't ask the questions I want to. Not now.

'We need to get back to them. Quickly,' I'm already turning and spurring my mount back along the track. I can only hope we get there in time.

I know the men follow me. I'm sure all of them have realised our mistake in thinking the Raiders travelled the same route we did.

Crouching low over Haden's shoulders, I focus more on the hoof imprints below us than where we're going. I curse when I see it, so obvious, and yet missed as we rode. I'm just about to turn my animal to the right, to crash through the undergrowth to where the wooded area truly begins, when I hear the sound I've been dreading.

'Hurry,' my voice is solid with the command, and I put my doubts and recriminations aside. There'll be time for those. Later. If we live through this.

I can clearly see where many horses have ridden over the ground, as though my band of warriors and hanger-ons had come through here. Which of course, they haven't. My eyes alight then on some bright splashes of red on green leaves. This is where Sæbald won free.

Somehow, Haden races ever faster, ears just as alert to the sounds coming from in front as mine.

I recognise the landscape keenly and abruptly rein in before we round the next bend. I want nothing more than to reach my warriors, but I need to exhibit as much trickery as the enemy if any of them are to live to see tomorrow.

'Dismount,' I call, turning Haden in a tight circle to take the speed from him. In a practised move I jump to the ground, grabbing my shield from the rear of the harness at the same time.

Edmund, Goda and Icel quickly follow my actions. The four horses eagerly take themselves to the side of the trackway, where a matt of green growth entices them more than the sound of battle up ahead.

I wish I shared the belief they exhibit that the battle would be easy and they'd soon be on the way again.

'I don't know how many there will be, but we need to take as many as we can from behind. They'll think that everyone is at the camp.'

I meet Edmund's eyes, they're filled with his usual fear, but I nod as he slips away. Next, I turn to Goda and Icel. I ask too much of my men. Always.

'Let's kill the fuckers,' Icel bristles with his desire for vengeance.

4

One by one, we work our way forwards, beyond the curve of the trackway, and only then do I see how truly stupid I've been.

There are probably thirty of them. None of them is mounted, although horses are muddying the scene. It seems that they arrived on horses, but will not fight on them.

That's sensible. For all of us.

But it's what's happening in the makeshift camp that horrifies me.

All of my men are up and standing shield to shield. At least they had enough warning to form up. It's small consolation but nothing else.

I shouldn't have left them.

My horses buck or shift uneasily, faced with the noise of the altercation. A few of the younger lads hide amongst the mass of horse flesh, as I've taught them to do if caught in the middle of a fight.

A swift glance their way, and I'm hoping the horses remember who feeds and grooms them, or my lads will be dead, as they mill around uneasily, their shrieks adding to the mass of confusion.

I can't see who directs the defence. All I can see are shields, and I note Hereman's the most easily of all.

But I can see who orders the offensive.

The warrior, I refuse to make an assumption as to whether it's a man or a woman, is sheathed in battle gear. It's impossible to tell, and more importantly, it doesn't matter. All warriors must possess skill. It seems this opponent does.

Edmund has chosen to make his way to the far side of the shield wall my men make, making his way beyond the backs of our distracted enemy. They have shields, but rather than forming their own wall, they're being encouraged to hack against my men's shields, and the sound splits the air, as iron hits the wood. It's a sound I'm used to, but today it feels different and filled with far more menace than I'd like.

Icel and Goda have made decisions about where they'll attack as well. It just remains for me to decide what I'm going to do.

Rationally, I should just kill anyone I can, but thrumming through my body is a desire to make sure their leader dies first.

I've fought Raiders all my life. I know that without a leader, their offensive will falter. But, and I squint, trying to decide how well they fight, both individually and as a unit, I'm unsure.

I shake my head. Frustrated by my indecision.

From behind one of the shields, I abruptly catch sight of young Rudolf's face, grimacing and streaked with blood, his eyes wild with delight.

The fucking fool.

Somehow, he sees me, and a grin splits his face, teeth flashing bright red before he's gone again, ducking down low, or swallowed by an enemy advance, I'm not sure.

Why the fuck is Rudolf in the shield wall?

And then I peer closer, quickly realising what's happening.

With no more time for thought, I stride into the clearing, banging my war axe on my shield, purposefully drawing attention to myself.

Twenty-eight pairs of eyes look my way. I know that, without counting, because only two continue to war.

The brief respite is all Edmund needs, and I watch with some envy, as he seems to leap over the enemy and the shield wall, to stand amongst my warriors and lads.

Goda turns to glare at me, confusion on his face. But Icel is quicker on the uptake.

He's charging toward the distracted warriors, shield high and axe gleaming. From the corner of my eye, I watch the bright streaks of blood that suddenly stain the air they breathe, before I stride to Goda's side.

What was moments ago an orderly attack has splintered. The two persistent attackers still strike my men's shields, but in the core of the enemy, confusion reigns. They thought the attack would be an easy one, but Icel's offensive has left some of them trapped.

'Let's do this,' Goda growls at me. Together, we rush our opponents. We might only be three men, against thirty, but it'll be enough.

It has to be.

My war axe is not my weapon of choice, but in this hacking foray, it's what I need. There's no room for elegant sword or seax manoeuvres. No, I need to knock as many of the shitting filth to the ground as possible. I can pick them off later, when the rest of them are under my control, or better yet, bleeding to death.

Outraged shrieks greet our actions, but I'm deaf to the complaints.

'Fucker,' I appreciate that my first true opponent has learned the fouler words of our language. It's always best to make yourself at home.

My enemy's voice is rough and deep as my war axe thumps against their right side, just above the elbow. I watch as his hands instinctively open and wait for the seax they carry to be dropped onto the grassy ground.

Somehow, the man recovers his grip, but in his distraction, it doesn't matter. I've turned my axe, well, more swung it really, and now it's embedded in his shoulder, and blood gushes freely. I lick it from my lips, grimacing it back at him with my teeth, as he realises what's happened.

But he's not done yet. A flailing arm, almost devoid of all strength, attempts to scratch my neck with a blade but I step around the action, shove the man hard. I watch with satisfaction as he crumbles to the floor and disappears beneath the feet of one of his ship brothers.

Before the dying man's eyes have even closed, I'm moving on to the next kill.

The figure that turns to face me wears helm and byrnie. The leather is so tight I imagine I can hear it creaking with each and every move, although it's impossible above the noise of the battle.

A scream of incomprehensible bollocks erupts from the warrior's mouth. I take a step back, predicting what will happen next. I'm not disappointed.

Both arms swirl, one with a seax, the other with a war axe, a glint of triumph in the man's eyes. I almost sigh with the predictability of it all.

I step into the range of his left arm, keen to have the seax out of the way first. It glitters menacingly in the sunlight, but no blood mars it, and never will again at his hand if I have my way. The war axe is well-made, the wooden handle gleaming as though sheened with honey, the blade sharpened, made for slicing, not hack.

I turn, showing the man my back, and then jab both of my elbows into his body. I hear the air leaving his lungs as I batter the seax away with my right hand. Unsurprisingly, it drops heavily to the ground, and I'm already reversing my position before the enemy realises what's happening.

Wide brown eyes greet mine, and I almost want to grin once more, but the man recovers more quickly than I expect, his war axe slashing down the front of my body, as I jump backwards.

Perhaps he has more skill than I imagined.

Or maybe not.

I slash with my axe, aiming for his hand that holds his weapon. He lifts his axe to block the movement, and I feel the reverberation of the weapons colliding shuddering up my arm.

Definitely more skilled than I thought.

I bend my neck from side to side, cracking the pain from my body. Determined I've had enough of such foolery, aware that the battle is still far from won, I raise my right elbow, in an action more used for felling a tree. At the last moment, I raise my arm yet higher, and aim for his neck, not his body. Despite his axe making a reciprocal move, it's my weapon that draws blood, his axe missing mine by a fraction of a heartbeat.

The warrior gasps, his lips burbling with fluid.

I wrench back command of my axe, exhaling heavily. The man still stands, and I snatch his axe from his lifeless hand.

'Fucker,' I spit into his face, using his axe against him. This time, the cut is even deeper, and I leave the weapon there, wedged in his neck, blood pulsing around it.

'Bastard fucker,' I complain again, moving beyond him.

I eye up who'll be my next target, my chest heaving, my rage under control, even though I've once more caught sight of Rudolf in the shield wall. I've realised what he's doing. The damn sod will feel my wrath when all this is over. He better bloody well live to let me flay him with my tongue.

Behind me, the sound of a heavy object hitting the ground finally reaches my ears.

I'm always surprised by just how long it takes an upright body to fall when life has fled.

I catch sight of Icel, weaving bloody violence amongst the enemy, but of Goda and Edmund, there's no sight. Not that it worries me.

The two know their business well.

I'm getting closer to the shield wall, pleased to see it standing still, even if bloody Rudolf is involved. The tenacity of my warriors is no surprise to me.

Those who've fought with me for many years have survived, where others have fallen. Those who are yet young in making war take heart from those with grey beards.

The next warrior I face is beardless and slight. I note it and consider that I face another woman. I tighten the grip on my war axe and then rerelease it.

The warrior wears blackened leather, and it doesn't creak but seems to move fluidly around the slight frame. There are scratches here and there, as though scoured with a knife. This isn't this warrior's first battle, despite the seeming youth.

Men who've fought for much of their lives quickly lose the speed of youth weighed down with experience and the bigger build it invariably brings.

I'm not lithe. But I have experience. Both advantages can quickly cancel each other out.

My opponent pauses, perhaps considering the best chance of survival, or maybe, just the best opening gambit. While they contemplate, I grip my axe in both hands, reversing my grip as I do so, bending my knees and slashing upwards. I don't expect the unexpected movement to work. Equally, I'm aware I need to pull up short or risk hitting myself at the end of the stroke, but a flicker in my opponent's eye shows me that they've been distracted.

I'm aware of movement behind me and broaden my stance, prepared to take a blow to incapacitate my current opponent.

Too late, my enemy focuses on me, and by then, surprising even myself, my war axe has impacted his exposed chin. For a moment, shiny red drops glisten in the sunlight, a hint of magic about them as they stay stationary, before they, and my enemy, are falling. Surprised eyes meet mine as the body tumbles, halfway down, the fall of the red rain meets the slower body, festooning it as though in jewels.

I turn, before the body has hit the ground, axe already swinging wide.

I catch sight of a blade out of the corner of my left eye, but it's the warrior I focus on.

All of these men, and women, are well dressed for war. Three dull silver rings snake up this warrior's right arm, a sign of a great wealth won in combat, and the man has the girth to go with it.

He breathes lightly, far from exhausted by his previous actions. Perhaps a worthy opponent at last.

'Lord Coelwulf,' the voice that calls to me is filled with derision, and heavy with the Danish tongue. 'They told us you were a warrior who couldn't be beaten. They told us we would never claim Western Mercia for ourselves.' The words ripple, rich with derision.

'Ah, so you've won Western Mercia already. You and whose fucking army?' The smile dies away, the lips purse, as though confused, as I consider how I'll kill this new man.

I've taken two men by the neck already, a constant weakness. This man covers his neck well with his leathers, but there's always fragility in any warrior. I just need to find it.

'Whichever force beat you. Why else would you be sneaking around on this track?'

I understand the belligerence now.

'This isn't a retreat,' I advise, enjoying the sudden look of unease, evident in the stubborn chin.

'Then what of Jarl Ragnar?'

'What of him?'

'His force, fifty of them. They went to the south of here.'

'Then they feed the crows and the wolves already, probably the boars and pigs as well,' I inform, jerking my chin back along the trackway we've ridden down.

'All of them?' there's no denying the slight catch in the voice.

'All of them. I didn't let a single one live.'

I think this might break the man's resolve, but instead, he tightens his hold on his weapon, bounces up and down on his knees.

'Then I'll have the honour,' he announces firmly.

'Of being the second jarl I kill, yes, you will.'

The conversation has run its course, and I strike quickly, moving to feint a blow on his left arm, only to reverse it and strike his right instead. The warrior, for all his silver, doesn't expect the change in direction. I've already made my hit before he's gathered himself together.

He grunts, readying himself now.

I wait.

I'm curious to see just what need be done to earn a silver armband amongst these Raiders. I've not yet discovered it to be more than luck, and only a little skill.

The Raiders pride themselves on being battle-hardened. But, it's not hard to be battle-hardened against men and women untrained in the art of making war, slain while going about their day to day business. The holy men and women who've lost their lives on the end of such sharpened edges, know only how to pray and farm.

And still, I wait.

In front of me, the shield wall remains firm, although I think I'll have to spend some of Rudolf's coin on obtaining the aid of a carpenter to repair the fractured and split pieces of wood that used to be shields. Not that I can't afford it. I could gift a horse in exchange, or perhaps this damn bastard's silver arm rings when he finally falls below my blade.

His strike almost surprises me, when it finally comes and I counter slowly, or so it feels. Still, I intercept the slashing seax easily. Although the warrior thinks to mask the second weapon he carries, I'm ready for the hastily swung axe that quickly follows.

The man thinks to use tricks. Perhaps his skill is just from being able to wield a weapon equally in both hands. There's no magic to that. Only time and training.

'Tell me who sent you?' My curiosity forces the question.

'Jarl Halfdan.'

'You're his sworn warrior?'

'Yes, he has my oath.' A long pause, and I think the conversation over.

'If I bring him your head, he'll reward me with great riches and another ship.'

'And what will he reward me if I bring him your head?'

'With death.' Hardly an original reply. But, enough of this. I'm aware the frenzy of the beginning of the battle is starting to drain away. The mass of dead and wounded enemy is mounting up. It seems that their jarl is the only one not to notice.

With a burst of speed, I thrust at my enemy, the four short steps having to be enough of a run-up, as I use my shoulder to unbalance him. He stumbles, somehow keeping his feet, one arm out for balance, the other hitting the ground behind him before thrusting him upwards. I almost fall over his tangle of arms and legs. As his body tries to rebound, his belly is exposed beneath the layer of his byrnie. I whip my axe across the mass of pink flesh, noting the red streaks that follow my blade.

It's not a deep cut, but the warrior buckles, desperate to protect the wound and to prevent me from attacking there again.

No one wants to die from a belly wound. It's an ugly way to die, the smell of your own body assaulting your nostrils.

As he buckles, his head pops up, and it's almost as though he slices his own neck on my waiting edge. I count that as one of his kills. Not mine.

'Coelwulf,' Edmund's voice permeates my senses, and I stand tall, seeking him out over the mass of bodies and fighting men. He peers at me from behind the shield wall, a hint of exasperation evident in his voice and stance.

'What?' I thought I was alert to everything. It seems not.

'They're fleeing,' he points, to where the abandoned horses are milling around, some tangled in harnesses, others taking unkindly to those who wish to escape.

'Fine,' I sigh heavily. I don't want to leave the shield wall, but neither can our enemy escape.

'Goda, Icel, with me.' Without waiting for a response, I'm striding toward the horses, ignoring any who try and attack me. Where that's impossible, I offer my casual attention to have them gone. Little cuts to the face, a slash on an exposed arm. The men would live to tell of their encounter with me. Only I doubt they will.

The sound of heavy breathing is loud in my ears. There are five or six warriors, all trying to escape.

If I had the breath, I'd laugh at their clumsy attempt to mount. I imagine when they began the journey, they had handy tree stumps to aid them. Now they don't.

The man who dangles from his harness, one foot in the stirrup, the other snaking half up the animal's back, is taken down with a hack across his back. It leaves him bucking, before falling to the floor, eyes frantic as I stab my axe down with all the strength I possess.

The resistance of the byrnie holds for only moments, before giving way with a whoosh of released air. The man kicks out with his one free leg, but the movement falters halfway, and all he does is add the horse to his problems. I turn aside. I don't need to witness the hoof impacting the skull.

My next target has faltered in his attempt to flee, his eyes watching me too keenly. Now, as I meet his startled glance, fear slithers over his exposed cheek, where the side of his helm has been ripped away.

'Going somewhere?' I ask, as his hands scrabble for purchase.

I don't like to attack a man in the back, but he makes it too easy. And in the next heartbeat, he too is sliding to the ground.

Icel has caught me, his heavy tread unmistakable.

'Get down here, you damn fucker,' he shouts at the only man who's made it into his saddle.

An incomprehensible stream of crap erupts from the man's mouth. His legs flail on top of the animal, but Goda has grabbed the harness. The animal is going nowhere. Not that the rider seems to notice.

Icel's rumble of laughter assures me that all is in order and, and I seek out the remaining men.

One, perhaps more intelligent, or by chance, has chosen an animal he can just about mount from standing. I watch the strain in his arms as he pulls himself upwards, his right foot seeking the stirrup.

It pains me to see the lack of skill.

'Arsehole,' Goda has moved on to face another. His voice is rich with disgust as he spits out whatever the man has thrown. Probably shit from one of the horses.

Despite my intentions, I laugh then, the sound overly loud. My target tenses, and why wouldn't he, as the daft sod mounts the horse, only to find himself facing the wrong way. I almost glide to him then, knocking a few of the horses to one side, my hand much softer than it appears. There's no need to wound any horse unnecessarily. I grip the horse's head harness, and without letting go, move to face the rider.

'Well, that went well,' I offer. Furious brown eyes meet mine, as he fumbles for a weapon from his belt.

'I think not,' I comment, a quick slash of my war axe, and his hand holds the seax, but he has no control over it as it tumbles to the ground, the blood rushing quickly from the severed arm.

'Go,' I encourage him then, a slap on the horse's rump and the animal is heading away, the dying man facing the wrong way and entirely out of control. I watch, for a long moment, as the animal picks up speed, and the sound of a body hitting the hard ground at speed reaches my ears as I turn aside with a wry smirk.

'He'll be dead then,' Goda calls contemptuously. All of the men who tried to escape are now dead. The danger that remains to Goda, Icel and I is the horses who're becoming distressed with the stench of iron and piss.

'Embarrassment,' is Goda's appraisal and I nod, eyes already raking back to the continuing battle.

'Come on. It's not over yet,' I indicate with my axe hand.

The enemy is outnumbered, but they still fight. They know, as I do, that they either manage to win, or they die. There's no means of escape available to them now.

'Stay with the horses,' I order Goda.

'Fuck that.' Goda strides back to the group of warriors still fighting.

'Do you want to stay with the horses?' I ask Icel, the threat of command absent from my voice.

'Nah, you can though,' Icel offers, following Goda with his loping stride.

'Fine, you fuckers, I will.'

But of course, I don't either. I do take the time to yank a water bottle from the harness of one of the horses. I sniff it first, just to be sure it is water, and then I gulp thirstily, keen to alleviate the salt of the men I've killed from my parched mouth.

Goda strides straight into the mass of heaving men, Icel picking his target more carefully. The well of noise has dimmed, and I can clearly make out Edmund's voice behind the shield wall.

'The bastards are nearly all gone. Well-done lads. Hold. Hold.'

I think they could easily survive without me, these days, but whether they would take commands that came only from Edmund and not from me is debatable.

My gaze is drawn to a violent spot of fighting, five of the enemy desperately trying to hammer down the shield wall before them. I realise why, and the water bottle discarded to spill onto the ground, I'm hustling toward them, a grimace on my lips.

The bastards.

They've found the weakness, and Edmund busy at the other end of the defences is unaware.

Pybba. He should have been with the green lads amongst the horses, not standing in the shield wall with Rudolf before him. I'll flay them both. Once I've rescued them.

Goda is busy, Icel as well, and I square my shoulders. I can take the enemy. I can do it easily, but whether I can do it before Rudolf and Pybba are wounded is beyond my knowing.

One man watches the backs of the other four, not entirely oblivious to what's happening around them. I heft my seax. An axe might not be the best for what I have planned now. I want more stabbing and less slicing.

The single warrior watches me approach scornfully, his posture assured as he clutches a spear. He thinks I'll do him no harm because of his fine battle gear. It surprises me. I wear only the red of my victims.

Without looking down to make sure I don't trip on the dead and dying, I menace him. It's evident he thinks I'll slow down when I'm close, but I don't, and although his spear glints threateningly, he's sluggish to aim it at me.

I cleave him with my seax, ramming home the point, spitting into his face as he slides from its end, his spear forgotten about, and his hands bloody where they cup the sharpened blade.

Now I'm faced with four well-covered backs, but who to attack first?

The decision is taken from me, when the second from the left, turns to ensure his ally still fights with him. He dies with his mouth open, the seax piercing his throat and grinding on his teeth as I yank it back.

The man next to him squeaks in horror when he sees me, instead of his friend, standing beside him.

He dies with the blade through his neck, gurgling on his blood, as I again use my free hand to hammer my seax through weak flesh.

That leaves me two warriors, and they do seem to be good at their work.

It's easy for me to hear Pybba and Rudolf now.

'Hold the damn thing straight,' Pybba's voice is reedy and weak, his good arm snaking around the side of the shield that Rudolf holds. I bend and retrieve the forgotten spear from the floor. I don't want to use it, but neither do I want my enemy to use it against me. I fling it with as much force as I can, back down the track and away from the horses.

'I am,' Rudolf's normally amused-filled words are filled with the stress of holding a shield in place for so long. It sucks the strength of a man. I doubt he's still grinning.

'Who's next?' I ask the question loudly, keen to take the attention of both men away from Rudolf and Pybba. I'm grateful for what they've done, but I'm still not going to compliment them when this battle is won.

But only one warrior turns to face me. The heavier of the two stays, pounding his massive war axe against the shield, so fast it seems to strike with my beating heart.

Fuck.

The shield falls, just a little, but enough that it exposes the shoulders of the two to either side of Pybba and Rudolf, and enough that the warrior must scent the victory.

Before I can step into the breach, the first warrior is attacking me fiercely with a hacking action, a long blade glinting menacingly in his hand.

Only his eyes and mouth show. I've no idea of his thoughts, but the stance that he takes, feet wide apart, shoulders square, assures me that he's not a green warrior. How could he be, to have survived so long in this bloody mess?

And I need to get through him to reach Pybba and Rudolf.

I use my blade to counter his attack, testing his strength and finding it prodigious as I do so.

I'm not fearful that he'll beat me, rather that killing him will take so long, Pybba and Rudolf will have fallen victim to the other warrior. How do the damn bastards know where my weakest men are? Not, I realise that I wouldn't in the same situation.

Turning my body to the side, I reach out with my seax, keen to score first blood against my opponent. He wears seasoned leather, and his byrnie is intact. He wears a second skin, as I do, and it won't be easy to get beyond it, even with my great strength.

He slashes with his blade, and I step back hastily, knowing I don't have the time to bend my knees and duck. He grunts with the wasted effort. I feint to his right, as though I'll attack him on the arm, but instead I slide beyond him, my weapon seeking, and finding, the shoulder of the warrior who attacks Pybba.

A howl of pain reaches my ears, but I've skipped back, in front of my first enemy.

When the other warrior turns crazed eyes on my opponent, I see Edmund, finally alert to the danger. He forces Pybba and Rudolf aside, none too carefully, taking their place before the man can even realise what's happened.

Now, I can concentrate on my opponent, while Edmund takes on the other man. Around us, most of the fighting has come to an end because while the shield wall holds, I can see it's much looser than it was before.

'You damn fucker,' I can hear Pybba's vitriol as well. His mood will be foul, and I look forward to further infuriating him. In good time.

Something changes in my opponent's stance. I consider that he realises he's alone, apart from the man in front of him. Only then, his body stiffens again, perhaps comprehending he must face his death either way.

'Lord Coelwulf, you can not win,' his mouth seems to struggle to form the words of my land, but I admire him all the same for trying.

'But I can't lose either,' I explain. Then I'm hurtling into him, turning to my right tightly. I make sure I get at least two full circles in, before I crash into him with my back, my free hand smacking into his with the added speed of my turns, so that the grip on his seax loosens, but the weapon doesn't fall.

It's enough though, to counter his skill and strength.

Before he can fully grip the hilt, I've rammed my blade backwards, behind the right of my body, and with my left hand, I hammer the seax in, and then further in, until I feel the body begin to sag.

Fearing his weight will settle on me, I spin back out of his embrace, taking my blade with me, in the opposite position to the way I started the action. I watch with some satisfaction, as he falls to his knees, his face pale, and a welter of black showing on his battle clothes. The stain grows quickly, but, with one hand on the ground for support, he unexpectedly pushes himself upright once more.

His lips are flecked with blood, his auburn beard as well, and I can hear his ragged breathing as though all other activity in the camp has ceased. And it has. Over the man's shoulder, Edmund is finishing his kill, the other warrior dead, although he doesn't seem to notice it yet.

Just like the man I face.

'Lord Coelwulf.'

'Yes.'

'We came to retrieve you peacefully. You'll die for this.' His final word is a bubble of blood, the sound escaping only as it explodes, releasing his air, and his words.

I nod, pulling my helm from my head so that I can see him clearly.

'If this is peacefully, then I fucking hate to see what you fuckers mean when you say you come to make fucking war.'

A grimace or a smile seems to touch his cheeks at my words. Damn the fucker.

'You will see,' he gasps, only to fall, straight as an arrow, to the ground beneath us, the final word coming to me from below.

I've heard enough.

'Rudolf,' I've already forgotten my dead opponent and his useless words.

'My Lord,' the head pops up from behind the shield wall that's being dismantled. The voice is far less cheerful than usual. His left cheek carries a slash of bright blood, while his right eye is already swelling from an impact, and I've not laid eyes on the rest of him yet. What damage has he done to himself?

'What the fuck were you doing?' I demand to know. 'And where's that arsehole Pybba?'

'I'm here as well, Lord Coelwulf.' Pybba sounds equally tired, as I stride around the shields that still stand, and turn to gaze down at a man I expected to behave far less recklessly.

'What the fuck?' I look at him, I look at Rudolf, my fists clenching with anger.

'Whose fucking idea was this?' Pybba has the shield tied to the arm where his hand is missing. The rope used has been expertly tied and fixed in just such a position where the movement, while not natural, might just be sustainable for long periods.

Rudolf has the weapon belt I gifted to him around his slim waist, and in his right hand, he continues to hold a bloodied seax, as well as his own shield. I can see that the war axe and sword have been used as well, from the glimmers of red that sheen there.

I look one from the other, the noise of the rest of the camp fading to nothing.

The silence is telling.

'Both of you! You're wounded, and you're too weak.' As I speak, I point at each of them in turn. I don't think I've ever been so furious in my entire life. Not even the thought that the Vikings have taken eastern Mercia makes the blood rush so loudly in my ears.

Pybba stands wearily. He's even paler than when I left him here, and a quick glance shows me that his wound is filthy and saturated with blood.

'Is that yours?' I'm still pointing, aware that someone is standing behind me. Not because I can hear them, but because Pybba and Rudolf's eyes are flickering from my face to theirs, as though expecting some help from them to appease my rage.

If it's fucking Edmund, I must just lose all control.

It's not his place to interfere. Not here. These are my men. They serve me. They pledged their lives to me, in exchange for my protection. If they won't let me protect them, then what fucking good was that damn oath.

'Only a little. Most of it is Sæbald's.'

'Good,' I release my pent up breath with the word.

'And what about you. Is all that your blood?'

Rudolf's face gleams with his triumph, not dissuaded at all, or fearful in the face of my evident, and unusual anger.

'No, Sæbald's. Although,' and he's pulling up his torn tunic with battered and bleeding hands. 'I think this bit is mine.' Rudolf's voice is rich with surprise and pride.

'It's the battle joy. You feel nothing. Until the end.' Edmund interjects into our conversation. 'Let me look at it.'

Edmund is rough as he turns Rudolf around, forcing the tunic higher, inspecting everywhere. He's taken the time to shake the seax from the young lad's hand, and it lands with a dull thud on the ground.

There's no more blood, but Rudolf's skin is shaded. By tonight, his entire chest will be purple and black. I want to smack him, hard, but I've had bruises like those in the past. I'm not going to make them worse.

I imagine Rudolf waits for me to praise him for such ingenuity. Pybba, however, knows me better than that.

Before my fury can get the better of me, I turn and march away. I'm breathing heavily, but I know that as angry as I am with Rudolf and Pybba, I'm more furious with myself. It's beginning to feel as though I've walked into a trap. It's beginning to feel as though I'm being hunted. Fuck King Burgred. He's told the Raiders who I am and where I'll be. If he weren't gone from Mercia, it'd be him that I wanted to take my revenge against, not the damn Raiders.

I don't march blindly. As I go, I take in the scene of devastation, and I look for my men. The young lads are out, looting the dead, while Ordheah scrambles amongst them, driving home his sword into any he fears might not yet be truly dead. He doesn't meet my eyes, either.

I go to his side.

'How many were there?' I ask, determined to decipher just what forces are arraigned against me.

'Thirty, including those over there.' Ordheah points with his chin towards the few who tried to escape.

'Good, we got them all.' It's small comfort. The Raiders have sent eighty warriors to track me down, and my men and I have killed them all. How many more have been sent, and more importantly, how long will the leaders, camped at Repton, wait until they accept these war bands have failed?

I'm used to being the hunter, not the hunted.

Next, I seek out Sæbald. He's sitting close to the remains of the campfire. Wulfhere is tending to him, offering him fresh water, and some rags to try and wipe away the worst of the blood.

Pybba needs a healer. I think Sæbald does as well.

I'll need to consider that when I make my decision as to what happens next.

'What happened?'

Sæbald glances at me with hazy eyes.

'Get some ale,' I turn and shout the command, fully expecting Rudolf to rush to fulfil my orders, even with his injuries.

'We felt that we were being tracked. We talked about one of us coming back to warn you. Gyrth was adamant that one of us should investigate, and he volunteered. I stayed on the track, but he went through the woodland. I waited, expecting him to return, and when he didn't, I went after him. More cautiously, but with my horse.'

'The woodlands were much deeper than I expected, and the floor was littered with roots while the branches routinely hung too low.

This,' and he points to a wide graze on his forehead, 'came from a fucking tree. Can you believe it?'

I can, and I note that some small splinters are deeply embedded, even now. They'll need to be removed.

'It was almost dark by the time the woodlands started to thin out. I'd not seen Gyrth and was beginning to wish I'd come back to find you. I knew you'd not see where we'd left the main trackway.'

I refrain from agreeing with him. It's Gyrth that concerns me.

'I saw the fire first, and then the sounds of men on the road. It was hard to see anything in the gloom, and the fire was no help. I hunkered down, to wait and see what was happening. I decided if I'd made an effort to come this far, then I needed to know what was actually happening.'

'It was then that I heard the shouts and cries. Mocking sounds the same, no matter the language spoken. I left my horse, and crept ever closer, desperate to see what was happening, but somehow knowing all at the same time.'

Sæbald pauses and swigs from the ale skin brought to him by Rudolf, who moves only less sprightly than usual. I'm almost looking forward to watching him when he wakes in the morning. He's not only going to ache. He's going to ache all over, and his body will be uncooperative as well. I might enjoy that.

'They didn't have canvasses, but they did have a picket of horses, and so I used them to cover my actions. They had Gyrth, of course, they did. I could see that he'd been beaten and was bleeding from a head wound, but he was conscious, and one of the fuckers was shouting at him. They were trying to find out who he was and where you were. It wasn't the most subtle of interrogations that I've ever witnessed.'

He holds his head to one side, his eyes far away, reliving the moment.

I wait for him to continue. When he doesn't, I reach out and touch his shoulder. He jerks at my touch, his hand already reaching for his discarded war axe before he remembers where he is.

Pybba needs a healer. And so does Sæbald. In the end, it'll be Pybba who heals the quickest from his wounds. I can already tell.

'They cut him, and then took one of his fingers, and still Gyrth said nothing. I could see how much pain he was in, and I, well, I could do nothing.' Sæbald's voice is thick with emotion. Even Rudolf, as oblivious of most things as he is, has settled to the ground, his legs crossed, quietly listening, and his shaded face lacking all mirth.

I think we all know how this ends.

'I decided to wait for the camp to settle and then try and free Gyrth. They set a guard over him, obviously, but the daft fucker fell asleep eventually. I snuck through the horses, and through the sleeping men, and Gyrth heard me coming. He shook his head, cautioned me to go back, but I didn't listen.

'I thought I was prepared to die for him. I know he'd have done the same for me.'

'I stabbed the guard while he slept. My easiest kill ever. It was more difficult to work the rope loose that bound Gyrth to a sodding stake in the ground.'

'We didn't speak, not until we'd made it back into the woodland without being discovered. He was limping and bleeding but was adamant he could go on. Only as the daylight began to infiltrate the woodland did we stop. He couldn't walk any further. I left him there, to go back and retrieve my horse, and his. If I could get it.'

I'm nodding. I expected Gyrth to be dead. The fact that he lives, or did live, and managed to escape from his captors surprises me.

'Before I left him, he told me that he'd overheard the leader of the Raiders bragging that they'd get the reward for finding you or killing you. They've sent six warbands to find you. Men hope to make their fortune from your apprehension.'

My face contorts. Three hundred warriors. To kill little me. I suppose I should be pleased, but it means I've killed less than a third of the fuckers. My fighting isn't over and done with. Far from it.

'So where's Gyrth now?'

'Still in the woods. We need to find him.' Urgency fills Sæbald's voice as he rushes to finish the story. 'I retrieved my horse. But the Raiders were in an uproar, arguing over where the prisoner had gone. I could hear them even from where I'd left my horse. I heard people in the woodlands and turned to make my way back here. I did well, for some time, but eventually, they tracked me down, despite my wandering ways.'

'There were four of the smug shits. They cornered me against a deep beck at my back and thought I'd be an easy kill. It was a fucking shit storm, but I took them all down. Not that it was easy, but then I couldn't risk going back for Gyrth.'

Sæbald swigs more ale, as though a man dying of thirst, and I consider what to do next.

'Did Gyrth say anything about where the other war bands were?'

'No, just that there were six of them. I take it that one three days ago was one of them. And this the second. So there's another four somewhere.'

I turn, gazing at the mess of my campsite.

I'm down to seventeen men, and four of them are injured, while Gyrth is missing. I can't leave him in the woods to die.

Neither can I take all these fucking horses with me.

If only I could arm the horses. Then the number of warriors at my command would just about equal those who are coming against me.

'We need to find Gyrth,' Sæbald is trying to stand, even though he winces, and his wound weeps at the action.

'Stay on your arse,' I instruct him. 'You can't go anywhere like that. Stay here.'

'Rudolf, see to his wound. Get Wulfhere to aid you. And Sæbald, listen to me, stay fucking still, or you'll bleed to fucking death.'

I turn and beckon Edmund to join me. He's been listening carefully to everything that Sæbald has told us.

'Fuck,' I share the sentiment, but don't comment.

'How do we find Gyrth? We can't leave him.'

'Neither can we go hunting with this bloody rabble.' Edmund indicates the men and horses, the lads as well. I swallow heavily. I left Gloucester five days ago with a healthy number of men, to fight a roving warband of men I'd assumed were from Gwent.

Now I'm a master of nearly a hundred fifty horses, but only eighteen warriors and one of them is missing. I sigh heavily, washing my face in my hands, noticing for the first time the dried blood and cracked knuckles.

'Give me Icel and Goda. We'll find Gyrth, and bring him to wherever you're going.'

Edmund knows me well. But not quite as well as he thinks.

'No. I'll send Hereman to Worcester, to lead the wounded and the extra horses to Bishop Wærferth. We'll have to hope the Raiders haven't turned him yet. I'll send nine of the men with him, including Pybba, Sæbald, Oda and Eahric and all of the lads. That stupid fucker will kill himself if he keeps trying to fight with his arm like that.'

'Then you're coming hunting with me?'

'Yes, and then when we find Gyrth, Goda and Icel can take him to Worcester as well.'

Edmund nods along with me, no fear as he absorbs my intention.

'What about this lot?'

'We bury them, as usual.'

He sighs heavily.

'We've always buried our kills.' I remind him.

'I know, but there's not normally thirty of the damn bastards.'

'Well, did you have something else to be getting on with?' I ask, and he shakes his head while rolling his eyes at me.

Edmund is bloodied from our battles, but it appears to be nothing too serious.

'We'll bury the dead, and then move on. I'm not stopping for the night here.' I grimace at the thought of sleeping with so many dead.

'Fine,' Edmund complains, moving off quickly, snapping his fingers to attract the attention of six of the men, including his brother and Goda. The lads have retreated from the bodies. Anything anyone wanted is gone, but they're still dressed. All of them. I consider ordering them stripped. There's good fighting equipment on all of them. I already have the horses, milling around, and being brought under control by a limping Ingwald. He should be resting as well. I fucking despair of this lot.

'Coelwulf,' Ingwald's voice is a slither of its typical robustness, but I hear him all the same.

'What?' I demand to know, my temper frayed enough as it is. He nods, as though understanding, but still waits for me, holding a horse I recognise far too well.

'Gyrth's?' I ask, noting the sandy colour and the one white hoof.

'Aye,' Ingwald bows his head low, as though accepting his friend is dead. I refuse to do the same, focusing instead on all the bodies still wearing battle equipment.

It's a waste to bury it all, but too much effort not to.

I peer, both north and south suddenly aware that I'm being watched, and yet it's impossible. Everyone is either dead or one of my warriors.

Unease prickles along my neck, and I walk to the side of one of the packhorses, yank a wood axe from the saddle pack, before joining the gravediggers.

Rudolf wisely stays out of view, Pybba as well. I try and force the unease from my body with each and every swing of the heavy weapon.

It doesn't work.

5

Only because of the long summer's day is it possible to break camp.

Pybba, although unhappy at being sent to Worcester, holds his tongue. Rudolf, his silence only lasting for the time it takes us to mount up, proves his youth with his steady litany of arguments as to why he should stay with me.

I let him witter away, occasionally grunting, as though I listen, even though I don't.

'For the love of fuck, will you still your devilish tongue,' Hereman's comment brings a wry smirk to my face. Rudolf looks outraged, and I reach over and pat his shoulder, noticing as I do so that he winces, and making my touch softer in an instant.

'You're going to Worcester, you daft shit.'

His abrupt silence makes me hear all the sounds of our party. The excess of horses, now linked together by their harnesses, making the most noise. Anyone coming the other way will think they face an army. I find the irony amusing.

While Sæbald is the most severely wounded of the men, Eoppa also has a long slice along his left arm, and Hereberht has a leg wound, that keeps oozing fresh blood, as he rides. Ingwald might have decided he's recovered, but Eahric and Oda still wear their wounds, and now Rudolf must be added to that number.

I rode out of Gloucester with my best men. More than half of that force is going to slink back to Worcester, and half of them are wounded.

Apart from Rudolf, no one has voiced a complaint about my recent decision to split the force. Worcester is less than half a day's ride from our current position, although it will mean finding a means to cross a river. Once we go our separate ways, the men will ride as hard as they can. I'm hoping that none of the four forces has yet made it any further east than the two warbands I've encountered. It's not much, but I can't be in two places at once.

Hereman has permission to abandon the extra horses if he must. I can't see them going far without a rider. I can't see the enemy wanting to encumber themselves with more of the animals they already struggle to ride.

'Here,' Sæbald's reedy voice calls out close to the spot where I first saw a collection of deep hoof imprints. 'I came out here.'

It makes sense, but it doesn't really give me any more of an idea as to where Gyrth might be. But, we've not yet come upon him, and so I take it as a starting point.

'Right men. Here's where we divide our small force. Hereman is leading those going to Worcester. He speaks for me in everything he now does.' I lace the words with force. I don't honestly think I need to, but I do all the same. We're in an unusual and unexpected situation. I don't want any of my warriors to panic.

'Hereman, you have permission to abandon the horses if you must and to offer Bishop Wærferth whatever you must to gain admittance. He's my ally. I hope he continues to be. And I charge you all with waiting for me in Worcester.' I meet the eyes of Rudolf and Pybba with my final comment. The two have proved themselves to be unexpected allies, and the two I currently trust the least to follow my commands.

Rudolf still looks mutinous, his face shaded in blacks and

purples, his two eyes pinpricks of white amongst the ruin. He's lucky he didn't break his nose or his jaw.

'Follow the trackway until you come to the first clearing that allows you to go east. Be alert and watch out for each other.'

I'm abruptly worried I might never see Rudolf or any of the other men again. But unlike the unease I felt earlier, this is just a flicker of fear. The warbands, if they are to the east of my current location, have no interest in my men. They won't even know their names.

'And lie, if you are attacked. Tell them you've never met me, or heard of me, or whatever you think will work. Tell them you found the horses on a battle site. Tell them everyone was dead, and send them south. Always south.'

Without pausing to reconsider my decisions any further, I turn towards the woodland, allowing the darkness caused by the tree canopy to cover me. I don't watch the men and horses ride away although I hear them well enough.

They'll be heard from bloody Gwent!

I listen carefully, assuring myself that my orders have been carried out before I consider the best way of searching for Gyrth.

Do we stay together, or spread out?

We need to cover a great deal of woodland. Gyrth could be anywhere. He might even have crawled out of the woods. It's impossible to know.

The growths here are all bashed and broken, showing the passage of the thirty-five warriors who came after us. It's impossible to decipher anything from the mass of hoof prints and footprints.

'We'll have to do this on foot,' I announce unhappily. 'Spread out, in a long line, so that you can see the man to your left and to your right. We'll have to adopt a systematic approach.'

I expect complaints, and I'm surprised when my instructions are carried out quickly, and without comment. I don't much like the subservience. It speaks to me of frightened and worried men.

'When he's found, shout to everyone. Then the man to your left and right needs to make sure the man next to them knows, and so on until we all know. Keep track of who is to either side of you. I don't want to lose anymore of you fuckers.' I try and end the comment with a lilt to my voice, but it falls flat, and I swallow unhappily.

It seems they're not the only ones to be concerned.

Icel takes the position to my left, and Edmund to my right. Beside Edmund is Goda, and beside Goda is Ingwald. To the left of Icel is Ordheah and Lyfing is the final man. It's not many to search such a massive area, but it's all I have. Gyrth better be easier to find than I fear he will be. I hope that like an animal that knows its death is coming he hasn't curled up somewhere, hidden, prepared to die.

I lead my horse, the animal breathing reassuringly in my left ear. It's been a long day, and yet Haden, his fierce eyes intelligent, as he seems to scent the air, shows no fatigue. I rub my hand along his nose as I search for any signs of an injured man in the undergrowth. The actions calm me just as much as it does Haden.

Yet, for all that, I can sense the frustration in his steps as our slow progress continues. I might have thought he searched with me, but he doesn't. His ears flicker but mostly lie flat.

The woodland grows quieter and quieter, before erupting in a cacophony of cries. I turn, startled, and gaze upwards, to where a flock of black rooks has abruptly taken to the skies. Whatever has disturbed them remains unseen.

I notice that the day is slowly drawing to a close, the bright blue sky fading, as though a bruise forming around the clouds, and still Gyrth hasn't been found.

I can't have my men searching in the dark. We'll trip, or the horses will trip, or we'll be consumed by the dark and unable to find each other.

Only then Icel shouts to me.

'He's been found.' The sound reverberates.

'Ordheah has him.'

'Thank fuck for that,' I mutter, and turn to move left, only to remember my instructions.

'Edmund,' I holler. 'He's been found. Ordheah has him.'

I see a flicker of movement far to my left.

'I'll tell the others,' Edmund responds, and I hear him bellowing to Goda. He takes up the cry to Ingwald, and the sound of horse's hooves and feet grows, disturbing a busy squirrel in a tree close to me. I watch it scurrying away, wishing I had somewhere safe and secure to dash away to when I felt threatened.

I wait for the three men, aware that if I don't, we might still all lose each other. Only then do I mount up, tired of walking, and allow my horse to take me to Icel. Together, the five of us make our way to where Ordheah and Lyfing have left their horses tied to a low branch.

I've not asked the question that makes the silence between us oppressive.

But then I can't put it off anymore.

'He's in a bad way,' Lyfing hisses, his eyes focused on where Ordheah is crouched down next to Gyrth.

I focus on Gyrth. He is, as I feared, curled up in a depression made by one of the tall oak trees that surround him, his eyes barely open, and his face a mass of bruises and shades of drying blood. His hand is wrapped tightly in a strip of tunic I recognise as belonging to Sæbald, and he's shivering.

Despite the heat, his entire body is convulsing, violently, his teeth chattering, and yet I feel the heat that emanates from him.

'Fuck,' I growl, jumping from Haden to land close to Ordheah.

'Fuck, fuck, fuck,' I complain, unsurprised to find Ordheah and Lyfing waiting for me to take control.

'He's not going to die,' I growl, feeling the truth of those words.

'Gyrth, wake up, you sod. Wake up you crazy bastard.' I'm crouched beside him now, considering what to do for the best. Darkness will fall soon, even if only temporarily because the moon has been bright of late. But, all the same, I know we can't leave here now. It would be too high a risk, even to make it from this spot back out to the trackway. And, of course, we've killed thirty-five warriors, from a group of fifty. Where those other fifteen have gone, I don't know.

If they come upon us now, they'll outnumber us two to one, and with Gyrth lying as he does, we won't be able to ride away.

'Fucking bollocks,' I complain. But Edmund, crouching beside me and peering at Gyrth is already standing, viewing the area around us.

'We make camp?' he asks, and I nod, unwillingly.

'We'll have to. We need a fire as well, and as many cloaks and furs as can be spared. Here, help me get him out of the hollow.'

Edmund moves away, to order Ingwald and Goda while Ordheah and Lyfing crouch as low as I am, preparing to carry Gyrth to where the fire will burn. Already, I can hear Icel tramping through the forest, picking up sticks and other fallen pieces of wood that he hopes will burn quickly and fiercely.

No one becomes a warrior to learn how to heal an injured friend. And yet, in time, we all learn some rudimentary ways of stopping blood flow, of closing wounds, and of trying to counter battle rot before it takes the life of a man, rather than just a hand or an arm.

The irony is never lost on me.

Gyrth is an ungainly and awkward weight to move. He's pulled his legs tight to his body. Now, although I feel the heat of him, it's as though his body has succumbed to the rigour of death.

'Fuck, he's a heavy bastard,' Ordheah complains. Gyrth's body seems to release from the hollow with a rush of sound, and then all three of us stumble, almost dropping Gyrth as we do so.

'He stinks,' Ordheah wrinkles his nose. I sniff, not enjoying the overripe smell, but need to determine whether he's just fouled himself, or whether the wound has already festered.

'He does,' I confirm. 'But it's a healthy stink,' I confirm, and then we're by the small flickers of flame Icel is coaxing from the twigs he's found.

Edmund and Goda are tending to all of the horses', the harsh smacks of horse flesh a reassuring sound as they move amongst the animals. They loosen harnesses but don't entirely remove them. We might need to ride out in a hurry.

With Gyrth on the ground, the flames rising ever higher, and Edmund and Ingwald moving to stand a guard around the impromptu camp, I begin the grisly task of trying to fix Gyrth.

'Ordheah, help me with his trews.'

Quickly, we peel them from his body, and then Ordheah moves

away, keen to fling the offending objects as far away from us as possible.

Pale and marbled flesh greets my eyes, and I curse softly.

Gyrth may be beyond saving, I admit it to myself, but not to anyone else.

'I need hot water, and ale,' I state, lifting Gyrth's hand and unwrapping the offending bandage.

The smell of corruption hits me immediately.

'Fuck,' I complain, noticing that the entire hand feels flaccid, and the finger stump is mottled. 'I'll have to cut more away. Here, put my knife in the flames.'

I've not had to sear so much flesh before. First, it was Pybba and now Gyrth.

I'll kill all the Raider fuckers when I get to them.

Ordheah moves more swiftly now, taking my knife, and returning from his horse with his winter cloak and the blanket customarily used to cover his horse. I rapidly cover Gyrth's nakedness. I need to remove his tunic, but my knife is turning orange in the flames.

'Give me your knife,' I demand from Icel. He does better than to hand it to me, but rather steps close, and slices through the linen, so that Gyrth's chest is exposed.

Only now do I see the welter of bruises, and burn marks that reveal the extent of his injuries. If I wasn't already angry, now I wish I could rush from here, find the damn fuckers, and slice their balls from them.

'Bastards,' the resolve in Icel's voice assures me that I'm not alone in such thoughts.

I stand then, keen to resolve the problem with Gyrth's finger. I slip my leather glove onto my hand and grip the knife.

Ordheah hovers at Gyrth's feet, Icel at his head, just in case what I'm about to do rouses him from his stupor. I hope it does, just as much as I wish it wouldn't.

I pour some ale over the wound site, and then lift the hand, critically examining where Gyrth has lost the middle finger on his left hand. They've taken the tip of the finger only, and I pause, head to one side, considering how much further to go. This might need doing more than once if I don't take enough.

'Bollocks,' I complain, laying the hand on the ground, and making a neat cut as close to the mass of his hand as I can. The finger doesn't snap cleanly off but instead breaks free with a reluctant sucking sound. It might not be enough. Even now. I place the end of my knife over the wetly pulsing wound, unhappy at the lack of blood.

The scent of burning flesh fills my nostrils, but Gyrth doesn't stir.

'Fuck,' I complain, gripping the clean linen Icel hands to me to bind the wound.

'It won't be enough,' Icel comments, and I nod.

'It's to be hoped it is. I don't want two men with only two hands between them.'

The words mask my sorrow, and Icel speaks as he finds. This isn't the first such wound we've tended. The men who lose their limbs often lose themselves as well.

There's a reason my Aunt cares for my warriors so well at Kingsholm. Not all of them will fight for me again.

'What now?'

'We need to get water into him and keep him as warm, but cool, as we can. Tonight he sleeps, tomorrow we ride for Worcester whether he can keep in his saddle or not.'

My words aren't comforting. I know that.

When the water has boiled, I return to Haden and my saddlebags. Amongst them, I keep a selection of herbs, prepared by my Aunt. I know which ones will assist Gyrth now, and quickly, I steep the mixture, only just allowing it time to cool, before I drip it into Gyrth's mouth.

His skin still shimmers with sweat, while Ordheah waits anxiously at his side.

Beyond our intimate circle of light, the sky has leached of all colour, and although I hoped for a full moon, a thick layer of cloud has formed, making it more challenging to see than I'd hoped.

We eat, but only cold rations from our saddlebags. The hot water is used to steep a herbal concoction for all of us, to drive away the fatigue. I gag on the sour drink but welcome the warmth. Despite the summer heat, I feel almost as cold as Gyrth's dead finger was when I severed it from his body.

I'm not one for portents or foreboding, but I feel too exposed in the haze of light. And there's nothing I can do. Not until the morning.

Every woodland sound prickles at my senses. By the time I relieve Edmund from his post, my senses are so attuned, I swear I can hear the breaths of every one of my seven men, as well as my own. His eyes are bright pinpoints in the gloom as he hears my steps.

'Will he live?' Edmund hasn't asked the question yet, and for that, I'm grateful.

'I can't promise. Tomorrow, Worcester, and the bishop's monks. They have more skills than I do.'

'I doubt that,' Edmund complains. 'They don't fight our enemy, but rather pray for our success. It's a different thing to curing an infected wound gained in combat.'

'I know,' I state, the words wrenched from me. I don't want to believe that Gyrth's best chance is if I tend to his ills. I've got other things on my mind.

'Do you think they tracked us?' Edmund asks, just before he walks back to the small campfire, no more than thirty paces away.

'I can't tell. We weren't quiet.'

'I'll sleep with my sword then,' he responds. It won't be the first time. I hope it won't prove to be the last either.

After the rustle of his departure, I make myself as comfortable as possible. I lean against the trunk of an oak tree, peering around me with so much fierceness, I almost feel as though the darkness dissolves when faced with my fury.

I shiver, wrapping my cloak around me with pleasure. I try and clear my thoughts, focus only on what must be done. I've done this many times in the past. Guard duty is a tedious business, and it's a skill that must be mastered. There's a key to appearing somnolent while being hyper-alert to every flicker of wind and patter of bird wings.

It's almost like sleeping, but with my eyes wide open.

When the first out of place noise reaches my ears, my hand is already on my seax.

We've been hunted. I suspected as much.

I call, the sound of a barn owl. It might pass for an actual owl to those not used to hearing them. I hope it wakes my sleeping men.

Not that we can move yet. We need the enemy to get closer before we attack.

They'll be able to see us, because of the campfire, long before we can detect them.

If these are the lost fifteen warriors, then we stand some chance of beating them. If they're another of the six gangs of fifty warriors sent to find me or kill me, depending on who you ask, then I think we stand no chance at all.

Not that it's going to stop me from trying, of course.

The horses' move uneasily from where they should sleep but evidently don't anymore. I bite my lip, adjust the grip on my seax, and shuffle my shoulders so that the cloak falls behind my arms as opposed to covering them.

Do they mean to use stealth, or will they come at us in a great rush?

It's impossible to tell, but the silence of the woodland is no longer that of night, but instead of heavy, and enforced silence.

It seems I'm not the only person waiting.

I detect movement in front of me, a figure, trying to move silently. But with the flicker of glinting iron from the distant fire, they come harshly into focus. I wonder how I couldn't have seen the enemy before.

And then I can pick out more of them. Not quite fifteen, but equal to my numbers.

It seems we have yet another battle to fight.

I'm unsure if they've seen me, and so I wait, tense but hidden until a foot nearly lands on me.

Only then do I erupt from my place of concealment, cloak flung to the ground, seax already reaching for the warrior. My reach is not quite what I would like it to be, but I make contact all the same, with the warrior's arm. My blade doesn't hack, but it slices across an exposed lower arm.

A squeak of protest comes from the warrior's open mouth, his eyes flickering nervously in the darkness for who attacks him.

My seax bites deeper on the second attack, and finally, the warrior reacts.

His blade flashes toward my left arm, his right arm pulled back, as though to stab, but I've already moved backwards, and his reach falters anyway, perhaps as a result of my first attack on him.

Other warriors are streaming towards the campfire, and I wish I'd thought more carefully about who should protect Gyrth if we were attacked. What point is there in risking our lives by staying here if Gyrth is the first to fall victim to this fresh wave of violence?

My worry makes me reckless, and I rush the warrior, my seax to the side of me so that I can use my weight against him. Only as he stumbles backwards do I realise his blade was in front of him. As he falls to the ground, I slice my seax across his chest, not quite reaching his neck, aware that he too has drawn blood.

'Fuck it,' I mutter, using my feet to keep him down, as I twist my grip and finally get a cut on his neck, as it flashes white with the impact. I turn, satisfied he's dead and rush to join my fellow warriors.

Someone has already fallen into the flames of the fire. A whoosh of yellow and orange temporarily blinds me so much so that I stumble into two warring bodies before I even realise.

'Fuck off,' Edmund grunts, whether aimed at the warrior he faces or me, I don't know. Regardless, I raise my seax and run it the length of the man's back.

The metal coat bursts open at the touch, as though severing a joint of meat, and I repeat the action. The man groans in pain, and Edmund's blade flashes. A wave of crimson covers me, and I spit, glaring at Edmund over the collapsing body of our enemy.

'What the fuck?' I demand, only to be ignored. There's heavy fighting elsewhere. Out of the corner of my eye, with the after-image of the erupting fire on the periphery of my eyesight, I see that

Ordheah and Lyfing are protecting Gyrth. Icel battles two warriors. Goda and Ingwald have one a piece.

Edmund has rushed off, something catching his attention, and I watch, always amazed by just how quickly human flesh burns.

The warrior in the fire is not quite dead, but neither can he move.

I stride to the fire, mindful of the heated flames, and reach in, slicing across yet another exposed neck. It's a mercy killing, nothing more.

By the time I've done that, an eerie silence has fallen.

I turn, there's the sound of heavy breathing, and the flicker of flames consuming the dead man. Other than that, it seems the attack is over.

'How many?' I demand to know.

'You had one, I took two, Icel took two, and Goda and Ingwald took one each.'

'Only seven then?'

'So it seems.' Edmund's voice holds neither rancour nor pleasure. Being attacked while sleeping is the work of the lazy or feeble. Our enemy does not deserve the swift deaths we've given them.

'There might be more,' I call, considering whether such an admission will bring the snakes slithering from hiding places or not. While the body burns, we've become an even bigger target than before, flames leaping higher, gobbling up the fatty tissue of flesh.

'Shit,' I complain, bending to find some part of the burning man I can yet grip and drag from the fire. I don't expect the touch of his hand on my arm, and I jerk, horrified by the blackened shell that reaches along my sleeve, threatening to pull me into the fire as well.

'You'll die, Lord Coelwulf.' The voice is stained with flames and smoke, the eyes flashing red and ruined, the tongue a slither of burnt meat, and yet I hear the words clearly all the same.

'So you fuckers keep promising me,' I complain, dropping low, to whisper into the blackened remains of his ears. 'But I still stand.'

Only the echo of death greets me as the grip drops away.

I drag the body away from the fire, keen to have it far from sight, eager to leave it as a mark of what I'll do to the next bastard who tries to end my life!

Only then do I turn to face my warriors. I don't miss the flicker of horror on all those faces other than Icel.

Icel cackles.

'Fuck that,' he offers, pointing with his bloodied blade to where I've left the body. 'We need to bury the bastard, or he'll come back again. Some of them are devils to kill.'

Icel's voice sounds too loud in the quiet that's fallen since the fighting ended and the flap of a bird taking to the air seems to recall him to the need for quiet.

I look back to the blackened body, and then I shake my head.

When I'm with my warriors once more, I speak.

'He's definitely dead now. Trust me. But where are the other sods?'

'They may have split up?' Edmund comments hopefully.

'They may yes, but I doubt it. A force of seven is too small to be travelling alone.'

'Then what do you suggest?' fatigue worries his tone, and I agree with him.

'Rest, we can't leave now, no matter what. I'll remain on watch duty, and there should be someone else as well. Let's hope we make it through the night.'

While the men eye each other up, all hopeful that another will take on the onerous task, I make my way back to my previous hiding place.

The woodland settles back to its nighttime activities. After only a brief burst of argument, Ingwald takes the other watch duty. I grimace. I would have preferred Edmund to do it. He has the gift of far-sight and quick wits. And everyone knows it. Perhaps though, he realises that as tired as he is, he'll do no good.

I make myself as uncomfortable as possible, keen to ensure I remain awake. I'll sleep tomorrow while I ride. Or perhaps another day.

Not that my mind wishes to allow me to rest. Far from it.

A great deal has happened in the last few days. I've lost good warriors. I've nearly lost even more. Mercia is genuinely threatened, and more importantly to me, the ancient kingdom of the Hwicce, part of Mercia, seems overrun by warriors out to kill me. Whether their leaders truly hold Repton or not, the imminent threat is here, where people look to me as their war leader.

I sigh. The weight of responsibility no new thing. I'm not fool enough to realise that I'm not suddenly a considerable part of the problem.

'Fucking bastards,' I mutter continually, the words forming time and time again on my lips, as I wait for the daylight to arrive.

I need to get Gyrth to Worcester.

6

Bishop Wærferth himself comes to meet our ragtag collection of men and horses.

Gyrth moans loudly as soon as his horse comes to a stop, and I think it's that cry, more than anything that makes Wærferth allow us entry.

It's been a difficult journey, and I've been forced to linger longer than I would have liked. The entire distance, I felt exposed. I've not enjoyed it, and my temper is foul to match to mood.

I know Wærferth of old, although he's only held his position in Gloucester for the last five years. He's a sprightly man, his intelligence evident in his hands that never stop moving, even when he's silent, and the rest of his body is so still, I might think him sleeping.

Now, as the monks take Gyrth away, on a stretcher because he can't walk unaided, those keen grey eyes seek mine out.

I slide from the back of Haden, more relieved than I care to admit on seeing Rudolf's cheeky face, with its shading of black and green, coming to care for my horse. The two greet as though they've been apart for years, and not the handful of days it's actually been. Haden almost licks Rudolf, and I turn away, trying not to snipe at them. Daft sods. The pair of them.

'I have news you must hear,' Wærferth's tone surprises me. I'm not entirely sure how I'd expected to be received by the bishop. It seems, dare I say it, as though he's actually pleased to see me. This doesn't bode well. Not if my past experiences are anything to go on.

I follow him, to the rear of the monastery buildings, to where the River Severn flows below us, the steep cliff acting as a source of defence far better than a ditch and earth mound. The air is ripe with the stench of stagnant water, and I wrinkle my nose. I'm not sure I wish to drink anything from that.

'It'll clear,' Wærferth's comments, noticing my disgust. 'It always does it at this time of the year. Too hot and too still. It'll disperse with a storm from the hills. But it'll clear.'

I nod, surprised that he's repeating himself.

Bishop Wærferth is a man who uses words sparingly. He never repeats himself.

I feel unease prickle my neck. What does he know?

'King Burgred is gone.'

I growl, low in my throat. 'Craven,' it's as polite as I can be, taking into account the bishop's sensibilities.

'It's not quite as bad as it sounds, although it's not good. The Raiders killed Beornwald. Everyone knows King Burgred and his wife couldn't breed. Burgred claimed his nephew instead, as the ætheling of Mercia. With his death, what point was there in the king continuing to fight?' There's no sympathy in the bishop's voice, but there might be understanding. I'm not sure yet.

'Another could have taken ætheling Beornwald's place. If King Burgred could make the witan acknowledge Beornwald as his heir, then he could have done the same with another man, however distantly related.'

'There was no other male in the family line. This line of Mercian kings ends with King Burgred, and he's dying too.'

There's a hint of compassion in Bishop Wærferth's voice.

'Then he should have stood in the shield wall and taken his death as a warrior king.' My words are filled with bile. There's always someone worth fighting for, even when your family are dead. And certainly, Mercia shouldn't be given away in despair.

'King Burgred had a responsibility to keep fighting and to hold the Raiders at bay.'

'I'm not going to disagree with you.' This is the closest to criticism I've ever heard from Wærferth. My eyes widen in surprise, not just at the disapproval. Bishop Wærferth and I never agree about anything.

The bishop believes the Raiders can be beaten with prayer and good deeds. I know they can only be stopped with cold iron and hard men and women.

'Wessex should never have abandoned their ally. This all stems from that.'

Now I know my jaw hangs loose, and Bishop Wærferth has the good grace to look contrite at the effect his words are having on me.

'A man can learn to change his mind,' he explains.

'I don't deny that, but I've never encountered a holy man capable of doing so.'

His laughter surprises me even more and puts me on alert. The man has never been this congenial before. What does he want from me?

'Mercia needs a king,' the words astound me.

'Yes,' I say slowly. 'It does.' I'm not sure what Bishop Wærferth has been conjuring in his mind, and I don't like the fact he shares his secrets with me. 'Is there a bastard son somewhere, or a forgotten half-brother?' It wouldn't surprise me. Not at all.

'No, the family line is ended, as I said. The ætheling had fathered no children. A disappointing end to that family.' Bishop Wærferth's mouth is a thin line of disapproval. All the same, I can decipher where his thoughts have taken him, and I don't like it.

'My grandfather was deposed fifty years ago,' I interject before the bishop can mutter the words I can see forming in his mind. 'No one made a fuss back then about it. They were content with the bastard who claimed the kingdom.'

The bishop is watching me closely, his eyes trying to seer into my soul. I feel uncomfortable under his stern gaze, and yet I can't make myself walk away.

'Your grandfather was not the warrior you are. The people of Mercia didn't realise there was a greater enemy than themselves.'

'Neither of those two facts are anything to do with me. I will protect western Mercia, as I've always done, my brother before me. I can't do more than that.'

'They mean to kill you.'

'I know they do. Fucking King Burgred must have told them about me.'

'Why would he do that?' Wærferth all but snaps, and any illusions I might have had about anyone but the bishop remembering my family line dissipates. That'll teach me to think of my predecessors so much.

'I think it more likely your reputation is known to them.' As the bishop makes his pronouncement, his mouth curdles into a line of displeasure.

'I kill warriors, and protect the borders from Welsh incursions, and I ride, with my men and horses. That's all I'm ever going to do.' I try to deflect him now. I don't want to be any more than that, even if I know it's not right.

'I don't think it is,' Bishop Wærferth says persuasively.

'It is. I've come here, to ensure Gyrth heals and to collect those other wounded men who can ride.'

'Why, where are you going?' His lips are pursed as he stares at me. Again, I don't appreciate his scrutiny.

'To face the Raiders, to Repton. Someone needs to drive them from Mercian lands.'

'So you've already decided to act as a king should?' Such delight fills his words that again I'm surprised by the emotions the bishop is revealing to me.

'Now, I've chosen to attack rather than be attacked. They've sent over three hundred warriors to find me, to take me to Repton, or to kill me, whatever must be done. I've only killed under a hundred of them. There's still two hundred plus to find on my way to Repton.'

Bishop Wærferth smiles at my words. I don't like the look of it. I'm sure he's never smiled at me before. I can't see how it makes his face appealing, but rather menacing.

'I have warriors who could assist you,' Wærferth offers. 'They're well-trained, and have good weapons and horses.'

'Why would you give me warriors?'

'If you were the king of Mercia, it would be my obligation to do so as the bishop of Worcester.'

'But I'm not the king of Mercia. The witan hasn't been convened, no one has been elected as king. Who even knows if there's a kingdom left to rule over?' I know my words are worthless. They were before I even tried to deny Bishop Wærferth's reasoning.

'No one will accept me as king of Mercia. I'm a warrior. I have no son, either!'

Bishop Wærferth continues to watch me, his eyes softening, but resolved all the same.

'Mercia needs a bastard warrior right now. Her kings have failed her. Her allies have failed her. But you haven't failed her. You've always fought for Mercia and the Mercians. I'm not the only one to think so.'

I scoff then. I can't help it.

'No one else thinks anything of me at all. I'd be amazed if the ealdormen and bishops even know who I am.'

Bishop Wærferth's chuckle is not reassuring.

'Shall I name those who know who you are? Who speaks of you with respect, even if it's always been in soft whispers so that King Burgred didn't become aware of the high esteem they all held you within?'

'My family was discarded. Our honour demanded we continue to protect Mercia. It doesn't require that I make a fool of myself by asking to become Mercia's king.'

'You'll not need to ask,' Bishop Wærferth is deliberately ignoring the words I say that deny what he asks. I feel my temper beginning to fray.

Before I can storm away, Bishop Wærferth grabs my arm, his grip stronger than I expect it to be. He holds me in place, his gaze filled with understanding.

'You and your family have been badly used by Mercia, or rather, by men who were foolish enough to think they should rule instead. I'll never deny that. And how have they fared for such impudence? They're all dead, or nearly so, their dynasties snuffed out as though they never existed. Yet you remain, as the final member of a dynasty from which great kings have come in the past. And that means far more than you imagine.'

'I know you'll not have it said that Our Lord God favours you, so I won't say that. But chance and happenstance favour you. You can't turn your back on Mercia, not now.'

I want to yank my arm away, but I don't.

'I haven't said I'll turn my back on Mercia. I've said I won't be her king.'

'You may not have the choice in the matter that you think you will.' Such ominous words, from the bishop, and then he drops his hold on my arm, an arch of his right eyebrow emphasising his words.

I want to say more, to deny his words, his inferences, and his damn interference.

But perhaps he's right. Even if I don't want to admit it.

'Mercia needs warriors, not kings,' I try, grudgingly.

'Mercia hasn't always received what she needs. She's been burdened with fools who couldn't see the Viking menace for what it was. Now, I fear, it is about to become the greatest it's ever been. King Alfred, in Wessex, holds on by the smallest of margins. Mercia however, stands proud and independent, but only if men and women fight for her.'

'Who then speaks of me?'

'Ah,' Bishop Wærferth's delight is evident in just that one sound. 'The ealdormen, and the other bishops, as well. And not just from eastern Mercia, but from the west as well.'

I'm shaking my head. I can't believe it. Whenever I've encountered these men in the past, they've dismissed me. No one has ever liked the fact that I roam western Mercia with my warband. I don't think that those I've helped have ever thanked me. Not that it concerns me. I just note it to myself.

'Bishop Eadberht of Lichfield and Deorlaf of Hereford have men they'll pledge to you.'

'They're holy men.' I can't quite keep the squeak of surprise from my voice.

'As am I. Holy men know just as well as the secular lords that someone must wield weapons against an enemy who threatens to extinguish the life of everyone they administer to.'

'Ealdorman Ælhun of central Mercia.'

'Hates me,' I interject quickly. Ælhun is the most influential of the ealdormen who helped King Burgred rule Mercia. The land he governs is close to mine. He resents me. He hates me, and I know all this without him having spoken to me even once.

His gaze has always spoken most eloquently for him.

Bishop Wærferth has the decency to look abashed.

'He does hate you, that can't be denied. But desperate men will overlook such small matters of love or hate to survive.'

'Ealdorman Alhferht.'

'Doesn't much like me either.'

Bishop Wærferth holds his hands to either side, a shrug of his shoulders telling me that the same applies to Ealdorman Alhferht as to Ælhun.

'Ealdorman Æthelwold.'

'I've never heard of him.' I look in surprise at the bishop. Has it really been so long since I attended the witan that a new generation of men has begun to rule?

'He's newly come to his position. You may remember his father, Æthelwulf.'

'He fucking hated me,' I confirm, respectful all the same. The man at least had the honour to die protecting Mercia. A pity really. He might have hated me, but he hated the bastard Raiders more.

'And now his son has taken his place and doesn't hate you. Yet. Of course, there's always time for that to happen,' the bishop's flippant tone almost makes me smirk.

'And you believe these men would support me?' I demand to know.

'I know these men would have no choice but to do so. They can agree on only one thing, and if it's that they hate you, then at least Mercia can be saved.'

I want to argue with Bishop Wærferth. I want to tell him that he's wrong. That Mercia doesn't need me. But I know that Ealdorman Ælhun, Alhferht and Æthelwold lack the skills I possess.'

'Then what of Ealdorman Beorhtnoth?'

After King Burgred and Ealdorman Ælhun, Beorhtnoth is the next most influential man in Mercia.

'He will be brought round, eventually.'

'That's far from reassuring. The bishops will tolerate me, and the ealdormen will hate me. There's still Beorhtnoth who will definitely refuse to acknowledge me.'

'I didn't realise you were wary of what others thought of you.'

'I'm not,' the words rip from my mouth before I can stop them.

Bishop Wærferth grins at me, his triumph souring my mouth.

'It'll not come to that,' I complain.

'I would suggest that you either do as I say, or those men will join the Raiders in trying to kill you. At the moment, you have just over two hundred warriors trying to kill you, and all of them are strangers to this kingdom. If the ealdormen add their numbers, it'll be another, what the same number again.'

'I don't know how many warriors they can supply.'

'I think you do.'

Again, I want to deny the bishop's logic, but it's becoming increasingly difficult.

Frustrated, I return our conversation to my primary concern.

'I need to go to Kingsholm, retrieve the rest of my warriors from my Aunt. Can Gyrth, Sæbald and Pybba remain under your care until my return?'

'Of course they can. They're not the ones with a bounty on their heads.' The response is not reassuring.

'And while you travel to Gloucester, with your handful of men, think about what I've said to you. You may have the command of the ancient Hwiccan kingdom, but you can't secure it. Not alone.'

Unconstrained, I finally manage to stride away from the bishop. But as I go, my eyes flicker all around me. The bishop's church is well protected. Worcester is well defended. But, it's still a river that sits at the rear of the defences, and the Raiders have ships. Lots and lots of fucking boats.

A shiver of dread runs down my spine. I try to ignore it, keen to see Pybba, Sæbald and Gyrth. Eager to know that the number of men killed in the recent attacks has stalled at two.

I've eighteen men left to me, but not all of them can fight. Not at the moment.

At Kingsholm, there are a further fifteen warriors I can call upon.

There are the young lads as well, but I don't believe any of them are yet ready to face our deadly enemy.

The kingdom of the Hwicce has had many great kings, but none since my grandfather was deposed. Since then, if anything, an attempt has been made by my family to keep out of trouble, even to hide behind who we were and what we could do. No doubt, I would have continued to do the same. If it hadn't been for the increasing frequency of Raider attacks.

Inside the monastery building, the smell of the river is still strong, but bunches of fresh herbs hang from the rafters, and they go some way to keeping the odour at bay.

My men are seated around a table, Rudolf amongst them, discussing the events since we last met. Rudolf rushes to my side.

'This way,' he states blandly, and I follow him, my heart thudding painfully in my chest. There's no mirth in Rudolf's voice. I've never known it to be missing in the past. What's happened to Pybba and Sæbald?

Then he begins to speak.

'We were set upon, not far from Worcester. It was a scouting party, nothing more, but the five men were handy with their blades.'

'Did everyone survive?' I ask.

'Yes. Pybba fought again. That man will not stop fighting. I think you could take his head, and he'd fight on.'

'And Sæbald?'

'He couldn't fight. By then he'd lost too much blood.'

'And did you fight?' The lengthy pause tells me all I need to know. But his silence again worries me.

'I killed a man,' Rudolf turns to look at me, the horror of his actions reflected in the dullness of his normally bright eyes. 'I killed a man.'

I swallow thickly. I hadn't wanted that. I should have been there for him. The others might not have realised the importance of such an act to Rudolf.

'How do you do it?' Rudolf asks then, jutting out his chin, as though he doesn't want to ask, but must do so.

'I do it because there's no choice. I do it because it's what will save Mercia and more importantly, because it saves my friends, and my warriors, and keeps the few people I care for, safe.'

'It hurts me,' Rudolf says. 'In here,' and he taps his chest where his heart would be, his voice cracking.

I reach out, wanting to shake his shoulder, to offer him my strength, but he shies away from me.

I had worried about this.

The joy of battle is in the killing, but the killing is not the joy it should be. For those who've never killed before, who can't imagine doing so, it's a strange realisation to discover that others can do something that pains you so very, very easily.

Instead, I grab his chin, force him to look into my eyes. I have to use more strength than I'd like to in order to keep his eyes on mine.

'If you want peace of mind and forgiveness for your action, then seek out a priest and perform your penance. For anything else, remember that if you hadn't killed that warrior, then he would have killed you, or worse, your friends and brothers in arms.'

I hold his gaze. I wish I could somehow gift him with my experience and reconciliation to who I am and what I am. But he'll only be as good as I think he can be if he learns his own lessons.

Rudolf lowers his lashes, and I see tears have settled there.

I want to drive away those tears, make him as impervious as I can be.

'It will get easier,' I assure him instead, a consolation I've never shared with even Edmund.

'But it never gets easy. Now, take me to my wounded.' Abruptly, I release Rudolf from my hold, and I think he might fall, but he staggers and regains his balance. For a moment longer, he glances at me, and then he seems to shake all over.

'Pybba is filled with complaints. Sæbald sleeps a great deal of the time.' Rudolf has searched for who he used to be and summoned a shadow of his previous cheeky ways. I appreciate that he makes an effort. Perhaps there's a realisation that I'm not quite the impervious bastard Rudolf takes me to be. Maybe he respects me more. It certainly couldn't be any fucking less.

'Then I hope you've been seeing to Pybba. He's to be esteemed.'

'He's a pestilence to be born with patience,' Rudolf comments, skipping in front of me to avoid the cuff I would give him around the head, while a wry smirk tugs at my cheeks.

'As are you,' I confirm, and Rudolf turns to glance at me, his tears dry, but his face still white with his worries.

'As are you,' he retorts, and then I fall silent because I've been led to a small building outside the main hall of the monastery and far away from the river. Rudolf holds the door wide for me, and the stench of the river is overridden by something even less pleasant.

I cough against the astringent smell as I lower my head to enter.

There are a handful of monks inside, walking amongst no more than ten beds. A body lies on every bed, some of them still, others bucking against whatever ails them.

Rudolf leads me to Pybba. Pybba is sitting beside the small hearth that burns at the centre of the room, peering gloomily into the flames.

His face is purple with bruises, but my eyes seek out his wound first.

As before the linen that covers his stump seems clean and clear. I almost dread to see it when the linens are no longer needed.

But Pybba doesn't sense my presence, and Rudolf hovers anxiously.

'Pybba,' I say the name softly, and while his head turns to me, it seems he's not aware of who I am.

'Pybba, it's me. Coelwulf.'

This time, there's more of a response on the lined face, but no recognition.

I turn to Rudolf, but it's one of the monks who speaks to me.

'His arm is recovering well. But he's taken a heavy blow to the head. It's to be hoped he'll recover. In time.'

'What happened?'

'In the battle. He was knocked down, by one of the Raiders. The one I killed.'

Ah, so much suddenly makes sense. I'm beginning to understand more of why Rudolf is so worried by the man he killed.

'You have my thanks for caring for him.' Into the hand of the monk, I press some of my silver pennies. They carry the head of King Burgred, but until there's a new king, they have value in Mercia. These pennies used to mean a great deal for me than they do now. Now I have horses, and each one is worth a hundred and twenty of these silver coins. Ten for the monks is really too little, but it's a great wealth for them.

The monk inclines his head.

'Where are Sæbald and Gyrth?'

The monk leads me toward another bed. On this one, lies the still figure of Sæbald.

I've always thought Sæbald a perfect warrior, the correct size, height and weight. He seems small and shrivelled beneath the furs that cover him.

'He lost a great deal of blood.' Sæbald seems to be myriad shades of blue, green and black, his right eye bulging, although not open.

'Will he recover?'

'It's to be hoped. He can remain in such a state for a few days more before it becomes worrying.'

I reach down, rub my thumb over Sæbald's arm. His skin feels dry and desiccated. I swallow around my sorrow to see him in such a state.

'And what of Gyrth?'

The monk leads me towards another bed. On this one, Gyrth lies, awake, and sweating, his finger unbound so that the air can get to it. I examine the cut I made. It's neat and tidy. And, despite my worries, it might well have been enough to ensure the wound-rot didn't set in. But still, he fights a high fever.

'The sweating is good. It should remove the contagion from his body. I believe, provided he recovers from the fever, that he'll be well.'

Gyrth turns to meet my eyes, a hint of his fiery desire to live clear to see.

'Don't worry about me,' he all but whispers.

If only it were that easy.

'I'll be back for you,' I inform Gyrth, my plans forming as I speak.

'In no more than a week. If you're not healed, I'll leave you here. If you're well, you can come with me.'

The monk startles at my side for my voice has dropped low, filled with foreboding.

Gyrth surprises me by grinning, his teeth flashing yellow in the dull light.

'You'll have to kill me from coming with you.' I grin then. Damn the fucker. He better be alive this time next week. I need him.

'And what of Oda and Eahric?' I can see the monks are no longer caring for them.

'They're with the rest of the men. They only have to come here twice a day to be assessed.'

That cheers me, to know that two of my men are near enough healed. I need them back to full fighting strength, and sooner than I'd like.

Resolved, I stride from the hospital, Rudolf accompanying me. I imagine he has many questions, and a sign of just how much he's changed in the last few days, is that not one of them slips through his lips.

I'll miss my young companion. I will. Now, I must learn to treat him as one of my warriors, even if I don't want to.

'Tomorrow, I'll travel to Kingsholm. I'm going to take as many of the horses as I can. You can decide whether to stay with Pybba or to come with me.'

I don't wait for an answer. The flicker of surprise on Rudolf's face alerts me to the fact that he too has realised the change in our relationship, even if only just.

I'll need a new lad to care for Haden. But that's a problem for another day.

I stride back into the bishop's hall and easily slide between Edmund and Icel. The two are eating and drinking as though there'll be no food tomorrow, and I join them.

It's an important lesson to be learned. Eat when you can, sleep when you can, drink when you can, and if you're that way inclined, fuck when you can as well.

I BANISH Bishop Wærferth's words about claiming the kingship from my mind. I don't have the capacity to think through all he's implying. First, I need to rebuild my ranks of missing men, but before that, I need to make it to Gloucester without being attacked.

'Take a ship?' Bishop Wærferth's suggestion isn't a bad one. But.

'I need to take the horses with me. It'll take too long to load them.'

He subsides, wisely holding his tongue. He's not spoken to me about becoming Mercia's king again. But his guarded looks are enough for me to know that he's not given up on the idea.

I don't think I have, either.

With all the horses we can manage, well over a hundred, we don't exactly make a timely escape through the remains of the ancient Roman defences in Worcester. I'm surprised that Rudolf rides with the rest of the men. I was sure he would stay with Pybba, Sæbald and Gyrth, as well as Oda and Eahric, who I've forced to stay behind. But he doesn't. Instead, Wulfhere remains in his place. I've not dared to make my farewells to Pybba. I don't think his complaints would be short, and in that time, I could have made it to Kingsholm and back.

Edmund and Hereman are engaged in a heated debate as we make our way to the riverbank, below Worcester. I don't ask what's riled them both, but rather stay clear of them. Brothers will always argue. It used to be the same while my brother lived.

The day is bright and clear, the river sluggish and rife with the smell that infected Worcester. I doubt it'll clear before we reach Kingsholm.

My thoughts turn to what I'll find in Kingsholm.

My father died a decade ago, fighting the Raiders. My mother lost her life birthing me, a guilt that's never left me. In place of parents, I have my Aunt. She's a formidable woman. If she could ride to war, then I know she would. And her reputation would then be far greater than any I've garnered in my lifetime.

She'll be displeased by the tide of change in Mercia. Of a generation with King Burgred, she never accorded him any respect. My father chose to keep her at Kingsholm rather than antagonise Burgred. After my father's death, she decided to seclude herself there. Some sort of punishment, but whether for her or my father, I've no idea.

The first I know that we're riding into danger is Hereman's bark of 'Raiders.'

I've not been riding blindly. Icel and Goda have been riding one to the front, and one to the rear of my small collection of warriors, and large group of horses. So where is Icel?

I peer into the near distance. I'd not expected more Raiders to infiltrate the Hwiccan kingdom quite so deeply. I'd assumed that they'd hover, on the edges, waiting for me to appear. It seems I'm wrong.

Ahead, I can clearly see what Hereman is warning me about. I can also see Icel, face filled with rage, as he races toward me.

Whatever apology he wants to make, I shrug aside, focusing on those who come against me now.

I can't blame Icel. Not for this. It's my mistake. I should have travelled via the River Severn as the bishop suggested. I only refused because of the smell. It's hardly an excuse worth dying for.

'Fuckers,' Icel complains. 'Hiding in the woods like sodding pigs looking for acorns.'

I allow that and turn to assess my force. Rudolf has stilled on his small pony, his face white, his teeth clenched. Fuck. I should have insisted he stay in Worcester. But I couldn't. Not now he's taken his first life.

I have fewer men than ever before. I wasn't going to Kingsholm because I fancied a hot bath.

I left Gloucester with twenty men, and the young lads, who number about the same.

I lost two good men, Athelstan and Beornberht in my first meeting with the Raiders.

Pybba lost his hand as well.

That's taken me down to seventeen men, although I should add Rudolf into the number, so that makes eighteen.

Only Sæbald and Gyrth are also incapacitated in Worcester, and I insisted that Oda and Eahric remained as well. So again, I'm down to fourteen. One of that number is a young lad, with his first blood on his hands. But I doubt the skill to fight as I want him too.

I should have left Rudolf in Worcester.

And of course, I have my young lads as well, all riding with three other horses under their command. Once more, I'm richer in horses than I am in warriors. And yet, I feel no fear, but rather a calm reckoning of what I have that the enemy doesn't have.

They number the usual fifty, or thereabouts, and they have horses. I can see where they've been discarded to the near side of the riverbank. The animals crop the lush grasses there.

The enemy also seems well provided with weapons, and battle wear, and already they taunt my force. Their words are incomprehensible from such a distance. The intent is not.

'Four each,' I call to Edmund. He and Hereman's argument has finally fallen silent, but only because of the coming altercation. I swear, if they live through this, then they'll resume it before they've taken their last kill. Blood will sheet blades, but the words will be about whatever the fuck it is they're arguing about.

'Easy,' Edmund licks his lips, his battle fears evident in the white of his face. As always, the thought of what's to come doesn't appeal to Edmund. Not until he's had his first kill.

I can hear the rest of my men preparing for battle. The mass of horses have been moved to one side by the lads, not the riverside, and I consider calling them back. Only perhaps not yet. I swivel on my horse, looking for Rudolf, and then beckon him to me.

He comes with mutiny on his young face, but when I speak to him, his tense shoulders relax.

'I fucking like it,' he comments, a hint of his former cheek restored to him.

'Good.'

While Rudolf directs his horse through my fourteen men, I squint into the bright daylight.

Fifty warriors. Without their horses.

Damn fuckers.

'We begin this on our mounts,' I inform my warriors. No one comments on the unusual battle tactic. 'That should reduce the numbers to more manageable levels.'

Hereman mutters something under his breath, but I ignore him. He'll be complaining, or praying, or whatever it is he does when he faces his death.

I reach down and lay my head along Haden's long neck. I don't want to risk my horse, but I can't ride another. I trust the damn bugger.

With no more thought, or consideration, or even time to take in the banner that the Raiders fight under, and which hangs limps in the summer heat, I encourage Haden to a fast gallop. In one breath, we go from stationary to flying, and I grin, despite it all.

The feel of my horse's steady gait beneath my body is invigorating.

I've done little but fight battles for the past eight days. And now I'll fight another.

The Raiders stand across the trackway, weapons gleaming, stances loose. I'm not sure who leads them. I don't much care.

I grin, thumping my helm over my mass of bright blonde hair, reaching for my seax, all while my horse flees, fleet-footed, over the summer-ripe trackway. It's not rained for days. The ground isn't yet hard-packed. It might be after this. Or maybe we'll water it with red rain.

Only when I'm close enough to see the flicker of unease in the eyes of the warriors who stand before the others, five men, weapons bristling, do I appreciate that they really expected me to leap from my horse.

With a light touch of my knees, Haden keeps his course steady but begins to move to face the front-most warrior.

My chosen opponent is not a giant, far from it, but he has the girth of a man who uses his weight to win. It'll do him no good against a charging horse.

Haden doesn't even hesitate, let alone consider that he's not customarily directed to ride through a man. His ability to follow my special instructions is born from our long years together.

Haden's hooves crash into the man, who's too slow to move, too dazed to realise what's coming. And then we're amongst the remaining warriors. A shimmer of panic seems to envelop some of them, as though time hangs unmoving. Into that void, my men and their horses gallop.

The first man is not the only one to fall beneath Haden's hooves. Another two also buckle from the knees and descend. Terrified eyes meet mine before I can get my horse under control and turn him to see the outcome of my unorthodox attack.

The screams of the wounded men are overridden only by the terrible screeching coming from Ingwald's horse.

'Fuck,' I complain, sliding from Haden's back and slapping his rump so that he moves away from the rest of the fighting.

It seems that every horse has taken down at least one man, often two. There are just over twenty men standing. But not all those on the ground are dead.

I watch as one man reaches for his lost weapon, his lips bloody, his legs shattered below the knees, pulling himself forward on his arms, fierce determination on his battered face although he leaves a trail of blood in his wake.

I grimace, take the necessary five hurried strides, and slice cleanly through his neck. His hand stills its frantic reach, but just to be sure, I stamp on the fingers, enjoying the crunch of broken bone as a counterpart to the clash of iron on iron.

Hereman is still mounted, turning his horse, which kicks out, front legs flying, against the two men who menace him.

I take the time to admire the action. I didn't know the damn thing could do that!

A grip on my ankle and my blade is moving before I've considered who might be there. Another lies dead, the fall of his blood on my hooded face, coming only after the breath has gurgled from him severed throat.

Another kill.

Edmund, his face finally robust with colour, faces two men, one to the side, and one to the front. As I make my way to assist him, my seax stabs down into the backs of two more men who lie, broken, but not dead, after the onslaught of the horses.

I leave the man with the broken skull alone. The white of the exposed bone casts the grey matter of his brain into sharp relief. I grimace. A quick death. But far from pleasant.

'Take the man to your left,' I call my instruction to Edmund, as I heave myself against the man in front of him. The blow catches my opponent on the shoulder, my blade glinting with ruby, but making no impact against the warrior's mail coat.

Damn fucker. I recognise the exquisite workmanship of the warrior's coat. This is Mercian. He's taken it from one of his kills.

It'll make him hard to kill, but I will, all the same.

My opponent turns to face me, his black beard flecked with spittle, a smirk on his face. I slice my seax as close to that smile as I can, only for him to counter, and thrust my seax away.

The blade he carries is good Mercian iron, I can tell from the way it reverberates along my arm. Made from iron mined from north Mercia, smelted with charcoal made from Mercia's vast forests. The man deserves to die for such an outrage.

Who did this bastard kill to take such prizes?

Soon, I consider, they'll be mine, and I might even take the time to find out who they once belonged to.

He tries to slice my belly, aiming his blade low, the shimmer of it reflecting the bright light of the day.

I step aside, aware that facing only one enemy, Edmund is enjoying himself by hammering his war axe repeatedly against the man's neck. Blood flies through the air. Edmund, it seems, has chosen to vent his rage at his brother, over whatever their stupid argument was about, on the enemy.

I'm glad he didn't so against Hereman. I would have lost yet another valued warrior.

I flick my right arm out, twisting the grip on my seax, stabbing, as opposed to slicing.

Such a movement makes the target too small for my enemy to counter easily, and his good Mercian sword slides effortlessly against my knuckles. They'll be bruised, maybe bleeding later, but it doesn't matter. My seax skewers the man, high on his shoulder.

It grates, as it slides ever deeper.

My opponent's attack falters but doesn't stop.

His breath is musty in my face, as I step in closer, and closer, keen to grip his blade, to ensure he knows I've taken it.

I meet fierce hazel eyes, the mouth moving, although no sound comes forth.

'Bastard,' I reply, aware that he can't see my arched eyebrows beneath my helm. Aware he probably doesn't understand what I say.

His response surprises me.

'Fucker, you'll lose your life for this.' The words are drenched in agony, as I twist my seax, just for good measure. His right hand hangs limply at his waist, his blade now in my left hand.

I'm considering stabbing him in the heart with the Mercian blade, ensuring he dies twice, both for invading my kingdom and for stealing from her. Only he speaks again.

'My father is one of the jarls in charge of the attack on Mercia. He wanted you alive. But now he'll want you dead.'

'A pity your father didn't come himself then, but sent the runt of his litter to do a man's work.'

The light in the brown eyes fades, and just for the fun of it, I stab with my left hand, the Mercian blade almost being repelled by the fine mail coat. Only then it does slide into the dying man's flesh.

I grin again. Lean forward, planting my lips on his feebly moving mouth.

'I'll tell your daddy how you died,' I confirm, and then move quickly back, thrusting him to the floor, both weapons wrenching free with a squelch of flesh and blood.

Edmund watches me, panting heavily, taking the time to restore himself before he finds another to attack.

Only the time has come for Rudolf's part in the battle.

Fifty or so men stood across our path, blocking the way to Gloucester, gleaming in the bright daylight, the intention to kill us all evident in their stance.

The initial charge of the horses took out at least eighteen of that number. I've killed a further four. But fierce fighting has broken out amongst the rest of the warriors.

''Ware' I shout, my warriors won't be expecting the next attack, but they'll quickly work it out. Or so I hope.

Thunder fills the air.

Edmund looks beyond me, his jaw clenching with fury at yet more enemy coming against us until he understands what's happening.

'You're a sick mother fucker,' Edmund shouts. He hastens to stand clear from the wreck of bodies, and dying men, to ensure the hundred horses being aimed toward the knots of fighting men, come nowhere near him.

I make to join him, only to catch sight of Ordheah, his back to the riverbank, an enemy advancing on him with confident strides, a long sword in his hand.

'Fuck,' I complain, trying to determine if I have time to reach him.

If Ordheah falls into the river, as turgid as it is at the moment, he might drown under the weight of his battle equipment.

It's no way for one of my warriors to die.

Ordheah's made mistakes of late. But such errors shouldn't be rewarded with death.

The crashing of hooves over broken bodies cuts off Edmund's cry 'Don't,' but I'm already moving. I won't allow one of my men to die like this.

A flash of brown, and then a flicker of midnight black buffet me. Both animals race beyond me, and I keep my feet only by dint of sheer fucking determination. My hand has been jarred, but both weapons are still firmly grasped.

But it's not the end of the horses' stampede.

I can hear Rudolf and the other lads encouraging the horses on. Through the flashes of light, I see Ordheah teetering closer and closer to the riverbank.

'Bollocks,' I can't see any way that I'm going to reach him in time. After this attack is done with, it seems I'm going to spend the rest of the day dredging the river for my missing warrior.

'Fuck,' I cry again, as a fresh wave of horseflesh threatens to overwhelm me. I've been a damn stupid bastard, and I fear that despite my best intentions, I might go down here. And not at the hands of the Raiders, but at my damn refusal to allow one of my men to fall.

I swallow my frustration, dance around the rear of one horse, only to find another charging down upon me. Time slows, as I consider the blades in my hand. Could I get the kill in before the weight of the animal takes me down?

Only then I notice the hand extended toward me, and Rudolf's bright face on the back of the animal.

It seems my young squire will rescue me.

I reach my hand to take his, digging my heel into the lush growths so that I have a small run-up. And then I release my back leg, feel Rudolf's weaker grip on my hand, and somehow, I'm on the back of his horse, and we're racing with the other horses.

I hunt for Ordheah, ignoring the crunch of bone splitting open, while the horses rush on, taking too long to come to a halt.

'What were you doing?' Rudolf's question is a fair one, brought to me from where he turns his horse around. I have no real answer.

'Take me back. Ordheah was under attack.'

'Lyfing went to aid him.'

'Take me back,' I command all the same. The horses are milling around on a gentle rise. Unsure what to do with themselves, they pluck at the grasses beneath their hooves.

I'm dimly aware that a handful of the young lads are tending to them, trying to gather together as many as they can.

Without further argument, Rudolf guides his horse back the way we've just come. A stray white horse flees beyond us, red streaks on its flanks attesting to the battle that's taken place.

I gaze forward, counting my men as I see them.

I look to where Ordheah was standing, and find Lyfing beside him, the pair slapping each other around the backs.

All is well there then.

Next, I seek out Edmund and find him disentangling himself from a thicket of summer weeds growing to the far side of the trackway. I keep my amusement from showing at his poor choice of places to wait out the stampede.

I've not yet found all of my men, although it seems that the only ones who walk amongst the ruin of the attack and the horses' stampede are men I recognise.

'Where's Hereman?' I call, slipping from the horse at the same time.

'My thanks,' I meet Rudolf's eyes, my hand on his arm, the pressure making him wince.

'I'm a warrior now,' Rudolf asks, and I nod, even though it hurts me to do so.

'The daft sods over here,' Edmund's call fills the silence where before battle raged.

'Does everyone live?' I can't afford to lose any more of my warriors.

A chorus of 'yes' reaches my ears, but still, I don't count fourteen amongst them.

'Who's missing?' I demand to know. Hereman erupts in front of me, Edmund at his side.

'What the fuck was that?' he calls, his face filled with fury, and worse, a slither of horseshit marring his clothes and weapons.

'A stampede,' I stutter, not wishing to get too close to him when he's so noxious.

'You nearly fucking killed me?'

'It was my intention to kill our enemy, not my warriors.' Hereman vibrates with his anger, and I'm unsurprised when Edmund marches up to him. The next words are a complaint, and I tune it out.

Who is missing?

Rudolf is riding around the scene of destruction, his head hanging lower than his mount's shoulders, as he looks amongst the dead.

There's more than one cracked skull. Now, the heat of the battle dissipating from my limbs, my stomach rolls with disgust at the destruction.

'Oslac,' Rudolf's cry reaches my ears, even above Hereman's complaints. Rudolf is off his horse, on his knees, as I rush to his side.

Oslac is lying face down on the ground, and Rudolf struggles to turn him. I bend, ignoring the creak of my back, and add my weight to that of the slight youth's.

I know, even before I see him, that Oslac is dead. No man alive would feel so damn heavy.

'Fuck,' I meet Oslac's staring blue eyes, his lips dyed with the green of summer growth, the wound on his chest, nothing compared to the ragged slices of the skin near his throat.

Rudolf stumbles away, his choking sobs the only sound, other than the heavy footsteps of my warriors coming to join me.

I reach out, take the useless helm from Oslac's head, rest it softly back on the ground, and then close his eyes. I don't need to see the endless question that will always be unanswered on his face.

'Bollocking bollocks,' Edmund roars, speaking for everyone. Silence falls between us all, broken only by the sound of the loose horses munching on the riverbank grasses.

My head hangs low. Each death is a blow for me. My warriors are my family. To lose three of them in such a small space of time weighs heavily on me.

But, I can't sit here mourning.

'Bring one of the horses, a sturdy one. We'll take him back to Kingsholm, bury him there.'

'What about the dead?' Edmund prompts me. I always bury my dead. Today I don't much feel like it.

'Pile them up over there,' I point to the hedge that Edmund emerged from.

'We'll bury them when we're back to full strength. I don't want to risk lingering.' What remains unsaid is that I don't want to have to face the bodies when I ride back this way. None of us does.

Rudolf returns, with Oslac's mount. The animal is splattered with blood, eyes rolling, but he quickly calms him. Then, with the aid of Hereman and Edmund, I lift the body, secure it to the saddle. Oslac's horse has one more journey to make with his master. It won't be a pleasant one.

'Loot the bodies, if there's anything of value.' I'm thinking of the man I killed, and the fine mail coat he wore. It seems Rudolf, for all he's a warrior now, has had the same thought. While his horse crops the grass, he's spidering his way amongst the dead, with the other lads.

Edmund stays beside me.

'More fucking horses.' I eye the additional animals apprehensively. There's so many now, it's ludicrous.

'Did Ingwald's horse die?' I think to ask. Edmund shakes his head.

'No. The damn thing stepped on a thistle. I thought it was dead as well. It screamed enough.'

'It seems I should have a war band of horses, not men.'

The grief that threatens to overwhelm me is uncomfortable, and my complaint is half-hearted.

'He died doing what he loves. They all did,' Edmund's voice is far from filled with the desire to reassure me.

I grunt. I can't deny the logic of the response.

'Right. Let's see if we can make it to Kingsholm without more fucking bloodshed.'

The bodies of the dead have been moved, the track way is clear again, the sounds of wildlife in the undergrowth resuming, the river running sluggishly behind us.

If it weren't for the trampled grass, the pile of bodies and the buzz of inquisitive flies come to feast on the cooling, sticky blood, I could almost imagine that nothing had happened here.

'Mount up,' I command, taking possession of Oslac's mount.

I'll lead the animal. It's my responsibility to do so.

Most of the horses have been recaptured. Each young lad is now responsible for four or five, not three. Above all the noise of horse and harness, I can hear Edmund and Hereman, their voices raised in argument, once more, as though nothing's happened.

I grin. It's a tight thing.

Another battle. The loss of another man I hope called me his friend, even if he fought as I instructed.

There'll be many more to come. Of that, I'm sure.

7

We reach Kingsholm without further trouble.
    But I can smell it in the air.
    There are men out there, trying to capture me yet.

Over a hundred and fifty of them, if the enemy we captured spoke the truth.

The cry of Wulfred reaches my ears, although it cuts off, as he truly catches sight of us from behind the defences that make Kingsholm secure.

The mood of the men is both melancholy and jaunty. After a battle such as that there are too many emotions to know what to do with them all.

Edmund has sung his songs of battle prowess, stringing together the list of our dead, in the same way that the Goddodin are immortalised by the scops. He, of course, ensures all is said in the correct order. Pedantic bastard.

'A man of the Hwicce,
He gulped mead at midnight feasts.
Slew Raiders, night and day.
Brave Athelstan, long will his valour endure.'
'Beornberht, son of the Magonsaete.

A proud man, a wise man, a strong man.
He fought and pierced with spears.
Above the blood, he slew with swords.'
'A man fought for Mercia
Against Raiders and foes.
Shield flashing red,
Brave Oslac, slew Raiders each seven-day.'

Hereman has finally stopped shouting at him to stop. And Rudolf has given me the hint of his former cheek.

But not all is well within our small group, despite the over a hundred and fifty horses we bring with us.

Wulfred's outraged comment echoes my own.

'What the fuck we supposed to do with all them?' Only then my Aunt is amongst my men and me, and Wulfred scuttles back to his post, head down, keen to avoid my Aunt's rancour.

She's spent much of her life listening to the battle talk of filthy warriors. She doesn't have to approve, though.

'What happened?' Her words cut through the air like lightning in a summer storm, recalling me to the here and now, dazzling my vision. I eye her, for once pleased to see the straight line of her thin lips, the harsh tilt of her chin, and the severe wimple that covers her long, grey hair. She looks like my father. The family resemblance has always been impossible to ignore.

'Aunt,' I incline my head, but her narrow hands swish through the air, dismissing my niceties. She wants news, not hellos.

'King Burgred has sold Mercia to the Raiders, in exchange for his life. Three hundred warriors hunt me. Or were. Half of them are now feeding Mercian soil. I hope the resultant growths are long-limbed.'

I expect to see no shock on her face, and she doesn't disappoint. Instead, her lips turn ever straighter as she appraises me.

'Are these the king's horses?'

'I imagine they were.'

'And they're yours now?'

'So, it would seem.'

'Excellent.' With no further words, she strides from my presence, her faithful hounds either side of her, weaving an unwavering path through the hidage of horseflesh. I know the conversation is far from over. I'll have to seek her out inside the priory.

I sigh, running my hand through my matted hair.

After all, I really could do with a hot bath.

'Stable them, where you can. They can graze, but only in the near meadows. I don't want them far from sight. The Raiders might think to steal them back.'

Wulfred's balding head bobs at my words. I can see his mouth trying to form a sentence, something that's not the filth he spouts typically, but I walk beyond him, into Kingsholm, the place of my birth.

It's a prosperous site. When my family were the kings of the Hwicce, this was one of their palaces. It's all that's left to my family now. But still, it's magnificent.

Just as Gloucester itself, it's built half in stone, quarried from the buildings of the Romans, and half in wood. The roof of the great hall sags a little sadly, and I recall that this was to be my task this summer until duty called me away.

My Aunt will be displeased to spend another winter with a dripping roof. I can already hear her sour complaints, little offered and holding more resonance because of that.

Wulfred guards the entrance to the enclosure, rimmed with a deep ditch that can fill with water from the River Severn when the tides are particularly high. A wooden walkway tops it, and from there, it's said, my ancestors protected their people from the Welsh.

I think the river in the way probably helped a great deal more than is ever said.

Piles of seasoned oak are waiting, inside the enclosure, to replace the broken and exposed areas of the walkway. Another job I should have performed this summer. And it's more critical than a saggy roof.

The space between the hall and I is blocked with horses. I can hear my warriors shouting for news from the returning men, and I also listen to exclamations of denial when they realise we're not complete.

I sigh once more.

My lost men had families. I seek out the women amongst the hopeful faces, unsurprised to find that Edmund has taken responsibility for the task.

All the same, I don't shy away from the women. One softly weeps, the other looks furious. I swallow down my sudden fear. Give me a wall of gleaming iron rather than a weeping woman.

'Ladies,' I bow before them both, Edmund's sharp intake of breath the warning I don't take.

And then hands are beating me, fiercely, bruising me as only hand-to-hand combat can. I allow it without trying to stop Athelstan's wife. She's always been fiery, and now, with her belly swollen against her dresses, I appreciate that she has every right to be angry with me.

Beornberht's wife watches on, blue eyes wide with shock and horror. Her grief is slower to arrive. I've seen it before.

Edmund moves to intervene, but I shake my head, meeting his eyes, pleading silently with him to understand. And he does. This isn't the first time that I've had to face angry women or bereaved children. It's my responsibility to do so.

And then a slight girl is stood before me, hair so blond it's almost blinding in the summer sun. Her lower lip trembles as she clutches a dirty cloth to her face. This then is Oslac's daughter.

I finally grip the beating hands of Athelstan's wife and lower them as gently as I can. I beckon the girl closer, the other widow as well, and throw my arms around them. I hold them all tight, pressing them to my chest, feeling them shake and twist with sorrow, trying to promise them my strength in place of their lost men.

'Your men died valiantly, fighting for Mercia and for their lord. You'll be honoured as their wives and children.'

I have horseflesh aplenty, and also a handful of women who live under the harsh, if fair, gaze of my Aunt. I'll never force any of them to leave, but they're welcome to go if they ever feel the time is right. They're also welcome to return if they ever have the need.

Eventually, as I hoped, the two women and the young girl, stand back, united in their sorrow and in hatred of me. I don't expect anything else. But I do demand that they support one another. They turn, stride away, and I watch, my jaw held tight. Edmund's hand on my shoulder is the strut that keeps me upright.

'And now for my Aunt.' The weariness in my voice surprises me. Edmund offers no empty words. It's not our way.

As I suspected, I find my Aunt amongst the gravestones of my ancestors, to the rear of the small priory, the monks from Gloucester maintain, at my expense.

Her hounds appear to be sleeping at her feet, but I know better. They're fiercely loyal and can be roused to snapping furies with just a word from her. One of the beast's growls at me, the sound more terrifying than iron being drawn from a scabbard.

'Down Wiglaf,' my Aunt snaps. I turn to meet the hound's eyes, and I fear that we both feel equally quelled by her tone. The hounds are named after the men who ruled Mercia after her father was deposed. Not that she had the naming of both of them. I consider that it might pain her, but then dismiss the idea. My Aunt is not the sort of woman to fear to speak a hound's name.

'King Burgred has always been a fucking coward.' Her coarse words shock me so much I feel my mouth drop open.

She turns to gaze at me, the hint of amusement in her eye, and I consider what she sees when she looks at me. No one has ever said that I resemble my father, but neither have I been told I take after my mother. My blond hair is a mystery to me, my build the result of my warrior skills.

'Did you think I grew deaf every time you and your warriors made Kingsholm your home?'

'I,' I stutter, but nothing else follows the words. She cows me as no one else ever has. Not even my father.

'King Burgred is a coward, and your father was a fool not to stake his claim to the kingdom.' My father could never have ruled. He was a weak man, tormented by the death of his father. I vowed to never be like him.

'You'll be king now.' It's not even a question, but a statement.

'How did Bishop Wærferth get to you so quickly? Did he sail

here?' I turn, as though to seek him out or spy the hint of sails to the west.

My aunt's sudden laughter takes me by surprise.

'So, he's already suggested it to you. Good. At least I don't have to force you to fulfil your duty.'

Again, my mouth opens, but no words sprout from it.

'The ealdormen will support you. All of them. The bishops as well.'

'I,' I try and speak, but she's walking to my side, her hand stretched out to touch my arm.

'Mercia suffers because our line has been broken. You'll heal it.'

'I.' I just can't find the words to say.

'I know you never wanted this. But I always knew. I think your father and brother did as well.'

'I can't be king,' I finally manage to force the words beyond my constricted throat.

'But you will be.' And she moves off, no doubt to find the bereaved women and the young girl. My aunt has never shied away from the responsibilities she feels to the people of Mercia.

One of the hounds follows her, but the other one, the one she chastised, Wiglaf, remains, head low and whining softly. I reach out. Cup the hound's muzzle, run my hand along his snout. His whining softens, dies away altogether.

Wiglaf was my brother's hound before he belonged to my aunt. That accounts for why she cares for it so well. He's old now.

Only when we're together, do we give in to our combined sorrow.

Together we walk to my brother's grave.

It's been over a decade since his death, fighting for Mercia. His hound is lined with grey and slow to move during the cold winter weather. Watching him struggle to his feet makes me realise how damn old I truly am.

I bend my head and rest my other hand on the gravestone that marks my brother's grave.

These warriors I ride with were his men.

Edmund was once my brother's closest ally, even closer than I was to him.

Coenwulf would have made a fine king of Mercia.

'Fuck it,' I complain, standing upright, shocking poor Wiglaf as he lies over my feet, and then struggles to stand.

'Fuck it, bugger it, arse it, shit it.'

There was never a choice.

There rarely is.

OSLAC IS BURIED CLOSE to the church. Not with my family. Instead, next to the other warriors who've fallen fighting for my brother and me, and for Mercia.

The ceremony is sombre, and difficult for the two widows who don't have bodies to bury. The young girl is quiet, supported by my Aunt. When the service is over, my Aunt leads the women away to mourn away from the fierce sorrow of the warriors.

Edmund joins me. I've taken the time to bathe and remove the muck of the dead from my body. Rudolf, despite his new status, has cleaned all of my equipment. Our parting is going to be difficult. On both of us.

'She told you to do it, didn't she?'

I used to think Edmund and my Aunt shared some sort of regard for each other. I'm not so sure anymore, and yet Edmund speaks of her with great respect, always. He admires her. I think she adores him. I've decided to ask nothing further from them. I really don't need to know that.

'She did.'

'And so, you will, because of your Aunt?'

'No, because she reminded me of my obligations.'

'Ah.' Understanding fills Edmund's voice.

'She used your brother against you.'

'No, she used my family against me.'

'And does she know that you're hunted?'

'She wouldn't care if I was. She believes in my talents more than I do.'

'So how will you do this?'

'I'll allow Bishop Wærferth to arrange everything. I have no time for tedious conversations. I came for my warriors. I have Raiders to track down and kill.'

Edmund grunts. He makes it impossible for me to decipher his true feelings on the matter.

Only then he says something never spoken about between us before.

'Your brother lacked your tenacity and genuine talent. He knew that. He didn't begrudge you for having it. He was proud of you. He would respect your decisions now.'

A hard lump forms in my throat.

Edmund and I are warriors.

We've fought in over thirty battles together, not counting the recent ones. Never once, in all that time, has he spoken to me of my lost brother, his greatest friend, and the man who should lead now, but doesn't.

It hurts to hear those words. I don't know if it's because I've been waiting to listen to them for so many years, or because my brother and I were never close while he lived.

'We ride out tomorrow, tell the men,' but even I hear the catch in my voice as I turn and stride away.

My Aunt has ensured there's ample food and ale that evening. I sit beside her at the front of the hall, trying not to glower, and failing. She remains silent at my side, although efficient. She has no qualms about ordering the servants as she sees fit, for all she leaves me well alone.

I want to thank her for all she does for my men and me, but I know she wouldn't appreciate the comment.

Just as I have duties and responsibilities, I have no control over, so does she. They're as much a part of us as breathing.

When she stands to retire for the night, I stand as well, bowing to her. She comes behind me, pressing my shoulders down and forcing me back onto the wooden seat that used to be my father's. I find it an uncomfortable fit. My brother filled the position better than I do.

Her touch is firm, and I obey without thought, almost as though I'm a child once more.

'You'll do what must be done, and when it's done, I'll welcome you back to Kingsholm.' She says nothing else, and I know I'll not see her when I ride out. She'll be on her knees, praying for me in the priory. I've never considered her piety to be worthwhile in the past, but, with so many warriors trying to kill me, I reconsider my original thoughts. Perhaps it's best if she prays for me, after all.

When morning comes, I've hardly rested, and yet I feel invigorated. I've made important decisions, and I know what I must do.

With my force added to by the men from Kingsholm, I once more have twenty men under my command. If my warriors in Worcester are well again, which I'm far from convinced about, my force will number twenty-four.

We retrace the path of our journey to Kingsholm, riding quickly beyond the mass grave that's been constructed while we've been gone to bury the dead, aware that others have ridden the path after us and cleared away the mess. I wish I knew if they were enemy or ally. But, I do know that Gloucester hasn't been threatened. That makes me hopeful that the three remaining bands of warriors might not have infiltrated into southwest Mercia just yet.

Perhaps the other war parties don't have mounts.

Perhaps the first three were just too damn cocky and thought I'd be easy to waylay.

The thought is not the comfort I hoped it would be.

Neither, it transpires was my thought about Gloucester remaining free from attack.

The sound of rushing hooves fleeing over the ground reaches my ears almost within sight of the joining of the Rivers Severn and Avon. The small settlement is a haze of grey smoke in the distance.

No sooner have I begun to turn Haden, keen to see what follows me, than I see Edmund, hand pointing into the distance.

'Fucking bollocks.' I don't really need the messenger, when he appears, sweaty faced and blowing harder than his horse, one of the new ones I notice. The lad is young, no doubt the son of one of my men. I don't think I know his name.

'My Lord.' He searches frantically for me, and I erupt from amongst my mass of warriors.

'Is Gloucester under attack?'

'Yes, My Lord. Your Lady Aunt sent me to bring you back.'

'Right,' I call, sighing heavily. 'We ride back the way we came. Gloucester can't pay the price for the Raiders frustration at not being able to find me.'

All of my warriors turn their horses, Edmund already riding on to bring back Icel and Goda to the body of the main force.

We can be no more than half a morning's hard ride from Gloucester, but it feels like too far as I turn my horse toward home.

The smoke rises thickly in the air, tainting the bright blue sky and I think this a new, but an old tactic, for the Raiders to use. So far, none of the three groups has advertised their presence to me. Perhaps they're not as desperate as I thought they were.

Or maybe, these lot have been sensible and made use of their fast ships rather than horseflesh to arrive in south-west Mercia. Did they risk the moody Severn estuary on a ship they could handle skilfully, rather than a difficult horse over hard-packed earth?

Within sight of Gloucester, I rein Haden in, my warriors following my actions. I turn to Edmund, my confusion reflected in the wrinkles on his forehead, his mouth hanging open.

'What the fuck?' His words speak for us all.

'Am I really seeing that?' I demand to know. 'Tell me I'm not really seeing that.'

'You're really seeing that,' Edmund replies, Icel beside him. His face mirrors Edmund's shocked one as well.

'Bollocking hell,' I shake my head, aghast.

Of all the things. Well, this was not what I was expecting to see. Not in Gloucester.

And not right now.

'Stupid bastards,' Icel's voice rumbles with his distaste, and I agree with him.

'Why would they do that?'

'Because they're fucking arseholes.' Edmund's voice is filled with part admiration and part outrage. I share his feelings.

'Just what we need. Stupid bastard Gwent Welsh Raiders on top of everything else.'

'What shall we do?'

'Kill them,' I state flatly. I've fought the Welsh men of Gwent almost as many times as I have the Raiders. Admittedly, I've never had to fight the Welsh and the Raiders in the same week, or even month.

The smoke that fills the air doesn't come from the settlement of Gloucester itself, still seemingly protected behind its three ancient Roman walls. But on the quayside, the settlement is threatened.

'Why would they burn the bloody bridge?'

It makes fuck all sense, but then, the Welsh of Gwent make fuck all sense to me most of the time.

'It seems they mean to cut off their own noses to spite themselves.'

Without the wooden bridge, that links Gloucester with the Mercian lands on the eastern side, the Welsh will have to use ships to cross the Severn if they wish to trade with the inhabitants.

'Right, stupidity or not, let's go and see if anyone needs killing on our side of the river.'

Kneeing Haden, I steer him quickly inside Gloucester. It seems our return has been expected, and the wooden gates are quickly flung open, the street just about deserted as we ride through it.

The town, like so many others in Mercia, is far from overpopulated other than by churches. In no time at all, my men and I are milling around close to the burning bridge.

The heat is surprisingly intense as yellow flames lick their way along the wooden struts.

I've nodded to those people I know as I lead my men on, the looks of relief on those faces, assuring me that Gloucester fears this new attack.

Edmund joins me, his hand already on his seax, death in his eyes, as we reach the quayside. He hates the Welsh. All of them. No matter their king or place of birth. If I allow him to, he'll kill all of the men marooned on this side of the bridge and not think twice about it.

I watch with mild interest as the twenty or so Welsh warriors realise they're not alone.

The tongue they speak is a gabble of too many syllables. But I've not lived all my life so close to the Welsh borderlands without learning some of the language.

A tight smile touches my cheeks.

It seems that facing me today was not their desire.

'Why?' I shout across the void, aware Icel has taken over the role of organising the men in light of Edmund's seething hissing going on beside me. The man is quite unmanageable where the Welsh are concerned.

One man steps forward. His long hair is tied back behind his neck, his beard and moustache trimmed close to his face. He wears excellent battle wear, but it's not going to help him if he needs to swim the Severn, for all it's much narrower here than downstream.

The man's Adam apple bobs, as he swallows heavily, his eyes widening with fear. I don't know what Icel's doing behind me, but I decide it's probably Edmund's wild features that cause so much concern.

'My Lord, My Lord Coelwulf.'

'Yes, and who are you?'

'I am Cadell ap Merfyn.'

'Well then, welcome to Gloucester, Cadell ap Merfyn.'

His grimace almost makes me smile.

'I.' He stops, and I wait, my hands still on the harness of my horse. The smell of the choking fumes of the treated, burning wood, is threatening to bring tears to my eyes. Any moment now, I think the flames will cover the twenty Welsh warriors, perhaps using it as a cover to slip back across the Severn.

Maybe, I consider, there's a ship waiting for them.

But, Cadell's nervousness speaks to me of an enormous fuck up.

'I. Well we. Well, it was our intention to trade in Gloucester. It seems that our enemies thought differently.'

Ah, now this I can understand.

'Did they, by any chance, wait for you to cross into Gloucester and then set the bridge aflame?'

Relief washes over Cadell's face, making him almost handsome if I avoid looking at his too sharp chin and elongated nose.

'How did you know? Did they tell you?' A touch of fury slips from Cadell's tongue.

'No, we didn't know. But you know, we have enemies too.'

From across the bridge, as the smoke blows clear for a heartbeat, I can actually make out a warband jeering at the enemy. Edmund growls, but I reach out and touch his hand, asking for a calmness that is never easily found where the Welsh are concerned.

'Is that all of you?' I demand to know, jerking my head to indicate the warriors surrounding their spokesperson.

'Yes, yes,' the head bobs too quickly.

'No fuckers are hiding along the quayside, in the boats or storehouses.'

The quayside could play host to five hundred enemy warriors, and I'd be none the wiser.

'No. We are all here.' But he turns, hesitant to show me his back, and picks out the faces of the men who serve him.

I shake my head, meeting Icel's amused eyes to the side of me.

'Edmund, do you want to fuck off somewhere else. I think I need to speak to this Cadell.'

'Speak, to the Welsh scum?' The outrage in his voice is evident.

'Yes, the Welsh scum. I have half an idea, and you won't fucking approve of it.'

Edmund's eyes are wild with fury, but I can see some understanding as his eyes flicker from Cadell and his men to my men.

'Well, yes, then. I think I'll just make myself scarce.'

'Find the portreeve. Make sure no one has been harmed. Take Hereman with you.'

Edmund opens his mouth to argue but snaps it shut. I've done him a favour, and it would be churlish to press the point.

With a jangle of harness, Edmund moves away from me, as Cadell abruptly turns his head, as though anticipating an attack while he's distracted.

I lift my hands clear from Haden's reins to show I mean no harm, while Edmund and Hereman peel away from the group.

Cadell watches Edmund keenly. I consider that they know each other. I consider that whatever is boiling Edmund's piss might not just be because the Welsh are in Gloucester. I dismiss the notion quickly.

Goda replaces Edmund. We're still mounted. I see no reason to dismount.

'It seems you might owe the people of Gloucester a new bridge?'

'We.' 'I.'

'Well, you either do, or you don't,' I press. Cadell's eyes boggle from his head.

'Perhaps an agreement could be reached,' Cadell eventually admits. He speaks my tongue as well as I do his. I approve.

'And what would that agreement consist of?'

'We could provide the labour force if Gloucester can provide the wood?'

It's a fair offer, after all, no one from Mercia would want Welsh wood on the bridge. Mercian oak is the best. And everyone knows that Welsh trees are a rarity. Not for them, the lush woodlands carefully managed and tended by the woods people.

'And you would feed the workforce, and ensure they slept on the other side of the river each night?'

'Of course,' Cadell is almost too keen to agree. I believe he thinks I'll let him live.

'And what will you do for me, if I allow this strange accord to happen?'

'For you, My Lord?' This has surprised Cadell, and I can hear, in his squeaked response, that he thinks he's already paid a high enough price for the deception foisted onto him.

'Yes, for me. I've been dragged back to Gloucester to fight the enemy, and all I face is a rabble of lost Gwent Welshmen. It hardly makes for battle glory.'

'No, no, of course not, My Lord.' I think Cadell takes offence, as do some of the other men, at being summed up as a rabble, and not the warriors they clearly are. Certainly, they're all well-armed, especially for the Gwent men.

'What can we offer, Lord Coelwulf?' Cadell makes it almost too easy.

'I need extra men to assist me, against the Raiders.'

Swift comprehension leaves a pensive look on Cadell's face.

'So, the rumours are correct?'

'What rumours?'

'That King Burgred has gifted Mercia to some of the Raiders?'

How Cadell knows this I don't know, and neither do I press.

'Perhaps,' I confirm non-committedly. 'But for you to leave here, alive, with all of your men, and no more ill-will once the bridge has been repaired, I want to know that you'll provide me with fifty warriors, and yourself, if I need to fight the Raiders.'

The Gwent Welshmen have no love for the Raiders. Their king recently won a great victory over a Viking horde. Cadell's flitting tongue slides over his lips as he considers. I'm surprised he doesn't turn, to ask the men who serve him their opinion. But he doesn't.

'It's agreed,' Cadell states, almost too eagerly. 'We'll provide the labour for the bridge to be rebuilt, and while that work continues, fifty warriors will be available to you. Once the repair work is done, our brief accord will be at an end.'

'And your fifty warriors will, of course, protect the settlement from the far side of the river bank. We wouldn't want your little enemies trying to start another fight or a fire.'

'Yes, yes, that as well. I'll oversee the arrangements. But, my warriors don't have horses. If you wish us to journey with you, deep into Mercian land, we must have horses, and an assurance that we'll not be attacked just for being Welsh.'

A fair deal, but I hold my tongue, considering before I agree.

'And you will, of course, pay compensation to those people whose livelihoods you've destroyed while the bridge is unusable. The price will be determined by the portreeve, who knows the businesses of his people well.'

'Agreed,' Cadell confirms.

I nod, slide from my horse, and hand the reins to Icel.

I stride toward Cadell seemingly unarmed, although my seax is fastened to the rear of my weapons belt should I require it.

Cadell walks toward me as well. Just two men with many watching on. Either of us could give the command, some flick of the wrist, and blades could fly.

A billow of smoke covers me, and I hear the tension in my watching warriors, as all of them must reach and grip a weapon.

But Cadell reaches out his hand, as I extend mine. Then we're clasping arms, one warrior to another, one lord to another, for I know who Cadell is, even if he's made no mention of it.

'Lord Cadell, tell your brother,' I offer, 'of what's happened here. Tell him to stay away from the Mercian borderlands, for now, or I'll send every Raider horde toward his precious kingdom.'

Cadell startles under my firm grip, dismayed to realise I've seen through his ruse, but he can't respond because the smoke abruptly clears, and all can see two men, arm in arm, agreeing to something that might well be temporary, but is no less extraordinary because of that.

'Lord Coelwulf.' Cadell inclines his head to me.

'Lord Cadell,' I confirm, following his example.

'Now,' and I drop his hand. 'Do you want a ship to take you across the Severn, or will you be swimming?'

Lord Cadell swallows heavily, perhaps unsure of the correct response.

'A ship,' he squeaks. 'If possible.'

'A ship,' I confirm, already turning to find someone of authority in Gloucester to organise it.

'A week,' I say. 'You have a week to be back with your labourers and warriors. If I'm not in Gloucester at the time, my warriors will be, and they'll know where to find me.'

'Of course,' Lord Cadell is keen to be gone, I can tell from the way he bounces on the balls of his feet.

'Until we meet again, then.' And I turn my back on him entirely, keen to be back in the saddle and back on the way to Worcester.

'Fucking mad bastards,' Icel rumbles, and I nod, not yet giving into my amusement.

Only when we're once more riding free from Gloucester, through the gates, closed tightly behind us, do I give into my glee.

'Did you see his fucking face?' I aim my comment at Icel. Edmund is riding with us once more, but he's sulking far behind me. He might not forgive me for my deal with the Gwent Welshman, but he does understand the necessity of it.

'Daft fuckers. If they didn't spend so much time fighting each other, they'd accomplish much more.'

'Then let's hope they never stop fighting amongst themselves. It's easier to handle them like this. But still, did you see their faces?'

My laughter takes me beyond the sight of the attack from the third group of warriors, and on so that we're once more at the spot where the two rivers converge, the Severn and the Avon. Worcester is waiting in the distance, and so too, I hope, are my warriors.

They better still live.

If they don't, I'll kill them myself.

8

The closer we get to Worcester, the more concerned I become.

The trackway is a riddle of horses' hooves. Only the lack of smoke rising in the air assures me that Worcester hasn't fallen to a Raider attack. Yet.

'Is there to be no damn peace today?' Edmund has recovered from his anger, and rides beside me, his eyes peering into the distance. I rely on that long-sight to tell me all that he can see.

We'll not speak of affairs in Gloucester. It would be impossible to do so without wounding each other. Our acceptance of what the other thinks will be enough to keep our friendship strong.

'I can't tell. It certainly doesn't look besieged,' Edmund complains, resting back on his saddle. His horse is docile that day. I consider the randy sod might have serviced some of the mares back at Kingsholm. I can't help thinking it would do Edmund some good as well.

'Let's hope Worcester remains intact.' I don't hold out much hope, and I'm surprised when we're quickly admitted inside Worcester and through the earthwork defences. I cast a glance at them. Would they survive an attack by the Raiders? Would they survive an attack by the bloody Welsh? Damn bastards, and bloody fools.

Unlike my previous arrival, Bishop Wærferth doesn't come to greet me personally, although Wulfhere does.

'The men are well, all of them. It's what the bloody bishop's up to that will boil you.' Wulfhere sounds so much like Rudolf, I turn, just to be sure that Rudolf is still mounted. I've forced him to exchange his small pony for one of the new horses. They've not yet made allies of each other.

'Why?' I demand to know, sliding from Haden's back and pausing to rub his nose and ears before leaving him to the care of one of the other young lads.

'He's been a busy little sod,' Wulfhere complains, and while I want to slap him for the disrespect, I refrain. Wulfhere isn't yet Rudolf. Not quite.

'He's been sending his minions to all the ealdormen of Mercia. Well, all those they can reach without encountering the Raiders anyway.'

'Already?' I gasp, trying to recall how many days I've been gone. Not enough, that's for sure.

'What have the responses been?' I ask. I don't actually know if I want to hear or not. I'm content knowing that the ealdormen all hate me. It's never concerned me in the past.

'Not good,' Wulfhere mutters, but before he can say more, Bishop Wærferth makes an appearance. He eyes me with a quizzical look.

'More Raiders?'

'There's always more of the pestilent fuckers,' I reply, Edmund's snort of laughter at my tone, turned into a hasty cough. I'm pleased his good humour has been restored to him. Bishop Wærferth doesn't seem quite as happy to see me as last time he was.

'Your men are healing well. Pybba has been causing trouble. That man will not do as he's told,' a flicker of frustration crosses Bishop Wærferth's face.

I nod. In all honesty, none of them ever do. As soon as Sæbald and Gyrth are up from their sick beds, the same will apply to them.

'I'll take him with me as soon as he's well enough to leave.'

'That would be for the best,' Bishop Wærferth admits. His rapidly moving eyes tell me there's something he wishes to speak with me about, and not in front of the audience I currently have.

'Come, Bishop Wærferth, I would speak with you, alone.'

With that, he gladly follows me to the same spot at the rear of his monastery, where we spoke a few days ago. The stench of the river is still ripe, and the fleet of four ships wallowing upstream, by the quayside draws my eyes. I have the hint of an idea rooting in my mind, but I don't need to discuss it. Not yet.

Bishop Wærferth sighs deeply, as though wishing he didn't have to speak.

'Went well, did it?' I prompt him. Consternation fills his intelligent grey eyes.

'Stubborn fucking bastards,' his explosion of bile startles me so much that I take an involuntary step back before I start to laugh. I warned the daft sod. One day, people will listen to me when I explain how much others revile me.

'Well, in that case, I shall brag that I've secured a temporary alliance with Cadell ap Merfyn. He'll provide me with fifty warriors, as well as a new damn bridge for Gloucester.' Confusion wars with respect on the bishop's stunned face.

'An alliance, with the Gwent Welshmen? Who's Cadell ap Merfyn?'

'Well that's the joy, he's only bloody Rhodri Mawr's little mentioned brother. Daft sod got hemmed into Gloucester. Seems he doesn't quite have the political clout of his brother.'

'So, you have an alliance with him?'

'For the summer, at least. After that, it'll be fair game again. So tell me, what did the ealdormen have to say about your suggestion?'

'Well, Ealdorman Ælhun doesn't believe that King Burgred has gone to Rome. He sends word that he's going to investigate for himself.'

'Good, once he's dead, his heir will be untried and untested and will have no choice but to do as he's told.'

'Lord Coelwulf!' Bishop Wærferth's explosion of shock alerts me to the fact the bishop has decided to re-exert his usual demeanour.

'Well, it's true. Without the older generation and their refusal to move on, it'll be much easier to react to the Raiders attacks. Tell me I'm wrong?' The sudden silence is all the answer I get.

'If Ealdorman Ælhun has any sense, he'll have sent scouts on in front of him, and he'll avoid the danger,' I say the words as a consolation. Ideally, I hope no such thing happens.

'Ealdorman Æthelwold was the only one to agree.'

I arch my eyebrows at Bishop Wærferth. He's just proved to me that I'm right with that statement.

'Then Ealdorman Beorhtnoth and Alhferht are not receptive to the idea either?'

'No, they're not. But the bishops are.'

'Well, bishops don't make a king.' I pause then, risk a glance at Bishop Wærferth. He doesn't say it, but I know what he's thinking. The bishops do make a king. Well, they perform the service that makes men kings anyway. I smirk at myself. Damn fool.

'So none of them have seen Raiders on the roads?'

'Not that they'll admit to. Although Bishop Eadberht has since sent a further messenger to tell me that the royal palace at Tamworth does lie deserted.'

'And what of Repton then?'

'I believe the scout was too terrified to venture that far.'

'I'd be surprised if he couldn't sodding see Repton from bloody Tamworth.'

Bishop Wærferth wisely holds his tongue at my exasperation.

'What of Bishop Deorlaf then? Is there no sign of attack in Hereford either?'

'Apparently not.'

'So they really are just coming after me then? Fuck.'

'Yes, they want you, Lord Coelwulf, and I know why. They know that you're the only one who could defeat them. The other ealdormen will realise in time.'

'Probably when I'm bloody dead,' I grumble.

The Mercians, just like the Welsh, are too damn keen to argue amongst themselves.

King Burgred has managed to keep his ealdormen aligned until now. The treaty with Wessex helped, but Alfred is king there now, not his brother, and I don't really think he's the man for the job. I hear he doesn't even fight his own battles.'

'Now, now,' Bishop Wærferth works to appease me, but I don't really need it.

'So, with your aid, and that of the other bishops, I have far more warriors than I did when I rode in here a few days ago.'

'Ah.'

'What?' I demand to know, beyond frustrated.

'That's not quite what they said.'

'Great, so they'll support me when I'm bloody dead as well. Fucking Mercian cock-suckers.'

Bishop Wærferth's face flushes with horror at my words, but I'm beyond pretending that his fucked up plan isn't entirely fucked up.

'What will you do?' the bishop finally asks me.

I'm pacing, measuring the space between the monastery and the cliffside. I have an idea forming. I don't believe it's a good one. But it might do. I just need time to think about it.

'I came for my warriors. I'll take them. If they're well enough to ride.'

'But what then?' worry laces his words, and in them, I hear the voices of every terrified man and woman, child and beast within Mercia.

'I'll think of something,' I offer with a shrug of my broad shoulders.

The bishop laughs.

'How bloody reassuring.' He stalks from my presence. And I can't help it, the words tumble from my mouth before I can stop them.

'At least I've killed a hundred and fifty of the damn bastards. What's anyone else done?'

My voice echoes too loudly, but I don't much care.

I stride toward the quayside upriver, curiosity getting the better of me.

Of course, I've been on a ship before, but not for any significant length of time. I remember it being an uncomfortable experience. I didn't like the motion even on the river, and the ship's captain laughed at me.

'You should feel her when she really starts to roll, far out to sea and far from here.'

I declined that offer. But, the Raiders use ships. All the damn time. In fact, riding a horse seems to be a weakness. And my weakness is being on a boat.

'Hum,' I make the noise out loud, only then aware that Edmund and Icel have joined me.

The two seem to be having some sort of internal battle as to who should always stand by my side. I leave them to it. I'm not settling an unnecessary argument.

'Sæbald is healing well. Gyrth more slowly, but he did seem to hear me when I called his name. Eahric and Oda are keen to re-join us.'

'Good. And Pybba? Is he really as much of a problem as the bishop implies?'

The silence that greets my question has me turning, first to gaze at Edmund and then at Icel. It appears I've found something that unites them.

'Well spit it out.'

'Pybba is not doing well.'

'Well, I didn't expect him to.'

'No, but it's worse than that.'

'Just bloody tell me before I go and find out for myself?'

'Wulfhere's done his best,' Edmund's excuse has me round on him in frustration.

'I blame no one, not even Pybba. Just tell me?'

'He's had Wulfhere attach a blade to the end of the bandages on his stump. Anyone who tries to speak to him gets threatened with blades in both ... well, hands, I suppose is the right word to use.'

Edmund offers the explanation, his eyes flashing at Icel for forcing him to speak.

'So Pybba's feeling vulnerable, and probably scared.'

'If that's what we're calling it, then yes, vulnerable and scared. I'd call it murderous and unmanageable.' Icel's rumble of words has me squaring my shoulders.

'Fine, I'll deal with the stupid sod.'

'I'd take your shield,' Edmund unhelpfully calls from behind me, and I don't even favour him with the foul words tumbling through my mind.

No wonder Bishop Wærferth's so pleased to see the back of Pybba.

'He's not in the hospital,' Icel offers more helpfully. 'You'll find him in the stables.'

I smartly change direction, shaking my head as I do. Why I consider, is he with the horses? He should be keeping his wound clean, not mingling with the horse manure.

It's Wulfhere I encounter first as I enter the stables. The creak of the door opening, brings him rushing from one of the stalls, worry etching his young face. Seeing me doesn't ease his concern. I sigh heavily. I'd expected something from Pybba. That it's only just happened doesn't surprise me. A man can convince himself losing a hand won't be a problem. The reality, when it hits, can be starkly different.

I resist the urge to ruffle Wulfhere's unruly hair as I pass him.

'Leave us. It'll be fine.' The look in his eyes is far from reassuring.

'Pybba, you daft fucker, I'm coming in.' I pitch my voice loud enough for him to hear, but not loud enough to terrify the horses stabled there. I don't need to be in the middle of a stampede.

I hear no response, and so round the stall, Wulfhere emerged from.

There's no horse inside, but there is a wide-eyed man, his clothes awry, his face sheeted in white.

'For fuck's sake. What are you doing in here?' I keep my eyes on Pybba's face, although I've already noted the two blades. The one on his stump looks as though he'll do more damage to himself than anyone else.

Pybba licks his lips, his tongue is small and reedy. He looks dry. Clearly, he's dehydrated as well as sodden with grief for his lost hand.

'Those monks kept lying to me.'

'So you what, threatened them? That's always my preferred option for obtaining the truth.'

'No, I protected myself.' Pybba's eyes search behind me. It seems he doesn't catch the sarcasm. 'Who did you bring with you?'

'No one. Why did I need to bring someone with me? You planning on attacking me?'

'No,' Pybba vehemently denies. And then in a smaller voice. 'No, I won't hurt you.'

I nod my head, stepping to slide down the wall beside Pybba. The place smells of horse and oats.

'What you doing with that?' I ask, pointing at his stump and the blade that shimmers there. 'Trying to lose an eye as well as a hand.'

Pybba has the good grace to look bashful.

'I was vulnerable. Those damn monks lied and couldn't have protected me from the damn Raider voices I heard.'

This makes me sit up straighter.

'What here? In Worcester?'

'Yes, or no, I don't know, I heard them all the same, looking for you.'

I look at my hands, noting that my scrapped knuckles are nearly healed.

'Do you think you might have been dreaming?' I ask, trying not to condescend to him.

'It felt real enough to me,' Pybba argues angrily.

'Aye, I know it can feel like that when the battle fever grips you.'

'I don't think it was the battle fever. I think Bishop Wærferth is helping the Raiders.'

'Bishop Wærferth? He's more bloody Mercian than I am.'

But Pybba refuses to be convinced.

'There was definitely something. I heard it, and I came here, with Wulfhere. He's a good lad.'

'Yes, I know he is.'

I'm pulling a long piece of straw between my hands, trying to straighten it, only it's bent and won't do my bidding. I consider Pybba's words seriously. I owe Bishop Wærferth nothing. And likewise, he owes me nothing. I've always been the unmanageable ealdorman of the Hwicce. A necessary evil, or so I believe.

I fight the battles no one else will, and I keep my lands secure. Or at least I did.

'Well, we're leaving tomorrow, so, take that damn blade off, or have Wulfhere do it, and for fuck's sake, have a bath! You stink. Now, show me your stump.'

Reluctantly, Pybba lifts his arm so that I can see the stump is bound tight, and clean. He winces as he does so.

'I've heard warriors say they can still feel missing limbs, even though their eyes tell them they're gone.'

His stricken face flashes at the words.

'It's only natural, or so they say,' I further comment. I'm not going to feel sorry for him. That would do Pybba no good. He needs to accept who he is, not what he was.

I go to stand as I speak, reaching out to grasp Pybba's complete arm. First, though, he has to attach his seax to his warriors' belt.

'That's going to need adjusting. You can't take that long, not in the shield wall.'

'I can't be in a damn shield wall,' Pybba complains, 'unless someone holds my shield for me or my weapon. I can't do fucking both.'

'I thought Pybba attached the shield to your arm back on the road.'

'Yes, he did,' Pybba complains. 'But it was painful and hurt like fuck.'

'Then what of Rudolf? He's taken a kill, and he's ridden his horses into the Raiders we met on the way to Gloucester. Do you want him?'

'Rudolf can fight with me. He's learning, he can't both fight and defend. Not yet.' Pybba's words are what I expected to hear, as he finally takes my hand and allows me to pull him upright.

He wobbles on his ungainly legs.

'You need to drink water, not ale, and you need to eat. I need your strength.'

'But what of the conversation I heard?'

'I'm not going to dismiss it, but tomorrow we leave. I don't see any danger, for now.'

'Then you think I rave like the men in the infirmary?'

'Did I say that?' I meet Pybba's eyes, noting the yellow tinge to the white of his eyes.

'Come on. We need food and water and then some bloody rest. You need to think about your balance more than you used to,' I offer, reaching for him as he walks from the stall. Wulfhere and Rudolf are waiting just the other side, clearly having heard all that we've said. Wulfhere moves with swift hands to undo the blade on Pybba's stump. His ingenuity surprises me, and yet it shouldn't.

A mind like that is always going to be seeking fresh challenges.

Once the handle-less blade is free, I grip it firmly.

'This stays with me. For now.' I force both Pybba and Wulfhere to meet my eyes, holding them until I see acceptance.

'Right, lead on Wulfhere. I could eat an entire boar all to myself.'

Emerging into the bright daylight, I'm aware of wary eyes watching the little procession.

'There's nothing to see here,' I snarl, and when no one moves away, I reach for my seax, hold it above my head and gnash my teeth, taking a few sliding steps toward the closest person. The squeals of horror bring a wide grin to my face, as does watching the crowd disperse.

'Do they have nothing better to do all day than gawk at the stables? A sad life for them. I'll speak to the bishop about it.'

Once inside the bishop's hall, closer to the quayside, I consider Pybba's words as food and water are served to me. Pybba drinks as though the well's run dry whereas I savour the fresh water, hoping it hasn't come from the turgid river.

Rudolf eats and eats and eats. In the end, I have to cover his hand with mine, shaking my head.

'Enough, or that weapons belt won't fit you when we head to Repton.'

The words remind me of Pybba's difficulties.

'Visit the tanner. See if they have any ideas for Pybba, and work out how he can affix his shield to his arm better. He needs to be able to slide it on and off, but keep it tight while he battles.'

Rudolf nods quickly, as though he's already considered the problem. The sod probably has.

When they stand to leave, Pybba bends close to me.

'You're a clever bastard, you know that, don't you.' I grip his good arm, meet his eyes.

'I serve good men, and they, in turn, serve me. We're not alone when we're together.'

He doesn't grin, but neither does Pybba look as haunted as he did when I first entered the stables.

As soon as he leaves me, Edmund and Icel thump themselves down on the seats next to me.

'What did you do?'

'I spoke to him, and more importantly, I listened.'

'To what, his mad mumblings?'

'To what he was trying to say around those mad mumblings, as you so eloquently put it.'

'Hum,' Edmund falls silent, considering what I've said.

'But he said that he'd heard the voices of Raiders.'

'He did, yes.'

'So did he?'

'Well, all we can say is that he believes he did, and we'll take that and be warier than before. Bishop Wærferth seems to be our ally, but maybe he isn't, or maybe some of his followers aren't. These people have the right to be fearful, and fear makes people act like arses.'

Silence greets my words. I turn to Icel, he nods, accepting my summation. Edmund looks as though he wishes to argue with me but then thinks better of it.

'So Pybba is coming with us?'

'Yes, but not Sæbald and Gyrth. They'll have to stay here.'

'Sæbald won't like that.'

'Well, Sæbald doesn't make the decisions. Anyway, I can't help thinking that we need someone here while we're gone. Anything could happen. Sæbald will protect Gyrth for me. I need that.'

'So we're still going to Repton?' Edmund continues his grilling.

'Yes, Repton. We need to find out the truth of what's been happening there.'

Edmund's face furrows with frustration before he speaks again.

'Coelwulf, they've sent three hundred warriors to track you down. How many do you think are in Repton?'

'More,' is my unhelpful response.

He rolls his eyes, opens his mouth to speak, but then snaps it shut and lifts his tankard to his lips. I know what he's thinking. I'm thinking about it too.'

'So we're going by boat then?' I turn, mouth open to glare at Icel. He shrugs at me, the movement rippling down his tall body.

'If you don't want me to guess your plans, then don't spend your time staring at them!'

I glare all the more, frustrated to know that my strategy has been so easily discerned. Not even the look of shock on Edmund's face showing that he's been taken by complete surprise makes up for Icel's correct guess.

'Yes. The Raiders have taken to riding our horses. I suggest we take to their ships.'

Edmund's forehead has once more furrowed.

'Can we even take boats to Repton? And are we taking the horses with us? And why?'

'As I said, we need to gain the upper hand. I can kill as many of the damn bastards as they throw at me, but I'd like to know exactly what's happening in Repton. The way to do that is not to be where they expect us to be.'

Edmund watches me with growing respect on his face.

'But are there rivers that'll take us to Repton?'

'I don't fucking know. We'll have to ask the boatman when we tell him he and his fellow ship's captains have new plans for the next few days.'

Icel remains silent beside me, and for a moment I do fear he'll disagree with me.

'If we can't get all the way to Repton on the River Severn, we can get closer to it than we are here. I like it.' He announces, leaning back and crossing his arms over his massive chest, trapping his long beard in the process.

Edmund startles, and then slowly begins to chuckle.

'You do know, Icel, that Lord Coelwulf wouldn't give a fart even if you didn't approve.'

Icel turns slowly to gaze at Edmund, a wide grin forming on his face.

'I know that. But still, a good leader benefits from knowing his men support and agree with him.'

Edmund huffs, and I push myself upright on my hands.

'I'll leave you two to sort out whatever's going between you. I need to sleep.'

I don't even look back as I stride outside into the darkening night.

9

I quickly regret my decision, and not just because looking at the boats and stepping onto the boats is such a different experience.

It transpires as I hoped that the four boats docked at Worcester all belong to the one captain. He watches me approach, in the early morning daylight, a flicker of respect and surprise on his wind-roughened face.

I waste no time with niceties.

'My men and I, horses as well, need to get as close to Repton as possible, by boat.'

Ships master Æthelred, as I've learned his name is, honks a bark of laughter at my question, while I stand, watching him, arms folded, not enjoying his amusement at the suggestion.

Eventually, he stills, looking from me to where Edmund and Icel still dog my steps.

'You're not joking?' Æthelred sobers eventually, and I shake my head.

'Not even a little bit.'

'But. But.'

'But what?'

'Well, I don't know. I've never been asked to do something like that before. The rivers are for trade, the trackways and royal roads are for riders.'

'That's as maybe, but I'm trying something a bit different.'

'A bit different! Well, fuck me. I just don't know.'

Æthelred turns to gaze at his boats, and as he does, I take in the sight of him. He's probably a little older than I. His face is weathered by the sun and wind, and his hands look strong and able. The lack of hair on top of his head, while his brown beard and moustache are neatly trimmed makes it difficult to guess at his exact age. His eyes are bright, and shimmering green, reminiscent of a deep pool of water. He's clearly a wealthy man to command so many crew and ships. Yet the boats he has are currently empty and riding high in the river because of it.

'Well, were you going somewhere else today?'

'No, not yet. I'm waiting for a shipment of quarried stone, that's why the boats are so light, but it's been delayed. I assume.'

'Then I can pay you for your service for a few days then?' I'm starting to feel frustrated that it's all taking so long to resolve.

'Well. Well,' Æthelred leans his head to one side, and then rubs his hand through his beard, as though seeking the answer there.

'Will it be dangerous? I've heard you're being hunted.'

'I don't see how,' I offer, 'not with all of my warriors on board.'

'So you are being hunted?'

'It would seem so. But the Raiders search for me on the roadways, and so I require a different mode of transport.'

Swift comprehension touches Æthelred's face, and then he nods his head, clearly reaching a conclusion.

'We'll take you, your men and your horses, but no further than the end of the River Stour. From there you can ride, or find others to transport you. But you'll protect my sons and I. No amount of coin would compensate me if one of my sons lost their lives.

'Agreed,' and I hold my hand toward him to seal the bargain. But he hesitates, and I realise I've offered no price.

'I'll reward you well,' I confirm, thinking of the coins that Rudolf found, and also all the new horses at Kingsholm. I wonder what the man would prefer?

'I know you will Lord Coelwulf,' Æthelred takes my hand, without agreeing to a price, but there's a firm look in his eyes. 'And if the rumours are true,' and he gazes upriver, as though expecting a Raider ship to appear before him, 'then I might well win acclaim for helping Mercia's saviour.'

Hearing those words gives me no satisfaction, but I seal the bargain firmly by gripping his forearm, keen to be on my way.

I have no idea how to load my men and horses, but Æthelred and his three strong sons don't hesitate to take charge, ordering men and beasts about with the sort of tone that brokers no argument.

I watch as Rudolf settles Pybba in the boat that Æthelred commands. It's a good choice, as is the weapons belt that Pybba now wears. I can see where it's been adjusted. It hangs heavy to the left side of Pybba's body so that he can reach for his weapons without having to stretch. Yet there's still a pocket to the right, and I imagine it houses his knife, the final choice open to a warrior when all other weapons have failed him.

Of all the horses, it's Haden that makes the most fuss about boarding. He rears backwards, threatening to topple me. In the end, he'll only step a hoof onto the boat if I lead him myself.

'Damn bastard,' I cajole, but it's as though he understands the intent behind the softly voiced complaint. His nip on my ear is probably deserved, for all I slap his inquisitive nose away.

When the boats move away, the people of Worcester stand and watch us, Bishop Wærferth leading them. His expression is difficult to unravel, and I turn aside quickly, keen to be out of sight so that I can slump to a sitting position. The gentle wallow of the boat makes me want to vomit, the stench unbearable. I curse myself for making an unwise decision.

I've forced my men to discard their full battle gear. I don't know how many of them can swim, or even how deep the river flows further upstream. Still, I don't want to risk losing one of them in an accident that could be so easily prevented.

Instead, our shields are to hand, our spears as well.

If the enemy finds us, then we'll protect ourselves while remaining afloat.

Æthelred leads the collection of boats. They're more flat bottomed than I expected.

'For the rivers,' he explains to me when he notices my interest from his place at the tiller. 'You need flat bottoms to prevent getting snared on the river bed. We don't use these out to sea. The waves would upend them in a heartbeat.'

I'm no expert on ships so I accept the information with a simple nod.

'And no sails either?'

We rely on the current or the oars. You might need to row yet!' The comment brings a whistle of laughter from between Æthelred's tight lips, and I scowl into the distance.

I've forced my force to split itself between the four ships. Pybba and Rudolf are with me. So are another four of my warriors, but only two horses, Haden being too big to fit many more in with all of Æthelred's four ship men. Edmund leads in the ship behind me. He has ten horses and only three warriors. Icel has an equal number of men and horses, those he leads being somewhat smaller than Haden. At the rear, Goda has everyone else.

It makes me feel vulnerable, and yet I chose this way to travel to outfox my enemy. I can only hope it's not been a waste of effort.

The day passes slowly. I'm overly alert to every sound, and my head bobs upwards every time a fish jumps clear from the murky water. I watch Æthelred shaking his head at my antics and curb my rising temper.

This must be what it feels like for the men and women of Mercia when the Raiders appear, exposed and yet unable to do anything about it.

Pybba's head nods in sleep, as does Hereman's. It takes a great effort to refrain from banging my seax against my shield to rouse them.

When the boats reach the confluence with the Stour, Æthelred's face focuses in concentration. Even I can tell that forcing the ship along the other watercourse is far from easy. A flurry of activity erupts on the boats, the shipmen rushing to fit oars, and then waiting for Æthelred's instructions.

The River Severn is broad, and sluggish, the muddy water brown until the Stour mingles with it. The smaller river seems to run much quicker, and I feel questions forming in my mind but refrain from asking them. Instead, I walk to Rudolf's side, determined to keep him from slipping over the side of the ship in his enthusiasm.

Pybba stirs in his sleep but doesn't wake. Haden whinnies for my attention, and I meet his startled eyes, considering that I look just as bemused as he does.

Only then do I realise that we're not alone, and instinctively, my hand reaches for my seax. But the people, who watch me, as I spy them on the bank of the Stour, are not Raiders, but young children, an adult with them.

They point and shriek with excitement, and even I feel caught up in their enthusiasm for the unusual sight of seeing a boat laden with horses and warriors.

I almost find myself waving, along with Rudolf, but a cry from behind me catches my attention.

Still wallowing in the River Severn behind us, Goda is pointing to the far side of the riverbank. I turn to realise that the children are not the only people who watch Æthelred's efforts.

Now I do grip my seax, aware that Goda has called his men to quick order, and that they all hold a shield before them, thinking to protect Æthelred's son as he works the tiller.

I've taken Eadric to be the oldest of Æthelred's sons. No vestige of youth remains on his face, and his frame has filled out, as only happens when a boy has truly become a man. His seriousness adds to my assumption. Here is a man considering how he'll make his livelihood when his father is dead.

Icel has followed Goda's actions, although Edmund hasn't, not yet, for his ship follows closely behind my own. I think we're out of spear reach if the men prove to be armed.

A tense silence fills the air, and I feel helpless again. It would take a great deal of skill to return my ship to beside Goda and Icel's. Those ships are almost within grasp, and yet I can't get to them, not now the current has taken hold of my boat, propelling it away from the rest of my warriors

'Fuck,' I grumble. Rudolf is tense as well. He's realised the danger and how helpless we are if there is an attack on the other boats.

Eadric, however, remains calm, and I watch as first Edmund, and then Icel and finally, Goda's ship make the turn without an attack. The men who watch us from the opposite bank of the River Severn have grown in number, but they don't menace.

'Ealdorman Beorhtnoth's men,' Edmund calls to me when he's once more close enough to do so.

'Ah,' is all I offer, but it makes me think. If they were so unsure of us, then why didn't they call out? Why didn't they menace Goda and Icel and their ships until they knew whether we were friend or enemy? Did they realise we were Mercian? I can't see how they could have done.

So that means they were pleased to just watch us pass by, content we weren't about to menace the lands they protect. It's not what I would expect from any of Mercia's ealdormen. It only adds to my unease following Bishop Wærferth's attempts to unite the ealdormen and bishops of western Mercia behind me.

It's going to be impossible.

'Coelwulf!' Rudolf's cry is urgent, his hand on my arm rousing me from my thoughts.

'Fuck.' Whatever my thoughts on Ealdorman Beorhtnoth's warriors, it seems the rest of our audience is now threatened.

From nowhere, I see a mounted warrior tearing through the collection of children, forcing them to scatter or be crushed beneath the powerful warhorse.

'Raiders.' I don't need Rudolf's observation to know it for the truth.

'Take me there,' I urge Æthelred, pointing toward the right side of the riverbank that has become pregnant with menace and threat.

The warrior doesn't ride alone, another has joined him, and even from a distance, I can hear the screams of the children and the sick sound of iron on flesh.

'You'll be too late.' Resignation labours Æthelred's response but I'm shaking my head.

'No, there, put me there, and I'll be able to help them.'

'There'll all be dead by then,' Æthelred complains, but he's already leaning hard on the tiller, trying to force the boat to where I want to go.

Behind me, I can hear Edmund having the same argument with the master of his ship. And still, the screams of the children reach my ears.

My seax is loose in my hand, just waiting for dry land so I can surge up the sharp riverbank and assist the children, only then it seems, I won't need to. Instead, I hear a thud and turn behind me, stunned.

A child, a boy I think, has raced to the steepest part of the riverbank and flung his body high into the air. I don't know how, but somehow he's managed to land in Edmund's boat. I turn, searching the bank for more children who might have had the same thought.

Icel is standing at the prow of his boat, head stretched as high as he can, although his shield hovers close by.

'Here, come here,' Icel cries, over and over again, but no other fleeing shape appears over the edge, and I feel my impatience growing.

When we're still too far from the riverbank, I thrust myself across the gap, dipping my back foot into the river as I stumble for balance.

'Here,' closer now, Rudolf throws me my shield. I surge up the steepness of the bank, ducking low, uncaring of the fact that there are at least two enemies above me, and I'm entirely alone.

Seax high, shield in hand, I take the last few steps, and then I'm looking to where the children were, to where the mounted warriors should be. My breath comes heavily, the climb up the bank far steeper than I would have liked.

But I see no trace of the mounted warriors. Alert to the danger of being alone, I stride forward, trying to seek the spot where the children were stood. The river grasses are lush, reaching almost to my knee, making it difficult to see anything, even with the advantage of my height.

A heavy thud behind me, and I turn, seax raised, only to face Edmund.

'Fuck,' he mutters as I almost slice his exposed chin.

'Where are they?' I complain.

'Ridden off, I imagine, the game of slaughtering children done with.'

I swallow uneasily. I was here. I should have saved those children.

'Well, we're here now. Let's check.'

We walk forward at a steady pace, ears cocked to where anyone might be hiding. Only now that we've reached the level ground once more, it stretches off into the distance, not even an old oak tree to provide a hiding place for two mounted warriors.

'Bastards,' the word erupts from my mouth as I almost step on the first body. A child, no more than five if I'm any judge, and I'm not, lies with his eyes forever staring, a skull caved in by what can only have been the hoof of one of the horses.

'Fuckers,' Edmund spits, bending to close the blue eyes forever, his touch surprisingly gentle. From the front, the child looks perfect, but the ruin to the back of her head speaks of instant death.

Another few steps and another sprawled body appears, a slicing wound oozing in the gentle sun, already attracting the attention of inquisitive flies.

Neither Edmund nor I speak. Our silence is more telling than any words we could offer.

But we keep walking forward, finding more and more children, all injured, all dead, and then finally, I stumble over the body of the adult who'd guarded them. The woman, not much older than the children, in reality, wears a slice to her neck, a gaping wound on her cheek, and her hands are a mess of darkening maroon.

'Fuck,' I sigh heavily, sweat beading my brow as I gaze into the distance. I can see a glimmer of smoke in the distance, no doubt from the settlement the children once lived in.

Another five of my warriors have joined me by now, Hereman spitting with fury, the others unnaturally quiet.

Warriors do not kill innocent children. Ever. And certainly not Mercian children.

'I'll hunt them,' Hereman is the first to make the suggestion, anger turning the day colder than winter.

'We can't divide the force,' I sigh wearily. I want nothing more than to do what Hereman suggests. And when I find the murderous scum, I'd inflict every wound on them, before silencing them forever.

'Then bring everyone ashore here. We can ride from here. I hate that bastard ship.' Hereman presses the point. The fact no one speaks against the idea reveals to me that if I force the men away from here, it will not go well.

I meet Edmund's eyes and then turn to stare at the thickening smoke. I should go to the settlement, I should help them bury their dead. These people might owe their loyalty to another ealdorman, but they're still Mercian, and that's all that matters to me.

Resigned, I sheath my seax, gaze down at the river, just visible from where I stand. The four ships have come to a messy halt, and many eyes look my way. I shake my head, and the young lad who survived begins to sob even harder.

'Right,' I announce. 'Let's get on with it.' The thought of what I must do presses on me more heavily than the threat of a coming battle.

'Bring all the bodies together, do what you can to cover the wounds. We'll get the horses and take them back to their parents.'

With the decision made, I stride back to the riverbank, and scramble down it, just as Rudolf begins to make his way up, trying to control a surging Haden. I narrowly miss being forced onto my arse

Æthelred waits there, two oars to either side of the boat as his shipmen try and hold her steady.

'A nasty business,' he says, voice filled with sorrow.

'Sorry that our arrangement must end so quickly.'

'Well, I'd think less of you if you just carried on your way. I take it none of them survived?'

'Just the lad who thought to throw himself into the boat.'

Æthelred shakes his head, anger forcing lines to form around his mouth.

'If you follow the course of the river, after, you'll get to where you wanted to go, anyway. If that's where you still intend to go.'

I reach out, clutch his forearm with my hand.

'Watch yourself on the way back. If it all goes to shit, seek out my Aunt, at Kingsholm.'

Æthelred nods, sucking his lower lip in thought.

'I will,' he confirms, his eyes following the progress of my men up the steep riverbank rather than focusing on me.

'Kill them all,' he states, turning to meet my eyes. 'Kill them all, and make Mercia safe.'

I nod, swallowing around the grief of what I've witnessed and wishing it could just be so simple as speaking the words aloud.

'I'll always fight for Mercia,' I confirm, turning to make my departure. 'For as long as Mercia needs fighting for,' I finish more softly. I can't see an end in sight. Not at the moment. And why should there be? While King Burgred ruled he was weak and ineffectual with the Raiders, managing only to unite the ealdormen around him, keen to demand support from Wessex.

But Wessex is now as threatened as Mercia. And Wessex won't be coming to Mercia's aid, not any time soon.

And honestly, I don't want Wessex to help Mercia.

Mercia needs to stand alone, but united, and only then will the Raiders be defeated.

But first, well first, I have the bodies of seven dead children, and a young woman, almost a child herself, to return to their parents. It will take more of my strength to do that than it will to kill the rest of the Raiders combined.

10

With the horses and men off-loaded, I bid farewell to Æthelred and his sons. I gift all of them with one of Rudolf's coins and promise more when they make it safely back to Gloucester. I don't want to make them rich men when it might encourage the enemy to attack them.

Their eyes reflect sorrow to me, and I find their grim smiles reassuring. It would be easy to disregard each stolen life, too intent on just surviving. I'm glad the Mercians are not yet that immured to the Raiders that the slaughter of the children can be disregarded.

When I once more mount the rise, my men are already milling around, Edmund having taken the initiative and sent someone for each body. Icel has the first child already slung over his horse's saddle, while he holds the reins, head bowed and grim-faced.

It's a terrible irony, the man who gains more life with each battle, and the poor boy, the one with his life stolen by a bastard warrior from the northern kingdoms before he truly had the chance to live.

Rudolf has taken command of the young lad who survived.

Hereman has been dispatched to find the girl, while Lyfing, Goda, Edmund, Ælfgar and Wulfred also have a grisly cargo. While the horses are pleased to be freed from the confines of the boats, they don't frolic. The mood of the subdued men has infected them.

'We all walk,' I announce, not wanting to strike fear into the hearts of the people when I must already destroy so many of them.

With our load, I lead the way, aiming for the thin trickle of smoke further inland. Slowly, for the land lies flat and the grasses and crops are tall, I begin to make out the first of the buildings. I swallow down my sorrow, fix an expression on my face that shows empathy but not my fury and deep grief, and consider the words I must say.

More and more buildings appear, and I appreciate that the village is more significant than I'd been expecting. The carrying cry of someone emerging from one of the buildings alerts me to the fact that we've been seen. I brace myself. I've known enough grief in my life. I've mourned for all those men who've fallen carrying out my orders. It's not an easy task to justify.

But this is so much worse.

The woman, I can tell only because of the skirts she wears, takes a step toward us, and then stops. I close my eyes. I don't want to see the moment of understanding. I don't. But I'm far from a coward, and I force my eyes open again. I won't allow myself to shy away from what comes next.

More and more people spill from the surrounding buildings in response to the woman's cry, and then she buckles, her hand covering her mouth, a scream filling the day.

I continue to lead my men. My gaze remains straight ahead, counting those who watch me approach. No one runs. No one attempt to stop me, but neither are they keen for me to arrive. I've witnessed such behaviour before.

Those few last precious moments, when everything is as it was, and the reality of what has transpired is still beyond confirmation.

'My name is Lord Coelwulf,' I call when I'm close enough. My voice catches, and I speak again.

'My name is Lord Coelwulf. These are my men. We are all Mercians. We were on the river, over there.' I stupidly point, although the people must know where the river is.

'There were two enemies. They attacked your children. I was on the river. I couldn't get to them in time. I'm sorry, only the child survived.'

Twenty or so shocked pairs of eyes watch me, flickering from my open-handed stance, Haden silent and still beside me, to my warriors who carry the dead children. And then to Rudolf, who escorts the only survivor.

'I will avenge them,' I state, knowing the words to be useless, but feeling compelled all the same.

The young lad jumps from his horse and rushes to a woman I take to be his mother. Yet she cries, and not with joy. I couldn't either.

The first woman I saw is on her feet now, dashing toward the horses, her arms outstretched, terror in her eyes and a low moan on her lips.

I look behind her, waiting for the rest to react. It seems to take an age, but then it's as though a wave strikes all of them. One by one they bob upwards and then downwards, some staying still, but others rushing with the tide to crawl amongst my men and the dead bodies.

The cry is terrible, the collective wail of grief setting the hairs on my arms on edge, and my neck prickling with unease.

I look to see if the settlement boosts it's own church or chapel, a place to lay the dead until they can be buried.

'Lord Coelwulf,' the voice is ancient, gnarled and cracked. My attention is drawn to an old woman, her hair covered by a wimple, her clothes more luxurious than I would expect.

'My Lady,' I incline my head respectfully. She cackles, showing me blackened stumps, and with the aid of a woman to either side, she makes her way before me.

'Thank you,' she gasps, her eyes clear from sorrow. 'The settlement has lost all of its young, apart from the survivor. We'll mourn deeply for the lost souls, and for our village. It will not survive to another generation.' The voice is warm and lost, all at the same time. I feel my throat tighten and hope she won't force me to speak.

'Ealdorman Ælhun was supposed to protect us. It was not your responsibility. You shouldn't wear it as though it is.'

'Where is the ealdorman?' I think to ask. I'm aware that my men have lifted the bodies from the horses, and that they make a sad procession, mothers and fathers clasping lifeless limbs, toward a small white building. A man waits at the door, his head bowed. The priest will be kept busy for the next few days.

'There are rumours of a battle, to the north of here, Raiders. But we'd seen none here, and I thought it to be nothing but idle scaremongering. The ealdorman would have sent word, surely, if we were threatened.'

The depth of betrayal is difficult to ignore.

'I'll hunt them down. Ensure they meet their deaths for such a crime.'

'It will not bring back our young.'

I have no reply to that.

She turns and follows the last of the bodies with her eyes as they enter the chapel.

'It began with such promise,' she whispers, and I nod, although she can't see me.

'We'll stay for the night. But we won't disturb you. We'll keep watch around you while farewells are made.'

'That is not your duty,' she states, but it's not a refusal. I bow once more, the oppressive atmosphere threatening to consume me.

When she turns to walk away, her steps are even slower than before, and I worry she'll follow the young to the grave in only a matter of days.

Haden is keen to follow my command when I lead him away. My men are returning from their trip to the chapel. All of them are bowed by the weight of what we've witnessed. There should be ale tonight, to help them sleep, but I need them alert and keen to fight. I'll not allow them to take the edge from their rage.

'Where the fuck is Ealdorman Ælhun?' Edmund asks as we make a rough camp beyond the settlement. My men will take it in turns to stand guard closer to the trackway to the west of the collection of buildings.

I must assume the enemy warriors are gone, perhaps re-joining the rest of the party, but I can't be sure.

'I don't know. Perhaps he already fights the Raiders. Bishop Wærferth said he was going to Repton.'

Edmund's rage boils from him. If I had iron to melt to forge a fresh blade, Edmund would have the heat to do it without the need for flames. I thought his reaction when I allied with the Gwent Welshmen was extreme. This is something else entirely.

'Don't make fucking excuses for him.'

'I didn't realise I was.' I retort. I'm not pleased with having my words questioned.

'We need to find out what's happened here. Are these rogue Raiders, or is there a larger force close by? These people will not want to leave this place, not now their dead lie here. It will bind them tighter than if the children lived, but they needed to flee to somewhere that offered more protection.'

'Send Icel and Goda. They've learnt to scout well.'

They haven't, but I don't acknowledge that.

'I won't send anyone alone. Two pairs, one to the north and one to the west. I'll ask for volunteers.'

I can't be sure that my four men will live, and right now, I don't want to add any more guilt to my shoulders.

'If that's what you think is best,' Edmund's tone assures me that I'm wrong. I meet his eyes.

'Do not be weak now.'

I would punch him. I would slice his neck wide open and watch his life-blood pulse to the floor, soaking the soil. But I don't.

He's right, and he knows it.

'Icel and Goda,' I shout for them, and they're before me, understanding on their faces. 'Guard the settlement to the north. I'll send Lyfing and Ordheah to watch the west.'

Icel pauses as though he'll say more, only then he walks away, determination in his strides.

My eyes track the near-silent settlement. Everyone is now within the chapel, and I think it must be crowded in there, as the priest speaks words the dead will never hear.

Frustrated, I turn away and make my way to Rudolf and the rest of my warriors. The mood is sombre. They feel it as much as I do.

'I'm going to ride the boundaries,' I state, although no one is asking. I need to do something to dissipate my sorrow and scuppered battle rage.

Edmund, of course, follows me. I knew he would. In silence, I direct Haden along the hard-packed trackway. We travel beyond the chapel, where the murmur of Latin reaches my ears, and then on, to the extent of the settlement beyond.

It's not entirely without protection. A deep ditch marks the limits of the easily defensible area, the river, as in Worcester and Gloucester, being used as part of the defences. Haden skips down the steep bank, and then back up the other side. The ripe smell of standing water reaches my nose. I realise the people of the settlement have been assiduous in their duties to do all they can to ensure their defences are well maintained.

No doubt they also have weapons with which to counter any who think to attack. So where then, did the mounted warriors come from?

Icel watches my progress and nods but does nothing further. Goda gazes northwards, without flinching, confident that Icel will warn him if there is danger.

I wish I knew what waited for us along the dried trackway that stretches before us. No doubt it joins one of the more well-travelled roadways further away, the river a distinct sound, but more distant than I would have thought.

But there's nothing to see. Not yet. I turn Haden and follow the line of the ditch to where Lyfing and Ordheah also gaze into the distance. They're more nervous, both reaching for weapons when they hear us approaching.

The tension drains slowly from Lyfing's taut body, and I understand his worry.

It seems too quiet. Far too peaceful.

Once more, I wish I knew more.

'I'll send Oda and Wulfred to relieve you.' But I'm still restless, and so I ride on, further west, my eyes scanning the low-lying ground for any sign of campfires or the dust of racing horsemen.

'There's nothing to see,' Edmund speaks firmly. His vision is so much better than mine that I have to trust what he says. There's no reason for him to lie.

I turn back, reluctant to return to the grieving families while knowing that my place is there. I think Edmund understands.

As I once more ride into the settlement, I catch sight of the men and women walking from the chapel. I force Haden to a halt, only for the old woman I spoke to earlier, to beckon for me to ride closer.

I slip from Haden, lead him instead. It's so silent that I almost fear to breathe too loudly.

'Tonight we were to feast. The food is prepared. Please, allow your men to eat it. There's no one here who will want it, and it must not go to waste.'

I want to argue with her, deny the suggestion, but I know it would not be the right thing to do.

'My thanks,' I bow my head low.

'Come,' she commands me, peering at Edmund. 'I would speak to your lord. Take his horse and inform the men of the food. They should come to the hall.' She points her reedy arm beyond the chapel, to where a steading stands, door open, the smoke leaching through the thatched roof showing me the cause of the grey cloud I saw earlier.

Edmund startles, no doubt shocked to be ordered about by someone other than myself. I nod to him, show him I'm happy to do as requested. He snatches Haden's harness from my hand, his aggravation evident.

It's been a long and strange day, and I know it's far from over.

The woman doesn't speak as we slowly make our way to the open door. No one watches us. The people mourn behind the doors of their houses, and I take some comfort from knowing it's my presence that makes it possible.

The building I walk inside is the largest in the village and is well constructed. It's an old establishment, some of the wooden poles aged, others sprightly and newly placed. That surprises me.

'Sit,' the woman orders me, and I do so, a tight smile on my face because I'm beginning to resent her attitude toward me as well.

She settles beside me. A young woman, a servant I assume, although possibly not because her clothes are far superior to most servants, rushes to bring a jug of both ale, and cold water.

I opt for the water, she chooses the ale.

'My name is Lady Eadburh.' I had suspected her of being a lady. Her attitude toward my men and I is more understandable in light of her name.

'I knew your grandfather.' This, I don't expect to hear, and I feel my body still, unsure of what she means by such a statement.

'He gifted me this land, and I have held it, safe from all ever since. I had great hopes for the future, but now my village will die with me. Without the promise of a new generation, my people will falter in their everyday tasks, and I'll be helpless to stop them.'

She speaks the truth and so I refrain from speaking, reminding her of the survivor.

Her face is lined and wrinkled, and her eyes gleam, but not necessarily with sorrow. Perhaps only regret.

'Your grandfather would have ruled Mercia well, but not as well as you will.'

I gasp at the words, looking around me, as though Bishop Wærferth might emerge from the shadows at any moment.

Lady Eadburh watches me, unsure of why I act as I do.

'What is it?'

'You aren't the first person to say that to me recently.'

'Ah, then it's not just my desire for the stability of the past that speaks. That pleases me.'

'I'm nothing more than a warrior, with a host of Raiders trying to kill me.'

'Ah, then they see it as well.'

I shake my head, lift my beaker and drink deeply, do anything other than meet her eyes.

'You shouldn't be ashamed of your family's past. You should revel in it.'

'I do what I must to keep it alive, for now. Like you, there'll be no one to lead after my death.'

'Perhaps not, but while you live, there's a great deal you can do.'

She falls silent, and I watch her fingers as they lightly grip her beaker. They're stick thin, and feeble, and yet not gnarled and twisted as I've seen the hands of other elders. She's still useful and resourceful. Perhaps she still sews, on days when the light is bright enough to allow it.

'Your grandfather was as handsome as you are. But more importantly, he was a ruler who knew his duties to the people of Mercia. Just as you do.'

'Why do you tell me this?'

'Because you need to know.'

'How did you know my grandfather?'

'Now that is a better question,' she chuckles, and I suddenly wish I hadn't asked.

'My father served him. I was often at court. I watched him from a distance and then when he was deposed, he spent some time here, helping my father build this house.'

I lean forward, resting my elbows on the table, peering into her hooded blue eyes as though seeking the truth of what she says.

'He laid the first posts upon which the roof was supported. He wished to be useful. He was a king without a kingdom.'

'Then what did he do?'

'He left, and I never saw him again. I imagine your father didn't either.'

I've never heard this story before. In fact, I've been told little other than that my grandfather lost his kingdom. I'd always assumed he lost his life at the same time. It seems that was not the case.

'I like to think he took the boat along the river and allowed it to wash him up somewhere far from here, where he would be appreciated. The Mercians are not always the wisest when it comes to choosing leaders. They've become used to listening to the loudest voice, and that's not right. Men who can lead, never choose to, not if they can help it.'

My men are making the way inside the hall, long glances seeing where I speak with Lady Eadburh, no doubt considering what it is we talk about. The smell of the cooked meat is making me hungry and yet I'm not sure I could eat. Not now.

I have more questions that I wish to ask, but Lady Eadburh stands and moves away, not quickly, but before I can form the words to ask just one of my questions. When she's gone, Edmund slumps beside me, his eyes intrigued. But still, words are beyond me.

The platter of meat and bread placed before me rouses my appetite, and I almost snatch for it. Edmund seems no less hungry as he does the same. Lady Eadburh personally directs her servants, and they dispatch the food as she directs. However, a man carves the meat for her.

The meat is well cooked, just tender enough to need little chewing, and it ignites my taste buds. I allow a moment to wish the villagers were here, to share in the delicious meal, but then I devour it.

A warrior always eats what he's given and when he's given it. Like sleep. Always best to get it when the opportunity allows it, and that applies, even more, when there is a war being fought. I finally appreciate that for all I've been fighting all my life, I'm only now in a war. It's a war for Mercian independence, not from the reaches of Wessex, but the Raiders.

Edmund remains silent, although my men are more talkative, subdued, but enjoying this unexpected feast all the same. Rudolf sits with Pybba, and I miss his inquisitive questions. No doubt Pybba is fighting to find answers to them.

One by one, a handful of the villagers enter the hall. They walk with bowed heads, and Lady Eadburh settles them close to the hearth, despite the heat of the day, and quickly they're given mead or ale to temper the grief. I watch her as she expertly weaves her way amongst them all. She reminds me of my Aunt.

This then is her skill. I would wish to have it.

At some point, Edmund stands and makes his way outside. I only notice when he strides back inside, his forehead wrinkled with consternation.

'Riders,' he explains, and nothing else, but I'm already standing, making my way to the door. Lady Eadburh watches me go, a question on her lips, but I can tell her nothing. Not yet.

I'm surprised to find the last vestiges of daylight still lingers. I thought it much later than that and expected to see the stars and the moon.

Edmund points and I follow his finger. Sure enough, there's a haze of something moving out beyond the ditch and the fire that my men must have built to ward off any enemy. I fear it's only drawn them closer like a beacon, but perhaps not.

'Fuck,' I mutter, but I move toward the ditch all the same. Edmund escorts me, and so do at least half of my men, although Pybba and Rudolf are not included in that number.

We've gone from feasting to facing our death in a handful of breaths.

Just like so many of our recent days.

The closer I get to the flames, the less I can see, and in the end, I angle away from the fire, heading to the north, where Goda and Icel meet me.

'Fifteen,' Goda states, 'all mounted.'

His voice gives no indication of his true feeling on the matter. It sounds suspiciously like the Raiders we've already encountered. Only the number gives me pause for thought. It's not the usual fifty who've been sent to hunt me down.

'Stand ready,' I instruct, 'but out of sight. I'll see what they want first.'

Only Edmund stays beside me, the rest of my men fading into the half-light. I can't see how the Raiders would have found me so soon. How would they even have known where I was?

The thudding of rushing hooves comes ever closer. I squint into the purple expanse of night, noting that the riders are heading for the flames.

The horses mill around, not wanting to cross the wide ditch in the dark.

'Why would they set a fire?' the first voice is querulous, but undeniably English.

'As a warning,' I call, striding toward the light now that I know the riders aren't Raiders.

'A warning against what?' I can't make out the face of the man, but his voice reaches me above the crackle of the burning wood.

'That Lord Coelwulf is here.'

'Lord Coelwulf?' Confusion fills the man's voice as I finally get close enough to focus on the riders. They're not at all what I expect to see. The lead man wears a helm, but I can see a black dent along the right side of it, and his face is sheeted in dried blood. His hand tremors on the harness, his other one held tight to his body. These men are no threat to us.

'What happened?'

'Ealdorman Ælhun sent some of his warriors north. We were overwhelmed by the Raiders.'

Fury laces the voice. I'm not surprised.

Edmund is moving amongst the other men, checking on them, seeing how severely wounded they are. I can hear him murmuring.

'Are you heading north?' The question doesn't surprise me.

'I want to determine the truth of what's happened.'

'No need. I can tell you,' the warrior states, but his voice is weakening, and I rush to his side to stop him from sliding to the ground.

Icel joins me, and together we lower him. His comrades aren't in much better condition.

'Come, into the village.' I inform the men who are still able to ride. 'But know that they mourn here as well. Their children were taken from them today, by mounted warriors who must have been Raiders.'

My words are greeted with even greater dismay, and an idea is already taking shape within my mind. I don't want to leave these people undefended. It seems I won't have to.

While Icel and I stagger under the weight of the fallen warrior, I realise that worried eyes have been watching my interactions with the potential threat.

'Rudolf,' I call his name quickly, aware that I shouldn't expect him to still run to obey my commands, but knowing that he will all the same. And he does, erupting before me and almost making me cry out in shock. I convince myself that the noise I'm making was too loud for footsteps to be heard, but I know better. Rudolf is nimble and fleet. I should be using him as a scout.

'Inform Lady Eadburh that we have wounded.' For a moment he hesitates, peering at the men, but then he's gone, following my orders.

The mounted men trudge wearily up and down the deep ditch, while Hereman and Ordheah remain to guard the ditch itself. Icel and I drag the man between us, the horse following on without needing to be lead. I need to know more of what these men have seen, but now is not the right time.

Lady Eadburh doesn't spill from the hall to watch my approach, but Rudolf has done his work well. When Icel and I do make it inside, the servants are ready and waiting. Small wooden cots are being prepared for the warriors to lie on, and I meet Lady Eadburh's eye with a hint of apology.

She shakes her head at me, to deny my intent, and I lower the man to a prone position. Now, in the glow of the fire, that's been heaped ever higher, I can clearly see his wounds. I leave him to the care of Lady Eadburh and move to mingle with the other men.

The majority of them can sit unaided, but their faces are smeared with blood and bruised badly. Wherever they've been, it was a hard battle.

One of the men beckons to me, his eyes the clearest of all, for all that his face is deathly white, and his hand trembles where he tries to grip a beaker of water offered to him. Rudolf hovers close to him, and I nod my thanks.

Rudolf, with his quick instincts, has determined the man most able to tell me what I need to know.

'Tell me, if you can,' I ask, settling beside him. 'I'm Lord Coelwulf.'

'My name's Oswald. I've served Ealdorman Ælhun all my adult life.'

I nod, keen for him to get to the point. He lifts his water to his mouth, and I extend my hand to provide some support so that he can drink. Oda does so, and then I settle the beaker back onto the table, where Rudolf quickly refills it.

'Ealdorman Ælhun wanted to learn the truth of Bishop Wærferth's message. He sent thirty of his men, under my command, to see what was happening in Tamworth and Repton. But we never made it. At the junction between Watling Street and Foss Way, we came upon a force of at least fifty Raiders. This is all that's left of the thirty warriors the ealdorman tasked me with leading.'

I bow my head low, thinking of yet more lost lives, and also reach out, touch Oswald's arm to convey my sympathy, but he flinches away. He doesn't wish to be consoled.

'Bishop Eadberht sent news that Tamworth was deserted, that's all I know.'

'They were hunting you, My Lord. They asked for you by name.'

I grimace, although the news is unsurprising.

'My men and I have already met three groups of warriors sent to hunt me down. They wished me to give oaths to the new Raider lords. I imagine those instructions might have changed now.'

'Where was Ealdorman Ælhun when he issued his instructions?'

'Warwick.'

'And he was staying there?'

'Yes, we were to report back, but we've lost our way and have been trying to re-orientate ourselves.'

'I'll go to Warwick, find the ealdorman. You and your men will stay here. Protect the village, help them as much as they help you.'

Oswald looks confused at my instructions.

'You and your men can't fight fifty Raiders, not alone. But you could protect this place from any more tragedy. My warriors and I will assist Ealdorman Ælhun, whether he wants our assistance or not.'

Abruptly the man sags forward, and I reach out to catch him.

'He has a wound, on his leg.' Rudolf's words reach me from the other side of Oswald.

'It looks bad,' Rudolf's eyes meet mine, and I nod.

'Right, let's get him with his fellow warriors.'

Oswald is not as heavy as the first man, but still, disentangling him from the table and bench he's slumped on is a tedious and cumbersome business. When he rests beside the fallen man from the horse, I'm breathing heavily.

'Bloody hell,' Rudolf points out the injury site to Lady Eadburh, and with swift hands, one of her servants has cut the trews free, and the puckered wound is exposed for all to see, as is the smell.

'Fuck,' the word is too loud in the hall, and all eyes turn to gaze at me. I bow my head in apology, but I know the wound is far worse than it looks.

'Come with me,' I lead Rudolf away, allowing the servants and some of the villagers to tend to the man. While all conversation is still muted, it seems Lady Eadburh has decided to call on those she knows have healing skills. The faces of all might reflect the grief of what's happened that day, but having something to focus on, is allowing them not to think of their dead children.

'What is it?' Rudolf asks, his voice has lost none of his typical cheek.

'I want you to stay here when we ride out.' I can already hear the complaints forming on Rudolf's lips, and I grip his upper arm tightly.

'You and Pybba need to learn to fight together before you have to fight together. I'm all for blind luck and good fortune but look at the state of those men. They've been fighting all their lives, and they're all wounded and bleeding and will be lucky to live. It seems to me that this new collection of Raiders might have more skill than the previous three groups.'

'Are you going to say the same to Pybba?'

'Yes I am, and I'm going to hope to fuck that he has the experience to realise that my caution is well placed. This won't be the last battle we fight against them. Far from it.'

'Then if Pybba agrees, so will I.'

I sigh and then smirk at Rudolf.

'Bastard,' I mutter at him, but I'm striding away, keen to find Pybba and have him know my decision.

I find him, as I suspected, sitting by the campfire set amongst where my men are sleeping that night. He's alone, and I suspect that he finds it challenging to be around people who grieve for lost children when he's still not reconciled to losing his hand.

'Yes,' Pybba speaks clearly above the rustle of the horses in their temporary picket and the rush of the wind over the crops growing nearby.

'Yes what?' I ask, crossing my legs and bending them so that I sit beside him.

'Yes, I'll stay here with Rudolf.'

'How did you know?'

'I'm not blind, just wounded. I can see your thoughts as clearly as if you'd written them in stones for me to see.'

'Good, Rudolf said he'd only stay if you agreed to it. He must have suspected you would be less easy to convince.'

'No, I imagine he hoped I would be. I don't wish to ride into a heated battle. Not yet. In a week or two, when I've worked out the best stances, then yes, I would object to being left behind. What are you going to do?'

'I'm going to find the ealdorman, and I'm going to kill the Raiders.'

'As always, small expectations,' Pybba's voice is rich with sarcasm, but I detect the flicker of respect behind it.

'The fuckers,' I complain, and he nods, and together, we stare into the heart of the fire, trying to un-see all that we've witnessed that day.

11

I don't direct the men to find the Foss Way, but rather hunt for the River Avon that will lead us to Warwick. The Foss Way is further to the east. It seems ridiculous to seek it out when I know Raiders are using it.

There have been surprisingly few complaints about my new destination. While none of the wounded warriors from the day before has succumbed to their wounds in the night, I worry it'll happen in our absence.

Rudolf bid me farewell, a furious expression on his young face while Pybba was smiling broadly. I imagine the two will be allies again by the time I return. Lady Eadburh watched us leave, a pensive expression on her old face, as she leaned against one of the women who aid her.

Mercia is in turmoil, but I imagine it's nothing she's not seen before.

I ride with my mind filled with the knowledge that another battle will come soon, and then perhaps another three or four. I need to kill the warriors who hunt me, and only then can I focus on Repton. But I also need to know what's happening in Repton before I kill all the warriors. I feel unsettled and yet resolved.

I've always defended Mercia. I might lead a small force of warriors, but we've proven effective so far. Far more effective than the Raiders and that's what matters.

The River Avon, when we find it, flows quickly, unlike the Severn and I wish I'd been able to have boats here to take us toward Warwick. I would have liked to arrive with rested horses and warriors. Ever since we left Gloucester to fight the first party of Raiders, the majority of my men have done nothing but ride, fight, eat and sleep where they can. It's exhausting. And we're far from done.

Edmund, as always rides at my side. Icel is away in front, with Goda, scouting, while Hereman and Ælfgar ride to the rear. I consider that Icel and Edmund have resolved their difficulties with each other, but I'm more pragmatic than that. I think they've just decided to ignore the problem and get on with doing whatever they think they should do.

As long as I don't have to chastise them like small children, I'm content.

'Riders,' the cry echoes itself along the line of men from Goda in front. I peer into the distance. With the river to our right, we're at both an advantage and a disadvantage. What we don't yet know is if they're enemy or ally. All the same, I prepare for what's coming next.

The crash of iron on wood is not long in reaching my ears, and I know it must be the enemy.

'Leave the horses,' I instruct, already leaping from Haden and tying up the harness and stirrups high on the saddle to enable him to flee if he needs to. His intelligent eyes watch me, and when I rub my hand along his nose, he reaches out and licks me.

'Get away with you,' I instruct him, a thwack to his rump, and he ambles away to the riverbank, keen to eat. The damn horse is always eating.

Nearly twenty horses take up more room than I'd like, especially when none of the damn fuckers does what I want them to do.

Hereman and Ælfgar quickly join us.

'Stay together,' I instruct my warriors who aren't yet caught up in the fighting in front. Goda and Icel don't hold off the advancing enemy alone, but I can see that's what they're trying to do, from the back of their mounts.

'How many?' I call.

'Twenty five.'

'Not bad,' I turn to meet Edmund's eyes. He almost grins at me, but the battle joy is absent from his face, and I know he'll be no good to me. Not yet.

'Hereman, with me,' I order instead.

'Fucker,' Hereman complains as he shoulders his way beyond his immobile brother. 'Fucker,' he mutters again, but with less force.

'Shield wall,' I instruct my warriors. 'But we'll need to let our men through, so be ready for them.'

The shield wall is only two men deep, but it'll be enough, I'm sure of it, as long as the enemy abandon their horses. I'm gambling that they will. I'm hopeful that men who can inflict such wounds as I've seen on Ealdorman Ælhun's men will know their limits. Fighting on horseback is one of those limits.

With Hereman to my left and Ælfgar to my right, Lyfing and Hereberht behind me, we begin to advance forward. My shield is lowered so that I can see where Goda and Icel battle from their saddles. The riverbank makes a sharp drop to the right, making it difficult for the enemy to make their way around the two horses. For all that, I think some of the warriors are trying it.

'Watch the drop,' I instruct, a whisper passed both ways down the shield wall, and also to those behind.

'Now,' I bellow, and Hereman and I step aside, Lyfing and Hereberht mirroring the action so that Goda and Icel can thrust their horse through the shield wall. I flick a glance at Icel. His beard is flecked with blood and spit, but he seems whole. Goda as well.

In their wake, I close the shield wall and raise my shield, waiting for the first impact.

The enemy has discarded the horses they've stolen, and they rush at my defence.

'Brace,' I instruct loudly, wanting my voice to carry. Others take up the chant. The shield wall seems to ripple as every man reaffirms his grip and prepares for the onslaught of warriors ready to risk it all by flinging themselves against the impregnable wood.

The blow, when it comes, is hard enough to jar my teeth, but I hold firm, pressing my shoulder into the shield with the left side of my body.

'Fuck,' Hereman complains to the side of me. It's as though a hundred men try to topple us. The weight is extreme, and then I feel the reaching attack begin.

The shields, as tightly packed as they are, still allow for small gaps. In to them, spears and seaxs are thrust.

'Hold,' I bellow, my breath heaving. I've not even taken a blow yet, but it feels as though I've been fighting all morning. I'd blame the heat or the enemy, but I know it's just fatigue.

'Hold,' I roar once more when I feel the shield wall falter a step.

'Hold,' if I could make men follow my instructions just by the force of my words, then the enemy would be tipped in the river by now.

And that gives me an idea. The enemy is determined to beat us, their weapons loud on the wood of our shields, and it seems as though they might be winning, for none of us have yet taken a killing blow. But, they're focus is only on that.

'Lyfing,' I breathe his name, the strain evident in my voice, but he hears me all the same.

'Have the left-hand side of the shield wall move forward. I want to push them into the river.'

Lyfing pauses only for a moment before I feel the hole of his absence behind me. If I'm struggling as much as I am, then I worry for the rest of my men.

We all have skills and weaknesses. But I'm the strongest of them all. Perhaps apart from Icel, and even Icel is getting slower.

To begin with, I don't notice the change in pressure. My shoulder is locked in place, my other hand busy knocking away probing weapons and avoiding those that I can't force back. But then, I realise that Hereman and the men are doing as I asked as a small crack opens up between Ælfgar and me.

'Careful,' I warn Ælfgar, and he immediately moves to fill the gap.

'Push,' I bellow, 'fucking push.' And now everyone is pushing, even my men closest to the river. We rode fully armed and ready for battle, and the river beneath us is fast-flowing and deep. If we can just get some of the enemy to fall in, I'm sure the rest will suddenly become much easier to kill.

Sweat beads my forehead, dripping into my mouth, turning my already dry lips even drier, but I can feel the motion of the shield wall now.

And the enemy seems oblivious. Whoever commands them does so in Danish, and although I understand much of the language, the accent is so strong that I'm struggling to hear everything they instruct. But, whatever it is, there's no hint of capitulation in them.

The first strangled cry of a warrior is followed by a heavy splash. I grimace, pushing, even more, wishing I could afford to discard my seax and use both of my shoulders to complete the manoeuvre.

The second and third splashes are equally loud, and I can hear the wet cries of men as water replaces the air they need to live. But it's only three warriors, and already, the shield wall, finally alert to my intentions, is trying to force its way back into the original position.

'Hold,' I instruct, the single word an effort to force out beyond my heaving chest and parched throat.

A blade threatens to slice my chin, the warrior on the other side of the shield less concerned with finding a watery death than those closer to the riverbank. I duck my head, keen to have the obstruction removed, but it's in an awkward place, and I can't lift my seax to counter the reach of the blade. If the shield wall continues to turn toward the river as it currently is, the weapon will strike me sooner or later.

But Hereberht has seen my quandary, and with an economy of movement that I admire, he lifts the shield he holds clear from above my head, and with his other hand, slices cleanly through the man's wrist.

The blade falls, and so does the twitching hand.

The scream of pain reaches my ears, and I spare a thought for Pybba before I follow the rest of my warriors, taking small steps so that I almost face the river now. The handless warrior disappears beneath my feet, Hereberht stabbing down. I doubt the warrior deserved such a clean and straightforward death, but sooner that than him screaming and getting entangled in my feet.

More splashes reach my ears, more frantic cries for help. Above it all, I can hear a heated debate between at least two of the Danish warriors that they need to escape the clutches of the shield wall.

I don't grin, not yet. Not until every man is dead, is it time to celebrate. And even then, any celebration will be muted. There are more Raiders out there to kill yet.

My shield wall falters to a stop, the shrieks coming from my own warriors, as all resistance suddenly melts away. The men are pulling Wulfred, closest to the riverbank of all, back to the other side of him as he falters, threatening to follow our enemy to a watery death.

I'm panting heavily. This hasn't so much been a battle as a shove. Each step has stolen my strength, and I gasp, my warriors doing the same.

Icel joins me, still mounted, his seax flashing darkly, his horse's coat stained stark brown.

'Is he wounded?'

Icel tears his eyes away from the sight of the men floundering in the river.

'No. Well, no, I don't think so,' but immediately Icel is jumping to the ground, soft words on his lips, as he runs his hand over his horse's right shoulder.

'What shall we do with them?' It's Edmund who asks the question. I'd not truly realised how deep the river was. At least ten of the enemy have already disappeared from sight. But a handful is struggling to the riverbank, desperate to escape a watery death. Some of them have used their intelligence and have opted for the far riverbank. But five of them are trying to make their way back to dry land in front of my warriors.

I sigh heavily. These men are strong warriors if they're able to haul themselves free from the river even while wearing all of their battle equipment, but that means that I can't allow any of them to live. Even if I felt any compulsion to do so.

'They must all die,' I state, and five pairs of eyes meet mine. That, at least, they understand.

'My Lord, my Jarl, will pay for my return.' The voice speaks English well, and with a start, I realise the boy who addresses me is no older than Rudolf.

'I've no interest in money,' I state flatly, while my warriors continue to taunt the dying.

'Bring me a spear,' I demand, determined to skewer the fucker who's trying to escape up the other side of the bank. There's no bridge close by, and so I must try and kill him now, or risk allowing one of the Raiders to live.

'My Lord, Jarl Anwend is my father, and I'm his only surviving child.'

'Then he should have thought of that sooner, as should you,' I comment, but with the spear in my hand, I'm sighting the other warrior. He lies gasping, helm lost in the flood of the river, on his back. There's no celebration from him that he's evaded death, but still, I can't allow him to live, no matter how easy the kill.

I take five steps back, my warriors clearing a path for me, and then I run forward, thrusting the spear high, hoping it will fall true.

Edmund, Icel and Lyfing have chosen to carry out my instructions regarding the survivors below me, but, as the spear seems to slip into the other man's body, I reconsider.

'Leave the boy,' I bellow, watching the body of my victim buckle around the spear, as though I've skewered a fish, and then it flops silent.

'I would speak with him,' I confirm, turning my eyes back to those below me. The four men are dead, but Edmund has held out his hand to aid the survivor. I've been reminded of the tactic I wished to employ the first time I encountered the enemy.

My warriors move quickly to retrieve what they can from the

trackway. The enemy might have fallen in the fast current, but along the way, they lost equipment, and it's worthwhile claiming.

'Tell me about your father,' I demand from the youth. 'And what's your name?'

'My father is Jarl Anwend, and my name is also Anwend.' The boy speaks well for all he's shivering violently and his teeth chatter noisily together. Only the fact that he reminds me so much of Rudolf has stayed my hand. All the other warriors claiming to be the sons of the Raiders have died at my hand. This boy though is different.

'Tell me, what's happening in Repton.'

Edmund hands me a cloak, and I wrap it around the boy's shoulders and in the same movement, grip his hands tightly in front of his chest and then tie them tightly together using a piece of hemp rope.

Anwend eyes me angrily and also gratefully from beneath heavy eyebrows, he still needs to grow into. I'm reminded of how young he is, for all I want to hate him, just because of who his father is.

'Who are you?' he asks, but I shake my head.

'I'm not a prisoner. Talk, or I might find it no use to keep you alive.'

'My father, Jarl Anwend, holds Repton with the aid of three other jarls, Halfdan, Guthrum and Oscetel.'

'And where is King Burgred?' the lad tries not to smirk at the mention of Mercia's king, but he doesn't quite manage it, and so I cuff the side of his head. I don't make him bleed, but it does startle a trickle of blood from an earlier wound.

Anwend is whiter than death, and I might not have done him a great favour in having him plucked from the river.

'He's fled Mercia in exchange for his life.' It relieves me to extract the same response from every Raider I speak to.

'And what does our father plan to do to Mercia now?'

'The jarls seek a Lord Coelwulf. King Burgred said he would be the only man capable of holding Mercia against them. King Burgred said it with a sneer.'

'So you search for this Lord Coelwulf?'

'Yes, I do, or rather I did. Perhaps not anymore.' The use of 'perhaps' almost has me slapping him again, but I restrain my impulse.

'And where will you find Lord Coelwulf?'

'Some place called Gloucester.'

'And what, they sent your force to track him down?'

The lad shakes his head or seems to try to, it's difficult to tell with all the shivering.

'No, each jarl has sent fifty warriors. Whoever finds him, dead or alive, can have his lands. But because of that prize, others have banded together as well.'

'So did you lead Jarl Anwend's men?'

'I did, well, I didn't really. He nominated Ragnar to follow my instructions, but really, I followed Ragnar's.' The fury is impossible to miss. Perhaps Ragnar should be pleased he's dead.

'Is this all of your force?' I point to the river, where a few items still cling to the surface of the water, the odd piece of clothing and for some reason, a sword. It should have sunk long ago, and only the shields should have floated.

'No, but the rest are dead. We met another group of Mercians two days ago. They didn't fight the way you did. Most of them were killed, but so were some of my force.'

'So, Repton. What do they plan to do from there?'

Anwend glares at me, his eyes showing his confusion.

'I. I. Why do you want to know? Who are you?'

The question is plaintive, but I ignore it.

'I would know what to do with you? Should I kill you now that you've spilt all the information you know, or let you live, only so you can fight the Mercians another day.'

Dark eyes watch me, the resentment an indication of Anwend's youth.

'My father will pay for my return. He has all of Mercia to gift now.'

'Surely he has a quarter of Mercia to gift if there are four jarls?'

'Well, if there are still four jarls.' Unexpectedly, I laugh.

'You're a feisty shit, aren't you? It's a pity you can't fight as well as you talk.'

'My father should have led the attack. Fucking Jarl Halfdan claimed the victory from him, but he lost many more men than my father did.'

'So there was a battle then?'

'Well. Sort of. A few Mercians against the might of the Danes. It was never going to end well, was it?'

Snot is dripping from Anwend's nose, and he raises his bound wrists to wipe it away. I watch him, aware my men are unsure why I've not killed him yet. I'm not sure either. But then I make a snap decision.

'Icel,' the tall warrior ambles his way to me, a keen look in his eye, as though he already understands my intent.

'Take him back to Repton. If they try and attack you, kill him, and try to escape. Find out what you can about events in Repton and how many warriors they lay claim to.' I've turned aside, to speak quietly to Icel, but Edmund is of course listening.

'Goda will tail you, and we won't be far behind. I would know all I can.'

Icel nods slowly, no hint of fear for being given such a difficult task.

'I take it I don't have to listen to the fucker speaking for the entire journey.'

A grin touches my cheeks, my eyes meet Icel's evenly. He accepts the task.

'You can do what you want to him, as long as he arrives back at Repton alive, or dead if the enemy tries to attack you.'

'Are you still going to Warwick to find the ealdorman?'

'Yes, I am, but I'll ride quickly. My plan is to follow you to Repton only a day later.'

'Then, I hope the little fucker knows when to keep his mouth shut, and when to open it.' With nothing further spoken between us, Icel strides away, beckoning for Goda to join him.

'Why?'

I expect Edmund's question.

'With the fucking jarl's son at his side, Icel will be able to scout better. The warriors from Repton won't want to risk losing their jarl's son, not when he's so nearly home.'

'But why risk Icel?'

'Icel will know what to do. I'd send you, but your reactions are not always the best, and you do tend to lash out without thought when roused.'

Edmund opens his mouth to complain but then changes his mind.

'A fair point, I suppose.'

Icel sighs heavily, and I notice that he favours his left leg a little.

'Are you wounded?'

'Bashed, nothing more. I can ride and fight and whatever the fuck else I need to do to get to Repton.' Icel sounds fierce, and I hold back any concerns I might have. I must trust Icel to know himself well enough not to exert beyond his level of endurance.

I stride from his side, mingle with my men to assure myself that there's nothing but bruises and shallow cuts to attest to our latest battle. Ingwald has gone on ahead, and comes back leading horses.

'More!' I exclaim. He grins and nods yes.

I turn and fix Anwend with a glare.

'Whose fucking horses were these?'

'King Burgred's.'

'And he gave them to you.'

'There wasn't much choice in it,' Anwend confirms jauntily, and I nod again.

King Burgred has been caught with his arse out, as so often is the case. Why he was Mercia's king, I'll never know.

Why King Burgred was so unprotected, I'll never know.

But, perhaps, I will.

'How did you make it to Repton?'

A furtive look covers Anwend's face. Perhaps he knows better than to share such information with the enemy. Maybe he realises there's no choice.

'Ships, down the Trent, from Torksey.'

So, King Burgred made peace with the enemy, thought the job done, and then allowed himself to fall victim to a peace that he believed in, and they didn't.

'How many?'

'Fifty.' Anwend spits the word and my eyes narrow.

'Fifty ships?'

'Fifty ships.'

'And how big are the ships?' Anwend shrugs, and I menace forward, my hand raised to slap his face. When he winces away, I hold my action in check. I know his kind. The answer will come from the threat, not from the actual act.

'There are near enough three thousand warriors. My father commands eight hundred of them.'

'So he's not the most powerful then?'

Frustration sweeps over Anwend's face as he realises his mistake in boasting.

'Jarl Anwend is the second most powerful jarl of the four. Only Jarl Halfdan has more men.'

I turn my back on Anwend. That number is massive. How can I, with only just over twenty men, hope to halt a force of so many?

'King Burgred fought, but his defence wasn't good. But still, some of the warriors fell, and several boats sank on the Trent in a storm.'

'So there aren't three thousand now then.'

'No, but more may come.'

I nod and turn to meet his eyes.

'Know this, young Anwend. I've already killed many Raiders. I've gained two hundred horses for my stables, and I'll add more to that number before this is done. But, I'll allow you to be returned to your father, for a price.'

Anwend looks concerned now. Whether he's realised who I am or not, I'm not sure, but after encountering Ealdorman Ælhun's warriors, I'm keen for him to appreciate that Mercia does have warriors who'll fight much harder for her. Anwend must realise that.

'My father will pay anything.' I don't think he would, but I'm not going to worry the boy with that.

'When you return to Repton, encourage your father to go back to his ships, and to leave Mercia.'

'He'll never agree to that,' Anwend is staunch in his defence of his father.

'Then Icel may as well take your head now.' Icel, a hand on his seax, leers at the youth, who screams. I can't say it's anything but a scream.

'I. I will speak with my father and convince him of your intentions toward our force.'

I grunt. I know the lad will have no success with his father, but I don't want to kill him. Not after what the Raiders did to Lady Eadburh's villagers. I'm not better than any warrior, but today I want to be. Tomorrow, I'll rue that decision. But not today.

The warriors who died on the riverbank have been hauled up the steep bank, and I point toward them.

'Was one of these men this Ragnar you speak about?'

Anwend swallows heavily, his mouth pressed tightly together. But I've seen his look, and I've noticed how well equipped the first dead man is. His face is bleached now, turning grey where it blends into the long blond hair that's been tied back in a myriad of braids, all topped with some small charm or other. A thin line of water trickles from his open mouth and staring eyes, and Anwend can't take his eyes away from the body.

With swift movements, I stand beside the body and then hack down with the war axe I've taken with me. It's not a clean strike.

But the second one is, and I hold it up using the hair braids to keep the severed flesh from my fingers.

'Ugly fucker,' Edmund calls, and I smirk at him. Edmund can always be relied upon.

'Bring a horse.' I don't know if I'm cruel, but I understand how important it is to be seen to be ruthless to your enemy.

Eahric walks with a suitable mount toward me. The animal steps well and has a build that will suit such a youthful and sprightly passenger.

'Here you go,' I indicate with my eyes that Eahric is to pick Anwend up and place him on the horse's back.

'Secure him tightly.'

While Eahric works, his fingers nimble, I'm busy to the other side of the horse. I don't want to scare the animal, but I do want to scare Anwend.

I step away from my grizzly work, and only then does Anwend realise what I've done.

'There, you're in charge of him now,' I offer, my tone ripe with condescension.

'Make sure your father know that I personally arranged this and that if he doesn't leave, I'll make sure I find him in the battle. I take it the family sigil is that of a one-eyed raven. Anwend opens his mouth to disagree with me, but snaps it shut as I point at his clothing.

The raven is everywhere, stitched into the tunic he wears; seen in the silver charm tied around his neck,to name just two places.

Anwend bows his head low, while Eahric turns the horse, preparing to hand the lead rope to Icel.

'Lord Coelwulf,' the voice is too high, and yet its evident Anwend is proud of his deduction.

'There's no one called that here,' I comment, fixing him with a firm glare. Anwend's confidence slips and then he's being led away. Icel is in front, mounted on his horse. Anwend doesn't realise that Goda is preparing to follow on behind. I would send more men, but I need them if I'm going to get fucking Ealdorman Ælhun to ride with me to Repton.

Edmund smirks at me, the sound of the headless body being dragged to the side of the trackway loud in my ears. No burial, but a pile of rocks will cover the three dead we've managed to catch. The body on the far side will have to remain there, perhaps a grizzly reminder to any who take this track. At least until someone steals the wealth from the body and thinks to hide it away.

'Right,' I state, mounting up myself, Haden unhappy at being dragged away from cropping the river grasses. 'Let's see if we can get to bloody Warwick without encountering anyone else. Hereman and Ælfgar, will you scout at the front. I'll take the rear, with Edmund.'

I take a last look over the site of yet another battle

How many more of the damn fuckers do I have to kill before I make it to Repton?

Too many.

12

Warwick comes into view as a haze of grey smoke. It's the worst thing about so many people living together in one space.

We've encountered no more Raiders, but the track is busy with the indentations of hooves, and I don't think it's because there aren't more Raiders. Instead, they've taken different routes to the one I'm using. It would be much easier for them to take the Foss Way to Gloucester, especially when they don't know the landscape well.

I imagine it depends on who leads them. Some of the groups show more caution than others, but even then, it's not a great deal of caution.

Warwick is on the same side of the Avon River as we are, and I'm hoping that accounts for the lack of scouts we encounter. Either that or Ealdorman Ælhun is entirely blind to the peril he's in.

But just in sight of the settlement, riders make an appearance, their intention to block the trackway.

I ride forward then, allowing Haden his jaunty steps, and taking an agonisingly slow time about it.

'Another came this way, earlier, he led a horse and a captive.' The words are barked at me. It seems there is a great deal of unease. Maybe Ealdorman Ælhun isn't unaware of the danger after all.

'Yes, he's my man. He's gone to return the runt to his father in Repton.'

'He had the head of a man on the horse.'

'Yes, well, it was better to take just a part of the body,' I state, considering why the men haven't asked who I am.

'Ealdorman Ælhun would know who you are.'

'Then tell Ealdorman Ælhun that Lord Coelwulf is being denied entry.'

The lead warrior looks temporarily confused, only to turn it to belligerence.

'You're not welcome here.'

'I'd rather Ealdorman Ælhun made that decision. Tell him that ten of his men are sheltering at a settlement close to where the Stour meets the Severn. They're the survivors from a meeting with the Raiders that decimated his force. Tell him, I've killed the rest of the Raiders for him.'

The lead warrior, no doubt sent more for his massive size than his quick thinking, looks confused. But the rider at the back quickly turns his mount and gallops across the short space of land being cultivated outside the settlement defences.

I relax on Haden, content to listen to the Avon rushing along its merry way to the side of me. If Ealdorman Ælhun denies me admittance to Warwick, I'll ignore it. If he refuses to let me ride around Warwick to reach Repton, I'll attack his warriors and forge myself a path.

I lick my lips. Without Rudolf, and the young lads, left behind either at Gloucester or Worcester for safety, I've been neglecting myself. I reach for my water bottle and empty the contents into my mouth. The water is tepid, but refreshing all the same.

I note my fingers in the bright daylight. They don't even have a scratch from the last fight.

In front, Warwick waits for me. It seems similar to Gloucester and Worcester in that it has encompassed the riverbank in its design. Still, it seems to lack any Roman fortifications. It seems an odd choice for Ealdorman Ælhun to decide to shelter within. Perhaps, I consider, he realises it wouldn't cost too much to rebuild, or even abandon altogether.

While I consider all this, five horsemen begin to make their way toward me. One I recognise, the others I don't until my eyes settle on Ealdorman Ælhun himself.

I incline my head toward him. His face is flushed red, probably with fury.

'Give him access,' Ealdorman Ælhun's voice carries the taint of command across the divide, and the four remaining men slowly move their horses from blocking our path.

I encourage Haden to ride forward, keeping my eyes firmly fixed on Ealdorman Ælhun.

'My Lord.'

'Lord Coelwulf. I didn't expect to see you so far north.'

'I didn't expect to find your stray warriors so far south, so it seems the day is full of surprises.'

'Were they your men who went by?' Ealdorman Ælhun redirects my strike, and I shrug my shoulders.

'They had a prisoner he was returning to Repton. The second shadows him.'

'You should have killed him.' I hope he speaks of the prisoner.

'Probably. But I was feeling magnanimous in light of what the Raiders did to the children of a settlement on the Stour. I'm not the monster that they are.'

Ealdorman Ælhun searches my face, as though looking for deceit, and I meet his eyes keenly. He's dressed for war, and his eyes are so strained that I almost think they might pop from his face. His beard is rimmed with frost, his hair almost non-existent. He's not an attractive man, and neither does he have the build of a warrior. I would expect to find him conducting a church service, not a defence against the Raiders.

Not that he is conducting a defence. Not really.

'The Raiders took the Foss Way, or so I understand it.'

'And you did nothing to stop them?' My tone is mild.

'They weren't looking for me,' he counters defensively. 'It's done you no harm, I see.' As he speaks, his eyes sweep up my body, and I wonder what he sees.

Does he see me as a warrior, or as a petty lord, or does he see me as no more than an annoyance. I reconsider. I don't want to know what he thinks of me. It's not necessary, I just need his warriors.

Ideally, I want to strike his head from his shoulders. But whatever Ealdorman Ælhun is, or isn't, he is most assuredly the ealdorman of this area, and I need his warriors to attack Repton. It would be fitting for me not to antagonise him.

'And you sent your men north?'

'I did, I needed to know what was happening in the wake of Bishop Wærferth's messenger.'

'So he did arrive here then?'

'You know he did, and you know I turned down the bishop's offer. But, well, that was before I knew what I know now.'

'And what do you know?'

'One of my warriors made it to Repton. He died, a short while ago, but he told me of the Raiders. Over three thousand of them, and fifty-odd boats clogging the Trent, and warriors imposing the will of their new lords over the people of Mercia.' I'm surprised that Ealdorman Ælhun sounds so choked, but then, he is an ealdorman of Mercia. This land provides his wealth and gives him his influence.

If the Raiders claim control over his people and his land, Ealdorman Ælhun will have nothing. Just like when my grandfather was deposed.

'I'm sorry for your loss,' I bow my head low, I never like to hear of a man being killed defending Mercia, although I would honour him.

'He was a good man. His actions aren't in vain. But it does put me in a difficult position.'

'Why does it?'

The rest of my warriors have joined me now. They mill around, unsure what to do while I talk to the ealdorman.

'I turned down the bishop's suggestion. But it is no doubt the correct one. Fucking King Burgred is gone, my man confirmed that there were no Mercians at Repton, other than those they've captured from the monastery. Tamworth is in the hands of men and women who once served the king and his queen, but no one is in command.'

'Then you would elect me as your king?'

I almost can't believe I'm asking the question.

'Yes, I would, and I'll ensure the other ealdormen do the same.'

'A shame there's no time for the witan to be called now, and I'm halfway to Repton.'

Ealdorman Ælhun twists his lips in thought.

'I'll send word to Bishop Wærferth and accompany you north.'

His words astound me.

'I didn't think you liked me?' I can't help it. I have to ask the question.

'I don't like you. I hate you, Lord Coelwulf. Everyone does. But I know that you can fight and I'll stand behind a man who can beat the Raiders.'

'Hardly a glowing approval, but it is a time of war. I'll take what I can. But I ride north now.'

'I'll follow you, in the next day, and I'll bring all of my warriors with me. Well, apart from those who must protect my dwelling here. It's hardly built at all.'

'Send your family with the messenger. Worcester has Roman walls. The bishop will protect them.'

Ealdorman Ælhun doesn't like the idea, that much is evident from the way his eyelid flutters, but he isn't a stupid man either.

'I will do as you say. My wife can speak for me with the bishop.'

'And I'll expect to see you close to Tamworth.'

Ealdorman Ælhun swallows heavily but then grunts an agreement.

'I'll not be called a coward, like King Burgred.'

'I wouldn't ever call you a coward,' I confirm, and then I smirk. I'm not good at lying, not at all.

I extend my arm to the ealdorman, and although he stares at it for a long moment, he leans forward and returns the gesture, our hands gripping arms. Mine, I note, is much tighter than his, my arm muscle much more developed.

'Our accord is sealed,' I confirm.

'It is. Do you need supplies?'

'No, we have everything we need. For now.'

'Lord Coelwulf,' I'm turning Haden away, already thinking of what awaits me as I get closer to Repton.

'Yes, Ealdorman Ælhun.'

'Thank you,' I'm unsure what I'm being thanked for.

'For this, for making me do more than cower behind my half-built walls and even smaller ditch.'

'I'm always keen to make men prove themselves in battle.'

His half-smile drops quickly. Only then he forces it back on his face.

'Then I'll prove myself, Lord Coelwulf.'

There's no further need for conversation, and I'm keen to be away from Warwick.

I knee Haden through the mass of horse flesh and ride at the front of them all.

From here on in, I have a feeling that it will not be easy to get to Repton. Not that it's been easy so far, but closer to Repton, there will be more warriors foraging and hunting for me.

I breathe deeply.

Now's not the time to second-guess myself.

My decision is made.

I will die, or I'll prevail. I can't do anything further.

THE DAY already feels as though it's been too long and yet there's still time to get closer to Repton. I encourage Haden to greater speed, aware that I lead my men. I hope that Edmund has sorted out who rides at the rear. Not that I don't trust Ealdorman Ælhun and our spoken agreement, but the path through Warwick could easily be taken by the enemy. I don't know if Ealdorman Ælhun would have the courage, alone, to stop them.

And when his wife goes to Worcester, Warwick will be all but abandoned. I should have considered that and told the ealdorman to burn it down when he left.

We ride to the side of the thick woodland that stretches to the west. It would be an ideal place for the Raiders to lay an ambush. I ride with half an eye to the west and the rest to the north. At some point, I hope we'll find the place that Ealdorman Ælhun's men fought the Raiders. I'd like to know the track they took, so I can avoid it, if possible.

Watling Street should appear soon, but also, so should the Foss Way, where they cross giving every person who travels the roads a decision to make, north or south, east or west.

I expect the Raiders to have used those ancient roadways to get to Gloucester, but it's possible they didn't.

'Will he do what he said?' Edmund as always comes to question my decision. I almost wish it were Rudolf and not Edmund. Rudolf's enthusiasm would be preferred to Edmund's reasoned questions and arguments.

'I don't think he has any choice, not now.'

Edmund's pensive silence tells me of his unease.

'What?'

'Well,' and Edmund pauses. 'How come he didn't know about King Burgred?'

This has given me some cause for concern, but I imagine the answer is simple.

'No one expected an attack, and, I think we'll find, that no one actually respected King Burgred. Ealdorman Ælhun probably took the extended silence as a good thing. The same charge could be levied at all the ealdormen and bishops, not just Ælhun.'

'I would think you'd be concerned at facing three thousand men more than whether Ælhun has decided upon treachery.'

'I was trying not to think of the three thousand warriors. So thanks for reminding me.' Edmund's tone is sharp. 'How,' he asks, 'do you plan on defeating them?'

'No fucking idea, not yet.'

'So we're just riding to Repton in the hope that you'll be struck with fucking inspiration?'

'Yes, that's about it,' I confirm. I don't have an idea, not yet. 'Bollocks.'

'What?' Edmund explains, hand going to his weapons belt.

'I should have told Ealdorman Ælhun to order the Gwent Welshmen sent north. I'm going to need them sooner rather than later.'

'Send someone back to pass on the message.'

'Um,' I consider carefully. 'I don't want to split the force, not here. We'll just have to hope that Bishop Wærferth uses his intelligence and sends everyone to Repton.'

'You do know that this is sodding madness, don't you?'

'I do, yes, but you'll still ride at my side, won't you?' I fix him with my sternest stare.

'You know, I will. But I would sooner live than die.'

'I don't plan on fucking dying,' I mutter.

'Then I would suggest that twenty warriors against three thousand aren't good odds.'

'There's not three thousand any more. We killed nearly two hundred of them.'

'Fine, then twenty warriors against two thousand eight hundred is not good odds.'

'That's better. I'd prefer accurate calculations when contemplating the battle that must be fought.'

Edmund hisses at me, and I turn to meet his eyes.

'Why the fucking questions now?'

'Because these fuckers will follow you anywhere, no matter how slim the chance of success, but for once, I don't think they appreciate just how slim that chance is. You've always won in the past.'

'They're not fools to follow me quite so blindly.'

'No, but they are fucking men who believe the legend you've created for yourself.'

I rein in abruptly and turn to look at him, incredulous.

'You were the one that said I needed a bloody scop!'

'And you do, to sing your legend before it ends.' Edmund's face is flushed with unease. I'm not used to seeing such unhappiness there, or to hear such words being spoken.

'If you're too damn scared, then you can go back to Kingsholm, and I'll never speak of this again.'

'I'm not fucking scared,' Edmund all but moans. 'But I am realistic. You're not.'

As angry as I am at having my decision questioned, I reach across the gap between us and grip his arm.

'This is what we've been doing all of our damn lives. This is what my brother died doing, the man you served before me. Just because the stakes have been raised doesn't mean we shy away from it. Think of those young children. What did they do wrong in this life? Fuck all, and yet the Raiders killed them for sport. If my men and I, you included in that, have to go down fighting, then we will. Someone has to stand up for Mercia. Wessex won't. Her own damn fucking king won't. But we will.'

'Fuck,' Edmund snatches his hand back, trying to avoid the too interested gaze of the warriors who make their way beyond us as we debate.

'I know it's fucking terrible. But it's what we fucking do. And you have to believe in that, and in our success. Or we will fail before we've even started.'

'But there's so few of us.'

'Yes, but more will come. Ealdorman Ælhun will send his men, and the others will follow suit. It might not be a force of thousands, but the Raiders think we're puppies who just want to roll over and have our tummies tickled. They see no threat from us, not after King Burgred fucked off to Rome. It's their complacency that'll kill them all.'

Still, Edmund looks dismayed, and a cold fear enters my heart that he must just ride back to Kingsholm. I don't want to do this without him, but I will if I must.

'Fuck it,' Edmund announces, kneeing his mount forward. 'But we still need a bastard scop.' I watch him ride in front of me, suddenly as pensive as he was. Only I shrug it aside.

It's always been my destiny to give my life to Mercia.

Facing two thousand eight hundred Raiders might not have been quite how I imagined the end coming about, but at least I'll be remembered for such foolery if I do meet my end on the edge of a Raider's blade.

13

Eventually, the daylight does start to leave the sky, the calls of the summer birds high with excitement as dusk falls. On the ground beneath us, the passage of many, many hooves finally makes itself known in the rich dirt.

'Here, Coelwulf,' Hereman calls me forward, and I grimace.

The Raiders aren't as tidy after a battle as my men, and I are. Mercian bodies are lying in tangled agony, and the scent of decay is strong, as is the buzz of flies.

'Fuck,' I complain, slipping from Haden's back all the same to walk amongst the detritus of battle.

'They didn't even bury their own dead,' I complain, kicking a body with my boot to disturb the horde of flies that covers the back. The area is sticky and black. A mortal wound.

'Tell the men to stay back, unless they can stomach this.'

This then is why we always bury the dead, even if we don't want to. No one should come upon such a scene unprepared. Even I feel bile rising in my throat, but I swallow it away.

Edmund has joined me, and together we walk among the dead, swatting the flies away, and trying not to see where the woodland animals have thought to feast. I appreciate that the dead feel nothing, but all the same, I'd sooner not see such ruin.

'Thirteen of Ealdorman Ælhun's men,' Edmund helpfully offers. I turn to glare at him, and he raises a shoulder at me as though to ward off a blow.

'When did you become a fucking mathematician?' Edmund grins without apology and continues to bend over the dead.

'They didn't even pillage the bodies.'

'No, they didn't.' I stand, hand on my hip, surveying the battle site.

We're still close to the woodland that covers the landscape here, but ahead, I can detect it growing less dense, and both the Foss Way and Watling Street must meet sooner rather than later. This area has been cleared by one of the ealdormen's forestry workers, and I imagine, new shoots will be planted soon to replace those taken. We've already ridden beside carefully managed woodlands, young trees in various stages of growth. I can't imagine it'll be any different here.

'It seems opportunistic, far from planned,' I muse. Neither force must have known that the other was there. They were both hunting blind. And yet. The imprints in the hard soil show only that a few warriors escaped this way.

'Perhaps they had a fire or something,' Edmund offers.

'I don't see any sign of it. Maybe they were being hunted after all, and this is where the Raiders decided to take a stand.'

'But how would they have found them? If they were using Watling Street.'

It's a mystery to me, and one I know I can't ask the dead men to answer.

'We'll have to bury them,' I sigh heavily, but behind me, I can already hear some of my warriors digging at the hard-packed earth with axes. I turn to watch Hereman, Wulfred and Ælfgar, beginning the process as close to the trees as possible.

'We should make camp for the night, but I'd rather not be so close to the dead,' Edmund grumbles under his breath at my words but makes no other comment.

'We better make two pits,' I holler. My men know me well.

Already Lyfing, Oda, Eadberht and Eahric have taken up defensive positions blocking the way we came, and the obvious way forward.

'Well, shall we?' I ask Edmund, and he grimaces.

'I hate touching the fucking dead.'

I agree, but it's not the time to show any squeamishness. The sooner the sixteen bodies are disposed of, the better.

I almost miss Rudolf, picking through the dead for treasure, for I find I have no enthusiasm for the task. It feels wasteful to consign so much iron and good leather to the soil. But equally, I don't relish the task of doing more than committing the slippery bodies to the earth.

Ordlaf and Wærwulf join Edmund and me in dragging the bodies to the growing grave. Then, as the bodies are lowered into the earth, Hereman bends and takes what he can quickly grab. By the time we're ready to close the ground over the sightless eyes, the pile of weapons belts and leather has grown more rapidly than I would have thought possible.

'They were well provisioned,' Hereman mutters. His face is rimmed with muddy streaks as he gazes at his hands, perhaps considering how he could have taken to the task so well.

'They were the ealdorman's sworn warriors, not the fyrd. Of course, they were well-provisioned.' But even I can see that the iron they carried was expertly forged.

'Take what you want,' I tell Hereman. 'You were the only one who could touch the dead. You get the first choice of everything.'

But Hereman is shaking his head.

'I didn't do it for the prize. I just don't like iron to be put to sleep beside dead masters when there's so much more fighting still to be done.'

I nod and smirk at his growled words. I understand what he's saying. Weapons are made to be used, not discarded.

'Such a way with words,' I thump him on the shoulder, while he nods, his head angled so that he looks both infinitely wise and impossibly stupid. He grins, his white teeth flickering for a moment in his dusty face.

'I think I need a good dunking,' he confirms, ineffectually brushing at the ingrained mud on his tunic and trews.

'There's running water, in the woodland,' Lyfing calls, hearing Hereman's words. 'Take your horse with you. Poor creature. Look at it.'

And Hereman and I do, but of course, the animal is not suffering at all, but rather eating happily, tugging at the long grasses that spill from beneath the tree canopy.

I become aware that Lyfing's not the only man to have discovered the stream, and although I didn't want to make camp here, a small fire has been lit, and Ordheah is fussing with it. My stomach gurgles loudly.

Beornstan erupts from beneath the trees, a broad grin on his slight face as he carries two handfuls of fish in front of him.

'Daft fuckers have clearly never been hunted before. They swam into my damn hands.' His incredulity brings a smile to my face, as he tries not to drop the slippery creatures.

'Now you just need to determine how to cook them,' I offer, making my way to Haden and leading him toward the stream as well.

It's quiet by the stream, despite my men and their horses coming and going. I hazard a thought that I could live somewhere like this if the wars ever came to an end. But of course, they never will. They haven't yet.

I shake my head, angry at my melancholy hope for a future that will never happen. Unless I am a king. And if I'm king, then I can never have such a quiet life.

Growling under my breath, I turn to make my way back to my men, but suddenly I realise I'm being watched. I slow my steps, try and sense where the eyes are coming from without alerting them to the fact I know they're there.

I don't feel as though I'm watched from behind, and certainly not from the front. I listen carefully, breathing as quietly as I can, pretending to fuss with Haden's hoof, as though I clean the muck from the day's riding, to prevent him from going lame.

Of course, Haden has no time for silence, and the damn horse huffs more impatiently than all the men combined. All the same, I decide I'm watched from my left. When I straighten myself, I peer into the undergrowth, hopeful that whoever watches me has become complacent and given him or her away.

But there's no such luck.

Frustrated, I make my way back to the camp, and gesture for Edmund to join me. He's not yet been to slack his horse's thirst.

'There's someone in there. Watching.'

'Fuck,' Edmund complains, peering at the rest of the men, biting his lip and considering what we can do.

'Send Ælfgar to aid me, casual like.'

'I'll send a few others as well,' I confirm, and Edmund lingers, as though looking for something lost on the ground. I make my way to Ælfgar, and tell him of the problem.

'Bastard,' Ælfgar confirms, going to join Edmund slowly, as though their meeting is unintentional. I take Haden back to the horse picket and gesturing for Eahric and Ordlaf to assist me, creep back into the woodlands. They're the smallest of my men, and I'm counting on them being the quietest. I don't go straight in at the same opening I exited, but rather twenty paces up.

The undergrowth here is sparser, and the going easier. I look all around me, searching the ground for signs of footprints or hoof prints, but find nothing.

Eahric is to my left and Ordlaf to my right. They follow my lead. We're not stalkers by nature, but every man must be able to hunt to stay alive.

We begin to make our way toward where Edmund and Ælfgar can be heard talking to each other, voices not overly loud but echoing under the thick canopy. I realise then that we might have attracted the attention of anyone making a home of the wood. I must remember that in the future.

Ordlaf looks at me and then indicates upward, and I follow his eyes. There's a figure up there, not really high up, but high enough that a casual observer might not see them.

'Circle the tree,' I confirm, and both men move with me to do just that. Only then do I make my presence known.

'What you looking at, you fucker?' the body startles, and there's rattling. Then a sword embeds itself into the ground, no further than a body length behind me.

'Get down here,' I bellow, furious at such a close call. For a moment, there's nothing but silence, but then the leaves rustle again, and I watch as the figure comes quickly into sight.

'Will you hurt me?' the voice is neither young nor old.

'Provided you have no other weapons then no.'

'You startled me,' the boy I face is younger than Rudolf, and his clothes are in poor condition. I don't think he's a threat, but then why does he have the sword?

'Where are you from?'

'In there?' the lad, longhaired but free from any facial growth, points deeper into the woods.

I reach for the sword, noting the runes that run down the side of it.

'A bit of opportunistic pillaging?' I ask, but the lad is shaking his head, about to deny my words.

'It's only what we've just done,' I confirm, already leaning to return the sword to him. 'Keep it, you found it.' Grubby hands grip the blade eagerly, a look of desire quickly quenched.

'Were you here when the attack took place?'

'Nope, I just came this way today. I was looking for fish, but I caught the shine through the tree trunks. I went to explore.' A wistful expression covers his youthful face then. 'I could have taken much more, and sold it, but you arrived on your horses.'

'Who do you live in the woods with?'

'No one,' he deflects, but I reach out and grip his arm.

'You're not in any trouble, but there are Raiders in Mercia. If you need more swords and seaxs to protect those you live with, then I want you to take them.'

The twin desires to have more weapons but to protect his fellow settlers, wars on his face.

'Really. My men and I have enough swords and shields and leather byrnies. We're going to fight the Raiders, to the north of here. If those you live with could use the weapons, you must take them.'

'Well, I could do with a few more then,' he eventually admits, and I nod.

'My name is Lord Coelwulf.'

I'm met with a blank expression, respectful, but blank.

'You've never heard of me then?'

'No, My Lord.'

Edmund has joined me by now, and so too has Ælfgar.

'What's your name, lad?'

'Eowa.'

'Then Eowa, come, decide what weapons are required, take as many as you need, and then go back to your people. Warn them of the Raiders. Tell them to take care and to hide in the trees if anyone comes with iron and shields.'

With a final lick of his lips, Eowa steps forward, and I walk with him, keen to ensure my men don't menace him. The youth is nervous, evidently not used to being around so many people. I don't want there to be any accidents or misunderstandings.

The eyes of everyone in the camp watch me emerge from the tree-line, but on seeing me with the lad, they quickly return to their tasks.

'Over here. We've buried the warriors but taken what we can from them.'

Again, Eowa licks his lips, and as he bends to examine the finds, a flicker of silver around his neck shows me that Eowa took more than the sword.

But I hold my tongue. I've no need for any more riches.

'You can eat with us before you go,' I offer, but Eowa shakes his head, looking longingly into the trees.

'Perhaps next time,' I say softly. Eowa's hands are now filled with five swords, a war axe and three seaxs. But he's chosen not to take a shield. I imagine it wouldn't be much use in the heart of the woods, with so many hiding places and trees to climb.

'Can you manage?' I ask. I don't want him to drop anything. 'They'll be sharp.' Eowa nods again, but I know he wants to be gone.

'If you ever have the need, you'll find me at Kingsholm, although you can also ask for me in Worcester or Gloucester.'

Eowa has clearly never heard of any of those places, and as I watch him go, I fear for him. But, he managed to evade my men and me for long enough. I'm sure the Raiders will be even less observant.

The fish, when it's cooked, is succulent, if too hot, and I burn my tongue and then swallow all my water to put out the fire. With the trees at my back, I feel more sheltered than usual, and so I determine to only set two guards and have them changed three times during the night.

Then I call Edmund and Hereman to my side.

'Tomorrow we ride north. The hoof prints are far from clear, but I think they came via Foss Way, not Watling Street. I want to find them, see if there are any more of these roving warbands out for my blood. As Edmund pointed out to me earlier, two thousand eight hundred warriors are standing between us and ejecting the Raiders from Repton. If we can shave that number further, then we should.'

'That will take us north of Repton?'

'Yes, it will. I don't want to meet them head-on.'

'But Icel is already going to Repton?'

'He is, and he offers peace, but he doesn't know where we'll appear from either. I would sooner everyone suspected us of travelling along Watling Street. I want the element of surprise and apprehension intermingled.'

I see Edmund bite back his response to my intentions, and I admire him for that.

'Tomorrow,' I confirm, and then I turn away and selecting a piece of likely looking ground, roll myself in my cloak and close my eyes. My men can keep watch tonight, I need to sleep.

14

But of course, I don't get to sleep for as long as I would like.

When the day is little more than a hint of bruised purple to the east, Hereman's hand on my shoulder roughly wakes me.

'Raiders,' he hisses, and I blink, trying to clear my vision and stand all at the same time.

'From which direction?'

'The north.'

'Ah, wake everyone,' I instruct, reaching for my weapons. I've laid them beside me during the night so that I don't cut myself while I sleep. Now I slide them back into position on my weapons belt. I've slept in my byrnie. There's not enough time to hustle into one of those when caught unawares.

'Fuck,' I can hear the men complain, as they stand and stretch and groan.

'No rest for you bunch of bastards,' I confirm, striding to Haden's side to slide his harness over him. I don't foresee fighting on horseback, but it's better to be prepared.

'How many?' I demand to know, as Hereman joins me in trying to decide the best place to stand and wait for the enemy.

We could ride away, of course, we could evade them, but why? I'm hunting these warriors. I want them dead, and they're about to make it sodding easy for me.

'Not quite fifty. Maybe the remnants of the last group, or perhaps another group entirely.'

'You hear that men,' I state, walking amongst them, checking they're all well-armed and that sleepiness hasn't made them do something stupid, such as forgetting their seax. 'Not quite fifty, two each, if we're lucky. It'll be like all the other times. The fuckers will think they can beat us because they outnumber us, but we'll show them that skill counts more.'

My men are slowly coming to, rousing from their sleep, and a few ragged cheers greet my words.

'I think you can do fucking better than that? I complain. 'A few Raiding bastards, before you break your fast, I'm sure some of you must be fucked off about that.'

'Damn right,' Edmund complains. His face is pale as he rubs his slick hand over his byrnie. When that fails to dry his sweating hand, he bends to run it through the tall grasses that have evaded our temporary campsite.

'Sodding gits,' Hereberht agrees, and the rustle of annoyance becomes more a river in spate. I nod, meeting eyes and making the same vow my men and I make before each battle. We fight together, we mourn together, and then we fight some damn, fucking more.

'Form up,' I command, and the clash of shield hitting shield fills the air. I take my place, not at the centre, but rather to the right a little. People always expect the leader to be at the centre. I don't like to do what's expected.

We're facing north. In the distance, the woodlands continue to our left, but to the right, there's open land, fields of crops nodding in the summer heat, as early as it is. I hope that no one comes to check the plants before the battle is done.

A thunder of hooves reaches my ears.

'Stand,' I order, Edmund, repeating my words, Hereman taking the place of Icel and doing the same from the right.

Lyfing is beside me, Ordheah to the far side. I turn to grin at them both, and mad eyes meet mine.

'Fuckers,' Lyfing grunts.

We hold our shields before us, interlocked and ready but they're lower than usual, so we can see who comes against us.

I expect it to be near enough fifty horsemen. I'm not disappointed.

The lead rider casually reins his horse to a stop, hand raised to advise those who follow him to do the same. I watch him. I don't know this man. Neither can I determine who rides with him because everyone wears a helm, more than halfway covering his or her eyes and chins.

Immediately, something feels wrong.

'Lord Coelwulf.' The man speaks English, and it's evidently his first language, missing the heavier accent the Danes use when they've learned to speak my tongue.

'Who's asking?' It's Edmund who calls, and the lead rider's head swivels from the centre of the line to the outer reaches. As he does so, I try and peer around him, keen to determine more about those he rides with.

'My name is Ealdorman Wulfstan of Mercia. I've come to join my force with yours, to attack the Raiders at Repton.'

I feel my eyebrows lift at the words. For a moment, I feel a flutter of triumph to know that the ealdormen of Mercia are finally prepared to unite behind me. Only, I pause, I've heard of Ealdorman Wulfstan, and I know that he served King Burgred. I also know that he ruled lands to the north of Repton, closer to Torksey than anywhere else.

That disturbs me.

'How did you know where to find me?' Hereman shouts the question and confusion wars on Ealdorman Wulfstan's face at being addressed by different people.

'It's widely known that you mean to stand against the Raiders.'

It's not a satisfactory answer. Far from it.

'How many warriors do you have?' Edmund this time. I'm silent, watching and considering. The riders directly behind Ealdorman Wulfstan are uneasy, the mounts trying to sidestep rather than wait quietly. These men are not skilled riders. I would expect such behaviour from the Raiders, not from Mercians.

'Forty-four,' the answer is more a gulp for air than an announcement of the intent to murder the Raiders.

'So who told you this 'widely' known news?' Hereman once more. Ealdorman Wulfstan's hands are lax on the reins, and I try and peer around them. He remains face on, making it impossible for me to see more than his head and upper body above the head of his horse.

His horse at least is docile.

And so is the ealdorman.

I try and catch his eye, try and determine the truth of what's happening before me. Only Lyfing inclines his head toward me, speaking with his lips barely moving.

'Hereman says the ealdorman's hands are tied.'

Ah. This makes a great deal more sense of what I'm seeing.

I've had enough of the bollocks.

'Ealdorman Wulfstan,' I state, erupting from the shield wall, and causing the man to jump. He's nervous as fuck, and he has good right to be.

'We welcome your warriors. Tell me, who here is your second in command?' I hear my shield wall close up behind me, and I also make out Edmund's oath of frustration at breaking from the ranks. No doubt he'll have some harsh words to share with me later. Or perhaps not. It'll depend on whether my suspicions are confirmed or not.

A flicker of panic over Ealdorman Wulfstan's face as I step ever closer. The riders behind him also shift uneasily, and I take the time to note how well armed they are, how much they carry with them, and whether they ride as though to war.

They do.

I smirk, pulling my seax loose so that I have it ready for when I need it.

Ealdorman Wulfstan still struggles for an answer. I'm close enough now that I can see the ealdorman's hands are tied together, his hands looped through the reins, rather than holding them.

His terrified eyes seek me out, but I make no effort to offer reassurance.

'You have no such warriors? Here, I'll show you, I have Edmund, over there,' and I point with my seax, 'and also Hereman over there. The pair of them can kill fucking anyone and more than anything, we hate traitors.'

I can see Ealdorman Wulfstan's throat bobbing as I speak. He's an older man, a firm ally and favourite of King Burgred, his chin showing the hoariness of his age. Perhaps he's as pissed off as I am at Burgred's betrayal, or maybe he encouraged his old friend to leave Mercia for the Raiders. Perhaps he even told the Raiders to take Repton, a calculated move on their part, bound to rouse the fury of the Mercians. I don't like the fact that the Raiders have control of the Mercian royal dead. I don't like it one fucking little bit.

I don't much care for Ealdorman Wulfstan's motivations, and I'm not about to find out, either.

'My warriors, all sixteen of them, are good men, fighting for Mercian independence. They're determined to drive back the fucking Raiders, and add more kills to our tally of over a hundred and fifty already.'

Just as I hoped, a flicker of unease betrays the riders behind Ealdorman Wulfstan. The horses shift because their passengers have startled and I know I'm right to suspect as I do.

Ealdorman Wulfstan is struggling for a suitable answer, as I turn my back on all of the riders attracting the attention of my men. We have no tell for them to know that the allies we face are really an enemy, but I've tried my best.

With barely time for more thought, I flash through the air, turning sharply as I do, aiming my seax at Ealdorman Wulfstan's throat. In the final moments, as he still fights to find answers to my questions, he determines my intention. Rather than anger in his eyes, a stray tear falls, a word forming on his lips that I take to be 'thank you,' and then the air is shimmering with an arc of escaping blood. I angle my seax once more, ensuring that as the movement is complete, a hail of blood covers the lead riders.

Ealdorman Wulfstan slumps over his horse's head, his body convulsing, as I whack the animal's backside, the scent of blood already turning it wild. Although I didn't plan it, the animal backs up, turns swiftly, the burden tied to the reins, as it races through the riders waiting behind.

I expel my pent up breath and meet the eyes of my enemy.

'You damn fuckers,' I bellow, and then I'm racing, not back to the shield wall, but amongst the churning mass of confused riders. These warriors, like all the others before, have little control over their mounts.

I narrowly avoid more than one horse hoof, more than one angled blade, and more than one fool slipping from his saddle at his mounts unexpected movement, and then I'm where I want to be.

The leader. Never at the centre of the attack. Only on this occasion, the wrong decision has been made.

I can hear my men begin their surge against the enemy. I hope they don't all fight mounted warriors. I hope the Raiders have dismounted as the attack comes. They might be skilled with blades but not with horses. I don't want any of my men to die, defeating those who would trick us.

The leader of this warband is easy to determine. He wears his helm, like all the others. But it isn't the usual everyday item, built for a single purpose, but rather an elaborately decorated one. I almost expect feathers to curl up from the cheek plates, but they don't.

I grin when I see him.

He rides a horse large enough for Icel or me, but he's a smaller man, his legs dangling from the high stirrups, as though a child on their father's horse.

'My Lord,' I call to him because I don't know his name. His reaction is immediate, as he attempts to dismount, only I've stepped close, turned his horse with just the weight of my arse, so that where before he was facing forward, now I get the side of him. And he's exposed.

The movement is slick and quick, the cut made before the jarl even notices that I've managed to take the time to plan my attack carefully. Already, his trews are staining dark, and not with piss. I turn to move away, rather than continue the attack, and the leader, confusion in his black eyes, tries to take aim at me with his war axe.

It's a heavy object and yet one he must clearly have been able to handle with ease.

Now, as he strikes out at me, his grip slips, and his reach falters, and then he's falling from the saddle, arms flailing feebly. He's dead before he hits the ground.

I find myself in a melee of discarded horses, and with no one aware that their leader has fallen.

'Fuckers,' I complain, trying to decide the best way to make it back to my men. With barely a moment's thought, I replace the seax on my weapons belt and mount the horse that recently carried the leader of the group of Raider scum.

With more luck than judgement, I leap, from one discarded saddle to another, and as I get closer to the line of fighting, I pause, eyeing up my men.

Unlike me, they've shown real discipline, and meet the enemy, shields interlocked tightly to protect everyone.

Those they face are clearly skilled and could be lethal, but the battle has gone from being a slow infiltration of my force to one of ferocious fighting. They've been caught unawares, and already a number of them lie, festooned in the leaking fluid of their bodies. I decide my involvement is not really needed.

Only then a high voice grabs my attention, coming not from in front of me, but from behind.

I imagine the words are something like, 'you fucking bastard,' but they're garbled by the heat of rage and fury and by the effort being put into trying to attack me.

I jump to the ground, shove a few horses to one side, and wait for the attacker to reach me.

The youth, I imagine the jarl's son, is slight of build, like the youth of yesterday, only wearing the best of equipment. The toughened leather of the byrnie flickers darkly, the sun's rays yet to penetrate so deep into the confused mass of moving horse-flesh, and the edge of the seax glistens only with the shimmer of iron.

'You don't have to do this,' I call. But I'm already moving my shield to counter the first blow from the seax before the final word reaches my mouth.

'I'll take that as a no then, you bastard.' The blow is more powerful than I expected and yet nothing compared to the force my shield can absorb. I hold my shield firmly before my body, almost decrying the fresh death that will follow shortly.

The feet of the warrior dance, from side to side, and forward and backwards, and the blows keep coming, accompanied by a running stream of Danish.

I don't understand all of it, but the actions speak louder than the words do.

I sense the fury and the anger, and I could, if I had the need to, end this game now. But, my warriors are winning their battle, and no one is interfering with us. I allow the youngster to vent his rage.

Only as the blows start to diminish, do I step around my shield, seax raised, ready to end the one-sided battle.

The eyes that greet me show shock that I'm entirely unaffected by what they've been doing. With quick strides, I'm in front of my enemy, their shield hanging uselessly in their hand. Even the seax is held point down, body heaving, sweating so freely that the hairless chin gleams.

My seax is ready to make the killing stroke, already hovering at the exposed threat. With no more thought, I make the cut clean, the slice immediately exposing the tangled web of body parts that lie beneath the weakness of a neck.

The youth slumps and I walk away, no remorse, just the stone cold knowledge that my enemy is not as proficient in warcraft as they think. Equally, that they try and cover that fact with tricks and boasting.

The shield wall has finally broken up into small areas of fighting when I emerge from the milling horses. My body is free of all marks, or it is until the lead horse bends down and nips my ear.

'Fucker,' I complain, batting the inquisitive head away. I work quickly to disentangle the mass of harness that makes it impossible for the horse to crop the grasses as his companions do.

'Where the fuck you been?' Edmund's angry words greet me. He glares at me, eyes blazing red with battle fury.

'Killing the fucker, back there. Well, two of them, actually.'

'While we took on the rest of them?'

'Well,' I stand, hand on my hip, meeting him above the moaning cries of a warrior who's not yet quite dead, 'we said two each. I killed my two.'

'For fuck's sake,' Edmund stabs down, his blade impaling the man through the neck, stilling the feeble cries.

'What?' I demand defensively.

'Nothing Coelwulf, nothing at all.' Edmund strides to the next malingering soul and stabs down again. I can see the tension in the movement.

'Did you miss me?' I call to his back.

'No, we didn't. See, they're all fucking dead. It would just have been better to know that you weren't fucking dead as well.'

'But I indicated what I was going to do.'

'How? How were we supposed to know what you were going to do?'

'I did the thing, with my eyes, rolling back in my head. I've done it before,' I counter, confused by the aggression.

Edmund strides to stand before me, the heat of his anger washing me. He jabs me with the handle of his seax.

'Whatever the fuck you think you told us, you didn't.'

Our argument has garnered the interest of all those no longer fighting.

Hereman is looking from his brother to me, a half-smile playing on his lips. His next words don't surprise me.

'I knew what you had planned, boss,' Edmund growls at the

words. I roll my eyes. Fucking Hereman. Always keen to infuriate his brother.

'You genuinely knew what Coelwulf had planned,' Edmund turns the force of his rage onto Hereman. A flicker of a smile touches my lips.

The daft bastards.

'Of course, I did. Don't you even know how he works?'

By now, I wish that Hereman hadn't decided to get involved.

'Right, let's vote. Who knew what fucking Coelwulf was about to do?' In the face of Edmund's roar at his fellow warriors, I'm surprised that anyone has the bollocks to respond. But they do.

'I did,' Lyfing calls. 'Me too,' Eoppa choruses, and more and more of them, as they bend and pillage, ensuring the dead are dead. Movement in the woodlands has caught my eyes. I'm already reaching for my seax when I realise it's Eowa and beckon him forward.

'So, you all knew, apart from me?' Edmund is still ranting.

'Yes, that's about the long and short of it,' Hereman calls gleefully. Edmund, with the barest of veiled threats at me, bows, the action jerky and ill-humoured.

'Then, Lord Coelwulf, please accept my most humble apology for my ill-conceived complaint.'

There's nothing for it.

'I accept. And my thanks,' I offer, my voice pitched only to reach his ears. Hereman is already back at his task, his back to us. At the same time, Edmund stands, for a moment longer, chest heaving, as he considers what, if anything, he's going to say next.

'Go and see what Eowa wants,' I command, pointing to the lad from yesterday.

Mumbling under his breath, Edmund marches off, and I go to Hereman and thwack him on the back.

'You shouldn't wind him up like that.'

'Well, he shouldn't be such a mouthy shit,' Hereman counters. I know that until the two are reconciled to each other, they'll be nothing but frosty silence between them.

Fucking brothers.

Wærwulf is moving amongst the horses, trying to get them into some sort of order, but my attention is on Eowa. He seems to be gesturing frantically, but Edmund, still furious, is being dismissive. I can tell just from the body language.

'What is it?' I ask Eowa, aware that the boy rears at my sudden appearance.

'I found more,' he explains, pointing toward the west.

'More what, bodies?'

'No, live ones. Like those,' and he points at the bodies being pillaged by my men.

'How many?' I ask although I expect the answer.

'Many,' he says, and I realise he might not be able to count.

'More than this?' I ask, pointing again at the riderless horses and dead warriors.

'About the same,' Eowa confirms, after screwing his face tightly in thought.

He still carries his seaxs and war axe. It's evident he's not yet made it back to the people he lives with.

'Can you show us where they are?'

He nods, although uncertainty tempers the movement. I'm not surprised. I have sixteen men and now nearly seventy horses under my command, and he makes his way through a densely packed wood.

I turn then, gazing at my warriors, and the scene we would be abandoning. But, I don't want to leave any of my men here. I sigh heavily. I don't like to do this, but if the sixth and final warband sent to track me down, is not far from here, then I must hunt them down.

A hundred fewer warriors might not feel like a great deal, but it's worth it.

Edmund is watching me keenly, his anger dimming with the knowledge that we're not yet done for the day.

'Take the horses into the wood. Make sure they can roam freely if they want to. We'll have to come back for them.' By this, I mean all of the horses, even Haden, and he clearly realises, his gaze as judgemental as Edmund's from where he grazes.

'We'll have to leave the dead, for now. Hopefully, Ealdorman

Ælhun will ride this way in the next day or so, but even so, we'll have to come back for the horses.'

'Tell the men to take all of their battle gear. No one is to leave anything behind they might need.' Edmund nods, and moves to walk amongst those still pillaging, drinking, or perhaps, considering eating. I expect some complaints, but there aren't any.

'You bloodthirsty bastards,' I holler, as they make ready to move away. The horses shelter under the trees, water close by, and plenty of green shoots to tempt them while we're gone.

'You know us,' Lyfing grins at me, his helm dented on the left-hand side, and a trickle of blood dripping down his neck.

'Who did that to you?' I ask, and Lyfing grins.

'The cut, myself, the helm, I dropped it, and the fucking horse stood on it.' He laughs, and so do I. Damn fool.

And then we're all under the tree canopy, and I stride to join Eowa, who watches my transformed men with only barely concealed fear.

'They won't hurt you,' I assure, hoping I speak the truth.

Eowa nods. He's evidently not one for using words and begins to lead the way. His steps are nimble, his feet almost silent over the matted ground, and I wish I still had the lithesome walk of youth. But I'm weighted down by the passage of years, my weapons, and perhaps even the men I've killed, who might, or might not, have stayed with me.

The thought makes me chuckle softly, and Eowa turns confused eyes glance at me.

'Nothing to worry you,' I try to reassure, but a man laughing for no known reason is hardly relaxing.

The sounds of the woods slowly overwhelm my senses, and all traces of daylight fade as we rush ever deeper into the trees. I realise then that we'll need Eowa to lead us back to the horses, when we win, and if we decide to go through the woods.

Eowa stops, every now and then, as though looking at the ground, or a tree, and as much as I stare, I can see nothing different from the hundreds of other trees. We all have our skills, or so I decide. I'm not a tracker, but Eowa is.

As the time drags on, the heat turns my face slick, and I can hear the grumbling of others as well. But Eowa presses on, with unwavering confidence, and I allow him to. The horses would have stood no chance here, where each tree presses closely to its neighbour, long arms reaching across the gaps above our heads so that they seem to merge into one continual mass.

When Eowa turns, his finger to his lips, I stop in my tracks, Edmund almost crashing into me, the group of men slowly falling silent. Ahead, I can hear the voices of others, and they're not speaking my tongue. Not at all.

I press on, leaving Eowa under the care of Hereman, with only Edmund for company. I need to see what the enemy is doing before I make any decisions as to what our next move will be.

I crouch low, hoping a fallen tree trunk will shield me from view, as I finally see my enemy.

As Eowa suggested, there are about fifty of them, maybe. It's difficult to tell because some of them are in perpetual motion and it's impossible to work out whether I've counted them already or not.

They have a small fire, and the smell of roasting flesh reaches my nostrils, as does the stench of a latrine. No doubt, I consider sourly, I'm standing in it.

There are horses tethered closer to the treeline. It seems that while we've walked through the dense trees, our enemy has been more cautious in their choice of campsite. But why, I consider, are they camping now? Surely they should be off, searching for me.

And why, I also want to know, are there no sentries?

A heated debate seems to be taking place between two of the men. They stand, one to either side of the fire, practically spitting with rage. The words they speak are Danish, of that I'm sure, but it's spoken too quickly for me to decipher more than that.

'They're arguing about what to do,' Edmund whispers to me, and I turn to him, surprised he can make out the individual words. He shrugs as though it's not important. And I remain silent. If he can hear them, I want him to listen to everything that's being said.

'They're waiting for word from a Jarl Sigurd, perhaps the fucker you killed, and then the skinny man wants to go back to Repton, the sturdier one wants to travel south. He says that Jarl Sigurd will never come and that they've been waiting an entire day already.'

'So not the man we fought then?'

'Maybe not. Have they sent some other poor bastard to hunt you down?'

'They've sent quite a few of the fuckers so far. None of them has managed to get a scratch on me yet.'

'No, they haven't,' Edmund's tone is far from complimentary.

'Are we going to attack them then?'

I've been considering the same thing. Better to kill them now, than when they're reinforced and likely to be more problematic.

'Yes, but I'm not sure how yet. A pity we can't climb the trees and just land on them from above.'

Edmund startles at the suggestion and then begins to chuckle.

'Maybe not, but I'd like to see it, all the same.'

'We'd have to come at them from all around their campsite to prevent anyone from escaping, and it'll be fraught with danger. No one will be able to watch another's back.'

'Hum,' Edmund's response is hardly reassuring, and I indicate we should creep back and re-join the rest of the men.

'What would you suggest then?' I demand to know when we're far enough away that we can risk whispering a bit louder.

'We could come at them from outside the wood.'

'We could, but then they'd melt away into the woods, and we'd have to hunt them down. It's not an efficient idea.'

'No, it's not, and there are probably warriors on fucking guard duty out there. After all, they're not expecting anyone else to be in the woods.'

'No, they're not,' I agree, rubbing my hand across my face, feeling the growth of my beard and wishing I could take the time to scrape it clear from my face. It's too damn hot for such a matted mess.

'So we need to use the element of fucking surprise as our extra warriors, and go from there.'

'I agree,' Edmund confirms, his eyes on where he steps, keen to avoid the multiple trip hazards.

'Fucking bastards,' I mutter. I don't much want to send my men to another altercation. I'd like to think we've killed enough, but the Raiders just keep coming. It's their damn luck if they meet us.

Eowa waits anxiously for us to return, and I grin at him.

'Well done,' I confirm. Meeting the eyes of the others who've all adopted defensive positions in my absence, all of them guarding Eowa.

'Right, they're in the woods. We'll have to go around them and encircle them. It'll be every man for himself. And we all need to stay hidden until the signal is given.'

'What will the signal be?' Hereman demands to know.

'Something they won't suspect. Something that you'd find in the woods?'

I'm not sure what it could be, and no one leaps to fill the sudden gap in the conversation. My barn owl impersonation will not do, not this time. It won't carry far enough, and anyway, I know it's a poor rendition.

If Rudolf were here, I'd know he'd have the answer, but he's not.

I look at Eowa. Maybe he has a suggestion, but the youth is hopping from one foot to another, and I'm sure he'd rather be gone from here.

'Well we'll just have to go with a war cry,' I suggest, but Edmund is looking pensive, his face drawn and his eyes unfocused.

'They have a fire burning, and we have a spear. Who's the best shot?'

He turns, gazing all around him, seemingly unprepared to hand the honour to his brother, even though we all know Hereman can hit a coin from fifty paces with a well-aimed throw.

'For fuck's sake,' I complain when Edmund refuses to answer the question he's asked, and Hereman is glaring at him. I like the idea, if not the way it's being arranged.

'Hereman, you take a spear, when you think everyone is in position, throw it at the fire, and then we'll all move to attack. It's going to be fucking rough,' I warn, picking out those who really need the warning, Ælfgar and Wulfstan amongst them. There's a reason I so often leave them at Kingsholm. They're good fighters, but not the best. It doesn't matter so much in a shield wall, but one on one, it's going to matter a great deal.

Hereman holds his spear high, showing it to everyone other than his brother, whose eyes he refuses to meet. The two always reconcile before a battle. Today better be no fucking different.

'Right, the force will be split as follows. Eoppa, Osbert, Hereberht, Lyfing, Ordheah, Oda, Wulfred, Beornstan and Ælfgar will take the far side. Decide amongst yourselves whose going where. The two closest to the end of the tree line will need to be doubly watchful and quiet. I'm assuming there will be lookouts, somewhere. I can't imagine the lax bastards are quite as confident as they appear.'

'I'll be at the point of deepest infiltration into the woods, along with Edmund to my right and Hereman to my left. The rest of you take the side closest to where we stand now. This isn't the way we normally operate. We're not one for fucking ambushes, but the objective is no different. Kill them all. We'll try and keep one alive amongst us, but only when we're assured of a damn victory. Is that agreed?'

We're in a sort of semi-circle now, bending low, heads together, everyone listening to what I say. Only one person remains standing upright, and that's Eowa. I look at him and gaze behind me.

'Will you wait here? High up in the branches. I don't want you to fight. You mustn't fight. If the enemy win.'

'Which they won't,' Hereman growls.

'If the enemy wins,' I continue ignoring the interruption. 'Go back to your people. Stay there, and keep safe.'

Eowa nods, a flicker of worry on his youthful face. I feel strangely protective of the lad, even though we've spoken only a handful of words together. Certainly, I would feel uncomfortable if he died while I was fighting.

'Right, then that's agreed. We go now, moving quietly, not

speaking to each other, and when we're in position, we'll have to wait for those on the far side to reach where they need to be. None of you fuckers die. None of you. No matter what, stay alive, even if you have to scramble up a tree and let some of your friends come and rescue you. We're few enough in number as it is.'

15

Without further words, I turn and stride away. With each step, I crouch a little lower, hunker closer to the ground. All this creeping isn't my idea of waging war. Still, the option has presented itself to me, and I'm not about to kick it in the face in place of being more fucking honourable.

It feels as though no time passes at all, and then I'm back at the spot that Edmund and I scouted, able to just make out the camp and smell the smoke from the fire. The enemy is far from quiet, while my men sound as though they're purposefully stamping on each and every twig they can find.

I've winced many times, and now I bite my lip, realising how thirsty I am, and try not to yell at the noisy fuckers to keep it quiet. I'm sure we'll be heard, but perhaps I'm just overly sensitive.

'Do you think this will work?' Despite our work at dawn, Edmund's face is white and sweating once more, his hands shaking with the fear of what will come.

'Of course, it will. We've killed all the other damn fuckers,' I state, the words more confident than my thoughts on the matter.

Hereman and Edmund have not spoken, and while we shelter

together, preparing to go to our assigned positions when the time is right, I move aside, giving them the privacy they need to reconcile.

I can see my warriors slinking through trees, and under low hanging branches, and to me, it seems impossible not to discover them. They're hardly dressed to blend in with the tree trunks. But, the enemy remains unaware. Sheltering within the woods has made them cocky fuckers. It'll be their death. But it works as a reminder that I never make the same mistake.

'Are we ready yet,' Edmund's voice almost trembles, and again, Hereman rolls his eyes, but with a thump to his brother's back. The two have clearly sorted out their temper with each other.

That pleases me more than it should.

'Just a few moments longer,' I hiss. I've caught sight of my warriors to the right of me, low and in position, weapons ready, shields resting on the ground. But to the left, the camp curves too tightly, and I've not yet spied whoever has the unfortunate task of reaching the further position.

Hereman meets my eyes.

'I like this tactic,' he rumbles. It's not often Hereman shares his true feelings with me.

'I don't,' I complain, but he smirks, his eyes flashing with the idea of the coming attack.

'It'll be good to be on the offensive,' he states, and then moves aside, keen to return to the place he's decided will give him the best angle to hit the campfire with.

'Well I'm fucking pleased he's happy,' I whisper, but Edmund hears me, and rarely for him before an attack, grins too.

'It's always best to keep the daft fucker happy,' Edmund assures me, reaching for my arm. We clasp forearms, and I feel him trembling but in control of himself. It'll take but the sound of iron slicing through flesh, and Edmund will be as keen as the rest of us to kill the enemy.

Eventually, I relent, the heat of Hereman's looks becoming too much for me to tolerate any longer.

'Do it you daft sod,' I hiss, and before the final word has left my lips, I can hear the spear flying through the air, the sound a soft hiss of deadly intent.

I reach for my seax, grimacing as I realise blood still covers the blade and stains the incised depiction of the double-headed eagle on the handle. I should have cleaned it. I'd berate my warriors for such an oversight. But there's no more time.

The spear hits the fire perfectly; a shower of sparks marking its arrival. Not one of the enemy notices. But I'm flying over the rough ground, and I can feel the rest of my men doing the same.

None of us is fleet-footed, they've proved that adequately already, but we act with a unity of purpose, and that is more important.

The first to notice the camp is under attack is a man sat by the fire, half-nodding in sleep as he rests against a tree stump. His yelp of surprise and warning is cut short when Hereman takes aim with another spear. I'd not realised that someone else had given him another to throw.

'Urgh,' I grimace, the spear transfixing the man as he tries to stand. It's a fitting tribute to Hereman's skills, as the body slowly begins to slide down the pole, leaving blood and torn flesh in its wake.

And still, the enemy hasn't realised the hunters are in the woods with them, not outside.

I determine on my first target, a man with his back to me, fiddling with harness or clothes or some such. I raise my seax, breathing heavily from running. At the last moment, the man turns, mouth open in shock, eyebrows almost reaching into his hairline, as I once more stab with the seax, aiming for the unprotected flesh that covers where his heart beats.

His death isn't instantaneous, a strangled cry issuing from his open mouth, and he's not alone. All of my men have chosen someone. As men caught pissing, or eating, or cleaning their weapons, become aware that they're under attack, their lives end on the end of a seax, the edge of a blade, or with the hack of a war axe.

But those outside the trees have finally realised what's happening, and they rush into the camp, weapons raised, murder on their faces and voices raised in incoherent fury.

They have no helms, and some don't wear byrnies, but their weapons are ready all the same. They carry anger and confusion, and we exploit it. As far from the treeline as I am, I'm aware of my other warriors taking their kills, while I wait for one of the faster-moving men to face me.

I lick my lips again, seax ready, shield poised to do its duty. I'm thirsty. I miss Rudolf's care for me.

The warrior who reaches me is of a slim build and fast. That's why his heavier comrades take longer to arrive than he does.

For all that, his face shows scars drooping down his left cheek, disappearing into his flimsy beard and I realise he's a survivor of battles. He carries a war axe, not a seax, and I raise my shield, ready to counter his attack. Only it doesn't come. Perplexed, I lower my shield a little, just enough that I can see, and almost shriek in surprise.

'Hereman,' I bellow.

'It seemed the quickest thing to do,' he retorts from behind me. He's probably right. Yet another spear has the man affixed to the ground, his mouth permanently open.

'That was my fucking kill,' I complain beneath my breath. Edmund is engaged with a warrior, and so is everyone else, but I have no one, not now Hereman has killed the man I was going to take.

With nothing else to occupy me, I stride amongst the small spots of fighting. All of my men are fighting well.

'Nice kill,' I call to Wærwulf, appreciative of the reverse blow he's used to knock the enemy to the ground, blood pooling quickly.

'Boss,' Wærwulf acknowledges, skipping around the dead man, and rushing to assist Eahric.

'Steady,' I bellow to Eadulf, noticing that his enemy has palmed a small knife into his free hand.

'I got this,' Eadulf grunts, and indeed, he has. I watch as yet another man surrenders to the ground. I turn then, my nostrils alert to the scent of burning hair, and watch Hereman kick his dead enemy clear of the fire, stamping on his body to extinguish the flames. The last thing the wood needs is to be burnt down.

I turn aside, watching yet more of the men, critically examining how they attack and parry. I don't often get to see them like this. I'm typically stood beside them, or they're practising, and not one of them ever fights as well as they could when they confront one of their friends.

'Watch out,' the cry is directed with no name, and I duck, all the same, feeling foolish when I realise it was intended for Eadberht and not me at all.

Eadberht ducks out of the way of a racing warrior, and I casually step into his path, offering an extended leg. The man goes down in a flurry of windmilling arms, and I bend to slice my seax across the back of his neck. The body judders and then stills, and I wish I'd killed him while he faced me.

I don't think I'll count that one.

The closer to the treeline I come, the more I'm aware that not everyone has run into the wood.

'Fuck,' I complain.

'Shield wall,' I bellow, and more than one startled glance comes my way.

'Bollocks,' Edmund is the first to realise what's happening. 'That must be Jarl Sigurd,' he states flatly.

'Let's hope he only has a handful of men with him,' but the thunder of hooves is clearly audible, and I know I'll not get my wish.

My warriors, heeding my words, rush from their individual combats when the opponent they face is dead. In no time the twenty-one of us stand side by side, shields down but in easy reach.

I glance up and down the line, seeing if everyone is well. I see a few with cuts and nasty looking impacts that will bruise or swell, provided we live beyond the third battle of the day.

'As one,' I shout the order, from my place not quite to the centre of the shield wall, and we walk firmly forward. There are still solitary trees to manoeuvre around, and we do so quickly. I'm not sure that

Jarl Sigurd has realised what's happened yet. Certainly, I hear no outraged cries from the fresh arrivals.

'Shields,' I bellow when we're beyond the last tree, and the shields lock into place, one into another, into another. Sweat beads my back, and stepping into the daylight is a new problem. We've been beneath the trees for so long, that we've become used to the dark. The stark sunlight is blinding in comparison. I raise my shield, and lower my eyes, for the time being seeing only horses hooves and men's feet.

Behind the shield wall, I take the time to re-orientate myself, and I imagine my men do the same.

Heated words fill the air, and I think Jarl Sigurd has probably seen us.

I see more and more feet in front of me, and then a force hits my shield.

'Hold,' I instruct my men, the cry echoed by Edmund and Hereman. I don't want to give them the chance to get organised, but I know nothing about the force I'm faced with, and so I choose caution over speed.

More Danish words are exchanged, heavily accented and hard to distinguish, and then I feel another impact against my shield. But it's not another shield that attacks me. The sudden weight makes my arm strain.

'Bastards,' I mutter. Someone has impaled my shield, rendering it almost useless. I'll not be able to keep hold of it, not with the added weight unbalancing it, and that makes me vulnerable, and I fucking hate being vulnerable.

I thrust the shield aside, keen to be done with it, and take my axe in my empty hand. In place of my shield, I must use my byrnie and my speed. I prepare to counter all attacks.

I can clearly see now. A swift reckoning tells me there are twenty-one men. Our forces are matched.

'Attack,' I roar, and we're moving forward, as the abandoned horses of the enemy rear and scream in horror. This new enemy hasn't yet thought to push them aside, and they will cause problems. For all of us.

Neither have they yet formed their shield wall. It's evident in the sudden shuffling of feet and the cursing that accompanies it. Or at least, I assume the angry words are cursing.

I can see everything clearly, although my focus is on avoiding the bucking horse in front of me. With a darting movement, I reach to slap the animal on the rump, avoiding the wild legs, and sending it on its way down the long line of men.

Before I can re-join my men, a warrior appears before me. He's encased almost entirely in blackened leather and iron. One quick glance tells me that this is perhaps Jarl Sigurd and he's come to fight me, man to man. I admire the thought. Not one of the war leaders I've so far encountered has thought of putting himself between his men and me.

His helm is heavily decorated with tempered iron. The impression of a dragon snakes down the right cheekpiece before wrapping its tail along the neck guard, where extra protection ensures I can't easily access his neck.

My enemy's shield is covered in the same image, the dragon turning to meet with glinting teeth that seem to drip blood. I arch an eyebrow, impressed despite my intentions not to be. Perhaps, when Jarl Sigurd is dead, I might have his helm and steal away his shield.

All I can see of the man is his blond moustache.

I raise my seax, not at all dismayed to find my opponent so well-armed.

Wealth will bring a man such excellent weapons, and that wealth need not come from battle spoils.

My war axe is loose in my arm, and I hear, although I don't turn to see, that the shield wall has closed around the space my departure has left.

'Fucker,' I drawl, considering the best place to try and land a strike.

The word means something to my enemy because he grins ever

wider. Heavily stained teeth warn me that if the fighting gets close, I'll have to combat his foul stench as well as his sword and shield.

The sword, like the shield and helm, is heavily decorated, and the pommel has a smaller image of the snarling dragon depicted on it. At least, that's what I assume it to be because I can't make out every detail, not with his gloved hand covering so much of it.

A sudden silence fills the air, the rest of the stray horses, finally finding what they consider to be a safe area. At the same time, both shield walls wait, no doubt to see what will happen between the two leaders.

I consider drawing the tension out further, making my enemy wait to launch an attack against me, but I'm fucking hungry, and I've really had enough of the day.

On light feet I aim for the shield, held in his left hand, with my seax, and only at the last moment, do I raise my elbow and swing the axe against the far edge of it, hoping to dislodge it.

My seax remains unused in my hand, and my opponent's shield wavers. Quickly, I raise my seax, keen to stab down, rather than slice, and aim at the uncovered right hand of my enemy.

The seax seems to slip over the thickness of his byrnie, rather than make an impact, and I have to step back quickly to avoid his sudden attack.

It begins with his shield, as he tries to thrust it at me. Without mine, to counter the move, I'm vulnerable. But, I realise, so is he. As the shield comes toward me, I again move on quick feet so that I can hack my axe behind the shield. I don't aim for my enemy, but instead for his shield.

It doesn't splinter, not straight away, but his grip slips with the unexpected movement, and while his sword impacts my byrnie, I hack with my axe once more. The top of the shield falls away, my opponent's hand holding the handle, but only half the wooden board remaining.

I grunt. The move took a great deal of strength, and now I'm unbalanced and heading toward where the other shield wall waits to attack my warriors. We've ended up turned around on each other, and I'm aware it would be easy for one of his warriors to drop his shield and attack me from behind.

I growl low in my throat. I like a good opponent, but I don't think he is one. He just looks the part.

I want to reverse our positions and quickly. While he's distracted with the fractured shield, I make a slicing attack on his right arm, keen to have him drop the sword as well. Only it seems to have no effect at all, and he's coming at me with the sword, and I have nothing but my war axe or my seax to prevent the blow from hitting me.

'Bastard,' I murmur beneath my breath, taking the time to decide which weapon is the best for the deflection. I can't risk losing either of them.

Only then I make a different decision.

As his sword impacts my byrnie, expelling the air from my mouth with the force of the thumping action, I stab down with my seax. We're close. Too close, and my seax makes a deep impact on his leather byrnie.

He's not as tall as me, I abruptly realise, as the seax rests against his chest, but doesn't quite reach his belly.

I'd hoped the action would draw blood, but it hasn't. I wrap my war axe around the back of his neck and bring him ever closer.

It's an action fraught with risk. Broken pieces of wood could impale an eye, or he might realise and use his sword to cut my belly open. But again, my enemy isn't expecting the action. With his head held close to my upper body, I use the pommel to stab down on the part of his arm that sends a strange sensation trickling down the arm.

The sword falls to the ground from suddenly lifeless fingers, and I'm sure I have the man and need only make the killing stroke as he struggles in my hold.

But his warriors feel differently.

The first I know is a sudden change in the atmosphere, not so much breathless anticipation but rather a thrum of denial.

And then two things happen at the same time.

'Beware,' Edmund's voice is the loudest I've ever heard it, but the sound is cut off almost midsentence by a heavy object falling.

I keep my enemy in front of me, a human shield rather than a wooden one. But the spear skewers the man lunging at me, his war axe already almost close enough to make an impact.

My shock at such a close call loosens my arm, and my enemy wriggles free as I look from Hereman to my enemy. Hereman doesn't quite grin, but there's a jauntiness about him that makes me want to belt the fucker in the eye right there and then.

'Another few inches,' I roar at him. 'Another few inches and I'd be fucking dead.'

'But you're not, are you, you ungrateful git,' Hereman retorts, already ducking back behind his shield. I languorously stretch out with my seax, and slice open my opponent's neck guard. It doesn't draw blood, but the man scampers back into his shield wall via the gap left by the transfixed warrior.

'Advance,' I call to my men, still fuming with Hereman but aware that he has probably saved me from an uncomfortable wound, if not death. All the same, I might kill the daft fucker myself. I can't believe he's taken such a chance.

While I silently fume, my shield wall envelops me once more, my quarry lost for the time being, and then the real fighting gets underway.

When the shield walls crash together, I'm in the second row, just waiting for an opportunity to kill someone, knowing I can't risk being at the front without a shield. Not while the shoving is taking place.

'Damn bastards.' I'm furious. I can't deny it. Their leader stepped forward, initiated hand-to-hand combat, and then when he was going to lose, another interfered. I might have admired Jarl Sigurd for taking the initiative, but I'm glad that Hereman killed the other man, or I'd have had no option but to hunt him down and kill him.

This battle shouldn't even be taking place.

But it is. Determined not to let my ill-temper get the better of me, I view the shield wall. From here, I can see nothing but backs, stretching away to either side. Every man has a shield, apart from me, and I'm the only one available to fill any gaps if one of my warriors should fall.

But it gives me more freedom than usual. Just like earlier, when I fought without my men, now I can consider other possibilities. And the one that calls to me is to mount one of the stray horses and ride through the enemy.

I grin, tasting my sweat and consider the possibility for all of five breaths.

'Fuck it,' I state, and then I'm running to where I remember the horses going. Down the line of my men to the right.

'Hold,' I order as I run, Edmund and Hereman repeating my words up and down the line, as they always do.

My warrior at the far end, Eoppa, has curved back on himself, just a little. It means an outcropping of tall trees acts as additional warriors for him, ensuring no one can come at him from behind. I step back into the woodland, manoeuvre my way around a handful of trees and then erupt to the other side of him.

I approve of the initiative Eoppa's taken. And then I see a flicker of black and know I've found the horses.

There are many of them, and they've not really gone far from the battle, but it must just be far enough for them to feel no fear.

From the edge, I can see the two shield walls easily, and I could just attack the rear of our enemy, for they've not taken the precautions that Eoppa has. But no. I decide the aid of a horse will make my endeavours quicker and more deadly.

With practised ease, I run hands over long noses, and along sleek backs, until I find a horse able to support my weight. The animal is brown, apart from where mud streaks the back legs, and there it appears almost black.

'Come on then,' I coax softly, trying not to focus on the increasing noise from the warring men. The horse whinnies softly, and I take it as an invitation to mount up. From his back, I can still see everything that's happening.

I don't like it. It seems as though the enemy men might actually be winning.

But enough of that. They tried their tricks on me, and I'll repay the favour.

With my seax in my left hand, I guide the horse amongst the other milling animals, and then, I kick him hard, hoping he'll leap to carry out my wishes, pleased when I feel his muscles bunch beneath me. We take off, almost too fast for me to strike the first of the warriors who face my men.

Only, I do manage to complete the movement. With satisfaction, my blade slices cleanly and deeply along the small area visible between the shoulders. The cut is just that, but immediately blood shows, only the horse has taken me on, to the next man, and the next. None of them is expecting an attack from the rear. Although gurgles of howling pain echo, their allies don't notice it, thinking it comes from where my warriors fight.

All along the rear of the shield wall, the horse carries me, and then, I turn him tightly and repeat the same action. Most of the men do still stand, but the shield wall is not as tightly held as it was, and with my next cuts, it fractures apart in confusion.

'Charge,' my men are swift to take advantage of the rupturing line of attack, and I turn the horse again, seeking out the man I almost killed before the real fighting began. From my vantage point, I spot him quickly and using my knees, direct my mount through the warring men.

The animal is more used to this than I expected, and in no time at all, I leap from his back and face the warrior with the dragon helm.

Hereberht has engaged him in battle, and when I appear, I think it'll be an unfair attack, two against one. Only then another two of the enemy join their jarl, and Hereberht and I are kept busy fending off swords and war axes. I hope it doesn't mean that one of my men has fallen. I don't want to lose another, not when we have more battles to fight after this one.

Hereberht works with his smaller war axe, and his shield, hammering into one of the enemy mouths. Blood erupts, and I can step in close, while the warrior's distracted, and slip my seax inside his byrnie, close to his armpit. The cut is deep and will be fatal when he realises.

Hereberht moves onto the next man, and I face Jarl Sigurd, my bloodied seax dripping menacingly.

At some point, the tie that binds the two sides of the chin guards has been sliced through. Despite his precautions, the jarl is as vulnerable as any other man.

I eye his neck keenly, as he prepares to attack with his sword. Neither of us has shields. We're equals, other than for my greater reach and his longer weapon, and the fact that I've already almost killed him. Something like that will weigh heavily on his mind, as I determine how to attack, and then just run at him.

His sword isn't pointed at me, but rather at the ground, and before he knows it, I'm close enough to lash out with my seax and take a swipe at his chin. The blade connects, although only just, and a flash of scarlet bubbles and drips immediately.

As he recoils, belatedly raising his sword, I follow up with my war axe, aiming for his shoulder, and hitting it, hard, although the leather holds.

His sword, without the room to move it in, is still far from attacking me, and so I jab with my seax, aiming for his throat. Predicting the attack, he's already moving away from me, and the strike does nothing more than rebound from his shoulder.

I can see, out of the corner of my eye, that Hereberht is closing on his warrior. I snarl with frustration. This warrior is no match for me and should be dead already. Certainly, many of his men have fallen beneath the blows of my warriors. I just need to kill him, and before Hereman can finish the job he started with his almost too close spear throw.

'Come on, you fucker, just die,' I breathe, and then I see his weakness. Not the exposed chin, but rather his need to fight only with the right side of his body. Even without his shield, he's not claimed another weapon for his left hand, leaving it empty.

Almost skipping closer and closer, I swing both of my weapons, making it impossible for him to know where to point his sword to best protect himself. He makes a movement to cover the left side of his body with his sword from my seax. I haul my axe back, preparing to finally slice through more than just leather and the first layer of skin. My axe hits home, on the left side of his body, and I force it ever deeper, relishing the flow of his hot blood over my hands.

I can smell it. I can fucking taste it.

But he's not done yet, and his hand scrabbles around my bloody one, his gloved fingers trying to fight me off. His sword hand struggles to manoeuvre it into position so that he can stab me with his dying breath.

But I can see what he's trying to do. I work my hand free from his slick grip and leaving my war axe in his neck, step out of his reach. He totters there, for a long moment, his eyes seeking me out, as though to ensure he knows who kills him. Only then does his sword drop to the ground, and this time, he follows it.

I'm heaving great gasps of air into my body, aware that the fighting is almost all over.

'Tricky bastard,' Edmund comes to stand beside me, gazing at the body thoughtfully.

'Aye, he was,' I confirm, about all I can manage as I recover my breath.

'What took you so fucking long?' Hereman bellows from where he stands over three dead bodies, one folded on top of another, as though he felled them to make a pattern like I've seen on ancient Roman floor tiles.

'You nearly fucking killed me,' I bellow, turning to stride toward him. Hereman's grin falters, and then it returns, just as cocky as ever.

'I knew you'd get out of the way. I'm not quite as bloody stupid as all that.' The final words die away to normal speaking volume, as I abruptly rear up before him.

'Then, thank you. For only nearly killing me,' I all but shout.

Hereman grins, even wider, even more delighted.

'You are most welcome,' and he inclines his head, as though addressing his king, and I thwack him on the arm.

'Daft bastard.' I turn to survey the scene of death and destruction, only then noticing that to the far side, the battle isn't yet over.

Not only is it not over, but three of my men are outnumbered, and two are lying on the floor.

'Fuck,' I exclaim, pointing, and everyone looks to see Eoppa, Osbert and Hereberht fighting on while Lyfing and Ordheah are on the ground. I can't see their wounds from here, but they must be severe if neither of the men is standing.

Oda, Wulfred, Beornstan and Ælfgar are closest, and with their enemy dead, they rush to aid their allies. I watch, trying to decide whether I need to interfere as well or not. In no time, Oda has used his seax to cut the throat of one of the enemy. In contrast, Wulfred has gone for the more confrontational approach of thumping the man's back so that he turns to face him, weapon raised. Distracted in such a way, Osbert stabs down into the man's back, and he falls to the floor without Wulfred doing anything else.

Hereberht and Beornstan work together then, to tire the remaining warrior, and sure that they'll kill him, eventually, I rush to Lyfing and Ordheah. Lyfing has a long leg wound that I'm sure will heal if only the bleeding will stop. His face is pale and lifeless, and I have to slap him to get him to look at me.

Ordheah has taken a wound to his stomach, and it looks deep, but also not long. It might heal.

I look around, Edmund and Hereman with me, as I try and decide what to do for the best. Help comes from an unexpected source.

'Put this in the wound,' Eowa states, waving a large piece of moss at me.

'My thanks,' I snatch the moss, rip it in half, and passing half to Ordheah, bend to cover Lyfing's wound with it. He moans at the touch.

'You'll be fine,' I tell him gruffly, not at all sure he will be.

'Bring him into the woods,' Eowa insists. 'I can help with the wounds.' I'm not sure he can, but all I know to do is to keep the wounds clean and free from infection. I have nothing to bind either wound with, other than dirty linen and I know that won't do. All of my supplies of herbs are back with Haden.

'Carry them,' I instruct. 'But four of you stay here, gather up the horses and watch for any other Raiders.' Hereman immediately takes that command, and calling Eahric, Wulfstan and Ælfgar to him, begins to issue his own instructions.

I help carry Lyfing back under the trees, grateful when the canopy above our heads disrupts the heat from the sun.

Eowa has made his way to the remains of the fire, and now he adds small pieces of wood and more moss to make it flame brighter and hotter. The Raiders had a temporary arrangement to hold a pot over the fire. Eowa discards it, and simply places the container into the flames, not seeming to heed the reaching yellow flickers that try to make the transition from wood to flesh.

Ordheah is laid beside Lyfing. Ordheah is groaning in pain, his face flushed, rather than white, and I bend to smell his wound. It doesn't stink.

'It might have somehow missed all the vital bits,' I confirm, and he nods, his hand bloody from holding the moss in place.

Eowa is busy, skipping around the outskirts of the cleared camp, picking up small green shoots, and then sniffing them. Some he keeps, some he discards, and then he thrusts them all into the pot, with a sniff of satisfaction. Then he stands again and goes hunting under rocks for more of the moss he's found.

I watch him, fascinated, the exertions of my day finally being felt. I almost fear to even blink in case my eyes close and never open again.

I can hear my men about the work of clearing the corpses and burying them, and I know I should help, but equally appreciate that I'm too exhausted. I'm hungry and thirsty, and I wish Haden were intelligent enough to come and find me with the supplies he carries.

Ordheah continues to groan and grumble, unhappy with his wound, but it's Lyfing that concerns me, for he's fallen back into a slumber.

'This,' Eowa flourishes a beaker in front of my eyes, and I realise that I've fallen asleep, sitting upright.

'For Lyfing or Ordheah,' I point as I speak, trying to focus on them both. Lyfing sleeps, but his colour seems to have been restored, and

Ordheah is also silent, his chest rising and forward in sleep. I notice then that both wounds have been dressed and packed with moss and strips of a torn tunic.

'How long was I asleep?' I ask no one.

'For you,' Eowa insists, and I take the beaker and sniff it suspiciously, only then realising that Edmund is also a member of our small party. He grins at me.

'It's fine. It'll make you feel better.'

I swig the warm mixture quickly enough that I can't taste it, but immediately I feel more alert, and my aching body seems much more fluid.

'Eowa has been treating our wounded. The dead are buried, their treasures taken and now we have a shit load of horses once more.'

I chuckle at Edmund's aggrieved tone.

'My thanks,' I bow to Eowa, and he grins, before scampering away to search a grassy expanse at the base of another tree.

'A strange creature,' Edmund comments. 'But skilled.'

I don't reply. There doesn't seem to be any need when I agree so wholeheartedly.

'I've sent Eadulf and Eahric to get our horses. They've ridden around the outskirts of the wood. I think they'll be fine, although Haden will be difficult, as usual.'

'He will, contrary bastard.'

'What were you thinking this morning?' Edmund asks, as though my words remind him of earlier events.

'I was just trying something different.'

'Well, don't do it again. The men need you to lead them. I've no interest in it, and Hereman has proven that he always acts without thought.'

I shrug away the comment, trying not to hear the fear that underlies Edmund's words.

'What now?' he asks, indicating the encampment, and the two sleeping men. They're not alone either. Eadulf and Eahric might have gone to get the horses, but other than the four that guard the treeline, almost everyone else is slumped in sleep.

My stomach rumbles loudly, and I look at Edmund, and he looks at me. And we laugh.

'I need to fucking eat,' I complain, standing and stretching my back.

'After that, well, we'll bloody well see, won't we?'

16

My concerns are mostly with Lyfing and Ordheah. I don't want to ride on with either of them, but neither can I send them back. Not with their wounds. It bedevils me as soon as my stomach is full, and I've mingled with the rest of my warriors, ensuring all are well.

There are, as I thought, cuts and bruises forming, and somehow, Eoppa has managed to get his helm wedged so tightly onto his head, that in the end, there's no choice but to slather the side of his head in the oil that's leaked from the fish taken from the river for another meal, and slip the helm free.

It comes away with a strange 'popping' noise, and Eoppa winces and then rubs his head.

'Bastard thing,' he complains, as we all examine his helm carefully.

'What hit you?' I ask, noticing how dented it is on the back of the helm. It makes no sense to me. It looks as though one of my warriors hit him.

'A bloody tree branch,' Eoppa offers ruefully. 'I walked into it, and it did that to me.'

'I hope you chopped it down,' Edmund laughs, and I'd join in, but my hands stink of fish and I'm desperate for something to rub them on.

'Fuck it,' I eventually complain when not even long grasses have rubbed the stink clear. 'I'm going to the stream.' It's only just out of sight of the camp, but I'm cautious all the same, Haden nudging me along. He's been a shit since he was retrieved from the other campsite.

'I know, I know,' I complain loudly. 'I've apologised. Can't we leave it at that.' I don't much mind that I'm speaking to my horse. Our conversation benefits from the fact he can't reply to me, other than by nipping my ear, or stamping on my foot, or generally being a total arsehole. He's opted for the last option, and now he shoves me with his nose, and refuses to go where I want to.

As I'm bending over, swirling my hands clean in the clear, but cold water, he nudges me, and I overbalance, landing almost face first in the water. I splutter, the cold permeating inside my byrnie immediately, and making me wish it were too hot, as opposed to too cold, I swear I hear him laughing at me.

'You damn fucker,' I complain, still standing, knee deep in the pool of water, determined not to give him another opportunity to dunk me.

Only then does he bend his neck, and lower himself so that he can drink deeply, and only as he does so, do I lift my hands clear from the water, liberally covering him with the water I dislodge.

His whinny of complaint brings a smile to my face as I stamp clear.

'Two can play, you know,' I laugh, resting my wet body against him. He stills, lowering his neck to drink once more. I could get used to such moments, but not while the Raiders still stalk me, and worse, have control of Repton.

The arrival of Jarl Sigurd, dead now of course, has me considering what the Raiders know about me. Do they know that my warriors and I have almost single-handedly killed every warrior they've sent to track me down? Or was Jarl Sigurd's arrival for a different reason.

By now, Icel might well have reached Repton, but sure as shit, there hasn't been enough time to send a fresh warband to hunt me down. If there had, I'm sure that Goda, if not Icel as well, would have escaped to let me know. I can't imagine we're difficult to hunt down, not anymore. Just follow the trail of burial mounds.

Disgruntled with my thinking, I lead Haden back the way we've come. I'm still dripping wet, and need to change, but the heat of the fire would make it easier for me. Movement in the woods has me reaching for my seax, sopping wet and slick in my hand, before I hear Edmund speaking to someone. There's no fear in his voice, and I deduce that one of my allies has finally decided to join us.

I'm not disappointed as I trudge into the campsite that's become our own now that the dead bodies have been buried, and find Ealdorman Ælhun. He turns to greet me, and then a smile touches his cheeks.

'I always thought you had to take your clothes off to have a wash,' he offers, and I wave my hand as though to disrupt his thoughts.

'Bloody horse,' I complain, as I slap Haden's rump and he meanders away to join the rest of the herd. It's quite large by now, but I'm aware that the horses my men and I ride, are not too keen on all the new arrivals.

'More enemy?' Ealdorman Ælhun states, a grimace on his face.

'They seem to be everywhere,' I confirm. 'I'm hoping I can make the rest of the journey without being interrupted, but it remains to be seen.'

'I've brought my warriors, and sent word that the rest should join us as soon as they can. I told them to follow the Foss Way and then take Watling Street west, if they don't find us first.'

'My thanks,' I incline my head.

'What will you do with your injured? They can't ride.'

'I know. I've a mind to leave them here, and collect them on my return. Lyfing can't ride, not without the risk of opening his wound again.'

'I'm sure the forest dwellers will care for them. The lad is already doing a good job.'

This stirs my interest. 'You know of them then?'

'Some of them. They keep to themselves most of the time. Sometimes they might make an appearance on a market day, but not often. They mean no harm, and so I'm content to allow them their obscurity.'

We've settled close to the fire, and I can feel the heat starting to dry my clothes out. Perhaps I won't have to change after all.

'Is there any news from Repton?'

'Nothing.'

I fall silent, my thoughts busy.

Perhaps, I consider, I shouldn't have sent Icel and Goda to Repton. Maybe they don't know I'm coming. But then I think of Jarl Sigurd. Maybe they do.

'We'll rest here overnight, and then tomorrow, I plan on scouting Watling Street toward Tamworth. I'm curious as to whether or not there are Raiders patrolling there. I can't quite work out how they made their way to Gloucester.'

Ealdorman Ælhun nods, as though in agreement, but he's here as my sworn man. While I'll listen to his arguments, the ultimate decision must be mine to make, or no one will have ultimate control of the men that Mercia sends to counter the Raiders.

'Your man told me about Ealdorman Wulfstan. It doesn't surprise me, although perhaps I'm being harsh. After all, Torksey was overrun last year. It makes sense that he might have divided loyalties.'

'Perhaps,' is all I'm prepared to concede. Would I, in the same situation, act as he did? I bloody hope not. I hope I'd be fucking dead.

Our conversation falls away then, my thoughts on what must be accomplished. For the first time, and despite my dismissive attitude to Edmund's questions, I consider the impossibility of what I'm trying to do. Not that I'm not going to do it. Far from that. But there is a distinct chance that when we make it to Repton, we will be overwhelmed.

How, I consider, can I stop that from happening?

. . .

I've been to Repton on numerous occasions. It's the ancient capital of Mercia. It housed the bones of many long dead kings and queens. I'm not convinced it still will.

I've never seen it like this.

The pale of grey in the distance that I interpreted as a rain cloud, is nothing of the sort, but rather the smoke from hundreds of cook fires.

The leaders of the Raiders sent three hundred warriors to track me down.

Those three hundred are dead, a few more as well.

I doubt they'll be missed, not with the horde that remains in Repton. I can see why they were content to squander so many on their fruitless task.

Even from this distance, I think I can hear them.

It feels as though I should be able to hear them.

'Fuck me,' Edmund's appreciative comment speaks for my men and I. I turn in the saddle, taking solace from the numbers who ride behind me. I might not have the same numbers as the enemy but I do have the reputation. That's what truly matters.

And a reputation that stems from having fought and killed many, many men, and never suffered a single injury in return.

'Look at them. Like a stain on the river.' I follow where Edmund points. I've been assuming that the Raiders rode to Repton. It seems I might have been wrong. Or, if not, then they've received no end of reinforcements who have arrived by ship.

The sails are a stunning array of colours. I can't see the designs in detail from here, but I can easily see that every shade is represented.

'How many of them did you say there were?' Edmund directs his comment at Icel.

'I said there were at least two thousand of them,' Icel's tone is ripe with annoyance. We've been arguing about the number, even though I fully expected to meet two thousand seven hundred based on my calculations.

'How many do we have?' Edmund joins me in looking over his

shoulder at the mass of men and boys behind us, out of sight of Repton.

'Four hundred and ninety three.'

'Four to one then, easy enough.'

Edmund, always slow to want to start a fight, seems keen for once. I note that but don't make reference to it, instead trying not to smirk at his instant dismissal of such huge numbers.

'If we fight,' I lace my words with calmness.

I've got my band of warriors, and also many warriors pledged to me from the lords of western Mercia who've elected me as their king, in my absence, and having turned me down first, now that King Burgred has buggered off.

Ideally, I want a pitched battle against the Raiders, but Icel, having returned to me from Repton, has already warned me it might not be possible.

I don't want to make a treaty with them. But neither do I want to lose a single warrior on the edge of one of their blades. We have few enough as it is, and this is our fucking kingdom.

'The fortification uses the church,' Icel repeats the information he's already shared with me when he came upon my enlarged force not far from Tamworth. This time satisfaction fills his voice at finally being able to prove that he speaks the truth. I've doubted him. I won't deny it.

'And the river as well. They're dug in like rats.' Without seeing it for myself, I've not been able to visualise what Icel meant when he returned from scouting Repton. Suddenly, it makes far more sense.

'The church is at the front, there's an earthen wall to either side, with a ditch, and it goes all the way to the river, at the back. The river's rather full.' Icel makes the last statement slowly, rolling the words around his mouth, as though we're unlikely to understand the importance of the statement.

'So you're saying we can't take the horses across the river then from the west?'

'Even if you could, there's nowhere for them to land inside the structure. The riverbank side is just as well guarded, only without the ditch and earthen bank. They don't need one there. Clever bastards.' The respect in Icel's voice doesn't surprise me. Not now I can see what they've done for myself.

'But they're still stuck in there,' Edmund's voice is equally valid, as he points out that while they might have built a fortification, to use it, they need to allow thousands of men inside. I don't see how it can be possible. Some will have to be sacrificed by their leaders, and that never goes down well with men who are still expected to risk their lives.

'They ride out, under heavy guard, to hunt and menace the poor fuckers who are still alive in Repton and the surrounding area.'

Icel speaks of the monks. There were nuns as well. There aren't anymore. Evil bastards, to do that to women who've dedicated their lives to God. Even Edmund has been filled with condemnation, and he's not always good at determining when a refusal is a refusal. They're so rare for him that it comes as a shock. Luckily, Hereman and I have always been there to hold him back.

'But what do they mean to do now?' This has been my main demand from everyone. The Raiders sent three hundred warriors to kill me, but other than that, and the attack on Repton itself, they've not moved from their temporary fort.

'Daft sods probably didn't expect King Burgred to agree to their demands in the first place.'

'Then why make him leave? It's not as though they've not reached agreements in the past.'

'They just mean to wait there, long enough that you get fucked off and attack them.' Edmund's comment is delivered flat, and I swivel my head to meet his gaze.

'You could have just told me to shut the fuck up?' I complain, not prepared to say anything more. I could argue with him. I could shout at him. I could tell him he's a damn waste of space. It won't enable him to answer my question.

'Could we attack them?' I direct the question at Icel. He shrugs his shoulders.

'Of course we could, but I doubt we'd live to see the next day.'

'So we can't then,' I retort. He shakes his head, a tight smile pulling at his lips.

'Why should we attack them when they're not doing anything?' I grunt. Icel makes a good point.

'The only people that I've seen leave the fort are those I mentioned. Other than that, the last people to ride out seem to be those who were sent to capture you. They're waiting for you before they do anything.'

I sigh heavily, running my gloved hand through my hair, and then patting Haden's shoulder, more to comfort me, than him.

I still don't know what to do.

They came for me, prepared to take me alive, only for it to become a killing spree, on my part, not theirs. Why do they want me?

'King Burgred has given your name as their greatest threat.' I can't deny that logic. And neither can I argue that I'm unimportant. I need only turn and see the warriors who ride with me now. They all owe pledges to their lords, and those lords have pledged themselves to me. That pledge is for me to rule over them, as their king. It's not even dependent on me beating back the Raiders. Bishop Wærferth wanted all contingencies covered.

Admittedly it'll help if I do. But it's not imperative.

They'll follow my lead. If I decide to attack the Raiders, their warriors will support me.

In all honesty, I know I'll struggle more if I don't attack them.

'And this Lord Anwend wasn't too keen on receiving his son and then retreating?'

'No,' there's a whole word behind that one word, but I'm not going to ask. Icel is back with me. That's enough. For now. Goda isn't. That worries me.

Into the silence, I muse about my position.

'How many warriors do I have?'

It's not Icel who knows this, but rather Edmund. He's good at keeping count, and has a far better memory for numbers than I do. I feel as though he's been counting ever since we left Gloucester for the first time.

'Four hundred and ninety.'

The number sounds huge. But it isn't.

'Only twenty of those are your actual, blood sworn warriors.' Edmund's lower lip turns as he speaks, but for once, he refrains from further comment. We all know, far too well, just what Edmund thinks of my current position.

It's not jealousy that makes him so unhappy. But fear.

I understand that fear.

It's not of death, but of losing what we've always had in the past.

I wasn't meant to be a king, and yet in lieu of anyone else having the damn balls to save Mercia, I find myself in that position.

'Tell me again who sent how many.'

Edmund's sigh is audible, but I ignore it.

'Bishop Wærferth, the first man to suggest you seek the support of others, offered you sixty of his retainers, only thirty three of which can actually fight.'

My glare of annoyance forces Edmund to his next emission.

'Could fight, could fight. Now all the damn fuckers know which end of a seax is which.'

'Bishop Eadberht, keen to emulate Bishop Wærferth, offered you the same advice, and sent thirty five warriors. All good warriors, I hasten to add.'

'Ealdorman Ælhun sent the most, nearly ninety, but to be precise, eighty-seven.'

'Ealdorman Æthelwold sent the least, only twenty-six.'

'But all good warriors,' I prompt.

'All excellent warriors and with equipment that makes me jealous.' The candid admission, brings a smirk to my lips.

'Ealdorman Alhferht sent seventy-two. Some of them okay, some of them not so good.'

'But they can all ride well.'

'Yes, they're good with horses.' Again, a sour admission.

'And what of Bishop Deorlaf.'

'He sent fifty-four.' When there's no other comment about their worth, I turn to arch an eyebrow at Edmund.

'All passably skilled, and I would be honoured to stand in a shield wall with them.'

'You do them a fine honour,' Icel comments, sardonically. Edmund ignores him.

'Ealdorman Beorhtnoth sent eighty-six. He was pissed he couldn't find another two to outmatch Ealdorman Ælhun.'

Edmund lapses into silence with his narration complete.

'I don't think that quite makes four hundred and ninety,' I prod. Edmund's sigh is heartfelt as he reflects on who else has joined our venture.

He's not happy about it.

But it's not up to him.

'The Gwent Welsh sent fifty.' Disgust fills Edmund's voice.

'We shouldn't ally with our enemies to fight our other enemies.' This isn't a new complaint, and Edmund is far from alone in being uneasy.

'No, we probably shouldn't. But we can't have two enemies. Not at the moment.' I speak with the fierce resolve I feel. I've never considered allying with the damn Welsh before, but I can't watch the east and the west. And I'd far rather have a Welsh ally than a Raider one. At least I can trust the Welsh to be deceitful fuckers.

'So are we fighting them, or not?'

This is the question, and despite Icel's observations, I'm still unsure, and I hate being unsure about anything.

'Maybe,' I muse. I've become king. I'd sooner not make the decision about such an enterprise though.

I have four hundred and ninety men at my command. If those men are lost in a battle against the Raiders, who will replace them and continue to keep Mercia safe?

I can't make a decision based on my personal desire for revenge. There's too much at stake.

Edmund's huff of annoyance almost makes me smile, but instead I grimace, showing him my teeth, and also beckoning him closer.

Icel, Edmund and I peer at the encampment from our place of concealment. I wish I could see inside the St Wystan's church that the

Raiders have taken command of. I wish I could determine how many ships were hovering just out of sight.

But I can't and I don't, and I must make a decision or we'll lose the element of surprise we currently have. Jarl Anwend doesn't think I'll attack Repton, not even after Icel's arrival with his son. They still believe one of the war bands will hunt me down and bring me here, to make my pledges of allegiance. Until their continued absence stretches too long, they'll wait. But it means my choices are time limited.

'We fight,' I decide, and when neither man argues with me, I know I've made the decision they expect me to make. And in honesty, I've made the decision I want to make.

I'll kill them all. The damn fuckers.

As we scurry out of sight, back to where my remaining warriors wait for me, I realise that I might have to make some sort of speech to justify my decision. Only then I don't have to.

'Look,' it's Edmund who draws my attention to the warriors who've ridden here with me, but my eye peers further back, to where Edmund truly points, his far-sight serving him well once more.

'Fuck,' I complain. I purposefully left those men behind, because they were all too ill to fight. It seems they've taken the decision from me, and I know I won't be able to send them away, not now they've come so far.

I expect an acerbic comment from Edmund, a counterpart to his on-going worry. His response puzzles me.

'Fucking clever bastards,' he mutters, laughing loudly as he continues to point.

I can't see well enough to know what causes the amusement, and when Icel's chest also starts to growl with laughter, I feel my temper beginning to build.

'Look,' Icel unhelpfully points as well, as Pybba and Rudolf make slow progress toward us.

'What have they got with them?'

A cart, pulled by an ox, is not usual when riding to war.

'You'll see,' Edmund chortles, and now I've had enough.

'Fucking pricks,' I grumble, striding toward Pybba and Rudolf. They might not think they make a fool of me, but I think they do, all the same.

I can't see, from my position, what's in the cart and I just hope the daft fuckers haven't brought the remainder of my injured men with them.

The sound of Edmund and Icel's laughter follows me and continues to grate. More and more of my warriors are turning to watch the strange procession, and on the faces of everyone, slow comprehension dawns, apart from mine.

'My Lord,' Pybba bows from his saddle, Rudolf grinning at me, more like the youth he was before I left Gloucester, than the young warrior he's been training to become. Even in the time we've been apart, I can see how his build has filled out. I imagine he can help Pybba much more now than previously.

'What the fuck are you doing here?' I demand to know, already walking around the side of the cart to see what the ox has brought me, fearful of seeing my other injured men, and perplexed when I don't see that.

Instead, heaped on with no regard for the skill and expertise that's gone into making the weapons and battle equipment, is everything that we've so far taken from the dead enemy, or at least I hope it is.

It gleams in the bright sunlight, and I can see why others were able to see it so much more clearly than I could.

'What the fuck?' I mutter, striding back to face Pybba and Rudolf. They're both smirking, and I consider a sharp swipe to wipe the good cheer from their face.

'We decided that this would be your only option, when all things were considered.'

'What would be my only option?' I still don't understand what this is about.

'To get inside,' Pybba says slowly, resolve thrumming through his words.

'Get inside what?'

'The fucking church compound,' Rudolf interjects, his smile wavering for just a moment, as though he can't believe my stupidity.

'What, you want me to give their equipment back to them?'

'No, we're going to wear it, and lead you inside as though you've been captured.'

I confess, my jaw drops open at the suggestion. I look from Pybba to Rudolf and then back again, but they're both nodding. Surely they're joking.

'You want to pretend to be Danish, or Norwegian, or whatever, and ride in there, with me as your prisoner?'

'We do yes,' Rudolf nods vigorously, while I turn to meet the amused eyes of Edmund and Icel.

'Have you fucking heard this bollocks?' I demand of them. Their silence assures me that they have. The fact that they're not vehemently decrying it worries me a great deal.

'You think this shit is a good idea?' I change tact, hoping someone else will voice incredulity for the ludicrousness of the suggestion.

'I think it's probably our only chance,' Edmund admits, his voice thrumming with laughter. He's enjoying this far more than he should.

'It has a great deal of merit to it,' Icel also agrees more slowly. 'It's not as though we can launch a full frontal assault, or even one from the rear. They've chosen a clever place to make their stand.'

'So you think we should willingly go inside?'

'We'll have weapons, and be well armoured, albeit with Danish iron and leather. They'll not even consider that we're not who we say we are, not with you bound and gagged as our prisoner.'

'So I must give them what they want? And do it without armour or weapons?'

'We can conceal a few about you, don't worry about that.'

'And how, exactly, would you plan on taking over the enclosure. There are many of them, and we would be few, and surrounded?'

'We'd have our allies outside waiting to get inside.'

I lapse into silence. I can think of so many ways that this could all go wrong that I can hardly order them into what aspect concerns me the most.

But, and I hate to admit it, it is the only reasonable plan that's been conceived to date. I might want to complain about being used as a sacrificial lamb, but I won't be alone, and it would ensure we were inside the fort before battle started.

'I don't like it,' I admit slowly, 'but it doesn't mean it's without merit.'

'I told you he'd go for it,' Rudolf's voice is rich with satisfaction.

'Did you think of this?' I demand to know, not sure if I'm angrier with Rudolf for thinking it is a good idea, or because he did think of the plan.

'Well, with some help from Bishop Wærferth.'

'Fuck,' I complain. 'No doubt he had some sort of biblical precedent.'

Rudolf's infuriating grin spreads even wider.

Only then does Sæbald step forward, a little unsteady, but walking all the same.

I watch him.

'You shouldn't have fucking come, look at you.'

Rudolf laughs again, but before he can offer another 'I told you so,' I walk to Sæbald and embrace him. It's good to see him, even if he shouldn't be here.

'Bishop Wærferth is keen for you to return to Worcester when all this is done,' Sæbald offers, with no trace of humour on his face.

'When what? When I've defeated the Raiders by pretending they've already captured me?' My anger has been sparked once more, and it only solidifies as I catch Sæbald smirking at Rudolf and Pybba.

Damn fuckers.

Too angry to speak, I stride from them, aware that they all watch me stalk away.

I can't believe it.

No really, I can't.

It's the most ridiculous, dangerous and outrageous idea I've ever heard.

I'm not one for great subtlety. Coming via the back route from Gloucester was about as devious as I get.

And yet there is something that I can't deny.

It is, undoubtedly, a fucking good idea.

Who would suspect us?

Not the Raiders, of that I'm sure.

Still, I walk and I think, trying to find another solution to the problem, desperate to in all honesty.

I don't want to lead my warriors into Repton as a prisoner. I don't want them to take such massive risks, because sure as day follows night, we won't all live through this. How can we?

But, I reconsider, is it really any different than the straight out attack I'd been planning? Is it any deadlier? Are we any more likely to die? I don't see how we can be.

I stalk back to my warriors. They are all haphazardly trying on the gear that Rudolf and Pybba have brought with them, pillaged from the scenes of destruction we've already left in our wake. It seems my warriors know I'll agree to it, even if I don't want to.

'Right, lads, let's get ready to infiltrate these fuckers and send them to their hell.'

17

My hands are bound too tightly. I've told the fuckers that, but they've ignored every word I've said since my capture.

My wrists, I know, are red-raw from trying to work my hands loose. The bastard who tied me up did far too good a job. And they enjoyed it too fucking much. I might never forgive the cock for this.

And yet I'm tied to the horse more by luck than any great skill. It seems they don't mind if I fall off, as long as my damn hands don't come untied.

It's about how it looks, I know that, and yet I'm furious all the same.

Ahead, the settlement of Repton is coming into view far too quickly for my liking. Not that I like any of this. That emotion couldn't be further from what I'm experiencing right now.

Inside my trews, my legs are slick from trying to grip the damn horse. And it's not even a bad horse. Still, without my hands on the rein, I can only use my knees, and the horse seems particularly stubborn about taking such half-hearted commands. I miss Haden's steady presence, but I didn't want to risk him.

I'd use my boots, but they've been taken from me, and my heels lack the impact they need.

The warriors who escort me are dour-faced and sheeted in their battle gear, complete with helms, and weapons close to hand.

I've tired myself out trying to talk to change their minds, and now I await my fate. I hope it won't be long in coming.

In the far distance, I can see the sails on the ships as they bob in the deep river the Raiders have used to infiltrate to the heart of Mercia. They flash in all shades of colour, from bleached white to vibrant red. I can't make out any decoration, but I'm sure that at least one of them must have the one-eyed raven of Jarl Anwend on it.

They're a stark reminder that the four men I'm about to face are allies by chance.

If only I can exploit that.

Beneath me, the horse stumbles, and a cry rips from my throat, fearing I'll fall and land head first on the hard-packed earth we travel over.

The summer has been hot, the threat of drought a persistent problem, although so far the crops have survived, and the people will be fed come the winter. I'm not sure that I'll be there to see it.

I angrily shake off a hand on my shoulder, righting me, aware that the fingers bite too deep.

Hard green eyes greet mine, and I decline to offer any thanks, even a muffled one. I refuse to even think it.

I do not like this. Not at fucking all.

I hope I won't soon become one of the Mercian royal dead housed within the church of St Wystan's.

It's not a huge settlement, but at the moment it stretches long beyond the bespattering of defences, crammed with Raiders and their makeshift canvas homes. There are thousands of them, and the jeering has only just begun to reach my ears.

The four jarls sent three hundred and more men to bring me to Repton. It was supposed to be a peaceful endeavour, but I ensured it was none of those things.

Now they bring me, bound and gagged, my tongue stuck to the

linen rag in my mouth, and if I could, I'd kill the fucking lot of them if only I had access to my seax.

My escort raises their heads at the murmur of noise. They're still helmed in iron, scrubbed black to look even more menacing, and with leather encasing almost all of their bodies. Only a flicker of flesh shows here and there, and mostly where chinstraps hold helms in place. They look fearful but take the acclaim as their due.

The fuckers.

A hand reaches over and grips the harness of my horse. I refuse to meet the green eyes that belong to the hand. I do prepare for my horse to come to a halt at the barricade that blocks the entrance to the interior of Repton.

Smoke erupts from many fires behind us, but inside Repton, only three tendrils of grey smoke drift toward the sky, one from the monastery building, one from St Wystan's, and I would suspect the third from a forge, no doubt inside the more superior defensive structure in front of me. I'll call it a fort. It's too complicated to think of it in any other way.

'Jarl Sigurd,' the voice sounds Danish, but I understand it all the same. I've been listening to the Raiders for almost all of my adult life. 'I see you've found him. The other jarls were becoming concerned.' I don't hear the rest of the conversation, my eyes raking in the scene in Repton itself.

Few people are walking about, but it's early, daybreak a myriad selection of oranges and mauves on the distant horizon behind me. I stare into the darkness of the day not yet touched by the sun, and I don't like what I see. Not at all.

My heart pounds in my chest, my breath coming shallow around the rag in my mouth. I wish it hadn't been needed. I feel my head pounding, my breath growing ragged, and then my horse lurches forward and once more, a hand reaches to hold me in the saddle. Fuckers.

Maybe I would rather fall here, splinter my head on the well-trodden ground and never know anything ever again.

But I'm not given the option, and then I'm through the barricade of tree trunks, barrels and carts, watched over by sleepy men, and being forced from my horse by eager hands, their breath too hot on my face.

I wince at the touch on my tied hands. My eyes bulge, and I start to choke.

In one swift movement, the rag is ripped from my mouth, and liberal water poured into my parched mouth. I swallow with the hunger of a starving man, beckoning for more, dismayed when the rag is once more thrust into place, and I'm being led to the next barricade.

This one includes the ancient church of St Wystan's, beneath which the royal families of Mercia have buried their dead. More warriors stand guard here, similar to those who escort me. They don't have helms, and I can clearly see eyes, moustaches, beards and the inkings that mark them as Raiders.

I don't need to see the iron around their waists, or their scars to know that these men are survivors.

Fucking bastards.

There are more derisive cries from them as they scamper to open the wooden door that allows me inside the most heavily protected area of the compound. There'll be no escape once I'm inside, and I struggle against my bonds again, uncaring of the fact that blood drips down my fingers, and that each movement is agony.

Two hands on my shoulder force me through the door, my feet walking over the rough terrain before finding the smoothness of well-worn stone. Fucking cold stone as well.

I shiver, the hands lingering on my shoulders for too long. I think to shake them off, but what's the point?

The interior of the church is dark and only a handful of fat, stinking candles blaze where the altar stands. There are no priests and no monks. I bow my head, mourning their loss.

All of my escort crowd into the church. I'm pushed deeper and deeper inside, blinking to try and acclimatise my eyes to the half-dark. The scratch of leather boots on the stone almost makes me wince, as does the vast quantity of weaponry on show, in a holy church.

It's not fucking right, and I'm not even overly religious. But there's no respect, and that boils me all over again.

Rough hands clamp over my tied hands, and I scowl at the touch. If I wasn't gagged, I'd have cried out in pain. Fuck. I mustn't appear weak, even here, and as surrounded by the blank faces of the helmed warriors as I am.

More and more warriors surge into the church, seeming to come from openings I didn't even know existed, and not just from the main door I've travelled through. Have they been sleeping in the smaller rooms of the building? Have they been in the crypt below my feet? I growl. The thought infuriates me. The fucking cheek of it.

The men, sodden with sleep and no doubt ale as well, barely perk up at the sight of their much-longed-for prisoner. I hear mumbled comments, as I swivel my head, trying to see all that I can.

There are shitting hundreds of Raiders, all wearing similar equipment. These, I deduce, must be the sworn men of the four jarls of Repton. Jarl Guthrum, Jarl Oscetel, Jarl Anwend and Jarl Halfdan, brother of the Ivarr who caused so many problems for Wessex before his fortuitous death.

I watch all of the men, making a note of how they line up, as though used to such summonings and wait, expectantly.

A large space remains around me, though, and my abductees. It's as though none of the others wishes to get too close to Jarl Sigurd and his men. I wonder then what sort of reputation the fucker has? Maybe he's a mean fighter, a terrible drunk or just a bloodthirsty bastard known for being cruel to the men who take him as their master.

I'll never know. Not now.

A hush falls.

In the distance, I can hear strident footsteps over the stone floor. From the door that leads into the area of the compound between the church and the river, four men emerge.

They're all shapes and sizes, the lead a large man, a wicked scar gleaming in the suddenly growing candlelight as more and more flames spring up, as though lighting the path for him. I take him to be Jarl Halfdan. He looks as mean as his reputation. That he comes without his byrnie or weapons speaks of a cocky bastard.

His blue tunic shimmers with golden thread, and on it, I see the eyes of a wolf watching me from his chest. Whoever made his tunic for him is well skilled. Almost too well skilled. The wolf eyes me coldly. It seems it wants to hunt.

Behind him comes a smaller man. I know him to be Jarl Anwend, although he doesn't know me. Surprised eyes rake me in from beneath the same heavy eyebrows that young Anwend had, joined by a long nose, and elongated chin. Not an attractive man, but he seems to make up for that in body tone. Here's a man who can fight, and probably very well. I'm not surprised to find his weapons belt in place, or his sigil of a one-eyed raven liberally festooning all of his clothes and weapons.

He can both fight and has learned to plan for all eventualities. I might have respected him had we met elsewhere.

Two men follow him, and I don't know which is Guthrum and which Oscetel. They could almost be brothers, for their hair is the same deep auburn, and they both wear it long and tightly braided down their backs.

They share many of the same features and walk like men who know the reach of their influence and power. Yet, they follow the two other jarls, and I think that must mean they're less powerful. At least, here, in the strange little collective they've decided upon to rule Repton from.

The sigils of Guthrum and Oscetel couldn't be more different. Guthrum has an owl, depicted on his tunic and also on his two arms. The sleeves of his tunic are cut short so that all can see the inkings that ripple as he walks.

Oscetel's serpent sigil snakes down his face, and perhaps even along his head and down his neck where his hair is so tightly bound. I can't see more than the inkings of teeth, and an open mouth with a slither of tongue. It's not a good look. When he's old, should he live to be old, the snake will either contract or expand, depending on whether he shrivels or swells. Either way, the snake will no longer look like a snake, but rather a ragged collection of teeth and tongue.

I'm shuffled forward by booted feet, hands on my shoulders, one digging in far too deeply, as though I'm their anchor and not vice versa.

A silence falls as the Raider bastards seek chairs and settle at the front of the church. It affronts me to see such men where a priest should stand, wearing only his holy robes and speaking the Latin of the church.

Jarls Guthrum and Oscetel mirror Halfdan in coming unarmed. Confident bastards.

Although I reconsider, there are near enough a hundred armed men in the church. Perhaps they're right to rely on them for protection.

More candles have been lit behind the backs of the jarls, and a fire blazes on the floor. I'd not noticed it before. Fuckers. The church shouldn't have had a fire in it, and it accounts for the thick air. I can almost taste it rather than smell it. For a moment the stench fills my nose, and I think I'll choke again, only then I'm distracted from my panic.

'Jarl Sigurd,' it's Jarl Halfdan who speaks. His voice is rich and commanding, and again, I understand him even though he speaks Danish.

Jarl Sigurd, now standing close enough to me that I can smell his fear, inclines his head quickly, his warrior garb covering him, so that little of him shows. If the other jarls think it strange, they don't show it. I wouldn't let a man come before me in all of his battle gear, no matter the prize he had with him.

'Jarls, I have your prisoner for you.' If the accent is less thick, and the words muffled, I'm sure that everyone will blame the swollen chin and cheeks that Jarl Sigurd has earned himself in capturing me, rather than anything else.

I wait, as does the entire church, expectant eyes on Jarl Halfdan as he gazes at me.

'Jarl Anwend, bring forth your son, I would know if this man is truly Lord Coelwulf, the murderer of my beloved son. He certainly doesn't look the part.'

I bristle at the words, even though I anticipate them.

A youth I know to be Anwend Anwendsson rushes forward to stand by his father, an awed expression on his young face as he looks from Jarl Sigurd to me. His heavy eyebrows are so high on his young forehead that they almost disappear into his equally abundant hair.

'Yes, yes, that's him,' Anwend splutters in Danish, his head bobbing in time with his words. The tension in my shoulders doesn't abate, not one bit, because someone else is being thrust through the crowd at the instigation of Jarl Halfdan.

'Fuck,' my head all but explodes, because I can't shout the word beyond the rag.

Goda, beaten and bloodied, his head hanging at a strange angle, turns pain-filled eyes my way, and startles, horror on his familiar face. His hair is tangled, his beard flecked with blood and what I take to be food. It looks to me as though they've been torturing my missing warrior, no doubt for information on me. My blood boils afresh, and I yank at my tied hands, even though I know it's useless.

How, I consider, did Icel manage to ride away unharmed, and yet Goda was captured?

'Yes, it must be, take him away,' Jarl Halfdan observes Goda's reaction, and dismisses him as quickly as he's had him brought in. I try to reassure Goda with my eyes, but I know I can't convey everything he needs to know, not without speech, and not looking the way I do.

Two large men drag Goda from the hall, his eyes never leaving mine. The black-clad warrior at my side stiffens, his stance no longer as casual as it should be.

I can't even hiss at him.

'So Lord Coelwulf, you have, at last, accepted my invitation to join me in Repton.'

This isn't my idea of an invitation, but I'm powerless to say anything. Not bound and gagged as I am.

'I expected someone with better clothes,' Jarl Halfdan laughs as he speaks, the rest of the warriors in the hall joining in, for all the jarl taunts me in Danish.

I can't reply, and he doesn't expect one.

'It appears that you don't wish to willingly pledge your oath to the new rulers of Mercia. We had, obviously, expected some resentment.' Jarl Halfdan has switched to English, perhaps worrying that I won't understand his gloating. I need only look at his eyes to appreciate his fucking intent.

'We allowed King Burgred to leave here, go to Rome to live out the last of his few remaining days.' Halfdan's tone is filled with false compassion, and I struggle against my bonds. For all I hated King Burgred, and would probably have killed him myself given half a chance.

'But of course, the agreement could only be reached after he'd informed us of all who might object to the change in .... leadership. Your name was offered immediately and alone. I can see I should have sent Jarl Sigurd to retrieve you first of all. My mistake.' Halfdan speaks as though he's the king here, and other than a reference to his dead son, there seems to be no desire for greater revenge. I can see unease on Jarl Anwend's face. His son speaks frantically into his ear, while he tries to listen to Jarl Halfdan at the same time.

Fuck, I should have realised the lad would be here. I'd overlooked the possibility.

Yet Jarl Anwend holds his tongue, uncertainty on his face, despite his son's increasingly frantic entreaties. Perhaps he's just pleased to be armed at this impromptu meeting.

'Now, the choice is yours.' It seems to me that Jarl Halfdan rather likes the sound of his own damn voice. 'You can still pledge your oath to my fellow jarls and me, or we can simply end your life. I'd sooner the latter. I don't believe you'll be a good ally, all things considered, and if you're here, then I imagine your men are dead. That means you're the lord of no one and fuck all.' Spittle flies from Halfdan's mouth, to fall, slowly, flames shimmering in them. I concentrate on that more than what Halfdan actually says. 'The fact that you killed my son, and also Guthrum's means we will never trust you.'

I incline my head, as though accepting the point. I can't speak, and the unease amongst the men who captured me seems to prove the point as well. What more should I say?

'So what will it be then?' Jarl Halfdan laughs as he imperiously asks the question, sitting forward eagerly on his chair and then turning to flick his eyes over the other jarls he says he rules with, but who've not been consulted.

Oscetel and Guthrum aren't enjoying this as much as Jarl Halfdan. Far from it. I consider whose son I killed on my way north. Three men told me that their father's led the Raiders. Only young Anwend was allowed to live, and only because of his resemblance to Rudolf. And because it suited me. Of course.

I already know I've killed one of Halfdan's sons. He's made no bones of that.

I remain still. I want to rip my bound hands free and grip them tightly around Jarl Halfdan's throat, but I can't. I feel small and insignificant, my hands covered in blood that I've spilt trying to uselessly fight my way free.

I don't fucking like it, not at all.

'As you will,' Jarl Halfdan leans back, a satisfied grin on his face, as he picks out members of his audience and offers them a jaunty smile.

'We should do this immediately,' Jarl Halfdan exclaims, standing, as though about to take a sword and swipe my head from my shoulders without further thought. Only then he pauses, glancing at Jarl Sigurd and the silent black-clad warriors who surround me. They're growing restless, a thread of disquiet about them.

Jarl Halfdan's eyes narrow as he acknowledges them.

'You found him. You shall have the honour, for exhibiting such restraint until now. Jarl Halfdan nods to himself, pleased with the solution he's proposed.

I turn aside from him, instead taking in the interior of the church, and looking for a chance to escape, even now. I count, in my head, the number of enemies arranged against me, feeling like Edmund, and I begin to appreciate just how fucking overwhelming the odds are.

There's a flurry of activity around me as men are pushed aside, and others come closer, keen to see the fabled Lord Coelwulf before death.

I would grin at them all, and show them my bloodied teeth, but the fucking rag is still in my mouth.

Do they fear me so much that they must kill me both bound and gagged? Is my reputation really so fearful?

I hope so.

Yet my guard of black-clad warriors stays close, fending off those who become too inquisitive, and not calmly. The one with the green-eyes is particularly violent. When a warrior with a shining baldhead attempts to head butt me, the green-eyed warrior raises his elbow casually and smashes it into his nose. Blood flows, and I think it'll only be the first such occurrence.

Leering faces swim in and out of my vision, and I stand tall, despite my shabby appearance. I'm a Mercian warrior, a man of royal birth. I've fought all my life for Mercian independence, both from Wessex and from the Raiders. While I face my death, I'll show them what that means. I don't believe they understand at all what being Mercian really involves.

Too soon, the Raiders are forced back, as Jarl Sigurd approaches me with a sharp blade in his hands. He wears a small smirk on his tight face, his steps almost jaunty and his blond moustache gleaming in the reflected glow from the fire.

The green-eyed warrior forces me to my knees. He might have sent the other man away with a bleeding nose so that he couldn't harm me, but now he's far from gentle, and I crash to the floor when he aims at the back of my legs with the end of his war axe. My entire body trembles and long-forgotten words of prayer form on my lips for the bastards haven't provided me with the opportunity to confess my sins.

I knew this moment would come, and yet nothing has prepared me for it. Nothing.

Strange thoughts cascade through my mind, and yet foremost of them all is the fact that I have fucking cold feet, and I hate having cold feet.

I fucking hate it.

A pair of boots strides into my restricted vision and how I envy those boots.

I don't lookup. I don't beg, and I don't plead. I am resolved.

But fuck, my feet are bloody cold.

I WINCE, preparing for the killing blow, but I know it won't come. How could it?

While 'Jarl Sigurd' steps close, Edmund with his green-eyes, and sure footing, steps even closer, his hand on the back of my head, as though to keep me in position. While his knife is busy at my ropes, Jarl Sigurd restricting the view of me from the front, and Hereman doing the same from the right-hand side.

My bound hands come free under cover of Edmund's actions, and I hear his soft whistle of dismay at the state of my hands.

'Maybe they were too tight,' Edmund curses, as I feel the reassuring weight of iron being pressed into my hand. Still, I stay, head down, just waiting.

Icel has been forced to remain outside, his height and weight too obvious when he's spoken to Jarl Anwend. In his place, Hereman serves me, alongside Edmund.

We wait, all three of us, the rest of the black-clad men as well.

I might have led my men here, but not all of them are in the church with me, and not all of them are my men. Others have chosen to accompany us. Warriors from all the ealdormen are represented. They've all sworn absolute loyalty to me, all of them making a vow that they would not watch me be killed by the enemy.

A vow that they would rather die than allow it. Most of them gave it eagerly. A few didn't.

Now we'll see how many of them can abide by that vow.

Jarl Sigurd, or rather, Wærwulf wearing his discarded equipment and suitable for the position because of us all, he spoke the best

Danish, hesitates, his sword loose in his hand. I don't meet his eyes, but rather wait.

It seems an interminable wait, but everything must be as we agreed before making this fucking foolhardy approach.

I see Wærwulf's sword move, I feel it as a rush of disturbed air over my head, but his sword never drops to my neck, and that, finally, is my cue to stand and meet the faces of my enemy.

I do so slowly, not wishing to startle anyone more than I already am. I spit the rag from my mouth and taste the thick atmosphere, as I pull the binding down, showing that I'm no longer bound. The thick fug of smoke and sweat makes me cough.

Wærwulf grimaces at me, as he stands with his sword raised, only to pivot away from me on sprightly feet. From behind him, I catch sight of Jarl Anwend already moving, but not toward me, as he is the first to determine what's really about to happen.

He's not a fool. That might just save him and his son. I hope they never darken Mercian land again.

My seax glitters menacingly in the candlelight as I hold it in front of me, enjoying the slow look of triumph on Jarl Halfdan's face turns to confusion and then drain entirely away. He's not even noticed that Jarl Anwend and his son have gone.

Jarls Guthrum and Oscetel, stunned by Jarl Anwend's quick movements, aren't even watching me. I turn to meet the jubilant eyes of every one of the fifty men who've come with me into Repton.

I raise an eyebrow, and abruptly, a helm is thrown my way, a sword as well. Hereberht and Eoppa have hidden them for me. I incline my head to them, and the moment seems to stretch and drag, as though time has somehow changed and nothing is happening as quickly as I thought it would.

And then everything crashes back in on itself.

'Attack,' I bellow, and it begins.

I should like to take out one of the jarls, but Anwend has already gone, the screech of the door that leads into the interior of the fort opening and closing attesting to that, and actually, it's not the jarls who threaten us, but rather their warriors.

They've been even slower to react than the jarls, and I watch with satisfaction as my fifty men sight a target, and strike them down without so much as a pause for thought. The first dead are the lucky ones. They don't even have a chance to raise their weapons or piss themselves with fear.

The next men to fall will have more than enough time to consider their imminent death.

I join the rest of my men, our circle pushing outwards. I take the first man with a stab to his eye, the second, a sharp cut to his exposed neck, and the third, well I'm sure the daft fuck actually aims for the edge of my sword.

He dies quickly, and I'm stepping around him, cursing the requirement that I give up my boots to look 'more like a prisoner.' Blood squelches between my toes, and I fear I might slide and slip and then wound myself as poorly as the third of my kills.

I have no byrnie, but beneath my torn tunic, I'm wearing extra layers of cloth, and they account for the sweat that quickly flows.

'The door,' I holler, relieved when four warriors rush to stop anyone else from escaping into the wider enclosure outside St Wystan's. I don't want those outside alerted to what's happening inside.

Jarl Anwend and his son took the door that leads into the protected area behind the church. I imagine they rush to a ship, with a bright sail because there won't be the men to row, determined to make a quick getaway. I want that door as well, but it's the one that leads outside Repton that worries me the most at the moment.

A warrior, his teeth gritted, slams into the side of me, and the foul bastard uses his initiative to stamp heavily on my naked foot.

'Fucking cunt,' I scream, so close to his face that he jerks away and that's all I need. My seax at neck height, I jab out and slice cleanly through his cheek and out the other side. He squeals, and I mean squeals, and then I yank my seax back, a dollop of blackish blood landing on my tongue in the process. I think the fucker might have broken my toe.

I suck on the black blood, making my dying enemy watch, and

then I turn away. He's dead. He's just not realised it yet. But fuck, my foot hurts.

I'm panting but no longer fearful, and Edmund is a whirling mass of blades, arms and feet. Whatever fear he might have had is gone. I duck quickly, keen to avoid the body of one of his kills as it rebounds from him.

'Careful you fucker,' I complain, and then I find another target.

This warrior is desperately trying to fight his way back through the mass of enemy who advances on us, wanting to avenge their comrades. Only his fellow warriors aren't keen to let him through, not at all.

While he kicks and screams to be allowed into the protection of their mass, his back toward me, they thrust him onwards. I raise my seax once more to neck height and then stab down, the weapon grinding over the bones on his back. He falls, but his hands are grabbing, frantic to find a purchase on one of the other men, and as he tumbles, he brings two others down with him. It's simple to stab them as well, exposed as they are.

I want to kick out, bring more of them to me, but my feet are still naked and slick with the blood of others. And I don't have my boots, and my feet are fucking freezing, my toe throbbing from the bastard who stamped on it. If I could kill him again, I would.

I grin, knowing my teeth are smeared with blackened blood. More of them flinch away, until there's nowhere else for them to go, for both doors are guarded.

'Dear me,' I speak with a smirk on my face. 'Maybe you shouldn't have come to witness this after all,' I comment, trying not to laugh at the terror on their faces or the pervading smell of piss that's filling the air.

These men will die, and they know it.

My blades are busy then, as are those of my other warriors. I'm not the only one to duck away from Edmund. He fights with all of his skill and without a genuine appreciation of who surrounds him. The battle lust has well and truly claimed him.

As I take the life of enemy after enemy, the blows all different, the end result always the same, I swerve out of Edmund's way time and time again, until Hereman, with all the familiarity of a brother, roars at him.

'Watch what you're doing you fucking bastard.'

Only then does Edmund seem to come to, aware for the first time of what he's doing, and he smiles. I've never seen such a terrible smile, and I hope to never do so again.

Edmund pounds his bloodied chest, and raises his weapons in front of him, as though making an offering to the pagan gods. The roar that erupts from his mouth brings dust raining down from the rafters.

'Fucking hell,' I complain, sneezing and fighting at the same time, blinking dust from my eyes, and spitting it clear from my mouth.

Only when I have nothing to attack but the walls of the building, do I pause again, turn and survey the terrible scene before me.

There are dead and dying men everywhere, and I mean everywhere.

Some have attempted to crawl away, trailing their innards in their wake. Others have curled around their pain, trying to drive it away. Others still stand, not understanding the wounds they've taken are lethal, while they cup body parts and watch blood pool through their fingers.

And then there are those that I count as friends or allies. Their deaths tear at me, for all I know they came willingly. Not a single man here was coerced into fighting for Mercia. Not a single one.

'Where are the fuckers?'

Now that every warrior in the church has been slain, it's time to hunt down the others who did manage to escape.

I want to find the jarls. I want to personally take their lives, although I think it impossible. I'm sure, like Jarl Anwend, that all four of the men must have escaped before we could seal the doors.

Now, is the time for us all to work together. The time for single-combat is gone.

We have no shields, those items being left with the horses that brought us here, but the church has tables. Wærwulf, still wearing

Jarl Sigurd's battle gear, and Ælfgar are busy dismantling one of them. We don't need the legs, but we do need the wood. I can see where they've flung bodies aside, and the wood gleams wetly. I know it's not with water.

'Are we ready?' I turn, keen to ensure my men have caught their breaths and can continue. Not a single one of them shouts for me to wait, even though many are gasping in great lungful's of air. Others see to injuries of a friend, and a few others just stare, as though perplexed by the success of the endeavour.

The men who held the door tight against any more escapees, Ordlaf, Eoppa and Beornstan carefully lift the heavy iron lock. The creak is overly loud in the church that's flooded with the final words of the dead and little else besides. Wærwulf and Ælfgar fill the gap with the enormous wooden tabletop. It just fits, as though we've taken the door from the hinges and moved it forward, a step at a time. That might have been easier to accomplish.

'Fuck, it's bastard heavy,' I can hear the strain in Wærwulf's voice, and wish I could assist him, but it's a job for only two men. There's no room for more.

The thunk of a heavy object hitting the moving door makes us all instinctively crouch lower. But when nothing else follows, I make my move.

Behind Wærwulf and Ælfgar, when they're far enough clear of the door, I slip, ten other warriors with me, Edmund and Hereman amongst them. I pause, risking a peek around the side of our shelter and then I allow everyone through because, surprisingly, there's no shield wall waiting to meet us.

This was my biggest fear about our plan.

But, while this area has clearly been lived in recently, and by many warriors, fires still smouldering with cook pots over them, it now appears deserted.

This is my first intelligence about the enclosed part of the enemy's fort. It seems to me, in the blink of an eye, that this is where the jarls and their favourites have been sheltering. There are four large canvasses, and many, many smaller ones, although not close to the larger ones.

I can see that items have been snatched in a panic. A scattering of coins lies forgotten about in front of me. A byrnie has been left hanging close to a fire, and the smell of pottage is ripe in my nostrils.

'Where the fuck are they all?'

But I've lifted my eyes, and I can see what they've planned.

'The ships,' I point to where the sails of the ships can be seen in the bright daylight, and where some of them make jerky movements forward. Now I can see the sigils on the sails. I'm unsurprised to see the one-eyed raven at the front of the group, followed by a wolf, an owl and a snake. And there are others as well. One of them surprises me by having a dragon on it.

It seems Jarl Sigurd had more warriors than just the fifty he took to find me.

We've planned our attack carefully.

We knew the ships would be a problem.

I rush forward, keen to make my way through the campsite and see what damage I can cause to the men trying to escape.

I confess I didn't actually expect them to do this. I thought they would sooner die than retreat. It seems I was wrong.

Only then, I'm not.

As I rush beyond the largest structure, a flurry of warriors abruptly pours forth from it, blocking my path with a thin, long shield wall. It aims to prevent me from reaching the object of my headlong thrust, wolves and owls working together to ensure their jarls manage to escape.

'Fuck,' I complain. We don't have shields. I didn't want to face a shield wall, and while we encounter one, I can see the ships beginning to move more smoothly. Perhaps the ships are clear of the quayside. Maybe the wind, beyond the slope of the defences, has quickened.

'Bastards,' I bellow, but already my men are joining me. We might not have shields, but we have our battle greed, and it's nowhere near sated yet. Hereman and Edmund ensure they surround me. I'm not surprised they've decided to work together. Not at our greatest moment of triumph.

The shields that meet us are various colours, only the sigils remaining a constant. With my first blow, I delight in seeing the colour sheer away beneath the edge of my blade.

My men are busy doing the same, but my eyes keep flickering to the sails. Why I consider would they have kept them up? I understood that any ship's captain worth his salt would bring the sails down when docking. Perhaps, this has always been their preferred method of escape, taking them back to Torksey and hopefully further away, to the Humber, and then back to bloody Denmark.

With my second blow, I feel my enemy falter. With a movement born of desperation, I jump, as high as I can, and slam my seax over the top of his shield, bringing it hammering to the floor. I only just miss my naked feet.

My arm moves instinctively, flicking over the Raider's tongue and then inside his mouth so that he chokes and bleeds, all at the time. I'm sawing my seax forward and backwards, enjoying the feel of bone over the blade.

Eadulf is the first to take advantage of the gap, sliding through and around, hacking at backs. The orderly shield wall disintegrates. I'm off again, running for the riverbank and the small guard that hovers by the gate. They wait to let their allies through and thwart us.

'With me,' I instruct, and the rush of feet assures me that I'm not the only one racing to force a path through the small gateway. The land has been built up in an earthen wall, even though the riverbank lies to the far side of it. Only one small gateway allows access either from the river or from the fort. At least ten warriors stand, weapons ready.

I'm so close now that I can't see what the sails do on the other side. That simply makes me more furious, and more determined to scythe through the waiting warriors as though they're no more than wheat waiting to be cut down.

I take a quick glance to either side, not at all surprised to find Edmund and Hereman still flanking me, although I do wish that

Rudolf and Pybba were not with us. But then, where would I rather they were? At least here I can keep an eye on them and support them if they need it.

Rudolf's eyes blaze fiercely from beneath his borrowed helm, the female warrior's weapons belt slick with blood but still around his waist. He holds his seax, and as though noticing my scrutiny, he meets my eyes and grins. I've never seen a more unsettling sight.

His teeth gleam maroon, his chin shimmering with his blood, and his nose at a strange angle. He's taken a mighty blow and can't feel it. Not yet.

I return his smile, allowing my delight at his successes to actually show.

I can't quite believe how successful we've been. Genuinely I thought we'd set ourselves an impossible task.

And then we're at the gate, and although I'd prefer to linger over yet more kills, I must get to the ships.

It's Pybba who taunts first. His lost hand has been masked, beneath a cleverly applied glove to his wrist, but now it's gone, ripped away, and all can see the puckered skin as he waves it before the ten fearful warriors. They've realised that waiting for their comrades was a bad decision. The only payment they're going to get is their death.

'Let a one-armed man kill you, would you?' I'm astounded by Pybba's threat, but equally, this is what he needs to recover his self-belief.

An opponent steps forward, his eyes gleaming with malice, and Pybba takes a few swings with his war axe. It's the easiest weapon for him to handle. I reach out and grip hold of the back of Rudolf's byrnie when he jerks as though to join in.

'Let the old man,' I caution him, as Pybba sweeps one way and then the next, drawing the warrior out so that he steps entirely clear of his fellow comrades.

A flicker of movement behind the warrior Pybba means to kill, and my eyes stay firmly on Pybba as he makes his attack. First one way, and then the next, and only then does the really dirty work begin.

When Pybba hits out with his war axe, his opponent goes to move away, but Pybba is too quick. With a too satisfying sound, he lets the axe fly, having tested its weight perfectly. The axe embeds itself into the enemy warrior's forehead, the bloom of red instantaneous.

Pybba's opponent drops to the ground more quickly than if he'd jumped from a great height.

Pybba yanks his axe clear, using his foot on the man's shoulder as leverage, twisting the body at the same time. The sound is terrible to my ears, but Pybba turns, grimacing to find his next kill.

Only there's no need.

'Sorry it took so long,' Goda offers, breathing heavily and clutching his side. He's appeared from the other side of the gate and quietly and quickly ended the lives of the nine warriors whose attention was on entirely the wrong enemy. For all that, Goda looks terrible, and blood laces his hands, adding to his battered face.

'Not mine,' Goda explains, when I look at him, eyebrows high, seeking an explanation.

'What of those retreating.'

Goda's words bring a smile to my lips, and I turn, gloatingly, to face Edmund, who merely shrugs as though unsurprised.

'The Gwent Welshmen have stopped all but three ships. They're lethal fuckers. They crawled onto those ships trying to escape, and killed every last warrior on them.' Goda's shaking his head. His surprise at the ferocity of the Gwent Welshmen assures me that everyone who tried to escape and was caught by them died a particularly gruesome death.

The knowledge cheers me, even though I imagine all four jarls have managed to escape.

Bastards. They left their men to die. They didn't fucking deserve the oaths of warriors if they were going to abandon them so easily.

I bend at the waist then, breathing heavily, peering at my bloody feet and wondering just what shit I've already stepped into. My toe is throbbing, sending pulses of pain along my leg, and I can see, beneath all the blood and crap, that it's already swollen. It better not be fucking broken.

When my breathing is finally under control once more, I stand and meet the eyes of my warriors who still stand.

Edmund is there, Hereman as well, the pair of them standing closer together through choice than I've ever seen them. Their black warrior's clothes are intact, but blood seems to run from them, pooling on the ground beside them.

Goda is there as well, laughing as he greets Ælfgar and Wærwulf. He admires Wærwulf's borrowed battle equipment because he'd already set off for Repton when we encountered Jarl Sigurd.

Pybba and Rudolf are picking through the dead, and I smirk to see Pybba so willing to pillage. It seems that young dogs can teach old dogs new tricks, just as well as vice versa.

Sæbald is clutching his side, a grimace on his face, but he shakes away my concern.

'Bruising, nothing more.'

Eoppa, Ingwald and Hereberht are kicking at corpses, ensuring themselves that they're truly dead.

Wulfstan, Ordlaf and Oda have found a jug of ale from somewhere and swig, each in turn, from their prize.

I lick my lips, considering that I'm thirsty too, but I want water, not ale.

Eadulf and Wulfred are peering through the gateway, pointing at what they can see. I stride to their side and turn and gaze as well. I can't quite believe how many ships are on the quayside.

'Fucking bollocks,' I whistle, aware than Osbert, Eahric and Beornstan have joined me.

'How many bloody ships?' Hearing the words 'fifty ships' and seeing fifty ships is very different. The river is filled with them. In fact, and I smirk to see it, the very number of them has been their downfall. I can see the Gwent Welshmen making their way from one side of the river to the other, just by jumping from ship to ship.

'Daft fuckers,' Osbert exclaims, but actually, I think it not a bad tactic to employ.

In the distance, I can see the three ships that managed to escape, and I do consider whether we could go after them or not. But there are at best about a hundred warriors on those ships. Outside Repton there are two thousand, perhaps more. They're my priority.

'Well that was fucking easy,' I exclaim, turning back to face into the fortress the Raiders have built at Repton.

The remaining warriors and I realise we've lost no more than one or two of the original fifty men that pretended to be Raiders to gain access into Repton, are milling around, kicking corpses, looking for treasure, generally exuberant to be alive.

They're all laughing and embracing, regardless of who pledges their oath to who, and fuck it feels good to be alive.

18

'Right, now for the easy bit,' I exclaim, and the men all grin, buoyant after what we've managed to accomplish. It makes no sense, and it shouldn't have been possible, and yet it's done, all the same. I'll leave the Gwent Welshmen to do what they want with the ships. I can only wonder that those men outside the fort haven't noticed and tried to gain admittance.

I lead the men back through the door of the church, trying not to look as I go. There are many bodies inside. The stink is obnoxious.

We've stolen their lives as surely as they attempted to take the whole of Mercia as well as my life. I didn't like them being in Torksey last year. I liked them being in Repton far less.

Those men left to guard the exterior doorway watch me with surprise on their faces at my sudden arrival.

I beam.

'It's done. The fort is ours.'

Relieved expressions flicker over tight faces, and then they grin, their disbelief at our quick successes evident.

'We need to take all of Repton for ourselves, and then we must battle any who still want to stand against us.' I don't anticipate many warriors making the second choice, but time will tell.

'Do we take prisoners?' It's one of Ealdorman Ælhun's men asking the question. It's been the subject of a great deal of discussion between the ealdormen who now call me their kin.

I don't want the blood of two thousand men on my hands, and neither do I want two thousand men in Mercia with twisted loyalties, forced to be slaves. It won't restore peace. But the other ealdormen do not want to let the warriors go. They don't want them to have the opportunity to return to Mercia. I'm happy for the apprehended to go anywhere, as long as they never return to Mercia.

Ealdorman Ælhun was aggrieved by that decision, citing that our neighbouring kingdoms might become inundated with the enemy. But Wessex has turned it's back on Mercia. They can have all the fucking Raiders for all I care.

Ealdorman Ælhun said he spoke of East Anglia and Northumbria, not just Wessex.

'If we must. Provided there are still ships at the end of this, they can leave, but only on swearing an oath to never return.'

For all my previous arguments, my blood is high, and I know I'll kill rather than accept capitulation.

'Ten men must guard the door. We don't want them coming back in here. Not when we've cleared it of everyone else.'

I leave the particulars to my warriors to thrash out, unsurprised when Ealdorman Ælhun's men determine to stay at the door. They think it'll be easy, but I know better. They don't seem to derive quite so much enjoyment from the kill as my sworn warriors do.

Desperate men are just that, desperate. I think the fighting will be hard at the door, should they be able to break through to it.

'Close it, after we're gone,' I instruct. 'Don't allow anyone in, or out. Not until you get a signal from us.'

'What will the signal be?'

Keen words, and for a moment, I have no idea what that sign will be. It needs to be specific, not something that others might guess at.

'Coelwulf's farts smell of roses.' Rudolf's cheeky voice echoes through the church, and we all turn to glare at him.

'Well they do, My Lord.' I grimace, but actually, it's a good idea to choose something so obscure.

'Fine, don't open the door until someone tells you that my farts smell of roses. Now come on. Anyone with an injury must stay here, keep safe, we've done the difficult part, let the other fuckers get on with clearing out the rats.'

I know that no one wants to remain behind, and yet, all the same, I hear a few shuffling feet and grimace tightly.

'Good. Now, open the door, and then close it again, quickly.'

I still hold my seax and my sword, but I bring them closer to my body, consider wiping the blood from my face but know it'll only smear more.

With a creak of the door, sunlight illuminates the space, and I pause, waiting for my eyes to readjust. For all the pageantry of my arrival, work inside the rest of Repton hasn't faltered, not at all. Not a single face turns with any interest at the creaking of the door.

I turn to meet the eyes of Edmund and Hereman.

'This might be altogether too easy.'

With confident strides, I walk from the church, my warriors following me. I allow them to streak off, picking their targets and deciding who they want to face first. There are a few screams, a ripple of cheers from the small remaining Mercian population trapped by the Raiders. Then the three of us are at the exterior gateway.

A crowd of ten warriors watch us arrive from various positions. They're hardly alert and ready for anything. I hide my surprise in check. How can such insolence have infiltrated so much of Mercia and Wessex? They don't even seem to recognise me, even though I was only brought through the barricade, bound and gagged earlier. I look down, expecting to see blood covering my body, but other than my naked feet, I appear relatively clear of the stuff.

'Oye, Oye lads,' Edmund calls, high on the successes we've already experienced.

Now a flicker of unease appears on the face of one of the men, the only one actually on his feet and appearing to pay even the slightest bit of attention.

'In case you wondered, the jarls are gone, see,' and Edmund points upriver, where one of the bright sails can still be seen.

Now all of the men are on their feet, fondling for weapons, as they sight the ships.

'Shall we?' I ask, but Hereman is already eyeing his first kill, and as he squares up, the sound of battle reaches my ears, and I know that we've been seen by the scouts hiding amongst the low lying ground. The Mercians are coming to make war on all the Raiders who've been abandoned by their jarls. Four hundred and ninety warriors against two thousand.

I began my day being trussed up like a prisoner, but I'll end it as the King of Mercia, in name as well as deed.

As I ready myself, choose my target, I allow a smirk to touch my cheeks.

Fuck, it feels good.

THANK YOU FOR READING THE LAST KING

I hope you've enjoyed The Last King. The series continues with The Last Warrior. If you've not enjoyed the strong language as much as I might hope, please do consider the Cleaner Versions - still with all the violence, but lacking some of the very strong language. These are available for the books in the series as ebooks.

Please do consider leaving a review on your platform of choice.

To keep up with all things Saxon England, you can join my monthly newsletter and receive a free short story collection via my website.

WHAT TO READ NEXT?

I hope you've enjoyed Coelwulf's newest tale. If you'd like to keep reading about Saxon England, and Mercia in particular, then please consider this series of interconnected titles, which I term 'The Tales of Mercia.'

Gods and Kings (Seventh century)
    Pagan Warrior
    Pagan King
    Warrior King

The Eagle of Mercia Chronicles (Earlier ninth century)
    Son of Mercia
    Wolf of Mercia
    Warrior of Mercia
    Eagle of Mercia
    Protector of Mercia
    Enemies of Mercia

The Lady of Mercia's Daughter (Tenth century)

A Conspiracy of Kings

The Earl of Mercia Series (End of the tenth century)
The Earl of Mercia's Father and subsequent titles (please note, perversely, I began this series first).

Enjoy

CAST OF CHARACTERS

Coelwulf – Lord of Mercia (western Mercia), rides Haden
    Edmund – rides Jethson
    Pybba – loses his hand in battle, rides Brimman
    Eadberht
    Rudolf – Coelwulf's squire
    Sæbald
    Ordheah
    Oslac
    Lyfing
    Ingwald
    Icel, rides Samson
    Hereman, Edmund's brother, rides Billy
    Hereberht
    Gyrth, rides Keira
    Goda, rides Magic
    Eoppa, rides Poppy
    Oda, rides Jaspar
    Wulfred, rides Cuthbert
    Ordlaf
    Wærwulf, rides Cinder

Eadulf, rides Simba
Eahric, rides Storm
Beornstan, rides Chocolate
Wulfstan, rides Berg
Ælfgar
Athelstan
Beornberht
Wulfhere – another of the squires

Bishop Wærferth of Worcester
Bishop Deorlaf of Hereford
Bishop Eadberht of Lichfield
Ealdorman Beorhtnoth
Ealdorman Ælhun
Ealdorman Alhferht
Ealdorman Æthelwold – his father Ealdorman Æthelwulf dies at the Battle of Berkshire in AD871
Ealdorman Wulfstan

Vikings
Ivarr – dies in AD870
Halfdan – brother of Ivarr, may take his place after his death
Guthrum - one of the three leaders at Repton with Halfdan (we will meet him later)
Oscetel - one of the three leaders at Repton with Halfdan
Anwend – one of the three leaders at Repton with Halfdan
Anwend Anwendsson – his fictional son
Sigurd (fictional)

The royal family of Mercia
King Burgred of Mercia
m. Lady Æthelswith in AD853 (the sister of King Alfred)
they had no children
Beornwald – a fictional nephew for King Burgred
King Wiglaf – ninth century ruler of Mercia

King Wigstan- ninth century ruler of Mercia
King Beorhtwulf – ninth century ruler of Mercia

Misc

Cadell ap Merfyn – fictional brother of Rhodri Mawr, King of Gwynedd (one of the Welsh kingdoms)

Eowa, forest dweller

Lady Eadburh, owns the village near the River Stour

Oswald, Ealdorman Ælhun's warrior

Shipsmaster Æthelred

Eadric – one of his three sons

Coenwulf – Coelwulf's dead (older) brother

Wiglaf and Berhtwulf – the names of Coelwulf's aunt's dogs

Places Mentioned

Gloucester, on the River Severn, in western Mercia.

Worcester, on the River Severn, in western Mercia.

Hereford, close to the border with Wales

Lichfield, an ancient diocese of Mercia. Now in Staffordshire.

Tamworth, an ancient capital of Mercia. Now in Staffordshire.

Repton, an ancient capital of Mercia. St Wystan's was a royal mausoleum.

Gwent, one of the Welsh kingdoms at this period.

Warwick, in Mercia

Torksey, in the ancient kingdom of Lindsey, which became part of Northern Mercia

River Severn, in the west of England

River Trent, runs through Staffordshire, Derbyshire, Nottingham and Lincolnshire and joins the Humber

River Avon, in Warwickshire

River Thames, runs through London and into Oxfordshire

River Stour, runs from Stourport to Wolverhampton

Kingsholm, close to Gloucester, an ancient royal site

The Foss Way, ancient roadway running from Lincoln to Exeter

Watling Street, ancient roadway running from Chester to London

HISTORICAL NOTES

This story of King Coelwulf is entirely fictional. Probably.

The story of the past, or rather the Early English period, was magnificently written down for future generations by two people, or rather, at the instigation of two people – The Venerable Bede (with his Northumbrian bias) and his history of the English Speaking People (as just one example of his vast work) and of course, King Alfred (with his Wessex bias), the man credited with beginning the Anglo-Saxon Chronicle upon which so much of the history of the period relies.

It is, the Anglo-Saxon Chronicle that's been used to write the history of the ninth century (Bede wrote in the eighth century), along with the letters that Asser wrote and information available from sources written in what is now Scotland, Wales, and Ireland, but which weren't known as such until much later. King Alfred, with the resources of all Wessex at his command, had history written precisely the way he wanted 'his story' to be remembered.

King Burgred, Alfred's brother by marriage, was ejected from Mercia by the Viking raiders, according to the Anglo-Saxon Chronicle in AD874, and lived the rest of his short life, alongside his wife, in

Rome. It's what happened afterwards that I find utterly compelling, and is the reason I've turned my hand to the ninth century.

I always try and find 'characters' that lived during the period I write about. For the names of the ealdormen and the bishops, I've made use of the surviving charter evidence as found in the Online Sawyer, a wonderful archive of all things Anglo-Saxon and which I spend a great deal of time studying. I don't know if the Raiders captured Ealdorman Wulfstan. I actually know nothing about him, other than his name appears in a charter of King Burgred's in AD968 but not in the later charters issued by King Coelwulf.

Bishop Wærferth, Eadberht, Deorlaf, Ealdorman Beorthnoth, Ælhun, Alhferht and Æthelwold do all witness the charters that Coelwulf is credited with having had produced.

Kingsholm was an ancient royal site, close to Gloucester, but outside the Roman walls of the settlement. I'm assuming it was connected with the kingdom of the Hwicce, which gave Mercia such great leaders as Penda (in the seventh century) and the rulers descended from his brother, Eowa. Coelwulf is believed to have been a descendant of Eowa.

The settlements I have used in this book, Gloucester, Worcester, Warwick, Repton and Tamworth are ancient sites. Warwick is most usually taken to first appear in AD914, although Bartlett has argued that it was probably a proto-ministry site earlier than this. I have taken some liberties.

Gloucester and Worcester have excellent articles available to read about them at this time. Repton is somewhere I've visited and Tamworth is somewhere I visited often as a child. For the evidence of the 873/4 camp at Repton, I've consulted the article available for free download, entitled, 'The Viking Great Army in England: new dates from the Repton charnel' by Jarmen, Biddle, Higham, and Bronk-Ramsey.

I've made use of a map from Anglo-Saxon.net, which also appears in Edward the Elder ed. Higham and Hill to determine what was what in England at this time. It depicts the ancient roadways of the Foss Way, Watling Street, Ermine Street and Icknield Way, and also gives some hints as to hills and forests, if not always rivers. I'm also lucky enough to have a 'mapman' for a father who has antique maps of every county in England stretching back to the seventeenth century. These are invaluable for gaining an idea of what everywhere looked like in the recent past.

The number of men in the warbands is fictitious. Historians have put a great deal of thought into the size of the 'Raider invasion' of the ninth century. At the moment, I understand there is still no definitive answer to the question of just how many Raiders came to what would become England.

I've yet to fully decipher all of the events of ninth century Mercia. But I will. There seems to be a confusion of royal men and women all usurping one another. But it is my intention, for the time being, to follow Lord Coelwulf, or King Coelwulf and see what else befalls him in the latter part of the ninth century as he fights to keep Mercia free from the Viking Raiders.

I have chosen to use the term Viking raiders as opposed to Viking, because the northern people went 'Viking' they weren't Vikings, but everyone likes to use the word Viking.

The song that Edmund sings is a mash-up of a translation of the Gododdin as shown at faculty.arts.ubc.ca and my own imagination.

My understanding of horses comes from teenager number 2, who spends a huge amount of time caring for a big beastie called Hayden. He's a lovely horse, and he 'stars' as Coelwulf's horse as Haden, a name that proved to be far more ancient than I realised.

The adventures of Coelwulf and his men continue in The Last Warrior.

MEET THE AUTHOR

I'm an author of historical fiction (Early English, Vikings and the British Isles as a whole before the Norman Conquest) and fantasy (Viking age/dragon-themed), born in the old Mercian kingdom at some point since AD1066. I like to write. You've been warned! My first non-fiction title is also now available.

Find me at mjporterauthor.com. mjporterauthor.blog and @coloursofunison on twitter. I have a monthly newsletter, which can be joined via my website. All subscribers will receive a free ebook short story collection.

https://dashboard.mailerlite.com/forms/699265/105452112446489757/share

BOOKS BY M J PORTER (IN CHRONOLOGICAL ORDER)

Gods and Kings Series (seventh century Britain)

Pagan Warrior

Pagan King

Warrior King

The Eagle of Mercia Chronicles

Son of Mercia

Wolf of Mercia

Warrior of Mercia

Eagle of Mercia

Protector of Mercia

Enemies of Mercia

The Eagle of Mercia Chronicles Book 7

The Ninth Century

Coelwulf's Company, stories from before The Last King

The Last King

The Last Warrior

The Last Horse

The Last Enemy

The Last Sword

The Last Shield

The Last Seven

The Last Viking

The Last Alliance

The Tenth Century

The Lady of Mercia's Daughter

A Conspiracy of Kings (the sequel to The Lady of Mercia's Daughter)

Kingmaker

The King's Daughter

Non-fiction title

The Royal Women Who Made England: The Tenth Century in Saxon England

The Brunanburh Series

King of Kings

Kings of War

Clash of Kings

Kings of Conflict

The Mercian Brexit (can be read as a prequel to The First Queen of England)

The First Queen of England (The story of Lady Elfrida) (tenth century England)

The First Queen of England Part 2

The First Queen of England Part 3

The King's Mother (The continuing story of Lady Elfrida)

The Queen Dowager

Once A Queen

The Earls of Mercia

The Earl of Mercia's Father

The Danish King's Enemy

Swein: The Danish King (side story)

Northman Part 1

Northman Part 2

Cnut: The Conqueror (full-length side story)

Wulfstan: An Anglo-Saxon Thegn (side story)

The King's Earl

The Earl of Mercia

The English Earl

The Earl's King

Viking King

The English King

The King's Brother

Lady Estrid (a novel of eleventh-century Denmark)

Fantasy

<u>The Dragon of Unison</u>

Hidden Dragon

Dragon Gone

Dragon Alone

Dragon Ally

Dragon Lost

Dragon Bond

<u>As JE Porter</u>

The Innkeeper (standalone)

<u>20th Century Mystery</u>

The Custard Corpses – a delicious 1940s mystery (audio book now available)

The Automobile Assassination (sequel to The Custard Corpses)

Cragside – a 1930s murder mystery (standalone)

Printed in Great Britain
by Amazon